BEACH READS AND DEADLY DEEDS

ALSO BY ALLISON BRENNAN

BEACH READS
AND
DEADLY DEEDS

ALLISON BRENNAN

/||MIRA

/IIMIRA˚

ISBN-13: 978-0-7783-8725-1

Beach Reads and Deadly Deeds

MIRA
22 Adelaide St. West, 41st Floor
Toronto, Ontario M5H 4E3, Canada

Printed in U.S.A.

For my daughter Mary, my sounding board
for all things Gen-Z and pop culture.
I love you to the moon and back.

PROLOGUE

"Death is so terribly final, while life is full
of possibilities."

—George R. R. Martin, *A Game of Thrones*

DIANA HARDEN HAD A plan, and the plan was good.

This little hiccup in her plan was merely an annoyance, not a roadblock. Sending her on a wild goose chase to St. John was childish and petty.

Ethan Valentine would pay dearly for wasting her time.

It was near dark when the water taxi returned her to St. Claire. The driver was barely more than a kid, but Diana paid him well. She'd had enough of this cloak-and-dagger bullshit, so she had the kid take her straight to Valentine's private dock in a sheltered cove on the southwest side of the island.

"Remember," she said, putting her fingers to her lips in the universal *be quiet* sign. She didn't want Ethan to know she'd figured out his ridiculous game.

The driver nodded and grinned, and she waved him off.

Ground lights lined the wood stairs from the dock to Ethan's house built on top of the cliff. The height dizzied her as she trudged up. The cool ocean breeze chilled her through the sheer scarf that she'd wrapped around her shoulders.

Ethan would pay first, and *then* she would tell him where she'd hidden the files. When she went out of her way to *help* someone, to give them information that would put them on top of the world, and they treated her like dog shit on their shoe? No way would she tolerate such disrespect.

The man had to be half-crazy to live like a hermit in the

middle of the Caribbean. All because he'd lost in a business deal? Coming here to lick his wounds and feel sorry for himself? He should be thrilled that she had proof he'd been cheated. Instead, he'd shunned her.

If someone had told Diana ten years ago that she'd fallen head over heels for a gold-digging con artist, she would have been grateful. Sad, angry, sure—who wouldn't be? But she would never have lost everything over it. Ethan Valentine should have been thanking her for the information that she had been willing to give to him practically for free yesterday.

Now the jerk would pay top dollar.

Diana stopped to catch her breath when she reached the top of the stairs. The view was breathtaking—the sun sinking into the ocean to her right, and the distant lights of St. John to her left. Almost as if on cue with the falling sun, several soft white LED lights flickered on, showcasing the house and garden, but darkening the jungle beyond.

Though the house was lit, she couldn't see through the privacy screens. She adjusted the oversized bag on her shoulder, then approached the frosted glass door and rang the bell twice. The chime sounded like a bird call. When no one immediately came, she rang again. And again. Nothing. She tried the door; locked.

Frustrated and angry after her crappy wasted day on St. John, she walked around the deck. The downstairs was almost completely enclosed by glass doors. She was looking for a way inside when a voice, heavy with an accent that sounded not quite Mexican, said, "Are you looking for something?"

Diana stumbled and knocked over a chair.

"Who are you?" she demanded.

Squinting, she saw an old man reclining on a chaise lounge on the far corner of the deck. He had brown skin and a white beard so long and thick she could barely see his face. She'd seen him at the resort, an annoying busybody. What was he doing at Ethan's house? How long had he been watching her?

"¿Quién crees que soy? ¿No has sentido curiosidad?"

Spanish? She didn't understand Spanish.

"No one is home," the old man said, in English this time. "Do you need help finding your way back to the resort?"

"This is Ethan Valentine's house," Diana said. "He said he would be here."

"He did? Odd."

Who *was* this strange man?

"When will Ethan be back? It's important."

"*Volverá cuando vuelva.* Perhaps you'd like to wait?" the man said. "It might be a day or two before he'll come by. Or a week. A month?" He lifted his hands in the air and shrugged.

Where the hell was Ethan? At the resort? Oh, that would be just her luck.

Irritated, she said, "I'll find him myself."

"Very well." The man leaned back into the chair and closed his eyes.

With an infuriated sigh, Diana traipsed along the gravel road that led to the main lodge, wishing she'd asked the kid with the water taxi to wait.

She didn't relish the two-mile hike to the resort, especially going over this mountain. Her flip-flops crunched on the gravel. She had wasted far too much time because of Ethan Valentine. He wanted to play games? Oh, she would play. And Diana was *much* better at it than he was. Her price had gone up tenfold.

The narrow road was poorly lit with sporadic ground lights. She didn't have a flashlight and her cell phone was dead, so she stayed in the middle of the path, knowing that there were sheer drops all over the place. Diana had never considered herself squeamish or afraid of the dark, but she couldn't even see the stars because of the thick canopy of bushy leaves hanging over the road.

Rodents ran from the trees right in front of her, then scurried down the cliff. She forced herself to breathe evenly. There were no dangerous animals on the island. The rustling leaves? Probably gophers or rabbits. She started talking out loud to herself, feeling silly, but hearing her own voice calmed her fears.

She stumbled and caught herself with a vine that was hanging from one of the trees, cursing Ethan. He thought a hundred thousand was too much? How about a million, Ethan? Pay up or she'd out him. Tell everyone what he had *really* been doing since disappearing from the United States. She'd start with the *Wall Street Journal* and *Variety*. Then maybe *Forbes* or *The Economist*. Hell, the *New York Times* might be interested in the scoop. See how Ethan liked the publicity. His ridiculous behavior certainly wouldn't help Valentine Enterprises.

She stepped into a clearing on the top of the mountain. Packed, flat earth free of rocks and bushes and lined in bright lights. Ethan's helipad, though there was no chopper here now. That *jerk*. That *asshole*. Chalk this up to one of the many lies he'd told.

Maybe she wouldn't sell him the documents at all. Maybe she'd sell them back to the man she'd stolen them from, and Ethan could continue to wallow in misery.

Angry but wholly determined to make these miserable men pay for the havoc they had wreaked in her life and the lives of those she cared about, she strode across the helipad.

The trees swayed in a sudden gust of wind, and a chill ran up her spine. She rubbed her arms and cursed.

Then the lights went out.

She froze in the sudden black. The jungle closed around her, and the trees groaned as if they knew something she didn't. Rustling to the left, then to the right. "Who's there?" she called out. "Show yourself, you prick!"

She heard the flapping of wings first. Then dozens of bats flew right at her. She screamed and dropped to the ground, her arms over her head, as the flurry of flying rodents rushed by. She could feel the air shift and change around her as they dipped so low she thought for a moment that she was prey.

Then the flapping faded into the distance, and Diana found herself huddled on the ground, filthy and sore.

"For shit's sake, Diana!" she said out loud. "Get up."

Determined not to let creatures of the night terrify her again, she stood, and her eyes readjusted to the dark. The lights flickered on, then went off again, but on the far side of the clearing, she spotted a wooden sign. She made her way there and came upon a forked path with two arrows. The path to the left was marked *The Falls*, and the path to the right went to *St. Claire*.

Finally! She hurried to the right, down the path toward the resort. All she could think about was stripping off her disgusting clothes and inspecting the cuts and bruises she felt all over her body.

Ten minutes later, faint music filtered up through the trees, and she thought about all her potential paydays—the conniving con artist with the super-rich, clueless boyfriend? Diana had had her pegged a mile away. *Don't try to con a con*, she thought with a smile. Or maybe she'd focus on the security guy with the gambling habit? The cheater? The thief?

So many to choose from . . . and then she got an idea, as if a light bulb went bright above her head. She slowed and reached into her bag to glance through her notes, then realized she'd left the book in her room this morning. No worries. It wasn't like she'd forget the most *brilliant* idea she'd had all week. After all, she was the heroine of this story—as strong and beautiful and smart as the treasure hunter in the novel she was reading. She laughed out loud. That's what she was, a treasure hunter! Only she hunted secrets, not gold.

Secrets that turned into gold. She loved the imagery.

She picked up her pace, eager to get back to her cottage. Her feet hurt, her head pounded, and all she wanted was a large glass of wine and a long soak in the hot tub with her book.

The path wound around as she descended. Diana avoided the main lodge because she didn't want to see anyone, especially when she looked like something the cat dragged in. Security lighting brightened the private patio of her cottage. She searched for her card key and as her hand grasped it at the bottom of her bag, she heard a voice behind her.

"Diana."

She jumped, whirled around. Fear bubbled up in her chest

until she saw who it was. Annoyed and tired, she said, "What do *you* want?"

"I've been waiting for you."

"We'll talk tomorrow. I'm beat."

She turned her back on her uninvited guest and started to insert her card key, but before she could open the door, she was grabbed from behind.

"Wha—" She tried to speak, but her words were cut off. Her scarf tightened around her neck. She couldn't talk. Then she couldn't breathe.

Her vision blurred. Grabbing at the scarf, she scratched her neck. Her knees grew weak. Her vision faded.

Scream!

No sound escaped her throat. She heard nothing except for her own pounding heart, fear wrapping itself around her like a vise.

Then, darkness.

CHAPTER
ONE

"Very few of us are what we seem."
—Agatha Christie, *The Man in the Mist*

I NEVER LEAVE HOME without a book.

The idea that I might be trapped somewhere without something to read gives me nightmares. Lunch break? That's a good chapter—ten if I'm reading James Patterson. Commute on the subway? *Easy* two chapters, each way. Doctor's office? Dentist? Waiting for my grandma to stop flirting with her doorman? A couple pages to pass the time.

I'm not antisocial, but *real* people—at least the ones I've met—are not as interesting, smart, or funny as the fictional characters my favorite writers create. I can solve a murder, climb the Himalayas, fall in love—all in four hundred pages or less. Much more exciting than my life.

And *this* book practically jumped into my hands at the Newark airport kiosk. The cover with the silhouette of a man and woman running from a raging fire and the title *Slow Burn* had my heart racing. The packaging didn't lie. The book was so engrossing, by the time I made the layover in Miami to change planes, only half the story remained. The suspense was pitch-perfect, drawing me into the tightening web of lies and deception as the title suggested. The sexual tension between Christina and John was intoxicating, leading to a satisfying love scene that was worth the wait, leaving me a bit overheated.

I could practically hear Grams. *"It's fiction, Mia. This is why you expect too much from your boyfriends."*

It wasn't just fiction, not to me. It wasn't that the men in romance novels were perfect—they weren't—but they had a spark with the heroine. Together, the characters found love. Sometimes, they worked together to solve a crime. Sometimes, they lusted for each other and discovered more than physical attraction. Sometimes they thought they hated each other . . . until the coin flipped and they fell in love.

Mostly, they weren't alone anymore. My career was right on track, but my love life had barely left the station. Every man who seemed interested in me, every man I gave a chance, failed in a fundamental way. Not just in bed, but in life.

Was I destined to either live alone with two cats for the rest of my life or settle for a man who didn't know how to cook or get me off?

There were still three chapters left by the time the plane landed at the small St. John airport. I'm a fast reader . . . but when a book is especially good, I replay every snippet of dialogue in my mind, every detail I consider might be a clue to the mystery, and then I savor the emotional connection between the characters as the ending draws near.

One of my favorite children's books is this *Sesame Street* story about Grover, who doesn't want to turn the page because of the monster at the end of the book. For me, it's not a monster I fear, but that the book will be over, that even if I reread it, the discovery is gone because I know what happens. So, the better the book, the slower I read, and I intended to draw out these last three chapters for as long as it took to reach St. Claire.

As I boarded the ferry, the quiet pulse of the engine and fresh salt air eased my tension. I watched couples board and realized I was one of the few singles heading to the resort. I figured there would be other single people on the island, but now that it was almost in sight, I wondered how I was going to actually find a vacation boyfriend, a guy I could have fun with . . . and sex with . . . no strings attached. When I was home, the fantasy of a week in paradise with a hunky man had been exciting; now that I was here, I was terrified that I'd be alone the entire trip.

I was just going to have to channel Grams and talk to every single man until one of them appealed to me.

I couldn't help feeling, again, that this trip was a waste of time and a ridiculous amount of money. I'd been with Mc-Mann & Cohn Financial Planners for five years, and this adventure was my nonnegotiable anniversary bonus—a trip to a private island in the Caribbean. As an accountant, I thought it was fiscally irresponsible to *force* an employee to spend a bonus frivolously, and the money would have done so much more for my portfolio if my boss had let me add it to my 401(k), but that wasn't an option. Believe me, I'd asked.

"Go, have fun, enjoy yourself! And remember—when you return, you have a promotion waiting for you. You've earned it, Mia. All we need is your signed contract."

The promotion was everything I'd wanted, everything I had asked for, everything I had been working so hard toward. They'd offered me a new contract complete with more money, more clients, and my name on the door.

But I also knew more money plus more clients would equal less time for the personal life I still meant to have one day. And my name on the door? *McMann, Cohn, & Crawford Financial Planners?* That honor meant more responsibility. And permanency. That engraved plaque was starting to feel more like an anchor.

The private St. Claire ferry was a sleek, sixty-foot-long yacht, so large that the group of ten men and women on board, plus crew, didn't feel crowded, and there were private nooks and crannies just begging for a reader. The other passengers ignored me, and I gladly reciprocated; I felt wholly out of place taking a vacation on a ritzy private island with the type of people I usually worked for, not socialized with.

And not one of the passengers was an unattached man.

Thank God for the champagne the server offered. The guy was cute in his crisp white uniform, but way too young. He probably couldn't even legally drink what he was serving.

I took a sip while avoiding eye contact and gawking just a little (okay, maybe a lot) at the couple who were making out in the corner and who also had made an exceptional PDA scene in the Miami airport. They were practically begging to star in a viral TikTok video, "The Couple Who Ate Each Other's Faces Off." Honeymooners, probably. Or maybe they were adulterers, stealing away for a week while their unsuspecting spouses watched the kids, fed the dog, and went to work.

A redheaded woman came in from the rear deck, her wide-brimmed hat hitting my forehead. "Excuse me," I muttered.

She didn't acknowledge me but gazed around the cabin as if looking for someone. She hadn't had a companion when I saw her at St. John. She'd been reading the local newspaper, which was now partly sticking out of her oversized yellow Kate Spade purse that matched her oversized yellow sun hat.

And she was gorgeous. My hopes for a vacation boyfriend fell to the bottom of the sea. If there was a single hunky guy on St. Claire, he would be all over her. What were the chances there were two attractive single men under forty?

The young server approached with a tray of champagne. "Ms. Jones, Ms. Crawford, it is a pleasure to serve you this afternoon. May I offer appetizers?" With a sweep of his free hand, he gestured to one of several food stations set up—far more food than ten people could eat on a thirty-minute cruise.

"Thank you," I said with a smile, too nervous to eat.

The redhead sized me up and, deciding I was no threat to her status as Queen Bee, smiled warmly as she lifted a flute from the silver tray, ignored the server, and introduced herself. "I'm Amber Jones."

She spoke in a tone that suggested she expected me to recognize her name. I smiled right back and extended my hand. "Mia Crawford."

Amber looked at my hand as if I had germs. I dropped it, self-conscious. My clients expected formalities like shaking hands and general politeness, but clearly that wasn't going to be the case here.

"Have you been to St. Claire before?" I asked, trying to minimize the awkwardness as I discreetly glanced around the cabin, looking for a place to hide to finish my book.

"No." She, too, looked around the room, overtly people-watching. "I wonder how long Nelson will keep his newest acquisition around," she whispered snidely.

At first, I didn't know what she meant, but I followed her eyes to where Nelson Stockton, one of the first black owners of an NFL team, stood drinking a beer while his much younger wife sipped her bubbly. Was Amber referring to the wife as an *acquisition*? I was all for being catty when having drinks with a girlfriend, but the comment seemed cruel when spoken to a stranger.

Assessing Nelson and his wife, I thought they made an attractive power couple. He was a large, fit, sixty-something former athlete who now co-owned the team he used to play for. Mrs. Stockton was as beautiful as Amber but in a completely different way. Amber was tall, rail-thin, lush red hair, hazel eyes, smooth translucent skin. Mrs. Stockton was voluptuous, with catlike eyes and light brown skin so perfect I couldn't even tell if she was wearing makeup. Her golden-brown hair was wrapped around her head in braids, and her jewelry, though a bit overdone, was classy. Thirty? Forty? Fifty with an amazing plastic surgeon?

Another server came over with more champagne. I exchanged my empty glass for a full one and tried to make an escape before I was roped into another conversation. I turned and headed out the back, where I nearly collided with two men.

"Hello!" they said in unison with smiles bearing equally gorgeous straight white teeth. The taller man said, "I'm David, this is my husband, Doug."

"Hi," I said. "Mia Crawford."

"You were on the plane in Miami. First time at St. Claire?"

"Yes. You?"

They laughed as if I'd said something hilarious when it really was just a polite question.

"Oh, no! It's our fifth anniversary. We've come here every year since our honeymoon." Doug kissed his husband on the cheek and grinned. "We're meeting up with friends who were celebrating *their* fifth anniversary during *our* honeymoon. They arrived earlier, but David here is a *doctor*," he said with pride, and to instill a bit of envy, I thought. "Works far too hard if you ask me, so we couldn't fly out until this morning."

"What kind of doctor?" I asked.

"Orthopedic surgeon," David said. "Not as glamorous as Doug would have you believe."

"David has saved the careers of more than a dozen baseball pitchers. Including Andrew Locke, who's also here this week."

"Stop," David said with a shy grin. "Are you here with your boyfriend? Girlfriend? We should meet up and have drinks later."

"Actually, I'm alone."

They glanced at each other, and I felt doubly self-conscious. Two happily married men feeling sorry for me because I was (possibly) the only single woman on a beautiful island. I should have thought about that before I agreed to come here with hopes of finding a boyfriend for the week.

"Be careful," Doug said with what sounded eerily like genuine concern.

"I think a private island in the middle of nowhere should be safe."

"You would think that, wouldn't you?" Doug said.

"Don't scare her," David said.

Now super curious, I asked, "What shouldn't I be scared about?"

David gave Doug a disapproving look, then said, "A woman went missing a couple days ago. We heard someone talking about it while waiting for the ferry. She took the ferry to St. John but never returned."

"Do you know who she was? Did she have a husband or something?" For the first time in years, I thought about my mother. She hadn't disappeared into thin air, exactly, but I'd never forget the day she walked out on my dad and me. I don't know what she said to Dad in private, but to me? *"Honey, I'm just not happy. It's not you, sweetheart, but this is the best thing for all of us."*

I had been six. I never saw her again.

Doug shrugged. "We don't know anything about her. People were talking about it while we were waiting to board, and the redhead over there—" he made a loose gesture toward Amber Jones "—was asking about her. She'd read something in the paper. The woman's name was Diane . . ."

"Diana," David corrected him.

"Right, *Diana*. Like the goddess. We gave Amber the same warning.

"That's why a pretty girl like you needs to be careful," Doug said, patting my arm. "While this island seems safe, you never know what might happen. If you need anything, find us. We're here for you."

"Um, thank you?" They seemed so sincere, I almost thought they were *too* nice.

"Doug worries about everything. Don't let him scare you," David said. "St. Claire is a wonderful resort. We've met some terrific people over the years. We'll have drinks later, get to know each other."

"That would be nice, thank you."

They went into the cabin and I was happily alone. The luxury yacht cut through the ocean like a knife, leaving behind a white, frothy wake and erasing all feelings of unease. *This* was peace. The fresh air, the splash of the water, the blue sky meeting the bluer ocean. Maybe a week in paradise wouldn't be so bad.

Several deck chairs were positioned facing the water, none of them occupied. I sank into one, finally removed from the super-awkward expectation of mingling and small talk. I pulled my book from my bag, but couldn't stop thinking about Diana, the missing woman. As I stared at St. John Island shrinking in the distance, I thought up a hundred scenarios for what might have happened to her. She left her husband and disappeared with her lover. Or she met with foul play, the victim of a robbery gone bad. Or she was single and met a hot, sexy waiter who swept her off her feet, stole a yacht, and sailed off to the Bahamas.

I sighed, thinking about how I wouldn't mind meeting a hot, sexy waiter to sweep *me* off my feet and take me to a beautiful island where we could run around on the beach half-naked and drink daiquiris out of coconut shells.

Of course, I didn't want to go missing. Because not all sexy men were good guys, and being whisked away was just a half step from being kidnapped. Maybe Diana had trusted the wrong person.

"Enough," I told myself, mentally making a note to ask the concierge about the missing woman. Right now, I needed to relax. And finish my book. I opened it to where I'd left my favorite bookmark—a laminated black card with a clear go-away message in white Courier font:

Thanks for not talking to me while I read.

It worked most of the time.

I was lost again in the book. No longer did I hear the chatter of voices from the cabin or the thrum of the engine cutting through water. All I heard were the voices of the characters in this fictional world I cared about as I followed them on their journey to solve the string of arson fires and fall in love in the process.

"Miss? Ms. Crawford? Are you all right?"

I looked up at the skinny server—with enough hair sticking out in all directions, I briefly wondered if he'd somehow electrocuted himself. He stared at me and asked again, "Are you okay?"

"What? Yes! He came back at the end! I knew he would, but I was a little worried that his stubbornness would get the better of him."

"Um . . . I meant . . . you're crying, and everyone else has already disembarked."

The ferry had stopped. The engine was off. The water was still. I didn't hear voices, no clinking of glassware. It was just me and the young server, wide eyes filled with concern.

Wiping my face, slightly embarrassed—yes, I had cried tears of joy that these characters had found their happily-ever-after—I said, "Whoops, I'm sorry. I didn't miss the shuttle, did I?"

"No, everyone is on the dock."

"I'll be right there, okay?" I smiled broadly as if I wasn't just crying over a book.

"Take your time, Ms. Crawford. We won't leave without you."

He left, and I breathed a long sigh of relief, got up and crossed to the railing.

This story had impacted me more than most, and I couldn't wait to gush about it. I would write a review, maybe record a reel for Instagram. I loved the community of readers I'd fostered online, where we talked about the books that swept us away. Maybe I could start a series of reviews, "Books I Read on Vacation." Ha, it would be a short series, considering this would be my last vacation for a very long time. Especially with the partnership waiting back home.

The unbelievably blue ocean beckoned me. As I leaned over the railing, I could see *hundreds* of fish swimming along the sandy bottom. An entire school of shimmery gray fish turned in unison and disappeared under the boat.

Never have I seen water so inviting that I had the urge to just jump in. *That* would be completely out of character. *Spontaneous* was my wild grandmother, not me.

I wished I had someone who'd jump into the ocean with me, someone to share this amazing, once-in-a-lifetime experience.

But I didn't, and I'd have to suck it up that I was here alone. *Being alone doesn't mean I have to be miserable.*

Maybe David and Doug could introduce me to any single straight guys they knew.

Confident that the tears were gone and my reddened face could be dismissed as a result of the salty breeze, I stuffed my book in my bag and followed the path of the server.

The main cabin was littered with the remnants of cheese-and-fruit platters, champagne flutes scattered around, as if the passengers had just vanished. Of course, that was silly—my over-active imagination at work. This wasn't a Stephen King novel, and the Langoliers weren't chomping their way to shore.

A door had been propped open on the opposite side of the room, and as I went through, I heard a collective gasp. Turning, I shielded my eyes from the midday sun and saw the passengers standing on the dock, all looking in the same direction—up. I followed their gaze.

Nothing. What the heck were they looking at? I grabbed my sunglasses and put them on, searching the sky for whatever had caught their attention across the brilliant crystalline bay.

Cliffs towered over the northern edge of the resort, and still I saw nothing. Then, at the top of the ledge, a giant bird—no, a *hang glider*—swept into view.

A man glided off the mountain until he was over the ocean, his body outstretched behind him, his legs encased in a sack, the large white wing that enabled him to soar like a bird glimmer-ing in the sun. Everyone gasped again—and this time I joined in—when the hang glider did a loop, like a roller coaster, over the ocean.

"Idiot," I muttered as *oohs* and *aahs* rolled through the crowd standing on the dock.

"Oh my God, that's so hot," a female voice said. A glance told me it was one of the horny honeymooners speaking.

Hot? Stupid show-off, more like it.

"I'll show you *hot*, darling," her husband said, and dipped her over his knee until her long hair touched the dock. Then he kissed her neck up and down while she giggled, "Oh, that tickles!"

I had no idea who the man was, and I wanted to ignore both the extreme sport spectacle *and* the PDA coming from the honeymooners, but I couldn't take my eyes off the aerial show. He swung side to side like a pendulum. Then he pushed forward, arching his back, and the glider went up again.

"How is he doing that?" Amber asked. "Is there a motor on the wings?"

"No," the honeymooner said, holding his wife close to his side while she gazed adoringly into his face. I didn't know if her expression was love or lust or witchcraft because it seemed unreal. "It's physics. He's using the wind speed plus air pressure plus his momentum to propel his wings."

His tone sounded like someone who made shit up to sound smart, but I had no other explanation, so maybe he was right. You would never see me do something so dangerously stupid.

The hang gliding idiot smoothly ascended. Then he did another loop and soared toward the rocks at the base of the cliff. The ocean swells splashed high, and I braced myself for his body to hit the boulders with a bloody *splat*.

"He's going to crash!" someone shouted, and a chorus of agreement rang through the group, followed by a collective inhale of breath as the glider pushed his arms straight up and flew parallel to the ocean, out to sea.

"Fool is going to break his bloody neck," the deep voice of Nelson Stockton proclaimed.

Yep. One hundred percent. The daredevil was going to crash into the ocean, drown, and put a huge damper on the first vacation I'd had in years.

As the gliding man disappeared from view, murmurs continued among the group. Admiring and critical, everyone had a comment.

"Is he flying all the way to St. John?" the bride—who had finally ended her creepy, doe-eyed gaze at her husband—asked.

Uh, no, that's like more than twenty miles. Maybe he wasn't the only fool on the island.

"There's probably a boat out there," David reasonably suggested.

The doctor. So he wasn't just a pretty face with an advanced degree. He had common sense too.

A boat would haul him in. Or maybe he really did crash into the ocean, body broken and floating for the seagulls to pick clean. Or dragged down by sharks and devoured. Or shot down by the coast guard, thinking he was a drug smuggler.

Hmm. Maybe I'd been reading too many murder mysteries these days. Might be time to switch over to romance again.

Movement on shore caught my eye. The crew was putting luggage into a van. Next to the van was an electric shuttle, presumably to take us to the resort.

Right now, all I wanted was to get away from the crowd, find the gift shop so I could buy a few books, and relax by the pool with a tall, frothy—and most importantly, strong—drink. From the pool I could check out all the men on the island and identify those who were alone, introduce myself, and hope for that spark between us, that *look*, that *feeling*, that flip-flop in my stomach that sent my libido into overdrive.

But no one was leaving the dock, all looking out to where the man had disappeared across the bay, and I was trapped at the top of the stairs because Amber of the Deadly Yellow Hat blocked my path.

"Excuse me," I said, and tried to step down.

She didn't acknowledge me, nor did she move.

I'm not confrontational. In fact, I go out of my way to avoid confrontation. Growing up, my dad and Grams would argue about everything—my dad was too stingy, Grams a spendthrift; my dad too judgmental, Grams too irresponsible. They argued about me, too. I hated when they argued about me. I would make myself as small as possible and hope they didn't ask for my opinion; hence, I was stuck here with a hat in my face and no recourse other than pushing Amber overboard.

It was a thought, but I didn't act on it.

"Oh. My!" The exclamation came from Mrs. Stockton.

"Is that him?"

"What is he doing?"

I couldn't see anything through Amber's hat, then realized the group was gawking at something behind the boat, out over the ocean. Standing on my tippy toes, I turned my head and saw the glider's wide wing coming straight for the boat. The jerk swooped right over us, banked right, then flew over the water only feet above the surface. He headed to shore, using the water to slow down as he unzipped the bag that his legs were encased in. As he descended, his legs touched the sand, and he ran along the beach, pulling his wing down as he slowed to a jog, then a fast walk. A rod protruded from the glider; he stuck that into the sand and stopped.

"Amazing!" a woman gasped. She sounded as if she'd just had an orgasm.

A man I presumed was her husband kissed her on the cheek. "We can do that," he said.

Right. Just jump off a cliff and hope that flimsy wing brings you back to the beach in one piece. Good luck with that.

No one—and I mean *no one*—would convince me to strap myself into one of those insane contraptions. I'll fly the way God intended: in a plane with an engine, trained pilots, and ten-dollar mini-bottles of vodka.

"Who *was* that?" Mrs. Stockton asked no one in particular.

The captain of the boat smiled as he approached us. "That, Mrs. Stockton, is Jason Mallory, our head bartender and part-time entertainment." He chuckled. "Your bags are on their way to the resort, where they will be taken to your rooms. If you'd like to follow me to the shuttle, the driver is ready."

I half expected him to bow and chirp, *Your chariot awaits.*

"I hope there's a backup bartender," Mr. Stockton said. "Mr. Mallory is itching to break his neck."

"He hasn't broken a bone yet," the captain said with a hint of pride.

There's a first for everything.

I could just picture it now, Jason Mallory stuck in a wheelchair with a broken leg à la Jimmy Stewart in *Rear Window*, resigned to watching the world from his apartment. I supposed if he lived full-time on the island, the view wouldn't be so bad, but the boredom might kill him just the same.

The passengers started down the dock. I was about to say *excuse me* to Amber again when I noticed she was looking in a completely different direction. Instead of the beach where Jason Mallory was packing up his hang glider, her gaze went south.

At first, I didn't see anything, only cliffs and a trail that went up the mountain. Then something moved—a man in khaki pants and a blue short-sleeved collared shirt. He was standing at the edge of the trail on an overlook watching the boat—or watching the people on the boat. I shivered, remembering what Doug and David told me about the missing woman—and my thoughts about a serial killer.

For my own peace of mind, I needed to find out exactly what happened to Diana. I really hoped she was having a lovely affair with a cabana boy and just lost track of time.

A laugh bubbled up in my throat and escaped. I slapped my hand over my mouth. Where had that come from? Amber shot me a dirty look, then followed the rest of the passengers.

I glanced back up to the trail; the man was gone. I counted to five before I followed Amber. I didn't want to be stuck sitting next to her, but I might not have a choice—only other single woman and all.

Suddenly, the sheer beauty of the island hit me. The bay with gently rolling waves, the staggering mountain that seemed to erupt from the water, the sprawling resort with buildings that practically disappeared into the lush green trees and flowering plants. I couldn't see the swimming pool from here, but from the brochure, knew it rolled right up to the sand.

As I started to follow the group, a folded newspaper tucked

partly under a seat cushion caught my eye. It was the same news-paper that Amber had had in her bag, but now I could read the headline.

AMERICAN WOMAN STILL MISSING
LAST SEEN LEAVING ST. CLAIRE

I picked up the paper. A photo accompanied the article: a stylish blonde with light-colored eyes and flawless skin.

Diana Harden, 32, of New Orleans, missing since Sunday morning.

Today was Tuesday.

I started to read the article.

"Ms. Crawford!"

Feeling guilty for no reason, my head jerked up. The captain smiled and waved. "The shuttle is ready to leave."

I stuffed the newspaper into my tote and climbed down the stairs. I definitely wanted to know more about Diana Harden. A single woman going missing at an exclusive resort in the Carib-bean? A chill ran down my spine remembering Doug's genuine concern that I was here alone.

Was Diana on St. Claire alone as well? Did Doug know more about her disappearance than he had said? Was my fan-tasy that Diana had gone off for a weekend of sun and sex about to be shattered?

Or maybe she did something stupid like hang glide off a cliff and drown in the ocean.

"Stop," I whispered. My overactive imagination had kicked into high gear.

Maybe she ran away from an abusive spouse, like in *Sleeping with the Enemy*. Or faked her own death à la *Gone Girl*. Perhaps she was an heiress, kidnapped for ransom. Or the victim of a serial killer who stalked rich tourists on remote islands.

At that moment, I was glad I wasn't rich.

The more likely story? Something completely innocuous, like she lost her cell phone. Or she was robbed. Or got drunk, fell off the dock, and was in a coma at the hospital.

Still, curiosity piqued, I was determined to learn more, starting with devouring this article—and anything I could find online about Diana Harden—as soon as I checked in to my room.

CHAPTER
TWO

"Push your boundaries, that's what they're there for."

—Colleen Hoover, *Slammed*

WHEN STUART COHN HAD handed me the brochure on St. Claire last month and said this was where they were sending me for R & R, the images were pretty enough. Blue ocean, green mountain, hidden waterfall, large, opulent rooms—each with a view of the water through wall-sized glass doors that opened onto a balcony or the beach. Private Jacuzzis, a pool that appeared to bleed into the ocean, beach volleyball, private cabanas, colorful umbrellas, palm trees, and flowering bushes taller than a man.

The printed photos had no dimension, though. Words were just words when you had no experience to give them life.

I felt like a tourist in New York, looking up and gawking at the simple majesty that was the St. Claire Resort, standing in the middle of the open lobby filled with more plants than people. Trees grew three stories to the skylights, some of which were open. Small, colorful birds flew inside and out, happily calling to each other—perhaps recognizing the luck of the draw being hatched in paradise. A waterfall seemed to come from nowhere out of the ceiling, cascading down rocks into a large pond filled with koi.

Every breath was a new experience. Jasmine and hibiscus

and a hint of something I couldn't place. Underneath the floral was the heavier scent of moist soil, then the fruity aromas of coconut and pineapple. I closed my eyes and wished for all the people to disappear so it was me and maybe a super-hot lifeguard with magic fingers who knew how to cook. Maybe that's why everyone called the Caribbean paradise. I wasn't simply on vacation; I had become a part of the island itself.

Unrealistic. All of it. What hot lifeguard would want me, Mia Crawford, who had to control everything and everyone for fear that something would go wrong? You know the phrase if you want it done right, do it yourself? My picture is plastered next to it. Letting someone else make decisions felt like I was on a roller coaster with no seat belt. Maybe that's why I felt so out-of-sorts coming to St. Claire—the decision wasn't really mine.

I wandered through the main building, in no rush to check in. Wide hallways, floors of large terra-cotta tile, potted ferns, and still more birds chirping. A pair of bright blue lovebirds perched on a branch above me as I strolled through the main hall. For a minute I thought they were fake, like in Disneyland's Tiki Room. Then they flew across the hall to another tree, where they looked down on me and chattered. The sounds of nature—birds, ocean, waterfall—replaced the need for music.

Enchanting.

Nooks abounded. A bench here, a comfy chair there, a café that oozed rich coffee and sweet pastries where a foursome—an older couple and a much younger couple—sat chatting. A family vacation? Grandparents taking their favorite grandchild and spouse on a special trip? Or did they just meet and hit it off, a multigenerational friendship? I pictured coming here with Grams. She would have loved everything about the island. Grams had genuine joy. Sometimes, I wished I'd inherited that trait.

"Remember, drinks later," a voice said. I jumped, then grinned when I saw David and Doug standing next to me.

"Yes," I said. "Here?" I waved to the bar next to the waterfall.

Doug linked his arm with David's and said, "Tonight, the Sky Bar, top of the mountain." He motioned toward a sign that listed times the shuttle left for the Sky Bar each night. "You'll love it. A buffet *to die for*, music, and the most exquisite sunset you will ever see. You're coming."

"I don't know," I said, feeling out of place. They were so friendly and seemed so genuine that I didn't want to decline, but I didn't want to intrude on their anniversary either.

"You *are*," Doug said.

"I'll try," I said. "Thank you."

An attractive forty-something man, lean and fit with black hair graying on the sides and dark blue eyes, approached us. "David?"

He smiled when David turned to him. "I thought it was you."

"Andrew, great to see you again." They shook hands, and David said, "You remember my husband, Doug?"

"Of course." Andrew shook Doug's hand.

"Andrew Locke, Mia Crawford," David introduced us. "Mia came over on the ferry with us."

Andrew smiled and took my hand. "Good to meet you, Mia. Is this your first time on St. Claire?"

"Yes," I said. Andrew was not only attractive, but exactly the kind of man I gravitated toward. I glanced at his hand. No wedding ring.

"What do you think so far?"

"Beautiful," I said. "I can't wait to hit the beach."

"My girlfriend and daughter are waiting for me there right now," Andrew said. "David, I'll reach out, and we'll have drinks to catch up."

Okay, girlfriend. Scratch him off the list. Also, he was at least ten years older than me. Not an insurmountable problem, but I didn't go after men who were taken, no matter how attractive and friendly.

"That would be great," David said.

Andrew smiled at me. "I've been coming to St. Claire every year for more than a decade. If you want any information about the island, let me know."

Andrew said his goodbyes and headed toward the beach.

David glanced at his watch. "Let's unpack. We're meeting the others in thirty minutes. See you tonight, Mia. If you don't come, you'll hurt our feelings."

They headed down a path that led to private beach cabins. I wasn't sure if David was serious or not, and I didn't want to hurt anyone's feelings.

I headed toward the lobby when I heard Nelson Stockton's familiar voice. "Anja, you don't know what happened, and I'm not going to take any chances with you."

The couple sat on a love seat in a nook that faced the waterfall. They were practically hidden among the plants that lined the alcove. A tiny bird hopped on the table in front of them, then flew away.

"Darling," Anja said in her subtle accent—not foreign, maybe a touch of the South. "I won't let you do this. Do you think I'm so weak I can't survive exposure?" She reached out for her husband, her diamond bracelet sparkling in the sunlight coming from the open roof.

"You shouldn't have to. Dammit, woman, I love you!"

I felt a jolt of compassion, the emotion in Nelson's voice hitting a chord deep down, the tone more than the words telling me how deeply he loved his wife. I didn't want to intrude on their private conversation any more than I already had, so tried to discreetly backtrack. Unfortunately, Nelson saw me.

"Ms. Crawford, yes?" he asked with a nod.

"Yes, hello," I said as if I hadn't noticed them.

"I'm Nelson Stockton. We met briefly on St. John. My wife, Anja." He took her hand, kissed it.

Anja smiled warmly. "We're going to have a bite to eat in the bar. Care to join us?"

"Oh—thank you, but I still need to check in."

"We'll be there all afternoon, I'm sure. The beachside bar—the Blue Dahlia—is quieter and more relaxing than the poolside bar. Stop by and we'll get to know each other."

It sounded like a genuine invitation, just like David and Doug's earlier.

"Thank you, maybe I will," I said with a smile and walked away. I wanted to know more about whatever had upset the couple.

Next to the reception desk was a long table with multiple glass canisters filled with icy water, a different fruit floating on the top of each one. Oranges. Lemons. Pineapple. Cucumber. I poured some of the lemon-infused water and drank deeply, looked around the lobby again, and spotted the most gorgeous man I'd seen in, well, forever.

I poured another glass of ice water. I needed it.

He could have walked right off the cover of a romance novel. Sun-kissed brown hair that curled at the collar, his eyes a deep green, like a lush forest at sunset. His skin light brown from both heritage and time outdoors. Like a Mayan god touched by St. Patrick. He was wearing khaki shorts and a lightweight jacket over a white polo shirt that might have been a staff shirt. Staff or guest, he was the most attractive man I had seen all day. All week. All year.

He was chatting with an employee and the honeymooners.

I couldn't help but stare.

He glanced over and caught me looking at him. Was I blushing? No, please no. No blushing.

He smiled. I melted. My face heated. Damn. Blushing.

The Irish-Mayan god stood between me and the reception desk. I would have to say hello. I wanted to say hello. I smiled. He nodded, motioning for me to approach. I took a step forward, but an overdressed older couple rushed over to him and began an animated conversation.

Dammit. Okay, I would wait around for him to be done greeting every guest. Maybe he was the manager, or the activities director, with a job to do.

I could think of a hundred ways he could entertain me.

He winked at me as if he could read my thoughts, and I abruptly turned and started walking. Right into the gift shop. Okay, good. I'd browse a bit, calm down, and when I was done, maybe my dream man would be free.

My cell phone rang, throwing me completely off-balance. I hurriedly pulled it from my bag and fumbled to answer, worried that there was an emergency at work. *I knew I shouldn't have come to a remote island!*

No emergency. It was Jane, one of my closest friends.

"Mia!" Jane squealed. "I'm with Amanda. I've got you on speaker. We were just talking about you and decided to call instead. How is the resort? How are the men on the island? Describe them all. *Every* juicy detail."

I glanced around to make sure no one could hear her side of the conversation.

"Stop. I practically just got here."

"Where are you now?" Amanda asked. "On the beach? In that sexy new bikini we forced you to buy?"

Jane said, "I'll bet she's in her room reading."

"Where are you?" Amanda demanded.

"I'm not in my room reading," I said as I stared at a rack of bestsellers.

"See?" Amanda said. "So, talk."

"About?"

"How is it? The island, the men, the drinks. Spill."

"I literally stepped off the ferry less than thirty minutes ago. I was about to check in when you called." I paused, glanced around, and then said quietly, "Almost everyone here is with someone, but there's this one guy. I think he works here. He's gorgeous." Understatement.

"Ohhh," the girls said together. "More," Jane added.

Talking to my besties helped. If I was going to have a wild and crazy fling this week, I needed to prepare.

"He's about six feet, lean, tan, muscles in all the right places," I said. "Dark hair that curls at his collar."

"Name?"

"I don't know. I just saw him across the lobby."

I glanced out and he was still there, talking to the same couple, laughing at something they said. Then he looked at me over their heads, and I froze as our eyes met. Then I turned my back on him. I needed more time to prepare.

"And you didn't introduce yourself? Right then and there?" Jane said. "Dammit, Mia! What did we tell you?"

I moaned. "Channel Elle Woods." *Legally Blonde* was our favorite movie. We'd seen it a million times.

"Channel Elle, channel Elle," they chanted.

I needed to radiate calm, cool confidence just like Elle Woods. And here I was, heart pounding, hiding in the gift shop.

"I'll try," I said.

"Just do it," Jane said. "This is the last time you can be wild and free. Next week, you'll be thirty and chained to a desk for the rest of your life."

I should *never* have told Jane and Amanda about the promotion.

"Love you too," I mumbled.

Amanda, the diplomat, said, "Jane, leave her alone. Mia, seriously, you want this. You *need* this. Have fun and don't think about anything except the moment, okay? Promise to be spontaneous?"

"Promise," I said. "Now I really need to check in so I can enjoy the beach."

"I swear," Jane said, "if you don't have sex on the beach, I'm never speaking to you again. When Robbie and I went to Miami, we . . ."

"Stop! I don't want to hear about your sex life, not without at least three margaritas," I said. Jane and Robbie had had sex in so many public places that I was surprised they hadn't been arrested for indecent exposure. "Love you both. Bye." I ended the call before they could say anything else.

I've known Jane and Amanda since college, and my life would be worse without them. Three years ago, I introduced

Amanda to my assistant, Braden, and they married last summer; Jane and Robbie had been together for nearly two years with their destination wedding scheduled for October. Which would just leave me, Mia Crawford, the unattached hanger-on, the fifth wheel.

Because even if I found a man to share my bed this week, it wasn't like he'd want to come home to meet my cats.

The gift shop was filled with clothing, bathing suits, hats, toiletries, souvenirs, and books. Lots and lots of books, more than just the bestseller rack.

You'd think someone like me, who reads every day, would have brought enough books to get me through the week. Normally, I would have, but Grams had called yesterday while I was in the middle of packing, needing help with a financial crisis. Hours later, I realized she was short this month because she had given four hundred dollars to an environmental group, two hundred dollars to an animal shelter, and fifty dollars to her distinguished neighbor who made six figures but apparently needed cash for a date.

The causes might be worthy, but not if Grams couldn't buy groceries. I'd already taken over paying for her rent-stabilized fifty-five-plus apartment, utilities, and insurance out of the trust I'd set up for her—a trust she couldn't touch because she'd give it away. But I made sure she had money in her personal account so she could get her hair done, buy groceries, go to a movie or lunch with a friend now and again. Yet ten days into the month, she was broke. She'd called me, and I had panicked more than she had, thus forgetting to pack my books because I was in a rush this morning.

And if I didn't have a book to read, I would literally die.

The clerk approached, a young woman with dark curly hair and a bright smile. In fact, all the staff I'd met smiled brightly—too brightly. They were the Stepford Staff, I thought. Should I be worried?

"Can I help you find anything?"

"Just looking for a book."

"This table here—" she gestured like Vanna White from Grams's favorite game show "—holds books about the islands, the history of the area, photography. Over there—" she again gestured broadly "—is the fiction section. We try to keep it stocked with newer releases, but if there is something you'd like that we don't have, I can order it from St. John. It'll be here tomorrow."

"Thank you," I said, and turned toward the rack of new releases. Nothing called out to me. The covers were uninspired, the titles boring, the authors not on my auto-buy list. And yes, some of the books I'd already read.

A table in the corner was tastefully decorated with flowers and a handcrafted sign:

BEACH READS!
Books left behind by guests
Free for your enjoyment

One of the books written by a popular author looked depressing. After I read the inside flap, my suspicions were confirmed—a story about a lying, cheating spouse. No thanks. I'd already had one boyfriend who'd cheated on me . . .

The next book was about a pathological liar. Also dated one of *those* . . .

And the third book was about love the second time around. Maybe . . . except, none of my ex-boyfriends ignited that spark inside me that made me think we could or should get back together.

Jane and Amanda agreed with my Grams. "Mia, your expectations are too high." "Mia, there are no Prince Charmings, only frogs." "The only perfect guys are in romance novels."

Yet Jane was engaged to Robbie, who ran his family's construction business, and Amanda was happily married to Braden, and I know that they didn't think *their* lovers were frogs.

They were partly right. I had high expectations. I didn't want perfection; I just wanted someone who was perfect *for me*. What was wrong with that? If I was going to spend the rest of my life with a man until we were both old and gray and needed hearing aids, shouldn't I have someone I enjoyed spending time with? Someone who was smart and interesting and liked my cats?

Frustrated that I couldn't even find one book that whispered "Read me," I spotted, tucked under a historical romance, a book with a torn cover.

It pained me—physically hurt me—to see a book in such distress. I picked it up, and though the lower right corner was completely missing, the cover was still intriguing—clearly a romantic thriller with a man and woman on a speedboat flying through the water while being pursued by men in black on a bigger, badder yacht.

Intriguing.

I read the back cover, noted the book was written by a debut author. In addition to the partly torn cover, the pages were gritty and slightly expanded, as if someone had left the book in the bathroom while taking a long, hot shower. Normally, I'd never read a book in such a sorry state, but it was the only story that spoke to me, and I needed *something* to read.

"Excuse me," a female voice said.

I glanced up, but the woman wasn't speaking to me. She hailed the clerk, who was straightening a display.

The clerk went to help her, and the guest complained that she couldn't purchase something without charging it to the room.

"We're not set up to take cash or credit," the clerk said.

"That's ridiculous," the woman snapped.

I tried to ignore the rude woman. I took a selfie with the book I'd read on the ferry for my review, then left it on the table.

"Look," the woman said. "I need to buy something and my boyfriend can't know about it, because it's a *surprise*, understand?"

She spoke so nasty to the clerk that I wanted to intervene. As I was about to lend the clerk moral support, a man of average height, dressed in an impeccable summer suit, entered the shop and immediately said, "Ms. Morrison, follow me, and we'll get this taken care of to your complete satisfaction." He motioned for her to join him, and Ms. Morrison said, "Thank you, Tristan. I should have come to you first."

I grabbed postcards for Grams, Amanda and Jane, Mr. Cohn, and my neighbor who was caring for Nick and Nora, my cats. I brought them to the counter and said, "Are you okay—" I glanced at her shirt "—Trina?"

She smiled. "Yes. How may I help you?" I figured she must deal with difficult guests all the time.

I showed her the postcards, and she provided stamps, all of which would be charged to my room. "There's a box in the lobby where you can leave them—the mail goes out to St. John every afternoon—or bring them to me and I'll see to it."

"I saw a newspaper on St. John." Slight fib. I saw it on the boat. It was now in my purse. "There was an article about a missing woman, Diana Harden. Did you know her?"

Trina didn't say anything for a beat, and I had this sense that she was going to lie. "I don't think she came in here while I was working. But I'm sure she'll turn up." Then she smiled her Stepford Smile and rushed over to an older man who walked into the shop.

Okay, I supposed it wasn't professional for staff to chat about missing guests with current guests, but that was weird.

I stepped out of the gift store half hoping the super-hot demigod was standing there waiting for me.

How may I serve you today, Ms. Crawford? Shall I bring chocolate-covered strawberries and champagne to your room? Would you like a private massage? Lavender lotion or vanilla?

I sighed, envisioning his hands working my sore muscles into complete bliss . . . but he wasn't standing there pining away for me. Such was my life. I pushed him to the back of my mind (not too far back) and checked in. I declined the escort but accepted the resort map. The clerk—Henry—had helpfully circled my room, a separate cabin north of the main lodge, down a trail that led to other private cabins.

"Have a lovely week with us, Ms. Crawford." Henry was as cheerful as Trina and the boat captain and everyone else who worked here. Pleasant on the surface, but with a hint of . . . of what? Like they all had a secret.

I thanked him and headed down the path that led to my cabin.

The resort was built at the eastern base of a steeply sloping mountain. Hiking trails marked with names like "Tiki Walk" and "Siempre Viva Vista" meandered away from the main area. A carved arrow pointed toward an eerie path darkened by a canopy of huge fanlike leaves dripping with sea grapes. The dark serenity drew me toward the forked path. The left headed up the mountain with a wooden sign that read "Hot Springs." To the right, a flatter, narrower path framed with vine-covered trees was labeled "Luz Luna Bahia." Both looked inviting.

The resort was a maze, and the main path curved around to the beach on the opposite side of the lodge. As my cabin came into view, voices broke the silence. A loud female voice said something indiscernible. Then a male said, "Keep quiet." They came from above one of the many paths that cut through the mountains.

Shielded only by the palm trees and flowering bushes that marked the stone path, I froze. One step forward and they might see me. Which wouldn't mean anything, right? Just walking to my room, don't mind me, continue with your argument . . .

I looked up. Partially obscured by the palm leaves, Amber Jones's bright yellow hat stood out among all the green.

So she *had* been meeting someone here. One point for Mia, the amateur sleuth.

Enola Holmes, eat your heart out.

I couldn't move. If I continued to my cottage, they'd see me and think I was eavesdropping.

Amber was arguing with a man who was probably her boyfriend. Or husband. Or maybe a married man she was having an affair with. Or a serial killer . . .

Stop. The unknown fate of the missing woman was clearly on my mind. Still, I didn't move because now it would be awkward and suspicious. Leaning into the huge jasmine bush, I was trying to make myself as small as possible when I heard, "You have until Friday or you're dead."

CHAPTER
THREE

> "The key to good eavesdropping is not getting caught."
>
> —Lemony Snicket, *The Blank Book*

DEAD. WAS THAT LITERAL or figurative? As in, I'm going to shoot you with the gun in my pocket *dead*, or I'm going to make your life miserable *dead*?

Amber's next words were lost in the breeze. Then she exclaimed, ". . . and don't threaten me!"

She didn't sound intimidated, so maybe *dead* along the lines of *I'm dead meat if I'm late again.*

At the age of nine, I'd convinced myself that Mrs. Horowitz, a woman I'd known half my young life, had killed her husband. I was wrong. But after devouring twenty *Nancy Drew* mysteries in a row and borrowing my science teacher's binoculars for the weekend, I saw murder, mystery, and mayhem around every corner.

Mr. Horowitz had simply been away on a business trip. But during the five days he was gone, I'd visualized more than a dozen ways Mrs. Horowitz could have disposed of his body.

"You have no idea what you've done," the man said. "You arrogant fucking bitch."

"That's rich, coming from you," Amber said. "I *said* I'd get everything back!"

"Do you know what will happen if those documents fall into the wrong hands?"

"Are you lost, Ms. Crawford?"

I jumped back and nearly fell into the vines. I was a poor excuse for a spy, hiding in the bushes but completely visible from the path in front of me.

A tall, lean black woman with short hair dressed in the St. Claire uniform of beige shorts and white shirt with her name, *Kalise*, embroidered in deep purple stared expectantly at me.

"No, I, just, was, um, enjoying the beautiful day."

Lying did not come easy to me. I smiled to show how honest I was. I don't think she was buying it.

"It is a lovely afternoon. I'm Kalise, the activities director. I hope you'll be attending the sunset dinner at the Sky Bar tonight? The shuttle leaves every fifteen minutes between six and seven."

"Sure, great, thanks."

"The details are in the guest portfolio on the desk in your cottage." She gestured down the path with her elegant hand.

"Thank you," I said and walked away, hoping and praying that Amber and the stranger hadn't realized I'd been listening to their conversation. I glanced back over my shoulder, waved and smiled at Kalise, and glanced up to the path above. No one was there.

Whew.

Amber and her lover/boss/enemy were arguing about some documents, and he *had* threatened her, but that didn't mean it had been an *actual* threat, and it really wasn't my business.

Though I couldn't help but wonder what Amber had done to anger the man. What documents had he been referring to? Financial? My mind usually went to money because that was my job, and as they say, money is the root of all evil. And the cause of most divorces.

"Stop," I said out loud as I opened the door to my suite. Mysteries were only in books. My life was far too calm and organized to have time for adventure—and I certainly wasn't looking for trouble. A risk-averse CPA–slash–financial planner? As boring as they come.

One step inside and I froze, mouth open at the view.

All rational thought disappeared. I had no words.

I never wanted to leave. To hell with responsible choices.

One entire wall of the beachfront cabin was thick floor-to-ceiling glass that folded closed, the seams barely visible. Beyond was a deck with a private hot tub, then three steps down to the sand. No other cottage in sight. An older couple with white hair and deeply tanned skin from too much time in the sun walked hand in hand fifty yards down the beach. Bushes of thick, vibrant greens bursting with colorful flowers surrounded my bungalow, providing privacy.

Turning a slow three-sixty, I absorbed the space. The muted blues and greens were soothing, the king-sized bed inviting with a fluffy white down comforter and a mountain of pillows. The bathroom—deep bathtub, separate rain shower with multiple jets, private toilet, large counter. Toiletries were tastefully arranged on a tray between the two sinks: shampoos, conditioners, lotions, toothpaste. A narrow closet held additional supplies and extra towels.

The walk-in closet was as big as my bedroom at home. Four robes—two plush, two lightweight cotton with the St. Claire logo tastefully embroidered on a pocket—hung neatly. A built-in set of drawers took up one wall. A wall safe was also provided. Convenient if you had anything of value, like Mrs. Stockton's diamonds.

After unpacking, I booted up my laptop. Fingers poised above the keyboard to type in my password, I froze.

What the hell was I doing? I had seven days to do anything I wanted, and my first thought was *work*?

St. Claire was literally paradise on earth, where the only people were guests and the staff who served them. How could I consider working when every whim and desire I had would be fulfilled? If I couldn't find the sexy should-be cover model, maybe a muscular, tanned lifeguard would cross my path. Or a limber, inventive yoga instructor. Or a sensuous cook to feed me grapes and fresh oysters . . . I needed to be spontaneous and confident. *Channel Elle Woods*, I heard Amanda and Jane instruct. This was my last free week. My promotion loomed ahead, and now was the time to throw caution to the wind, as they say. Do *something* so I had stories to tell my girlfriends when they thought I was a boring workaholic who lived for spreadsheets and fiscal accountability.

I shut my laptop, put my phone on the charger, and changed into my new bikini and wrap-around sundress.

It was three in the afternoon: I would socialize, eat, drink, be merry. And track down that gorgeous man who'd smiled at me in the lobby.

This was my vacation, maybe my last vacation for years. The irony? With my promotion, I'd have more money—enough to pay for a trip to St. Claire myself—but no time to take even a three-day weekend. I'd never really cared about the trade-off until I got here, and now the thought of this trip being the first and last for me was depressing.

But money meant security. It meant helping Grams, paying my rent, saving for retirement. My dad had thought of all that and created a modest trust for me in the event he died . . . and then he'd died. How could I forget all he'd taught me, the responsibility he'd instilled in me, and turn down a promotion that included my name on the door?

I had a week to make my decision, and there really was only one decision I could make. Why was I doubting myself?

I knew who I was at work: Mia Crawford, CPA, Financial Planner. My clients respected me. My boss valued me.

But numbers didn't keep me warm at night. If I took the promotion, I wouldn't have time to find love. I would be alone for the rest of my life.

I had to work. I had to take care of my Grams and make

sure my future was financially secure. But what if I never found anyone to share my future with?

The thought made me surprisingly sad.

Maybe I'd never find my forever love, but I damn well could find a lover for the next six days.

CHAPTER
FOUR

"The fear of death follows from the fear
of life. A man who lives fully is prepared
to die at any time."

— Mark Twain

I CONSIDERED THE MAIN outdoor bar options from two perspectives: comfort, and the ability to meet single men.

The circular bar in the center of the pool, accessed by a bridge, would make me feel onstage. It was a focal point of the resort. I noted that Doug, David, and their friends sat under an umbrella table, laughing. Another couple—a fit forty-something man and a woman ten years younger—sat with an older teenager who looked exceptionally bored. The girl wore jean shorts and a hoodie and stared at her cell phone, clearly not wanting to be there. When the man turned his profile to me, I recognized Andrew Locke, the very handsome, slightly-too-old-for-me former baseball player who had a girlfriend.

I shielded my eyes and squinted. His girlfriend was the rude woman from the gift shop. Silky brown hair cut stylishly to fall perfectly on her shoulders, large designer sunglasses, long tanned legs. She leaned over and kissed Andrew. The teenager got up and left.

The pool had the benefit of allowing me to show off my

cute bikini. But everyone was in couples or groups, and swimming solo would make me feel even more isolated.

The Blue Dahlia connected the main resort building to the beach with the bar dividing indoor and outdoor seating. Dahlias of every hue—except blue, which didn't exist in nature—filled colorful vases on the tables, with additional displays of the flower mixed with wide, green stalks in tall urns in the corners.

I crossed the threshold. The lazy overhead fans moved the flowery scent of the dahlias and jasmine around. Neither too cold nor too hot, as if the island itself was the perfect temperature.

The honeymooners—I still didn't know their names—had their faces together in the corner, alternately talking and kissing, ignoring their rapidly melting drinks. Hadn't I just seen them making out in the lobby? I didn't see the Stocktons—I would have enjoyed getting to know them better. Maybe because Nelson had the same sensibilities as I did about the hang glider, or maybe because Anja seemed genuinely friendly.

I approached the buffet of snacks and selected plump grapes, cheddar cheese, and a spear of fresh fruit I didn't recognize that made my mouth water. Pineapple-glazed meatballs on toothpicks smelled great, so I took a few.

"Ohmigod, this is amazing," a woman said as she approached the buffet. "I just *can't*." She picked up a plate and put one fruit spear on it. I glanced at my very full plate and bit my lip, but didn't say anything.

The woman—a little younger than me and pretty in an exaggerated way with dyed blond hair, too much makeup, and boobs that might have been fake (but I wasn't going to touch to find out)—spoke rapidly. "I'm Candace Tremaine. My friends call me CeeCee. My boyfriend and I have been here since Friday, and I swear I've already gained five pounds. And I'm going to the gym every day!"

I spied the bar, but CeeCee blocked my path.

"Did you just come in today?" CeeCee asked. "I haven't seen you before."

"Yes," I said. "I'm Mia."

"Where's your boyfriend? Husband? *Girlfriend.*" She winked and laughed. "I had a girlfriend once. It was great, you know? Have to try everything once! But I prefer men."

"Me, too."

I immediately second-thought my response. Did she think that meant *me, too*, that I'd once had a girlfriend but preferred men? Or that I just preferred men? Or . . .

"And," CeeCee continued, "this is the most *amazing* resort, isn't it? Have you been to the Sky Bar yet? Or the waterfall? Ohmigod, it's incredible! We went there Sunday—you have to go with a group because the trail is totally dangerous and someone actually *died* there years ago because they went at night and fell—and the water is, like, totally clear and the staff packs a picnic and it's *so* romantic. Oh, right, you just got here. Maybe the four of us could picnic together!"

It took me a beat to realize she was asking if I wanted to double date. "I'm here alone," I said.

CeeCee frowned deeply, seemed genuinely sad for me. Or maybe I was reading my emotions in her expression. "I'm *so* sorry. Oh! I know! Do you like yoga? The morning class is *great*. Trevor runs a super-huge business empire, so he works half the day. Maybe we could meet up tomorrow?" She seemed hopeful.

Before I could respond to her invite, she waved at a man who walked into the bar. "Oh! There's Trevor. Trevor!"

Trevor was twice CeeCee's age, early fifties. Hair more gray than brown. Dark eyes. A firm jaw and no-nonsense expression. He didn't smile, and a chill ran down my spine as he walked up to us. I tried not to instantly judge people, but I didn't like this guy.

"Candace, I thought you were at the pool."

"I *was*, but I got antsy. This is my new friend, Mia. Mia, this is Trevor."

CeeCee beamed. Trevor did not.

"Nice to meet you," he mumbled. "Shall we rest before dinner?" He took CeeCee's elbow.

"Oh, yes," she said, then winked at Mia and mouthed, "*Sex*." Then she giggled and wrapped her arm around Trevor's waist.

I felt like I'd just listened to an audiobook on double-speed. CeeCee was friendly, and I had the impression that what you saw was what you got. A younger, chattier version of my Grams.

I walked over to the bar and sat on a stool, looking for the bartender. I was more than ready for a drink.

A man rose from where he had been squatting while organizing bottles under the bar. My mouth dropped open, so I put a grape in it and chewed. This was the man from the lobby, the sexiest man on the island, the demigod. My fantasy. He wore no wedding ring, nor was there a telltale white band of flesh where one had recently been. Fate or divine intervention, I didn't care—this was a sign from the universe to take a risk and enjoy myself.

"What may I get you?" he said, his dimples deepening. He, like most of the staff, wore a white shirt with the St. Claire logo embroidered on the pocket. "Wine? Something more fruity? A mai tai maybe?"

I stared at the name under the logo.

Jason.

Jason was the name of the insane hang glider. *Jason Mallory, our head bartender and part-time entertainment.*

Fate, you are a bitch.

"Still thinking?" Jason asked. "May I recommend . . ."

"Piña colada, please." My heart was pounding. Just my luck that the cutest single guy on the island was also insane.

"One piña colada coming up," Jason said.

His experienced hands moved across the bar, grabbing bottles, shakers, mixers.

"I saw your . . . stunt." Why had I said that. Why, why, why? I didn't want a conversation. He was gorgeous but he was reckless. I weighed the pros and cons. I didn't know if I could have sex with a crazy daredevil no matter how pretty he was. Though it would probably be fun. Wild. Adventurous.

I should only care about this moment in time, but I wasn't

wired to live in the moment. I blamed my father *and* my Grams. They were yin and yang. I was the spot trapped in the middle.

He stopped what he was doing and tilted his head in confusion. "Stunt?"

I waved my right hand vaguely in the direction of the cliffs.

He grinned, and my heart skipped a beat. How many beats could it skip before it became a medical emergency? The blender whirled at high speed for a few seconds. Then he poured the frothy white beverage into a hollowed-out pineapple with a skewer of fruit and a bright pink straw. A chunk of coconut, a chunk of pineapple, two strawberries, and three cherries. Practically dinner on a stick. He placed it on a coaster in front of me.

I took a sip. Heavenly. I smiled and took another sip.

"I'll take you up anytime you want."

"Up where?" I was still tasting the pineapple and coconut and rum and feeling decadent and surprisingly happy. I ate one of the cherries.

"Hang gliding."

"Hang gliding," I repeated. I pictured myself jumping off the cliff. In my vision, my body soared straight down into the mouth of a hungry shark. I shivered.

Jason's smile widened. Had he noticed my reaction? Read my mind?

"I teach a class a couple mornings a week. A small group . . . or we could do one-on-one."

One-on-one . . . I shook my head to clear the image that popped to mind: Me, Jason, naked.

"I'll pass." My voice cracked.

"It's fun."

I ate a pineapple wedge, chased it with more piña colada. Yes, Jason Mallory looked like fun. And where would that get me? Grams had a lot of fun in her twenties and ended up pregnant and didn't know who my dad's father was. Fun was . . . *fun*. But there were consequences. I felt wholly out of my element. All I knew was that there *had* to be more than one unattached man on the island. Someone less . . .

"It's risky," I said. "Dangerous. And you're . . . you're . . ." I twirled my fingers in circles to indicate his acrobatic loops, but stopped when I realized it was the universal sign for crazy. "The loops were insanely risky. The resort insurance must be through the roof."

"Insurance?"

"The captain said you were part of the entertainment, so I assume this is your job."

Jason laughed, and I immediately repressed my smile. I might not be able to help being attracted to the man—he was gorgeous, and he had to know it—but I didn't have to succumb to his charms. I wanted risk-free sex. A man like Jason Mallory was *not* risk-free. If he behaved wild in life, what would he do in bed?

My insides nearly exploded at the thought. So I stared at my drink, sipped, let out a low moan of pleasure. I kept drinking, trying to forget that he was watching me.

"I'm just the bartender," Jason said lightly. "I hang glide for fun. Water ski. Windsurfing—that's probably my favorite. We even have a helicopter. There's nothing better than seeing the island from a thousand feet up. Well, maybe *something*." His tone was light and all too sexy.

I choked on a cherry. Coughed, drank more piña colada.

"I would hate for your pretty face to be smashed on the rocks when your parachute fails or a gust of wind slams you into the mountain," I said.

"I take it you're afraid of heights."

I hesitated. Had he been flirting with me? I looked up at him, and his eyes sparkled. Jason was intoxicating.

"I'm afraid of falling," I said, chin up, holding his gaze. "Like every sane person."

"And your name?"

"I thought the staff knew everyone's name." I didn't mean to sound so snarky. Was I disappointed that he didn't know?

"Mia Crawford," he said. "But I thought I'd be polite and ask. Excuse me." He walked over to where a couple had just sat down on a love seat facing the ocean.

He'd been friendly, flirty, and I had offended him. I hadn't meant to, but I felt wholly out of my element here. I tried not to be obvious as I watched the man. I could look, right?

Look, don't touch. Everything about Jason Mallory went against my sensibilities. Maybe it was best this way—I could find another guy. I mean, if it was this easy to flirt with Jason Mallory, then I could surely flirt with the other men on staff. Men less likely to risk breaking their necks on a daily basis. But, I reminded myself, no matter how much I safeguard, even risk-free men could be the source of unplanned heartbreak. Like my dad.

He'd died suddenly, in a stupid car accident that wasn't his fault. A jerk who'd driven all night had fallen asleep at the wheel and hit my dad head-on when he was heading to work early in the morning. That's when I learned the hard way what financial havoc Grams's free and fun lifestyle had wreaked on our family. I finally understood my dad's frugal nature—it was directly related to growing up with financial insecurity and general chaos. Now I take care of Grams—just like my dad had done. Because for all her faults, she had the kindest heart, and we both loved her.

A girl walked in—the bored teen who'd been sitting with Andrew Locke and his girlfriend at the pool. She slumped at the end of the bar, reached over the counter, and grabbed a premade fruit stick from the tray. She called out to Jason as he walked back from serving the couple. "Hey, Jason, can I get one of those strawberry daiquiris you made me yesterday?"

Jason said, "Now that you're legal, you can have anything you want, within reason."

Major eye roll. "I already have one dad."

Jason started making her drink. Fresh strawberries, a light touch of both light and dark rum, lime, ice. That looked good too.

"And where is your overbearing brute of a father?" Jason asked lightly.

"One guess."

"What are your plans?" Jason said without guessing.

"If I said I was going to get drunk, you probably wouldn't serve me."

"I don't want your dad to get me fired."

"He probably wouldn't notice," she mumbled and took the drink from him. "Later." She looked me up and down long enough to make me uncomfortable, then headed toward a lounge chair on the beach.

Jason wiped the counter as he made his way back to my side of the bar. "Brie's dad has a new girlfriend," he said.

"Is she really old enough to drink?" It came out before I realized it was a dumb question.

"Eighteen is legal here," he said. "But I wouldn't let her get wasted." He paused, then added almost as an afterthought, "She's apprehensive about college and the fact that her dad has a serious girlfriend."

Observant *and* cute. What wasn't to love about this guy? Maybe I could overlook his risky nature . . .

"Her dad really isn't a brute," Jason said. "He's actually a pretty cool guy. Former baseball player. Andrew Locke?"

"I met him earlier," I said. "The orthopedic surgeon who apparently saved his career introduced us."

Jason laughed. The sound was genuine and filled my heart. He seemed to be as happy and content as I wanted to be. Jason acted like he loved his job and his life, and suddenly I wanted to love *my* job and *my* life just as much.

"Dr. David Butcher," Jason said. "David and his husband visit St. Claire every year for their anniversary."

"I heard the story on the ferry," I said.

Did everyone know everyone else's business on this island? Were there no secrets?

Suddenly, I thought, *What does the staff know about me?* It wasn't that I had secrets, but the idea that my life was ripe for analysis among guests and staff made me squeamish.

"Andrew pitched for the Dodgers for six years, had surgery, then was traded to the Braves for another six years, had even better stats. Retired at thirty-five."

"He must have a good financial planner," I heard myself saying, then mentally slapped myself. *Stop thinking about work!* Yet . . . retiring at thirty-five and not having to work was a huge accomplishment. I might have to ask him who he worked with—I was always interested in new ways to safely build my clients' portfolios.

He nodded to my drink. "Another?"

"I'm not done."

"You're almost done," he said as he started mixing another drink. *Sure, why not?* I thought. Maybe a couple drinks would loosen me up.

"Sherry is the first woman he's brought since I've been here," Jason said. "It was always just him and Brie. She's feeling displaced."

I was getting an overprotective big brother vibe. I felt for the sulky teenager.

"Being a teenager isn't easy," I said.

"But it's fun," he said with a flirty grin, placing the fresh piña colada in front of me and removing my nearly empty drink.

"Nothing about being a teenager is fun," I said, twirling the little umbrella in the icy concoction. "It's all about navigating shark-infested waters and coming out with a diploma and your sanity intact."

"I can't imagine that a cute girl like you didn't have every teenage boy begging for a date."

The comment almost stunned me into silence. "Me?" I said with a squeak. I forced a laugh. "I was a very awkward, somewhat nerdy teenager."

"Who grew into a swan." He really was flirting. If I had any doubts before, they were gone. He was smiling and friendly and had a sparkle in his eye, as if he was both having fun *and* enjoying my company. My heart pounded and I feared I was blushing as I picked up the fresh drink.

"Thank you," I said. "I'm going to check out the beach."

"If I can do anything for you, let me know," he said. "I mean it, Mia."

Come to my room tonight for no-strings sex . . .

But I didn't say it. He watched me leave, and I didn't look back.

Men like Jason Mallory who were born attractive and outgoing probably had the time of their lives in high school. He wasn't built like a football player—maybe baseball. Soccer with those lean muscles. Or maybe the class clown. Someone that everyone liked because he made them laugh. I liked him. A lot.

Not your type, Mia, I told myself.

Who cares? I heard Jane and Amanda echo in my head.

It's not like I had great success with the men I *thought* were my type.

The beach looked inviting, and I needed time alone to decompress. I passed several guests lounging in cabanas or soaking in the sun by the pool. Many were reading books, including an older woman lying on her stomach reading an erotic romance, one I'd heard a lot about but had never read. Maybe she'd leave it on the free table when she was done.

Another woman was reading in a partly shaded cabana while her significant other appeared to be sleeping. I tilted my head ninety degrees to see the cover—a domestic suspense I'd read when it first came out last year. A terrific book by one of my favorite auto-buy authors. An older man in another cabana was reading on a tablet. I hated when I couldn't see the cover.

An empty lounge chair with a large adjustable umbrella beckoned me. The only thing between me and the ocean was white sand. No people, no headaches, no annoyingly sexy, hang gliding bartenders.

Brie the grumpy teen was sitting two chairs over, reading on her phone, which always gave me a headache. Give me a solid book over technology. She wore a black bikini on her tall, lanky body, her shorts and hoodie dumped in the sand.

I sipped the piña colada and put it down on the table before adjusting the huge umbrella to provide just the right amount of sun. I lathered on sunscreen—the last thing I wanted was to nurse a sunburn all week—then leaned back on the wide chair, tattered romantic thriller in hand. I was *so* looking forward to getting lost in a great story about love the second time around against a backdrop of hidden treasure, pirates, and race-against-time suspense.

When I opened the cover, grains of sand fell out. I frowned and wiped them off my chest. The previous owner had really abused this book. I flipped through the front matter and found the opening chapter.

Three pages in, I gasped.

Someone had written in the margins of the book.

Only *monsters* wrote in books! (The same kind of monsters who left books in the sand.)

In college, I was loath to write in books even if the professor said to do so. Sticky notes became my favorite tool. Why mar a perfectly good book with ink or even pencil?

Someone—a woman, judging by the neat, flowery handwriting—had written next to the paragraph that described the lost treasure:

A treasure hunt! Sounds like fun, haha.

It was a free book; I shouldn't get so upset about the violence done to it. And I happened to agree with her sentiment here: a treasure hunt would be fun. Who didn't love stories like *Uncharted* and *Outer Banks* where the journey was just as exciting as the discovery of something special? I felt an odd kinship with my fellow book lover and vaguely wondered if she was still here on the island, if I could track her down to have a drink or three and see if we had anything else in common.

I jumped back into the story, ignoring the bold penmanship.

The author did a great job integrating the history of the fictional Santa Regina into the first chapter, describing the lost treasure, and introducing the main characters who had once been lovers until Juan disappeared with a treasure he and Gabrielle had found together.

Jerk. He probably had a good reason, but what it was, I could only guess. Gabrielle certainly didn't believe anything he said. Smart woman.

After reading a particularly biting comeback from the heroine, I smiled. Gabrielle was more confident, more sarcastic, and bolder than I'd ever be. There were so many times my manners prevented a witty response. Or I'd think of something perfect to say . . . ten minutes too late. If I were the author of my life, I could go back and edit all those conversations where I'd bitten my tongue, misspoke, didn't say what I should have.

I'd love, for example, to have stood up to Amber Jones when she blocked me on the boat. Or told Andrew's girlfriend not to be rude to staff.

On the next page, another passage was underlined.

Gabrielle tied back her thick red hair to keep it out of her face while she cleaned the deck. Why pay deckhands when they did such an awful job?

The previous book owner had written:

Sounds just my type. I hope she's not **TOO** mad at me . . .

What did that mean? Why write it in the book? Should I take the book back and find another? This running commentary distracted from the story.

I drank more, adjusted the umbrella to block the sun because I was overheated, and turned the page.

The end of chapter one had Juan showing Gabrielle what he'd found. The last paragraph was underlined:

Three gold pieces stamped with the royal crest, hidden away from the world, buried on an island, until someone found them. *Why couldn't it have been me?* Gabrielle thought. *Why couldn't it have been my dad?*

The book vandal had drawn an arrow and written at the bottom of the page:

He just walked by on the way to the bar. How much will he pay for the truth? How much will he pay for me to keep his secret?

CHAPTER
FIVE

"All human beings have three lives: public, private, and secret."

—Gabriel García Márquez

SECRET. WHAT SECRET? WAS THIS unknown destroyer of books writing about people here on the island?

That seemed far-fetched and rather ludicrous.

Yet . . . I felt surprisingly like her confidante, her friend. As if she were writing these notes for me. Silly, I know, but still . . . it was exciting to be privy to information both tantalizing and intimate. She was Harriet the Spy, and I had found her secret diary.

Over the top of the book, I looked around, sunglasses masking the direction of my gaze.

David, Doug, and the two men they'd been drinking with were now playing a friendly game of beach volleyball, away from the reclining sun worshippers.

A couple—the couple from the ferry who I hadn't spoken with—argued in a nearby cabana. I only recognized them from the man's bright flowered shorts. What were they fighting about? Maybe this vacation was their one last chance to save their marriage.

I glanced down at the book, half expecting to see commentary about the couple in the margins, but they were new on the island, and my compatriot couldn't have spied on them.

Brie watched her dad and his girlfriend walk hand in hand along the edge of the water. Though Brie's face was blank, her body was tense, practically screaming in silent rage. She watched until they disappeared from view. I could relate to Brie in some ways—my mom had walked away when I was six and my dad had dated on and off. He'd once told me that after my mom left—a beautiful woman who was never happy—he didn't have the energy to fall in love again. I asked him if he was lonely.

"No, I'm content with my life."

I wanted to be happy, but I didn't know how. I didn't want to end up like my mother, never happy with anything or anyone, or my father, being merely content.

"Stop being so melancholy," I whispered and opened the book again.

How much will he pay for me to keep his secret?

Whose secret was she keeping?

One of the guests? One of the staff? Maybe there would be more clues in the book.

Both stories were interesting—the book *and* the writing in the margins. A thrill ran up my spine and had me reaching for my drink. I had two mysteries to solve. I had the missing woman *and* the identity of Harriet the Spy. Plus, who were the people she was writing about? Were they still here? The idea that I might share in this treasure trove of secrets kept me reading, book in one hand, drink in the other.

At the end of chapter two, the graffiti artist had penned:

Money or love? Money, of course—he's worth a small fortune.
Does he know all the dirt on his new girlfriend?

Below that, written in a different color, as if added later:

112 ~ est. net $80-90m, AZ residence $5m+, vacation
house $3m

Why would this person be tracking anyone's net worth? Maybe the second note had nothing to do with what was written above. It was the same person—I could tell by the penmanship—but written at a different time.

Harriet was being catty. Why was anyone who dated someone wealthy, man or woman, suspected of being a gold digger?

She could be right. Harriet might in fact have a better grasp of human nature than most. Bookish people were often more observant.

I have more than one wealthy client who had been the target of unscrupulous con artists. One of my favorite clients, a sweet seventy-year-old retired secretary, had invested five percent of her paycheck every week and every bonus for over forty years in the company she worked for—IBM. When she retired, she was worth more than $10 million. She'd been scammed once—lost over $100,000—and then was romanced by a younger man who wanted her to cash out her investment fund so that they could travel the world together. Fortunately, her children talked her out of it.

So yes, there were assholes out there in the world, though preying on a senior citizen was a lot different than dating a wealthy man.

The running commentary in the margins was both salacious and addictive. Who was Harriet writing about? Trevor and CeeCee? Andrew and Sherry? Another unmarried couple on the island?

I flipped through the pages, looking for something like a receipt or a room key that might identify the previous owner. Dozens of passages were highlighted. Notes dotted the margins, all written in the same handwriting.

About two thirds through the book, the writing stopped . . . and at the page headed *Chapter Thirty-Two*, I found a business card that had likely been used as a bookmark.

She writes in books but doesn't dog-ear pages . . . she gets a point for that.

The business card read:

Broussard Antiques & Collectibles

The address was in New Orleans, Louisiana. Why did that sound familiar? I had never been to New Orleans. But I knew I recently read *something* about New Orleans.

I left the card sticking up and continued to read, finding myself reading faster than usual with an eye on the margins to discover what my new friend wrote next. A few words in the text were underlined or circled, but I couldn't make any sense of them with no accompanying notes. *Home? Child? Port?*

In the middle of chapter three, an entire paragraph was underlined:

"I told your dad years ago, when you were just a pup, that the Santa Regina was cursed. He told me curses can be broken. Be careful, Gabrielle. The coins showing up now . . . I don't think this is the work of divine providence."

In the margins was written what appeared to be a math equation:

$2.7m—bonds + $350K - bank + property $4m 5% @ $200K— convert into gold? Check business net. 2012, $1m liquid—more? (If I'd have known there was so much potential here I would have come years ago!)

Potential? What did *that* mean? Whoever she was writing about didn't have the wealth of the first person with more property and net worth, but they certainly weren't paupers.

I started flipping through the pages, not reading the book but looking for the comments, more interested in the story in the margins.

At the end of one chapter, Harriet had circled a snippet of dialogue—an argument between the hero and heroine—and written:

Fool me once, shame on me? Hell no. Why do people think they can walk all over anyone they think is weak? Do they think I'm *stupid? I haven't been stupid since I walked out of the house when I was 18 and took control of my life...*

I leaned back and wondered about this woman. She was self-confident, a take-control type who didn't let people push her aside. *She* would have told Amber Jones to move out of her way.

A scream from the ocean startled me. I looked up and didn't see anyone. The volleyball players were gone. Brie had left. A couple I hadn't seen before were walking south on the beach, toward the dock. A family played a good fifty yards away, kids running in and out of the surf, laughing.

It must have been the kids, I thought, scanning the ocean.

A head bobbed up out of the calm water, then went back down again. I jumped up, the book falling to my lounge chair. Someone was in trouble.

I called out, "Help! Someone's drowning!" as I kicked off my flip-flops and ran to the water's edge. The lazy waves rolled over my feet, then back. Was there an undertow here? Or had a swimmer cramped? Or maybe someone was tangled in seaweed, the tide rolling in and out over them.

Quickly, I waded into the water, then dove against the gentle surf, taking long strokes toward the bobbing head. The water was refreshing, not cold. A minute later I stopped, looked around me for any sign of life, fearing I was too late and a freak accident had taken someone's life. My toes just barely touched the sandy ocean floor. Flora or fauna caressed my ankle, and I shivered in surprise. The water was clear. I could almost see the bottom. Something bright pink was floating under the surface.

Twenty feet from me, a man surfaced and groaned. He was hurt. "I'm coming!" I called out to him, and swam over.

He looked at me, his face twisted, and he groaned again, his entire body convulsing. He must have been stung by a jellyfish and was having a seizure.

"Take my hand. It's not too deep. I'll help you to shore," I said, reaching for him.

At that moment, I recognized him. The honeymooner. Where was his wife? Was she lost at sea?

Then she surfaced, taking a deep breath and laughing. "Oh, God, honey! That was amazing. I lost my bottoms. Let's go find it." She was about to go under again when her husband pulled her toward him and stared at me.

"Hi," he said.

I wasn't an idiot. Okay, I was an idiot, I just wasn't stupid. I put two and two together and got *sex on the beach.*

"I—didn't mean—sorry—I thought—" I was making the uncomfortable situation even more awkward.

The wife finally noticed me. "Oh," she said. Then she brightened. "Mia?"

"Yes?" My voice was a whisper.

She pointed next to me. "Grab that for me, will you?"

I looked. Her pink bikini bottoms were floating just beneath the surface. I tossed them to her. She wiggled into them, half swimming, half bouncing off the ocean floor. I wanted to disappear, to float out to sea and never be seen again. Instead, I was frozen, looking up at the sky to avoid looking down through the far-too-clear water at their nearly naked bodies.

She smiled at her husband and said, "I love you, Mr. Kent."

He grabbed his wife's waist and pulled her to him, making her giggle. "I love you, Mrs. Kent."

I stared. They weren't going to—not with me just five feet away. Then they smiled at me, and Mrs. Kent wiggled her fingers and said, "See you later!" They half swam, half walked to shore.

I stayed right where I was, the waves softly hitting me, worried that someone might realize what had happened. I watched the pair walk up the beach, heading toward their cabin, her hand down the back of his swim trunks. The family was still playing, oblivious to what had just happened.

Movement near the lounger where I'd been reading caught my attention, and I put my hand on my forehead and squinted against the bright sun. Someone was next to my chair. Between the sun and the salt water and the umbrella partially obscuring the person, I couldn't see anything other than a blur. Were they going through my things? I called out as loud as I could, "Hey! That's my stuff!" then swam to shore. By the time I walked up from the water, no one was there.

But my book wasn't on the chair where I had dropped it; it was now on the table next to my drink. Why would someone have moved it?

"Mia, you're making a mountain out of a molehill," I muttered. A staff member might have been cleaning up. They didn't take anything—my book was here, my bag, my nearly empty drink.

After what I'd interrupted in the ocean, I needed another drink. But it was getting late and I should shower and get ready for dinner at the Sky Bar—and maybe take a few minutes to lament one of the most embarrassing moments of my life.

As I stuffed the book back into my beach bag, the newspaper fell out. I picked it up and glanced at the caption.

New Orleans.

I unfolded the newspaper, sat on the edge of the lounger, and reread the article.

Diana Harden, the missing woman, was from New Orleans. The article didn't say what she did there, where she worked, if she worked, but it couldn't be a coincidence that the book I now held contained a business card with a New Orleans address.

Had the owner of this tattered book known the missing woman? Maybe they met on the ferry. Or had a drink together. Had something in common—reading, antiques, two single women traveling alone? I *really* wanted to find the book owner now. She might have an idea what happened to Diana. It could be as simple as her mother having a medical emergency. Maybe Diana didn't tell the resort she was leaving.

Or maybe . . . could Diana Harden, the missing woman, have left the book herself? Could *she* be the one who wrote these notes? Was she my Harriet the Spy?

A thrill ran through me. I would find out *exactly* who had this book before me, and I knew where to start. Trina at the gift shop. I might even have time to talk to her before I went to dinner.

"May I see that?"

I jumped up, hit my head on the umbrella, stumbled backward, tripped over the table, and knocked over my near-empty drink, leaving a trail of fruit in the sand as I fell heavily on my ass.

"Shit," I muttered.

"I shouldn't have snuck up on you."

The man smiled and offered his hand to help me up.

Flushed and embarrassed, I took the hand because it would have been more awkward to ignore it.

He pulled me up quickly, as if I weighed nothing, then grabbed my elbow to steady me. "Thank you," I managed to say.

"I'm Gino Garmon, head of security."

"Oh. Hi. I'm Mia. Mia Crawford. I just arrived today." I saw my reflection in his mirrored sunglasses.

He dressed like all the other staff at St. Claire, but then I saw that instead of his name, *Security* was embroidered under the logo.

"It was quite heroic of you to risk your life to save that couple," he said, motioning to the water.

He sounded like he was mocking me, but I couldn't tell because his eyes were hidden behind his shades.

"I heard a scream—I was wrong."

"Too many people don't pay any attention to others." Now he didn't sound insulting, but I was certain he was laughing at me on the inside. "I saw the headline you were reading. We don't get the St. John paper here. May I?"

He extended his hand, and I reluctantly gave him the paper.

Gino read quickly, and I tried not to stare. Tall? *Check.* Dark? *Check.* Handsome? *Double-check.* Broad shoulders with a tapered waist and well-defined muscles. I swallowed and wished I had another drink.

Gino shook his head and made a *tsk-tsk* sound. "Tragic." He folded the paper and handed it back. "I can assure you, St. Claire is a safe island."

"Did she disappear here or on St. John?"

"I couldn't say."

"But the article said she boarded the ferry, right?"

He smiled. "Curious, aren't you?"

"When a single woman traveling alone disappears, it makes other single women traveling alone curious as to why."

"Do you feel unsafe?"

"No, but I'd still like to know if she disappeared from St. Claire or if she disappeared from St. John."

"The St. John police chief has been keeping me informed. She left St. Claire early Sunday morning, was seen exiting the ferry on St. John, told our captain that she'd hire her own boat for the return trip because she didn't know how long she'd be. And no one has seen her since. The private taxis have all been questioned, and none brought her back to the island."

"So she *was* traveling alone? The newspaper didn't say either way, but that's what I'd gathered."

"She didn't check in with another party."

That was an odd way of phrasing the answer. "Did she meet someone here?"

He wasn't smiling now. He looked like a stern, no-nonsense cop more than a resort security guard. A bit intimidating. "If I was privy to any information that would assist the police in their investigation, I would have told them, and them alone. St. Claire prides itself on our privacy policy, which means no discussing the lives of our guests—on or off the island."

I would not be deterred. "What do you think happened?"

"I don't have enough information to make an educated guess."

"People don't just disappear."

"I'm confident that the police will find out what happened. Do not worry about it, Ms. Crawford. Enjoy your vacation."

Gino smiled and walked down the beach, greeted each guest he passed, then stopped at the poolside bar. He glanced back at me; I quickly averted my eyes.

No, I wouldn't worry my pretty little head about it, Mr.

Security Chief. He might be eye-candy, but his attitude ruled him off my one-night stand list.

At least Jason the bartender wasn't a jerk.

Hungry and frustrated, I stuffed the newspaper into my book bag and headed for my cottage, taking the beach path instead of cutting through the lodge.

As I passed the bar, I heard a brusque male voice that I immediately recognized as the man who had been arguing with Amber. I stopped, partially blocked by a trellis. He was standing just outside the ring of tables, his back to the bar, phone to his ear, and clearly angry. Bermuda shorts, sky-blue polo shirt, designer sunglasses. The shirt—the man on the cliff when we were getting off the boat had been wearing the same color. One and the same?

His tone grated on me—the whiny, arrogant lilt of someone who always expected to get his way. If he was in a romance novel, he'd be the heroine's emotionally abusive ex-husband. The type of guy a girl fell for because of his good looks (and maybe ability in bed), who later made her question her judgment. The manipulative jerk who made the heroine swear off men entirely, until the right guy came along and convinced her that not all men were assholes.

I couldn't get to my cottage without passing him, unless I wanted to go the long way through the lodge. Which I didn't, because I really didn't want to see the honeymooners for the rest of my life—or at least for the rest of today.

"You can't make up something?" the jerk was saying. "Tell him you can't reach me? Fine! Put him on, but next time, you'd better come up with a good excuse or you'll be looking for a new job."

A second later, his voice completely changed. "Dad? Hey! Yeah, reception isn't great, but I wanted to talk to you . . . Spontaneous, I know, and I'm sorry I didn't tell you before that I was going to St. Claire, but Amber and I are trying to make it work . . . Of course I'll be at the meeting on Monday . . . Sure. Anything you need, let me know. Love ya, Dad."

Silence. I peered through the trellis. He was standing there, looking at the ocean. I couldn't leave without being seen. Damn. Just do it.

I plastered a half smile on my face and walked briskly from the edge of the bar, down the path that led to my cabin.

"Hello," I said cheerfully as I passed by.

He whirled around, his face rigid and angry. "Hello." Gruff, but he relaxed a bit when he saw me.

"You weren't on the ferry this afternoon," I said. "Have you been here long?"

"Yesterday," he said, his voice clipped.

"It's so beautiful." I waved my hand toward the ocean on one side, the lush mountain on the other. "I don't think I ever want to leave, though my boss probably won't like that." I laughed while cringing inside. Why had I said that? I wanted a rewrite, but that was the problem when you said the first thing that came to your mind. Sometimes it was smart . . . sometimes not.

"Oh. Yes. Pretty," he said vaguely. Then he looked around as if he hadn't really noticed much of anything.

"I'm Mia Crawford. From New Jersey." I extended my hand out of habit and wished I could pull it back.

He pumped my hand once, dropped it. "Parker Briggs."

"Nice to meet you, Parker. See you around."

I walked away and immediately breathed easier. Okay, at least I knew who he was. He wasn't just Mr. Asshole. He was Mr. Parker Briggs, Asshole.

I thought about Parker's conversation with his father. He'd been talking about Amber, about wanting to "make it work." Did that mean they were together? Like, *together* together? If he wanted to make it work, why had he been yelling at her? I was nonconfrontational, sure, but if a man yelled at me like that, I wouldn't be wanting to get back together with him. I had one boyfriend years ago who snapped at everyone—me, servers, his staff. I was so tense and stressed waiting for him to snap some order to get him this or that or do some such thing that I called it quits.

Some people seemed to thrive in those kinds of relation-ships, the big blowout fight followed by the great make-up sex. Or so I've heard. And read. Just not experienced. And honestly? It sounded exhausting, never knowing where you stood with someone.

What had Amber said?

"I said I'd get everything back!"

That didn't sound like a relationship, but what did I know? Every man I'd dated was not *The One*. I had the urge to tell Amber to run far, far away . . . but it wasn't my place. Besides, Amber had been rude, certainly no shrinking violet. If *she* were in a romance novel, she'd be the stalker ex-girlfriend of the hero. Maybe she and Parker Briggs were made for each other.

Still . . . I wanted to know what was going on between Amber and Parker, and not just because I'm naturally curious. They were arguing about documents, not their love life. Why? What made these two people tick? What split them up? I might not *like* them, but I wanted to understand how their relationship worked—and didn't work. If I could dissect other relationships, maybe I could fix my own love life.

There I went again, spiraling into worrying about the im-pending doom of my future as a lonely workaholic, which I'd promised myself not to think about this week.

For now, I should focus on finding answers. Not about my long-term love life or the job that might kill it, but what hap-pened to Diana Harden. Why did she leave, where did she go, and what happened to her?

I also wouldn't mind finding out if Amber and Mr. Asshole got back together. They deserved each other.

CHAPTER
SIX

"Things'll get worse before they get better."
—Karen M. McManus, *One of Us Is Lying*

WHAT DID ONE WEAR to a sunset dinner?

I stood half-naked in the glorious bathroom and took advantage of the complimentary lavender lotion. I pinned my dark blond hair up and decided to leave it that way—the damp curls fell in a casual but attractive way. Getting fancy didn't appeal, since this was an island vacation, so just a touch of makeup to highlight my light brown eyes and I was done.

I had considered not even going to the Sky Bar tonight, but I wanted to find out more about the missing woman. If what Gino the head of security said about privacy was true, then trying to talk up Trina in the gift shop or Kalise the activities director wasn't going to get me anywhere. But several of the guests had been here at the same time as Diana, and they might be chattier than the staff.

Diana Harden was a curiosity, a mystery to be solved. Like me, she had come to the island alone. We shared an exclusive club. Even Amber and Parker, who had traveled alone, weren't *actually* alone, considering they knew each other.

It wasn't just Diana's disappearance, which most likely had a logical explanation, that piqued my interest. But the book . . . her attitude seemed whimsical, flip, superior, interesting. She watched and assessed people from a distance—

like me. It was her writing comments in the margins that had me confounded. Was she a novelist, penning ideas as she thought of them? That didn't seem plausible, considering she was writing about real people from the island . . . Unless, a reporter? A reporter for a gossip rag? *That* made sense. Where did the antique store fit in? Just a convenient bookmark? Or something important?

Her life observations, about betrayal and lies, intrigued me. There was far more to Diana than her Harriet the Spy persona. I wanted to know why she felt the need to take stock of the people on the island. What compelled her to write down all the gossip she learned? A treatise to the idea that people didn't live up to expectations? Or that people were, at their core, liars, cheats, and scoundrels?

I didn't believe it, because there were good people I trusted— Jane, Amanda, Braden, my boss. Yet . . . I'd been burned more than once. A high school friend who'd betrayed my trust. An internship where my boss had promised me a full-time job . . . if I agreed to have sex with him. Assorted boyfriends who'd lied, cheated, or both.

Maybe I understood Diana Harden more than I thought. Maybe I was more like her than I wanted to believe.

I put all those thoughts aside and dressed in one of my new sundresses, a comfortable white mid-calf dress with blue and green flowers. Took one look, deemed myself presentable, and left.

I chose the most direct route to the lodge, passing the marked trails I'd seen when I first arrived. I wanted to hike all of them. The hot springs were really hot, the path marked Luz Luna Bahia led to a hidden lagoon, and the Siempre Viva Vista was a steep climb to the top of the cliffs and promised one of the best views on the island.

Each path was marked with pinpoint white lights wrapped around the trees, and ground lighting to make sure you didn't tumble down a slope. If I wasn't so hungry, I would have made the detour now.

Music at the Blue Dahlia was lively. The rich smell of barbecue had my stomach growling. The restaurant in the lodge was half-full with diners. I spotted the Stocktons, Andrew Locke and his girlfriend, Sherry Morrison, and the honeymooners sitting in a booth side-by-side taking pictures of their food. They didn't have their faces smashed together—a first. I pictured the wife popping out of the water after giving her husband a blow job, and my face instantly reddened.

I was relieved to see David and Doug at the shuttle, where they introduced me to their friends. Brie the brooding teen was sitting in the back of the shuttle, ignoring everyone who boarded. Just as Henry, the driver, was about to pull away, Amber Jones approached. "The Sky Bar?" she asked.

"All aboard," Henry said.

She glanced at me, then the others, but the only available spots were next to me and in the back with Brie. She chose me, then pulled out her phone and scrolled. Where was her boyfriend? She couldn't like me any less, so I decided to chat her up.

"Hi, I'm Mia, from the ferry?"

Her eyes slowly tore themselves from her phone as she looked at me through long fake lashes. "Yes. I remember," she said flatly.

"Where's your boyfriend?"

She stared at me with a bored expression. "Boyfriend?"

"I saw you with a guy . . . I just assumed."

She didn't say anything for a long moment. I almost squirmed. "Oh. Parker. *Not* my boyfriend," she added with an eye roll.

I guess this little vacation wasn't going to reunite Parker and Amber. I mentally patted myself on the back for solving *that* mystery so fast. I could only hope solving Diana's disappearance was as easy.

I bit back a smile. I was grown-up Nancy Drew, or Veronica Mars from the reboot, determined to find the truth, wherever it led. No more cozy mystery book club, solving crime from the security of a library or tea shop. I was in the middle of a *real* mystery, the Case of the Missing Blonde.

Books weren't real life. I wanted the adventure to continue beyond the pages—not just learning the truth about Diana Harden and what happened to her, but figuring out what I was doing with my life, where I was going, who I wanted to be. I was tired of hiding in the library stacks. I wanted to shape my own story. Which is why I was surprised—almost as much as my boss—that I hadn't signed my promotion contract before I left. It was completely out of character. I should have committed; I hadn't even asked to be a partner—that would have been a huge swing—but Mr. Cohn had offered it anyway.

It was an honor.

It was final. You couldn't quit if your name was on the door.

The winding one-lane road up the mountain wasn't paved, but the gravel and dirt were firmly packed. At first, I couldn't see anything through the thick trees, but as we rose in elevation, the resort came into spectacular view below us. The ocean was calm, the buildings and cabins awash with twilight, the grand lodge growing smaller as we reached the top of the mountain.

Heavenly.

I let everyone disembark first so I could spend another minute in the midst of such beauty.

"Paradise on earth," Henry said quietly.

"It is," I agreed. "You're lucky to work in such an amazing place."

"I am."

"There's no town here. Do you live here all the time?"

He nodded. "The buildings south of the dock? Employee housing."

I only vaguely remembered them when the ferry docked. My attention had been on Jason, the cute hang gliding fool.

"Not everyone lives here full-time," Henry said. "Many live on St. John and commute. Mostly those with families, kids in school. A few people live in the States and work seasonally. Me and my wife, we're what I think is called empty nesters? When our youngest went to college, we applied for jobs here. Millie is head of housekeeping. I do a little of everything. Management is good. We take one month off a year, paid vacation, and visit our children. But here, even working is like a vacation."

I glanced to the east one more time, with the resort and beach spread out below.

"Look," he said, and gestured to the west.

I turned around. It was heady to see the ocean on both sides. The sun made the water sparkle like diamonds for as far as I could see. "Don't miss the sunset," he said.

"I won't." I thanked Henry and followed the music.

The Sky Bar was a large, partially open building with a re-inforced thatched roof, kitchen, and full bar. Tables surrounded a dance floor, and the DJ played in the corner. White string lighting liberally decorated nearby trees. Benches and lounge chairs were perched on the edge of the mountain for viewing the sunset. The room glowed orange; the sky a brilliant rain-bow as the sun continued its descent into the water.

More than thirty people were eating appetizers and min-gling. Jason was working the bar. I watched his easy moves and comfortable smile as I grabbed a glass of champagne from a tray.

Doug pulled me into his group. It was fun being around men who were good friends, animated, intelligent, and full of humor. Maybe a little too *much* good humor, but they were on vacation.

Brie was standing to one side, and I wondered why she'd come here alone. After a few moments, I excused myself and walked over to where she watched the sunset.

"Hi," I said. "Brie, right?"

Brie gave me a sidelong glance. I guess I would, too, if some stranger came up to me and started talking.

"You're the accountant from the bar."

How did she know?

"Mia," I said.

"So, first day here. What do you think?"

"It's beautiful." That seemed like an obvious thing to say. "I've never been to the Caribbean before."

"We come every year. Well, since my mom died when I was five."

"I'm sorry."

She shrugged. "Yeah. Well."

I felt a surprising kinship with the teen. My mom had left when I was young, and while that wasn't the same as dying, I hadn't seen my mother since. She sent an annual birthday card, then a card with a hundred dollars for my high school graduation, but no acknowledgment when I graduated magna cum laude from college. She hadn't even attended my dad's funeral. I didn't love her or hate her; I had no feelings about the woman who gave birth to me.

"Jason said you're going to college in the fall."

Brie rolled her eyes. "Can't tell him anything."

I had questions about the missing woman, and Brie had been here for several days. I wondered if she knew anything.

"I liked college a lot more than high school," I said. It was the truth. "I hated the drama, always feeling like I was walking across a minefield."

Brie grunted a laugh. "True. And there's no drama in college?" she added sarcastically.

"There's plenty, but it's easier to avoid. Where are you going?"

"University of Arizona, my dad's alma mater. It's a good school, close enough to my dad that I can visit on the weekends if I want." She paused, glanced over at me. "I've been talking to my new roommate. She seems okay, from a tiny town near the Arizona-California border, population one hundred." She waved her hand. "You don't care."

"It's interesting."

"Are you one of those adults who misses college and wants to go back?"

"Absolutely not," I said, and laughed. "I liked college, but I'm definitely not going back."

Now or never, I thought. "Um, you know, I was wondering. Did you meet the missing woman? Diana Harden?"

"Why?"

"Just curious."

She eyed me as if she didn't quite believe in vague curiosity as an excuse.

"She got here on Friday," Brie said, "and spent all day in the spa getting a complete makeover. Then she spent all Saturday at the pool reading—pretty much like you did today. Then I saw her walk down the South Trail. It's the only off-limits hike."

"Why?"

"Steep drops. Five or six years ago two people jumped into the lake at the top and wham! Hit rocks just under the surface that they couldn't see. Now, off-limits. And it's the only way to get to Ethan Valentine's mansion, other than by boat."

"Why is that name familiar?" I wondered out loud.

"Reclusive dotcom billionaire? Sold his company, made a fortune. A genius, invented a microprocessing chip, like the kind that is super small and does the work of a chip ten times the size."

Brie clearly knew a lot about the history of the island.

"And he lives there by himself?"

"He bought the island three years ago and planned to close down the resort, which would have been a bummer because it's nice and I'd have missed it. But I guess he decided to let it continue, did a full renovation. The place needed it. Kalise says he has an agreement with management to leave him alone."

"That's sad."

"He's just weird, and I've heard he's rarely at his house anyway. He has his own yacht and a helicopter and comes and goes as he pleases. Pretty cush life." Brie glanced over at the DJ. "We need better music. This is ancient shit." She walked away.

Ancient? NSYNC and Destiny's Child? I wasn't even thirty (not for two days, anyway), and I didn't think my music was *ancient*.

I headed to the bar and looked over the alcohol selection. Jason said, "I just made a pitcher of sangria. It's the best you've ever had."

"Confident, aren't you?"

"Always."

"Ever wrong?"

"Rarely."

"I'll try it."

He poured the sangria with fresh orange, lemon, and lime in a hurricane-style glass, set it in front of me. Waited.

"You want me to praise you?"

"I want you to be honest."

I sipped. It was the best sangria I had ever had. I sipped again.

"Very good," I said with a nod. I wasn't going to stroke the man's ego—his was clearly big enough already.

His eyes sparkled and his dimples deepened when he smiled. "Admit it, it's the best you've ever had."

I melted when he smiled. "Okay, you win. It's the best I've ever had."

Laughing, he walked away to mix up a pitcher of margaritas.

The music changed, and Dua Lipa rocked through the speakers.

I watched Jason out of the corner of my eye. He chatted with everyone, completely at ease, but I supposed that's because he was a bartender. His movements were fluid. He seemed to be both busy and having a good time—like everyone else. There were more than thirty people here, a good crowd, friendly, and no one—not even Brie—seemed lonely.

I mingled with an ulterior motive. Introduced myself to people, then managed to ask about the missing woman.

"Did you hear about the missing woman?"

Or, *"I read the newspaper about a guest here who just disappeared! Were you here this weekend?"*

Other than Brie, no one had known who she was, except David and Doug's friends, who said they'd come over with her on the ferry Friday and she didn't talk to anyone.

When the servers put food on the buffet, I groaned. I'd eaten so many appetizers I didn't think I would be hungry, but the shrimp and steak made my stomach growl, and the salad looked refreshing. I filled a plate and sat at the bar because it had the best view of the room. I noticed Amber wasn't here—had she left early?

The meal gave Jason a lull, and he came over to top off my sangria as I stuffed my mouth with a giant shrimp. He leaned against the bar across from me.

"So, Mia the accountant. What do you do for fun?"

"Read," I said without thinking.

"I noticed." I must have given him a suspicious look, because he continued, "I saw you reading on the beach. What do you like to read?"

"Mystery, romance, pretty much anything. I'm reading this romantic thriller right now. It's pretty good. What about you? Read much?"

"Mostly nonfiction."

"What was the last book you read?"

"A book about AI."

"Really?"

"It's interesting."

It was the last thing I expected from a bartender. I guess I figured his tastes would be more in tune with popular fiction, if he read at all. I realized that wasn't fair to bartenders in general.

"Now I'm reading about pubs in England," he said. That fit, I thought.

"Have you been?"

"To England? Sure."

"A jet-setting bartender."

He shook his head. "Not really."

He left to mix another pitcher of margaritas and pour a round of sangrias for Doug's group, then returned as I was eating the last bite of steak.

"So, you like your job? Being an accountant?"

"Yes."

"You don't sound like it."

"I'm very good at my job."

"Of course you are."

What does that mean?

"But being good at something doesn't necessarily mean you enjoy it," Jason continued. "I quit my last job because, even though I excelled, I grew to hate everything about it."

"I'm mostly a financial planner. I help people manage their finances. Make smart investments. Give them the assurance that they'll be safe and secure in their retirement. It's rewarding."

"Low-risk investments?"

The way he said it raised my hackles. "There's nothing wrong with being cautious, especially with money."

"Life is all about risks."

"Life is about *living*."

"But if you don't take risks, are you really living? Or just counting the days until you die?"

I frowned. "Taking risks with money, mine or my clients', is as foolish as hang gliding off a mountain."

"What about your clients? Don't they push you to expand their portfolios? Bet on a new venture? A company that might explode and be the next Apple or Amazon?"

"There's a far greater chance that new ventures will implode," I said. "Costing my clients their hard-earned money and control over their future."

"Not everything is about security."

Now I was mad.

"My dad worked his ass off his entire life because my grandmother had no concept of saving for a rainy day," I snapped.

"You don't like your grandma?" He looked at me as if I had just kicked a puppy.

"I love her," I said, surprised that he would think that. "You'd never know she was seventy-five, doesn't look or act it. Always the life of the party—she'd be dancing there with Brie right now. Has amazing stories from her Bohemian lifestyle. Literally traveled across Europe when she was twenty-one."

"She sounds like a blast."

He said it as if that was the opposite of me. My grandma *was* my opposite, but it rubbed me wrong, the way he said it, the unspoken criticism of my life choices. "Then when I was fifteen, my dad died. She sold the family house and took me traveling the world for six months."

"What an amazing experience."

"Sure, it was fun. We went everywhere I wanted. Saw the pyramids in Egypt. Went to the top of the Eiffel Tower. Lived on the beach in New Zealand for two weeks and took an Alaskan cruise. But when we got back to Connecticut? No place to live and no money in the bank. She'd spent every dime from selling the house for a six-month trip around the world. We barely made it, surviving because I budgeted my very small inheritance to make it last, and Social Security payments from my dad's death, and worked through high school. The only reason I could go to college was that my dad had set up my college fund the day I was born and contributed to it every month, *and* I got a scholarship. I realized then that it's all fun and wonderful to do whatever you want whenever you want, but someone has to pay for it in the end. I make sure my clients are safe and secure for their future, so they don't have to worry about their mortgage or living expenses. That's my job, and I'm *very* good at it."

"But you're here," he said with a shrug as if he hadn't listened to a word I'd said. "St. Claire isn't known for attracting the frugalminded, so you must have a wild streak in you."

"I'm here because my boss made me come. My five-year work anniversary just happens to coincide with my birthday on Thursday, so this trip was my bonus. Believe me, I asked for the money to put in my retirement instead. He said no."

Jason looked at me in shock. "You'd rather take the money to use in forty years than enjoy a week at an all-inclusive resort on the most beautiful island in the Caribbean?"

"Yes. This—" I waved my hand to encompass the whole decadent island "—is not practical." As I said it, I believed it . . . yet I loved this island. I would never admit *that* to Jason.

"Don't you have a dream?"

"Don't you?" I snapped. "Or did you always want to be a bartender?"

I regretted the words as soon as they slipped out. I didn't realize I sounded so mean, that Jason's comments about my life had made me so defensive.

He stared at me and didn't look hurt, just surprised. I wanted to apologize, but I said nothing, and Jason left to fill orders.

Jason had irritated me, true, but I hadn't wanted to insult him. That wasn't me. Why had I even come? To the Sky Bar *or* St. Claire? Maybe I should have put my foot down with Mr. Cohn. He couldn't have forced me to go. I could have forfeited the trip, not boarded the plane, stayed home for a weeklong staycation.

Now, *that* sounded depressing.

I took my sangria glass and walked down a well-lit path to a bench that had an amazing view. The bench was framed by trees covered with the same white lights as along the path. The sunset was even better than I could have imagined. As the sun disappeared, I thought about what Jason had said.

Don't you have a dream?

I didn't dare give voice to my dream. It was foolish and fiscally irresponsible. Small businesses started and shut down every day, and the business I wanted? I wouldn't get three years before losing my life savings. Success would be out of my control. The thought gave me heart palpitations.

I refused to risk everything—my financial security, my future—on a whimsical dream.

The music played and laughter filtered through the warm air, but I felt alone. Maybe I should have asked Adam to come with me this week.

Adam, my most recent ex-boyfriend, wanted to get back together. Amanda and Jane liked him, but . . . well, I don't feel much of anything when I think of him. He was *fine*. Had a good job, was responsible, practically perfect on paper . . . except there was no chemistry. No romance. My heart didn't beat for Adam.

He was comfortable, and I didn't want comfortable. I had

that in my work life already. I wanted passion and fun. To look forward to dates, not find excuses to avoid them.

Maybe my expectations *were* too high. Impossible dreams, just like my dream of owning my own business.

Enough *woe is me*. I faced the most gorgeous view I'd seen, and I would enjoy myself, dammit.

I rolled my shoulders, stretched my jaw, and practiced smiling. Then I took out my phone to film my book review. I would edit in the book cover before I posted it online.

"Hi, it's Mia. I'm on vacation—my first real vacation in years—on a beautiful Caribbean island! Isn't it gorgeous?" I panned the camera around, then turned it back to me. "I'm here to *rave* about the book I read on the plane . . ."

I gave a two-minute review, which was the sweet spot—neither too long nor too short. I saved the video to my phone because the resort Wi-Fi didn't reach the top of the mountain. I'd edit and post it when I got back to my cottage.

Done with that happy chore, I pulled out Diana's book. I reread the previous chapter because I'd been distracted by the notes. Then I started chapter four, really got into the story because Gabrielle, the heroine, was smart and sassy and everything I wished I could be.

Five pages into the chapter, Diana's script practically screamed at me.

> The old man should mind his own business. Someone needs to shut him up.

A chill ran down my spine. Was she talking about the mentor character in the book who was trying to get Gabrielle back together with her ex? Or someone here, on the island? Was it a threat?

I flipped through a couple pages to see if there was any more about the old man. At the end of the chapter were several cryptic notes.

A little heart with My #1 won't be here until Tuesday! followed by a sad face.

Totally broke, he'll help. Followed by the number 77.

Then: 1419 is worth at least $100K. Maybe more.

Under that: Finally! Scored with the big cheese. Hahahaha. 2012, future deal.

2012? That was more than a decade ago. How could it be a future big deal? I was getting a headache trying to figure out Diana's shorthand.

The last point on the list was interesting. There was no doodle, no numbers, no dollar amount. Only the comment meet two-face @ 8 Sun.

Who was two-face? Diana left early Sunday on the ferry—was she meeting someone on St. John at eight in the morning? Or was she supposed to be back for a meeting on St. Claire at eight that night?

Before I could think more about this information, the DJ announced that the last shuttle back to the resort was leaving in ten minutes. The sun was gone; only a thin dark red line now edged the ocean. I wanted to get back and find the lagoon since, surprisingly, I wasn't tired. As I started up the path, I heard three female voices gossiping in hushed tones. The scent of marijuana drifted down.

I stopped, not wanting to interrupt. Eavesdropping had become a really bad habit today.

A server I'd spoken to earlier—a young woman named Leesa—said, "Did you see what Mrs. Craig was wearing? No one over fifty should even attempt such a thing."

"Shows off her new boobs," another woman said.

"Sometimes less is more."

Giggles, then a *shh*.

"Did you hear that Kalise was in Tristan's room all night?"

"He's gay," Leesa said.

"No, she was definitely in there all night, and they weren't watching movies."

"She's entitled to some fun," Leesa said. "The St. John police are still asking about Ms. Harden. Tristan is *very* concerned. So is Kalise. Liability issues."

"Good riddance," a third voice, much deeper, said, then coughed. "She was a bitch."

"Stop—if anyone hears you talking about guests like that—"

"They would agree with me. Entitled and rude. She made Ginger cry after her spa treatment. Ginger!"

The others murmured something, their tone implying that this was particularly egregious.

"And it's not like she's a regular," the gruff woman said. "Never been here before, and it wasn't planned."

"How do you know?" Leesa asked.

"I read the guest profiles. She registered *literally* two days before she showed up Friday. That's unheard-of."

"Surprised we had room," another said.

"She's not the only one," the gruff woman said. "The actress? Who brags about being in a Tom Cruise movie where she had *one line* and was on screen for a nanosecond? She *also* registered last minute. And she's been asking questions about the Harden woman. Wanted to know what room she'd stayed in, can you believe that?"

I bit my lip. Why was Amber asking questions about Diana? I would need to be very careful how I approached the subject of the missing woman with staff.

"She left all her stuff behind," Leesa said. "We had to pack everything up and—"

"Enough gossiping!" a new voice, a brusque female, snapped. "I was wondering where everyone had gone off to. Do I smell weed? While on duty?"

"No, ma'am," the sweet girl said. "Must be a guest."

"Must be," the woman said in a disbelieving tone. "Come on, Jason's already shut down the bar, and we're just waiting for the last guests to board the shuttle. We'll be out of here in five minutes if you double-time it."

The women walked back into the main building, and I breathed easier.

Last shuttle leaving!

I didn't want to walk back in the dark, so I ran up the trail and burst onto the dance floor. The empty room was disorienting as I looked around for the exit to the shuttle.

"Now, that's an entrance," Jason said from the bar as he locked the cabinets.

"I didn't realize how late it was. Has the shuttle left?"

"You have a few minutes."

"Water?"

He smiled, as charming as ever, and put a water bottle down on the bar. I felt doubly bad for being rude earlier. I was about to apologize, but he walked away.

I couldn't blame him. I had been rude. It was for the best. We were totally incompatible.

I pushed Jason to the back of my mind and thought about what the staff had been talking about.

Diana Harden had left without packing her belongings. That suggested that she didn't plan to leave, to run away with a sexy chef or even have a family emergency—she would have called the resort, let them know. She left the island for St. John—perhaps to meet Mr.—or Ms.—Two-Face, and she never came back. There were now two things I wanted to do: go through her belongings and talk to the ferry captain who took her to St. John. Maybe she met someone on the dock. Maybe she said something to staff.

I just had to figure out how to do both without arousing suspicion.

CHAPTER
SEVEN

"Some things in life are out of your control.
You can make it a party or a tragedy."

—Nora Roberts, *Vision in White*

AFTER UPLOADING MY BOOK review and changing into jeans and a T-shirt, I studied the island map. The lagoon was a half-mile walk down the Luz Luna Bahia trail. Though it was after ten, I was too wound up to sleep, tipsy but not drunk, so figured a little exploration would clear my mind.

I stepped out on my patio. Faint music came from the main lodge. I loved the lights wound among the trees and the peace of the starry night, stars I couldn't see living in the city. I'd been a bit rough on Jason when I told him I hadn't wanted to come to the island. Now I was glad to be here.

I headed down the beach and was about to turn toward Luz Luna Bahia when I smelled the distinct foul aroma of a cigar.

A man with a mop of white hair and a long white beard against brown skin lounged against a palm tree, framed by subdued ground lights fifty feet beyond my patio. His eyes were closed and he had a half smile on his face, as if listening to good music or reliving a happy memory.

I didn't want to disturb him, so walked as quietly as I could past him, toward the path.

He opened his eyes.

"Hello," he said.

"Hi. I'm sorry to disturb you."

He smiled. He looked like Hispanic Santa Claus with his white, white hair. "You're new here."

"Yes. My first time. You?"

"I live here." He puffed on his cigar, blew out rings of smoke.

"You do? That must be nice. It's beautiful." Beautiful. Why couldn't I think of another word?

He kept smiling. "I keep an eye on things. It's the least I can do."

Odd comment.

"Oh. Well, I'm Mia. I'm just going for a walk."

"Mia, Mia," he murmured. He looked at least eighty.

He might be older than eighty. Was he all there? Maybe I should find someone to help him.

"Do you need help getting back to your room?"

"Oh, no. I'm fine. They don't let me smoke in there, but I can sit here every night and have my cigar."

Anyone who made it past life expectancy should be entitled to do whatever they wanted. At least, that's what Grams told me every time I questioned her decisions.

"I'm Luis," he continued. "Nice to meet you, Mia. I hope to see you later."

"That would be nice," I said and meant it. I had a soft spot for old people. They had wonderful stories, sometimes humorous, sometimes sad. Grams's friend Minnie rambled but always made me smile with her tales of working in a factory during World War II when she was sixteen. Or Hank, Grams's neighbor, who embellished his Vietnam War stories. He'd served, I knew, but what was truth and what was fiction? In the end, all they wanted was someone to listen, someone to care.

Someone to remember.

Luis closed his eyes again and smiled as he inhaled his cigar.

I headed to the path, but almost stumbled when the words from the margins flashed through my mind:

The old man should mind his own business. Someone needs to shut him up.

I glanced back at Luis. He might know something about Diana Harden and who she was writing about—and what she was planning. The more I thought on it, the more I wondered if she'd been up to no good.

Before I could think twice, I turned around and walked back. "Luis?" I asked.

I thought he might have fallen asleep because he didn't immediately answer. Then he opened his eyes and said with a twinkle in his voice, "Yes, Mia?"

"I, um, well, thought maybe you'd like to have breakfast with me? Tomorrow? I came here alone, and if you don't have anyone to eat with, I'd love to talk to you about the island."

"Breakfast would be very nice."

A smidge of guilt crept in because I planned to pick his brain about Diana, but I would also just enjoy talking with him. Even if he knew nothing about the missing woman, he probably knew everything about the island and the Caribbean. He'd be fascinating to listen to.

"Great. Is eight okay?"

"The Blue Dahlia. Eight in the morning."

"That's the bar."

"The chef makes crepes fresh every morning at the Blue Dahlia. You want them. He stops cooking at nine."

"Okay," I said with a smile. "Eight at the Blue Dahlia."

Smoke slowly meandered from his lips as he smiled and waved me off.

THE LUZ LUNA Bahia path was mostly flat as it wound into the jungle. I didn't know if this would be called a *jungle*, but the trees and bushes were so thick there was no easy way to walk through them. The path had been trimmed, but the canopy of trees blocked the sky, the only light coming from the ground lighting and strings of tiny white bulbs woven through the plants.

The air was moist and earthy the farther I trekked, with intermittent whiffs of honeysuckle. It wasn't long before the path ended and I stepped into a huge cavern.

The light from the path cast shadows on the rocky mountain that jutted up on three sides. The ocean rolled in through an arch to the east, the sound of waves echoing against the mountain walls. As my eyes adjusted to the semidark, I realized the sky above was lit with stars.

Slowly, I walked around the edge of the inlet. It was almost completely round, the size of a large planetarium. The beach was about ninety feet wide. I didn't know if it was high tide or low tide. The sand was moist, not wet. I kicked off my sandals and wiggled my toes, smiling, inching toward the edge of the water, the gentle waves lapping against my feet. The water was surprisingly warm. Why had I put pants on? I should have brought a bathing suit.

I heard nothing but the water. No music, no people. I thought about all the wild things my grandmother had done. This was my moment, my time to let go. After all, I was alone. Who would know?

I stripped down to my panties and left my clothes folded on a rock. Giggling, I walked into the surf. None of my friends would believe I went skinny dipping. Acting out of character was both terrifying and exhilarating.

I dove into the water, then surfaced, worried for a minute that I might be pulled out to sea. But the current was so weak I could have been in a swimming pool. I swam to the rocks, on the edge of the lagoon, then across to the other side. I floated back to the middle and stared up at the sky and had the overwhelming and heady feeling that I was the only person in the world. The rhythmic splash of water against rocks outside the lagoon seemed so distant, yet also comforting.

Believing that I was the only person on the island who knew of this place was foolish, but for the next fifteen minutes, I indulged in the fantasy. I didn't want to leave, but I could feel wrinkles on my fingers and knew it was time to get out.

I walked out of the water. Goose bumps rose on my skin. Tomorrow I'd bring a towel, swimsuit, maybe a snack. I definitely planned to return.

"Maybe you do have your grandmother's wild streak after all," a male voice said from the darkness.

I screamed, then clapped my hand over my mouth, heard a brief echo, followed by hearty laughter.

"I'm sorry," he said with humor. "I didn't mean to startle you, but I'm glad you're here improving the view."

I knew that voice.

"Jason?"

"The one and only."

I dropped back into the water, embarrassed. Excited. Nervous. A small thrill shot up my spine. I tried to ignore my reaction to Jason and reached deep down for some anger but couldn't find much ire to hold on to.

"Damn you." Okay, maybe a *little* anger. Because he *did* startle me. And I wasn't quite sure why I wasn't more upset about it.

"I come here to decompress," he said as if I hadn't spoken. "I rarely see guests at night."

My feet touched the sand, but I squatted to avoid exposing myself, keeping my breasts just below the water's surface. I gazed up at the cavernous space, the trees and cliffs and the stars overhead. "It's truly stunning," I said, the residual anger and embarrassment fading away.

"This place suits you," he said.

"Why?" I didn't know what else to say.

"That it's beautiful isn't enough?"

"That sounds like a line."

Jason smiled and I thought he might be making fun of me. I don't know why it bothered me so much. I'd already decided that no matter how attracted I was to the man, I wasn't going to choose him for a fling.

"Not a line," he said. "This is the most beautiful spot on the island, but it's also mysterious, with trails no one knows about even though they're practically in plain sight. Everything is open, asking to be enjoyed, to be appreciated . . . but it's also a lonely place."

My stomach twisted in knots as I viewed the hidden cove as Jason saw it. For a brief moment, I felt he understood me.

When I looked back toward him, I watched him pick up my bra from the rock.

"Are these your clothes?"

"Put that down!"

He was grinning. "Definitely a wild streak. Maybe I should join you. It's a good night for a swim."

"No!" A flush of fresh embarrassment washed over me. "I need you to leave, Jason."

He sat on the rock, still holding my bra. A playful gleam in his expression told me he had no intention of leaving. I imagined him throwing off his shirt and pants and joining me in the water.

Fine. I stood, walked out of the water and up the beach, right over to him. He was still smiling, looking right at me, his green eyes sparkling. In humor? Appreciation? I had no idea.

Jason Mallory was still too gorgeous for words. He wore swim trunks and a tank top, as if he'd planned to do exactly what I had done. But with his risky behavior, he'd probably scale the cliffs and dive headfirst into the rock-strewn cove.

I hoped it was too dark for him to see my red face, raw from embarrassment as I snatched my bra from his hand. He didn't look away. I wanted to run behind a tree and dress, but I didn't. I stood in front of him, put on my bra, then pulled my shirt over my head. I was wet; now my shirt was wet. This night was getting better and better.

With humor, he asked, "You didn't bring a towel?"

"I wasn't planning on going swimming."

"A spontaneous streak, too."

"Argh!"

He was impossible. Why oh why had I gone skinny dipping? I was smarter than this! Yet . . . it was thrilling that he was here. Amanda and Jane wouldn't believe that I'd jumped naked into a lagoon or that the hottest guy on the island watched me dress.

I wished he'd shown up sooner, before I decided to channel my inner Grams. It might have been nice, sitting on the small beach, looking at the stars with someone who—even though he was absolutely not my type, and I wouldn't in a million years have sex with him—seemed smart and fun and probably knew everything about the island and the people on it.

"Goodbye," I said.

"You're going to walk back to the resort like that?"

I knew how hard it would be to pull on jeans over wet skin. "Do you have a problem?"

"Nope. No problem at all."

I waved one hand at the formerly blissful cavern and grabbed my jeans with the other. "It's all yours."

"Stay."

"I—what?" I must have heard him wrong.

He gestured to a picnic basket I hadn't noticed before. "I have some snacks, a couple beers. I don't mind sharing."

Could he see the surprise on my face?

"Um—" *No. No, I'm not staying.* But I didn't say that.

"You're cute when you're flustered and blushing." He grinned. "You're kinda fun to throw off-balance."

I literally froze. I had no idea what to say or do. He was definitely flirting.

"One beer," he said. "We don't even have to talk. We'll just sit here and enjoy the peace." The way he looked at me, as if he could see inside me, had me wanting to do anything he asked. "Then I'll walk you back to your cabin. The island is safe, but you never know."

"The missing woman." I cleared my throat, my mouth suddenly dry. "Diana Harden."

"I figured everyone heard about what happened. She disappeared on St. John, not here."

"Did you meet her?" I needed to get Jason to stop looking at me as if he wanted to know more about me. As if . . . as if he was attracted and wanted to kiss me. Because if he asked me a question, I'd tell him anything he wanted to know. Right then and there, I was an open book.

"I meet everyone." He shrugged. "I'm the bartender. Everyone comes to the bar."

I knew I shouldn't stay. But . . . what could go wrong? Jason was friendly, and I no longer felt nervous around him. In fact, he was a bit hard to resist. I might as well embrace the wild side I didn't know I had until tonight.

"Okay," I said. "One beer."

Jason looked pleasantly surprised that I had agreed, and pulled two beers from the basket, popped off the tops, and handed me one.

"To new friends and new adventures," he said, and clinked the neck of his bottle against mine.

I had nothing better to add, so I nodded and drained half the beer in one long gulp.

Jason's gaze turned intense, all his focus and attention aimed at me. It was heady and disconcerting, almost overwhelming.

I wanted to kiss him.

My lips parted, and I tried to say something, anything, to break the surprisingly easy silence. Did he know what I was thinking? I think he did . . . and he was thinking the same thoughts.

He touched the sensitive skin behind my ear, and a shiver ran through me. The good kind, the shiver of anticipation, the heat of expectation that when our lips touched, it would be perfect.

He smiled, just a tiny curve of his lips. I could swear I was releasing pheromones right and left, and they were calling this man to me. He leaned forward. I could almost taste him.

It was going to happen, and I knew it would be everything I expected from a man like Jason Mallory. Everything and more.

A scream pierced the night.

The scream sounded straight out of a horror movie.

CHAPTER
EIGHT

"You only live twice:
　　Once when you are born
　　And once when you look death in the
face."

—Ian Fleming, *You Only Live Twice*

JASON TOOK MY BEER, put it down next to his, and clasped my hand, motioning for me to come with him. He didn't have to ask twice; I wasn't staying here alone after that scream.

Now I knew exactly what authors meant by *blood-curdling*.

Jason set a brisk pace down the main path, never letting go of my hand. We turned left before we were halfway back to the lodge. He knew the island better than I did, but this path wasn't well lit. No pretty white lights wrapped around tree trunks, just a few lights embedded along a narrow stone path.

A minute later, we were on the beach, close to where the water rolled into the inlet we'd just left. Giant boulders separated us from the cavern.

At first, I didn't see anyone, though I heard sobs. Jason pulled me close to his side as we approached the shoreline, and that's when I saw the newlyweds huddled together in the sand. Had they seen a shark? Were there sharks here? Maybe a jellyfish, or the carcass of a swordfish that rolled up with the surf.

"Mr. Kent, what happened?" Jason asked.

Mrs. Kent was sobbing, and Mr. Kent pointed toward the rocks.

"I don't see anything," I whispered.

Still holding hands, we walked carefully toward the rocks. The waves came in, went out. In, out. Gentle and constant. Seaweed dotted the wet sand, but nothing out of the ordinary. Then the waves rolled out, revealing a large pile of kelp. I saw something twisted inside the kelp. A large fish? Maybe garbage, or debris, or . . . I gasped when I thought I saw a hand.

It couldn't be a hand.

The waves rolled over the mass, went out again, and then I stifled a scream.

"Ohmigod, Jason," I said, my voice squeaky.

It *was* a hand. And the hand was attached to a body.

"Stay here," Jason said.

I didn't. I followed him as he stepped closer to the pile.

Kelp wrapped around the body so thickly I almost couldn't tell if it was male or female, but the hand was elegant, the chipped nails polished a bright pink. Each time the waves came in, they pushed her body an inch up the shore. When they rolled out, they took her body half an inch back. The rhythm was grotesquely hypnotic.

The tide had dumped her here. She wore a long sundress, but I couldn't tell what color it might have been. A scarf was wrapped around her neck. Slowly, Jason and I walked around the body, keeping several feet away. Her eyes were open and opaque, her mouth a loose O shape, her body bloated, skin mottled.

I'd read enough crime novels to know she'd been in the water for more than twenty-four hours.

"Oh, shit," Jason whispered. "That's Diana Harden, our missing guest."

Before we could go to the lodge to find help, Gino Garmon and three security officers approached. They must have heard the scream as well. Gino took one look at the body and swore, then said, "Jason, take the guests back to the lodge. Tell Tristan what happened and ask him to contact the St. John police chief. We'll stay with the body."

Jason didn't move. He was still staring at the body.

"Now, Jason," Gino commanded.

Then he noticed me. "Ms. Crawford." He looked down, saw I was wearing only underwear and my T-shirt didn't quite cover my ass. I had lost my embarrassment with Jason. Now I found it again, but was too shocked at our discovery to blush.

"Jason," I said quietly. "We need to go. Let them take care of her. Call the police."

"Yeah. Right. Okay. Thanks, Gino."

We went over to the newlyweds. Mrs. Kent was still sobbing. "Let's go," I said to her. "We need to contact the authorities, and they'll secure the crime scene."

I almost laughed at myself. I sounded like a detective from my favorite police procedural.

Mr. Kent helped his wife up. Okay, I know seeing a dead body is shocking—this was my first in-real-life dead body, too—but this woman's near paralysis was a bit much.

"She's dead! Who is she? Ohmigod!" Mrs. Kent whirled around and clutched Jason. "Is that *her*? The missing woman?"

He nodded.

"What happened?"

"I don't know," he said. "She could have had an accident. Maybe a boating accident. She didn't return from St. John on Sunday."

She must have returned because I don't think a body could have floated nearly from St. John to St. Claire in two days. I didn't know exactly how tides worked, but it didn't seem realistic—especially since she didn't appear, at first glance, to have been nibbled on by fish.

Mr. Kent put his arm around his wife's waist as the four of us walked along the beach until we reached the lodge. It was after midnight and the Blue Dahlia was closed, but the bar in the main lodge was still open. The music was low, and several guests talked and laughed.

"I'm taking my wife to our room," Mr. Kent said, breaking the awkward silence.

Jason said, "The police will want to talk to you."

"Tonight?" Mrs. Kent asked, her voice high and whiny.

"Maybe," Jason said. "I don't know. I'll tell them you went to your suite."

I asked, "How did you find her?"

The couple glanced at each other. "We, uh, were having a moment on the beach. And, um, something rolled up next to me," Mrs. Kent said.

A *moment* on the beach. Just like the *moment* in the ocean this afternoon that I'd interrupted. They must have been rabbits in a previous life.

"I thought it was a giant clump of seaweed, but then I saw her eyes." She shivered. That's when I noticed that they weren't wearing shoes and, in the lodge lighting, I could see Mrs. Kent had no clothes on under her filmy cover-up. Mr. Kent's shorts were on inside out.

Maybe a dead woman interrupting their sex on the beach rendezvous would turn them off of excessive PDA. Yet my "rescue" this afternoon hadn't stopped them from sex in public, so I don't know what would.

Then I looked down at my bare legs. I wanted to disappear.

"Don't think about it." Mr. Kent steered his wife through the lodge toward their cabin.

"Are you okay?" Jason asked me.

"I should be asking you the same thing. You look like you've seen a ghost. Cliché, I know, but truth."

"I didn't—I mean, I knew who she was. I didn't think she was dead. I thought she went to St. John to wait for her girlfriend."

"Girlfriend?"

"She complained Saturday that her girlfriend was late and ruining their first vacation in a year. She was irritated and—I shouldn't be telling you this. We have a strict policy not to talk about other guests. I'm sorry. I need to talk to my manager. I'll walk you back to your cabin."

"I'm fine," I said. He didn't look like he believed me. "Really, I promise I'm okay."

"I'm still escorting you back to your room," he said and took my hand. We walked down the path that led to the private cottages.

It seemed I was less disturbed by the events than Jason was. I thought there must be more to this than he was saying—things he must know about Diana and her disappearance. But like he'd said, staff wasn't supposed to talk about guests. But they *would* talk to the police.

Maybe, deep down, I'd been thinking all day that Diana Harden was dead. People didn't just go missing and leave all their stuff behind on a Caribbean island unless something bad happened.

We didn't speak on the short walk to my cottage. The silence wasn't uncomfortable, though. I'm sure Jason was thinking about all the things he needed to do, and I was wondering how Diana Harden had ended up dead on the beach.

I stopped outside my door. "If the police want to talk to me, I'll—" My voice faltered as he gave me a half smile, and it was so sexy that all thoughts of the body on the beach disappeared. I blinked as he stared, a jolt of lust hitting me. Jason stood so close, too close, and then he brought our joined hands to his lips. The feathery kiss on my palm left me speechless.

He said, "I'd like a do-over."

"What?" I knew what he meant, but now I was stalling, trying to regain my balance and composure.

"At the lagoon. Tomorrow? Same time?" He leaned in, almost kissed me. "Please?"

"Okay." I couldn't believe I'd agreed. A thrill ran up and down my spine in anticipation. And nerves. And lust. And a hint of fear. These feelings, this attraction, wasn't just in my imagination. It was real. For both of us.

"Great." He casually ran his fingers through my damp hair, then stepped back. I breathed easier . . . yet I had hoped he would kiss me.

Really? Now, right after seeing a dead body, you're thinking about kissing an almost-stranger?

Well, they did it in all the romantic suspense novels I loved. Why not here and now?

"Be careful," Jason said. "I mean, I don't think anything criminal happened to Ms. Harden. It was probably an accident, but until we know exactly what happened, watch yourself."

"I will. You too."

I reached for my pocket . . . but it wasn't there. My room card key was in the pocket of my jeans, which were still at the lagoon.

"Dammit!"

Jason reached into his pocket and pulled out a card key. "I have a master," he said. "Do you mind?"

"Thank you," I said as he unlocked my door. "I'll get dressed and go get my things."

"It's late. I'll have someone bring them to you."

"You don't have to—"

He put his finger on my lips. I couldn't breathe as my pulse quickened, and I could feel my heart pounding in my chest. I almost asked him to come in, but didn't. All these unexpected feelings washed over me. I needed to sort through things, regain some control over this situation that had gone from flirting to lust way too fast.

"Stay put," he whispered.

I nodded because I couldn't speak. He smiled, then walked away.

It took me a minute to breathe normally again, and I was grinning—until I saw my reflection in the bathroom mirror. My hair was tangled and frizzy. No sexy windswept-in-the-sea-breeze look. The makeup I'd put on before the Sky Bar had given me raccoon eyes because I hadn't planned on diving into the ocean. And my filthy shirt stopped halfway down my ass, revealing now grubby-looking pink underwear.

I took a very long hot shower, shampooed and conditioned my hair. My feet were sore, and when I got out, I saw little cuts on them. I rubbed lotion all over my body, put fuzzy socks on my feet, then wrapped myself in one of the fluffy bathrobes. I grabbed a can of nuts from the gift basket in the living area of the cottage and went out to the beachside patio.

On the beach where we had found Diana Harden's body, there were bright lights set up highlighting several people, but they were too far away for me to make out what anyone was doing. I ate the nuts and considered what might have happened to her. Accident was the most likely answer, but her disappearance was suspicious. She had a scarf wound around her neck in a way that didn't look like she'd have done it herself.

The book.

I went back inside, pulled Diana's book out of my bag, then sat down on the comfy bed and read through the comments in the margins.

Everything began to click into place.

Comments about people on the island—other guests that she seemed to know a lot about, including their net worth and properties they owned. The old man, the catty comments, numbers that made no sense at all to me, but must have meant something to Diana.

It was the dollar signs and calculations of net worth that gave me the final clue.

Was Diana Harden blackmailing someone? She was obsessed with money. The comment about scoring and including dollar signs. Had she been paid to keep a secret? Or had someone agreed to pay her, she met them Sunday on St. John, and something very bad happened?

Maybe her death wasn't an accident.

Maybe someone had killed her.

CHAPTER
NINE

"It's only gossip if you repeat it. Until then,
it's gathering information."

—Mercedes Lackey, *Intrigues*

I DIDN'T FALL ASLEEP until nearly dawn and woke up after eight.
My first thought was Diana Harden and her book—should I
give it to the police? What could they do with it if I did? Would
they even believe my theory that it had once belonged to Diana
and that she might have been blackmailing people on the island?
Last night, it had seemed the most plausible explanation . . . in
the light of morning, it sounded foolish and paranoid.

I needed to think more about this. I had a theory . . . and
no way to prove it. I should work through all plausible answers
before I discussed it with anyone, even Jason, for a second opinion. I mean, it was sort of unreal to think that I, Mia Crawford,
found myself in the middle of a murder mystery.

A not-so-little thrill ran through me. I had the book. I could
figure out what Diana was up to. I wondered if . . .

Breakfast.

I was late to breakfast with cigar-smoking Luis. I felt awful.
Not just because I detested being late for anything, but because
he was expecting me and probably thought I'd bailed on him.

I jumped out of bed, brushed my teeth, quickly pulled my
hair into a messy bun, and slipped on shorts and a tank top before half running to the Blue Dahlia for crepes.

Before looking for Luis, I glanced to the bar, hoping to see Jason.

He wasn't there. A pretty woman in her early twenties with caramel skin and sun-bleached hair was busy prepping the bar. Doug was drinking a Bloody Mary at the bar with one of his friends, their spouses nowhere in sight.

Of course Jason wasn't working; he'd worked last night. He had to sleep sometime.

I spotted Luis at a table drinking coffee from an oversized mug and staring out at the ocean. I sat down across from him. "I'm so sorry I'm late," I said.

He turned to smile at me. "I heard you had a busy night." He flipped a second mug over and poured me coffee from the carafe on the table. The smell made my taste buds leap with joy.

Did everyone know about what happened? Did they know I had walked back to the resort in my pink underwear? I supposed my state of undress was a minor point of gossip considering the dead body on the beach.

"It was eventful," I murmured.

"Go get your breakfast before the chef closes up. He's stubborn, won't stay open a minute past nine. I'm ready for a mimosa. What would you like? I recommend the pineapple or guava. Both mmm." He closed his eyes and kissed his fingers.

"Pineapple, thank you."

The chef was indeed grumpy. I couldn't make up my mind, so asked for one of each crepe. Strawberry, mango, chocolate, blueberry, and a ham and cheese. He looked at me as if wasting food was the greatest sin, so I said defensively, "I'm starving, and they smell so good."

Both statements were true, and I gave him my best smile.

He didn't smile back. He prepared the five crepes with quick, sure hands, sprinkling powdered sugar and fresh whipped cream on the chocolate, pureed fruit over the fruit crepes, and a sprinkling of cheese and onion over the ham and cheese.

I thanked him profusely, then went back to the beachside table where Luis had returned with the mimosas.

Luis smiled and held up his flute. "To new friends," he toasted.

I clinked his glass, sipped, then dug into the crepes.

"Oh. My. God," I said through a mouth full of blueberry crepe.

I spent the next five minutes in silence. I really was famished, and Luis didn't seem to mind that I was stuffing my face.

I followed Luis's gaze to the beach. The ocean was mesmerizing. The water rolling in and out, clear near the shoreline, bluer and more vibrant farther out.

Nelson and Anja Stockton were walking hand in hand, just out of reach of the water. They each wore hats to protect from the sun, and Anja rocked a long animal-print skirt and loose blouse. Her jewelry sparkled in the morning sun. Diamonds at dawn, I thought with a half smile. Wholly impractical and flashy, but for some reason, Anja was able to pull it off.

Far down the beach, two families with kids played, the occasional squeal of happiness reaching my ears. Near where I sat yesterday, a yoga class was wrapping up, six women facing a super-fit male instructor all in white. Hmm . . . I *really* needed to make time for yoga on the beach.

"Okay," I said after I had eaten most of the fruit crepes, "I need to slow down. You're right, these are amazing. Would he give me the recipe?" I was a decent cook. I just didn't have anyone to cook for. A brunch might be fun. Invite Jane and Amanda to my place, tell them all about my trip—the lagoon and finding the dead body would definitely be the highlight— and make these crepes.

"No," Luis said with a chuckle. "He's prickly. But I will get it for you."

"I don't want you to get in trouble."

He laughed at my comment, which seemed odd, but Luis wasn't the usual guest here. I wondered if he was the father of one of the employees, remembering what Henry said about employee housing on the south side of the dock.

I heard rather than saw CeeCee walk in and squeal as the

crepe stand was being carted away. "Oh, Trevor! We missed the crepes!"

I glanced over as CeeCee rushed the angry chef. "Are you sure you couldn't just make a couple of your yummy crepes for *me*?" She batted her eyes and smiled hopefully.

The chef started yelling in a language that sounded like French. He pushed his cart out of the Blue Dahlia while continuing to rant.

"Oh, Trevor, I'm so sad," CeeCee said. Then she saw me and waved. "Mia! Hi, Mia, remember me from yesterday?"

"CeeCee," Trevor said quietly—but loud enough for me to hear, "you're shouting."

CeeCee kissed him on the cheek, then ran over to me.

"Would you like one of my crepes?" I said. "I'm stuffed." Which was true.

"You're *so* sweet. But we'll go to the restaurant." She glanced over her shoulder. Trevor was talking to the bartender and didn't look happy. The few times I'd seen him, he had never smiled.

CeeCee plucked a strawberry off my plate and ate it. Normally, such an act would annoy me, but with CeeCee, I didn't care. Maybe because I felt a bit sorry for her. She seemed so clueless about what an asshole her boyfriend was to her. Plus I *had* offered her a crepe.

I was about to introduce CeeCee to Luis when she sighed dramatically. "I *love* this bar and how it just opens up to the beach and *everything*!" She spread her arms wide, closed her eyes, and smiled up at the sun.

A comment from the margins of Diana's book popped into my head.

Why do unhappily married men always go for bimbos?

I'd stayed up way too late last night reading Diana Harden's cryptic notes. And they might not mean anything. She could have simply been catty and bored waiting for her girlfriend. She probably wasn't talking about Trevor and CeeCee.

But she could have been.

"CeeCee, let's go," Trevor said from the bar. He looked pointedly at his watch. "I have a conference call in ninety minutes."

"Mia," CeeCee said, "do you want to go on a hike with me this afternoon to the top of the mountain?" She pointed vaguely north. "Trevor will be in meetings *all day*. It's not a difficult trail, but it would be fun, and the pictures I saw are *so pretty*."

She looked . . . well, a bit too hopeful, as if expecting me to say no.

"Sure," I said. "After lunch?"

CeeCee grinned widely. "One thirty. We'll meet right here." She patted the table. "Ta-ta!" She waved and walked off with Trevor.

I realized then that CeeCee hadn't said anything to Luis. "I'm sorry," I apologized. "I tried to introduce you, but . . ." I didn't finish what I planned to say because I didn't want to be rude. "I think that's just how she is. I don't think she meant to offend you."

"No offense taken," he said with that knowing half smile again. "People see what they want to see. You see quite a bit."

Luis's comment was cryptic, but maybe that's just the way he talked. I preferred cryptic Luis over melodramatic CeeCee.

"Not enough," I said, thinking about how I'd "saved" the honeymooners in the ocean. I finished my mimosa and leaned back in the comfortable chair. I couldn't eat the last few bites of crepe. I didn't know if I'd be able to eat for the rest of the day.

"How are you doing after last night's grisly discovery?" Luis asked kindly.

"Okay," I said. "It feels surreal now. Had you met her? The guest who went missing. Who, um, died." I hoped I didn't sound too nosy.

He turned to me, eyebrow raised, as if he knew there was more to my question than vague curiosity.

"I saw her several times," he said. "When you're old like me, people tend to not really see you."

That made me sad, though Luis didn't go out of his way to be noticed. Maybe he liked being invisible.

"Do you think her death was an accident?" I asked.

He shrugged. "I don't know."

"But you must have an idea."

Did I sound overly eager?

"I mean," I continued quickly, "it seems suspicious that she goes to St. John and no one sees her for more than two days, and then she washes up on the beach of St. Claire. It's too far for a body to float that fast without, um, a lot of damage."

He must think I'm completely morbid. Yet he seemed to consider my words, then said, "You're right." But he didn't elaborate, and I felt awkward continuing to pump him for information.

I sipped my coffee and poured more from the carafe to heat it up. Here I was, having a conversation with a man older than my Grams about a possible murder.

"How long have you lived on the island?" I asked, changing the subject.

He pondered. "A few years now."

"Do you work here?" That seemed unrealistic, considering his age.

He smiled. "I help when I can, doing this and that, but no one expects me to work."

"It must be nice to live here for your retirement," I said wistfully. I thought about my own retirement plans. By fifty-five, I would be able to comfortably retire and live within a budget for thirty years, but I doubted I'd retire that young. Ideally, when I accepted my promotion, I would put my raise into a second retirement fund and build up a larger portfolio. By sixty-five, I would be able to take one very nice trip a year. I'd never be able to live like this—full-time at an all-inclusive private island like St. Claire. While the resort was beautiful and peaceful, it was also extravagant and wasteful. Even if I *had* the money, I wouldn't squander it.

But for the first time, I considered maybe retirement could

look different from my plan to buy a small house in Connecticut and travel two weeks a year. I wouldn't live on an island, but maybe a quaint beach town in South Carolina or Florida. And if I planned carefully, I could take a vacation to the Caribbean every couple of years.

I would be thirty tomorrow. I was planning my life after sixty-five and all the things I would do *then* because I had a compulsive need to be financially secure *now*. What about the next thirty-five years? Was life about working hard and then having fun? I thought about Jane and Amanda, who'd balanced their careers with dating. Now Amanda was married and trying to get pregnant, and Jane would soon be married, and they'd both have families, and I would still be alone.

Suddenly, my eyes burned with unshed tears, and I felt so sad that it made me angry. I was here on the most beautiful island on the planet, and I was making myself depressed.

I saw Luis watching me. What was he thinking? Did he feel sorry for me? Because right now I felt sorry for myself. I forced a smile.

"You are a very serious young woman," Luis said. "But when you smile, you're as beautiful as a dahlia."

"Thank you," I said, knowing he was trying to cheer me up. "What did you do before you retired?"

"Oh, this and that," he said.

That wasn't an answer.

"Where are you from?" I asked.

"Everywhere."

"I mean, where were you raised."

"I was born in Texas."

I don't know why, but his answer surprised me. His slight accent sounded more foreign than Texas, as if he had been born here in the islands.

"My father enlisted in the Navy after the bombing of Pearl Harbor. That was nine months before I was born. He'd never been on a ship before, but he loved it. When he came back, I was a little tot. He had jobs that took him to the sea. He shared his love of the ocean with me. Then he got into a bit of trouble with the law, and we—my dad, my ma, me—we traveled on a boat all over the world. Settled for a time in Spain, where I met the love of my life. I was sixteen. She was nineteen."

His eyes became glassy with the memory.

"My parents left. I stayed. Married Maria, and we had a wonderful life."

I could picture their epic love story and wanted to know more. What happened to Maria? How did he end up on the island? They must have had children, and one of his children, or maybe grandchildren, worked here. The way he spoke was both old-fashioned and romantic and everything that made a great historical romance. A young boy from Texas whisked off because his dad was a criminal, traveling the high seas and finding true love in a faraway land with a princess . . .

Well, Maria probably wasn't a princess, but a princess in Luis's eyes.

Before I could ask more about his story, I spotted Brie walking up from the beach and heading right to our table.

"Hi, Luis," she said, then turned to me. "Spill the tea."

"What?" I was confused.

"Ohmigod, you *know* what I mean! You found Diana Harden's body!"

I glanced around to make sure no one was listening. I didn't want to be a gossip, though I was sort of *dying* to talk to someone about it. So what if the only person interested was an eighteen-year-old?

"I didn't *find* her body," I said.

Brie leaned forward. "I heard the sex addicts rolled on top of her."

With a glance at Luis, who seemed amused at our conversation, I said, "That was my impression."

"And?" Brie pushed. "I know you were there. Gino was talking about it with Tristan. I tried to get Kalise to spill, but she can be *so* tight-lipped. And I can't find Jason anywhere."

Now I was blushing.

"Ohmigod!" Brie exclaimed again. "You were with *Jason*."

"I wasn't *with* Jason. We were, just, well, at the same place at the same time."

Brie wasn't listening to me. Her mouth spread into the first real smile that I'd seen in the twenty-four hours I'd known her. Her clear blue eyes lit up with humor. "I totally knew it."

There was no way I was talking about Jason with a teenager and in front of Luis. Last night was all mine, and I wanted to keep it that way.

Clearing the hot bartender from my thoughts, I said, "*Anyway*, yes, Jason and I heard screams and went to see what happened. Diana was dead, tangled in a pile of kelp. She must have been brought in with the tide, but she'd been dead for a while. Maybe even since she went missing on Sunday."

"Were you there when the police came? What did they say?"

I shook my head. "There was no reason to stay. I thought they might talk to me last night, but no one came by. I'm sure they'll be around to ask questions."

I glanced around the resort, but nothing appeared different from yesterday. People on the beach, a few lounging in the sun, a small water aerobics class in the shallow half of the pool. The yoga class had broken up, and one of the women was talking to the instructor, standing *very* close. More people had come into the bar, laughing.

Did no one else care that a woman had died?

Maybe no one knew. CeeCee hadn't said anything, and I suspected if she knew, it would have been the first thing she mentioned.

"How did you hear about it?" I asked Brie.

"Who *doesn't* know? I was chilling on the balcony last night—" she vaguely gestured to one of the larger private cabins on the cliffs "—and saw two boats come in late. No one comes at night, so I went down to see what was going on. I thought maybe a celeb or something, though they usually come in on a helicopter. I got real close to where they were set up and hid in the trees until Gino saw me and *actually* called my dad." She rolled her eyes. "Jerk. I'm eighteen, a legal adult."

"Did the police say anything?"

"Not much that I could hear," Brie admitted. "The coroner from St. John was there, said she'd been in the water for around forty-eight hours."

I glanced at Luis, but he didn't appear to be listening to our conversation. He was looking out at the water again, his eyes shaded by sunglasses, and I wondered if he had fallen asleep.

Diana had disappeared Sunday morning. She could have died anytime between then and maybe Sunday night, which was forty-eight hours before she was discovered. How long could a body stay submersed? Had she been there all along, weighed down until a rope broke? I hadn't seen a rope, but that didn't mean there hadn't been one.

Kalise entered the Blue Dahlia and walked over to our table. "Ms. Locke, Mr. Caruso, if you'll please excuse me, I need Ms. Crawford."

Brie looked excited. I thanked Luis for having breakfast with me.

"Anytime, Mia, anytime," he said. He rose, stretched, bowed to Brie, and headed leisurely down the beach.

I glanced at Brie as I walked out of the Blue Dahlia. She pointed to herself and made a motion with her hand, indicating she wanted me to find her later, probably to tell her what I learned about Diana's death.

Maybe I would.

CHAPTER
TEN

"No. You never apologize for something
you didn't do wrong. You say 'excuse me.'
Never 'I'm sorry.' If you spend your life
apologizing you'll never gain any confidence."

—J. T. Ellison, *Good Girls Lie*

KALISE LED THE WAY toward the resort offices in silence.

"Any news about what happened to Diana Harden?" I asked.

"If you have any questions or concerns, you can speak with
the resort manager."

"Is that where we're going now?"

"We're going to the security office. There's nothing to be
concerned about. Mr. Garmon, our head of security, simply
needs your statement."

"What about the police?"

"We're cooperating fully with St. John police, of course,"
Kalise said.

"Then why aren't the police taking my statement?"

She glanced at me as if it was an odd question. "St. Claire
is a private island. Gino Garmon *is* our police."

That surprised me, and I expected more of an explanation,
but Kalise remained silent as she led me to the security building south of the main lodge. It was set back from the other

structures, partly hidden behind flowering bushes and bamboo fencing. Kalise badged in at the door, and it opened.

A security officer smiled at us. He was dressed in khakis and the standard St. Claire polo with *Security* under the logo instead of his name. "Thanks, Kalise. I'll take her from here."

Kalise nodded to me and left.

The officer led me past several small offices to a conference room at the end of the wide hall.

Gino Garmon, the security chief, was just as hot as I remembered from the beach: dark Italian looks, firm, muscular body. But he was still an ass, I reminded myself. He sat at the table with a man in a summer-weight light gray suit with a pale pink tie. Tristan, who had helped Trina in the gift shop with the rude Sherry Morrison. The Tristan who, according to staff gossip last night, was sleeping with Kalise.

Gino glanced at me without smiling. Tristan rose, smiled, and extended his hand. "Ms. Crawford, thank you for coming in so promptly. I'm Tristan Dubois, the manager of St. Claire." He had perfect posture and a slight French accent.

I couldn't picture it. The tall, dark, stately Kalise with the shorter, pale, wiry Tristan who lived on an island but didn't look like he spent a minute in the sun. Not to mention he had a receding hairline and funeral home demeanor.

Maybe I wasn't being fair, judging books—or people—by their covers. And Tristan had a warm, pleasant smile that would have put me at ease if Gino hadn't been glaring at me.

"Of course," I said belatedly. "Anything I can do to help."

Tristan said, "You've met Gino Garmon, our head of security. We just have a few questions, but you are of course not a suspect in Ms. Harden's death."

That comment surprised me, that he felt like he had to say it out loud. I hadn't even been here when she disappeared.

"I thought the police would be here."

"St. Claire is a private island," Gino said. "*I* am the police."

I really didn't like this guy. His tone and body language screamed intimidation. I steeled my spine, willed myself not to be cowed by him. I found myself playing with the ends of my hair, twirling the waves into tight curls. A nervous habit. I forced myself to stop by clasping my hands on the table in front of me.

Tristan said in a more conciliatory tone, "We are *of course* working closely with the St. John Police Department. They have retrieved the body and are performing the autopsy, and they are leading the investigation on St. John. But you don't need to worry about any of that. We simply need a timeline for the record. May I bring you something to drink? Water? Iced tea? Something alcoholic perhaps?"

Was he trying to throw me for a loop? I tried to picture being interrogated by the police in New York City and being offered a glass of wine. It almost made me laugh.

"No, thank you," I said. "Maybe water?"

Tristan walked over to a mini-fridge and retrieved a bottled water, put it in front of me, then took his seat again, giving me an encouraging smile. Maybe Kalise liked him because he was a genuinely nice guy.

Gino said, "What happened last night? How did you come upon the body? Where were you, what did you hear, what did you see?"

All humor disappeared, and I was immediately self-conscious about last night. What exactly did I say? What had Jason said? I assumed they spoke to Jason, but what if they hadn't yet?

Why are you even worried about it? Just tell the truth.

"I heard Mrs. Kent scream," I said. "I mean, I didn't know it was her at the time. But I heard a scream and ran toward it."

"Where were you?"

"The lagoon at the end of the Luz Luna Bahia trail," I said.

"Alone?" Gino asked with a smirk. Of course he'd spoken to Jason—Jason worked here. Or he remembered me in my panties and shirt last night. Plus, Jason had been holding my hand. Was I blushing? Dear God, I prayed I wasn't blushing. The more I thought about not blushing, the hotter my face felt.

"At first. Then Jason Mallory, one of the bartenders here—" Of course they knew Jason was a bartender. *Stop rambling*, I told myself. "Um, Jason showed up as I was getting ready to leave. We were talking when we heard the scream."

"What did you see on the beach?" Gino asked.

"The Kents were very upset. There was a body twisted in a pile of kelp. And Jason said it looked like the missing guest, Diana Harden. By that time, you arrived with security, and we were instructed to leave."

Gino stared at me. Intentionally to make me even more uncomfortable? Tristan, in a much kinder, even tone, asked a few clarifying questions, specifically about time, whether I touched the body, and if I saw anything else that might be helpful.

When neither of them had additional questions, I asked, "How did she die?"

They both stared at me, Tristan with a neutral look, and Gino with a hint of . . . anger? I thought it was a logical question.

"I mean, was it an accident? Did someone kill her?"

"We haven't received word from St. John as to cause of death," Tristan said. He stood, signaling for me to do the same. "Thank you so much for your time." He walked me to the door. Gino remained seated at the table, writing in his notepad.

"I am so sorry about all this," Tristan continued as we stepped outside. "I understand how traumatic and disturbing last night must have been, and I've been authorized to extend you an all-expense-paid three-night package to use at your convenience."

"That's not necessary."

Shut up! I practically screamed at myself in my head. A free vacation? *Here? On St. Claire?*

Stop being so damn conciliatory, I told myself.

Tristan smiled at me and said, "On behalf of St. Claire, we are deeply sorry for the trouble you have had during your stay. If there is anything I or any of the staff can do for you, please do not hesitate to contact me directly." He reached into his breast pocket and pulled out a business card. "This is my personal number. I am available any time, day or night."

What, he didn't sleep? Eat? He was on call 24/7?

I took the card. "Thank you." I had questions about Diana and her murder, but nothing Tristan could answer.

"I know Gino can be intimidating, I'm sorry if you were uncomfortable," Tristan said. "He was a police officer in the States and works well with the St. John Police Department. I'm hoping this was simply an awful accident. If there was foul play, please, rest assured, the police will be leading the investigation, and we will assist in any way we can."

That made me feel marginally better, though I still didn't like Gino. If someone here was responsible, it would benefit the resort to cover up a murder.

Murder. No one said she was murdered.

It could have been an accident, like Tristan said.

I didn't believe that for a minute.

CHAPTER
ELEVEN

"It is a capital mistake to theorize before one has data. Insensibly one begins to twist facts to suit theories, instead of theories to suit facts."

—Sir Arthur Conan Doyle, *A Scandal in Bohemia*

THINKING ABOUT EVERYTHING GINO and Tristan told me, I headed back toward my room on autopilot and ran into Andrew Locke and his girlfriend. Literally. If I'd been holding a drink, it would have been all over his shirt.

"I'm so sorry," I said, my hand splayed on his chest as I reached out to stop myself from falling. It was a very firm, very nice chest, and I supposed I touched it just a moment too long, based on the angry glare coming from Sherry.

Andrew smiled warmly and cupped my elbow to steady me. "No harm, no foul," he said. "Mia, right?"

"Yes, hi," I said.

Had Diana written about Andrew in the book? Which note? She'd written about the value of a house in Arizona, and that's where Andrew and Brie lived. I couldn't remember the details. Could she have been blackmailing Andrew? Or his girlfriend?

"This is my girlfriend, Sherry Morrison," he said. "Mia came over on the ferry with David and Doug," he added to Sherry. "You met them yesterday."

"Nice to meet you," I said automatically. "I don't know where my head is. I'm not usually so distracted." I knew exactly where my head was—thinking about murder.

"I daydream a lot around here as well," Andrew said.

I realized then how much Andrew and Brie looked alike, with the black hair and vibrant blue eyes. He seemed so nice and genuine and was very attractive. I wished he was a few years younger. I wished he didn't have a girlfriend.

"Honey, we don't want to be late meeting the Stocktons," Sherry said. Her tone was pleasant, but she possessively laced her fingers with Andrew's.

"We're on island time," Andrew said lightly. "Would you like to join us?" he asked me.

The offer surprised me—and clearly it surprised Sherry, though she hid her irritation well. If I hadn't been looking at her, I would have missed it.

"Yes," she said with a fake smile, "why don't you?"

Her voice was definitely more pleasant than her expression.

"Oh, well, thank you, but I can't." Though I suddenly wanted to. I didn't know why Sherry had this almost . . . jealous? . . . vibe. Of *me*? Why? "Maybe later?" I said.

"Absolutely," Andrew said. "See you at the luau tonight?"

"Sure," I said, though I had no idea what he was talking about since I hadn't looked at today's resort schedule. "See you then."

They walked away, and I caught Sherry looking over her shoulder at me. Then she made a point to kiss Andrew on his cheek as they walked hand in hand toward the Blue Dahlia.

I never wanted to be that girl—a woman so territorial over her boyfriend that she had to make a point of PDA to flex her feminine muscle. Sure, the Kents' PDA was over the top, but I didn't think the wife was jumping on the husband as a sign for all the other women to back off.

I pushed the encounter aside and continued down the path to my cottage.

My door was open.

For a split second I worried that someone had broken in, that they were searching for my book, or waiting to kill me like Diana Harden . . .

Stop it! I told myself. Imagination in overdrive, I approached cautiously, just in case.

Then I saw the housekeeping cart and two maids in black shorts and white polos efficiently cleaning my room. "Hi," I said.

"Ms. Crawford," one of the maids said, "we'll be not ten more minutes."

"Don't rush," I said. "I'll sit on the patio."

I walked through my room and picked the book up from my nightstand, along with the notes I'd taken the night before when I couldn't sleep. My spine tingled as the housekeepers watched me exiting through the sliding doors. Had they read what I'd written? The first page was pretty damning:

> Diana Harden: arrived Friday on St. Claire. Who else was
> here? Was anyone on the ferry with her Sunday morning?
> Did she return to the island before she was killed? Who is her
> girlfriend?

Even last night I'd thought murder, not an accident. Now I was positive she was killed even though Tristan said they didn't have the report from St. John authorities.

Last night, I'd copied everything Diana had written in my notepad, using her shorthand, then my thoughts on what she might have meant—including passages and words she'd highlighted within the text. I reread the comment about the house in Arizona.

> Money or love? Money, of course—he's worth a small fortune.
> Does he know all the dirt on his new girlfriend?

Then, written with a different pen: 112 ~ est. net $80-90m, AZ residence $5m+, vacation house $3m

AZ residence. That had to be Andrew Locke, right? Unless someone else on this small island was from Arizona. And maybe the comment above about dirt on a new girlfriend was about someone completely different . . . like Trevor's girlfriend CeeCee. What did the 112 mean? A room number? I could easily check that out.

"We're done, Ms. Crawford," one of the maids said.

I jumped, completely lost in my work. "Oh. Sorry. Thank you." I gave her a smile that felt lopsided.

She looked at the book and frowned, then left with her partner, whispering something in her ear. Had she seen this book before? Was she suspicious of me?

I was reading *way* too much into one glance. Still, I watched through the glass wall until they were gone before turning back to the book.

112. It had to be a room number. Not a cottage, because cottages were letters—I was in K. But the main building had rooms. I went inside and picked up the phone, read the instructions for calling a room. Dialed.

"St. Claire desk. How may I help you, Ms. Crawford?"

"Uh—I was trying to reach room 112."

"There is no room 112, so your call was routed to the main desk. Who are you trying to reach?"

I was at a loss. I needed to lie. I was an awful liar.

"Luis Caruso? We had breakfast this morning. I had a question for him. I might have gotten his room wrong."

"I can get a message to Mr. Caruso," the clerk said.

Oh, God, I was at a complete loss. "It, um, is sort of personal? We had a long conversation, and I . . . well, just, uh, tell him I called and I'll look for him." That sounded so lame. I thanked the clerk and hung up.

So much for being a private investigator. In one of my favorite series, PI Elvis Cole lied so smoothly whenever he was investigating. Why couldn't I lie like Elvis Cole?

So 112 wasn't a room. I went back outside and picked up the book. I was only a few chapters from the spot where Diana had left the business card as a bookmark. I turned the page and frowned.

Chapter Twenty-Nine.

The pages must have been stuck together. I rolled them in my fingers, trying to separate them, but they weren't stuck together.

The last page of chapter twenty-eight was missing.

Why would Diana have torn out a page? She was reading the book as well as writing in it, which was clear from some of her comments about the characters and plot.

Had one of the maids done it? Doubtful, but possible.

Then I remembered what happened yesterday.

After I jumped in the ocean to "save" the honeymooners, I'd seen someone squatting next to my lounge chair. I closed my eyes and tried to picture him—I think it was a him, that was my impression, but I couldn't be sure. My sight had been blurry from the water (and my deep embarrassment), and I had been at least a hundred yards away. Just a sense that it was a guy, but I couldn't even say with certainty what race. He'd worn a light-weight jacket and shorts. I hadn't noticed the torn page then, but I hadn't read that far.

Could the stranger have torn out the page?

That seemed more likely than the maids, no matter how far-fetched it sounded.

"Mia! The tea!"

I yelped and jumped up, knocking both the chair and table over. Diana's book and my notebook slid across the tiles as I fell to my ass.

It was Brie, in jean shorts and a bikini top, coming up from the beach to my cottage.

"Dammit," I said, picking up the furniture.

"Sorry," Brie said, not sounding sorry. She picked up the book. I tried to grab it from her hand at the same time I was picking up my notebook. She pulled back and I fell on my ass again as I overcompensated.

"Whatcha reading?" Brie asked. She sat in the chair I hadn't knocked over and opened the book.

"That's mine," I said. I righted my chair and reached out for her to hand it to me, but she didn't.

"This book has seen better days," she said, shaking sand out from the pages.

If I made a bigger deal about the book, she would be even more curious, so I tried to divert her attention and asked, "What do you want to know?"

"The police—what they said, what you said, what they know. I need the deets."

"The police weren't there."

"What do you mean they weren't there?" Brie looked up from the book, and I judged whether I could grab it away before she could pull it out of my reach. I decided no. "Isn't that why Kalise grabbed you? To talk to the police about the body?"

"Tristan told me that St. Claire has its own security because it's a private island. St. John is doing an autopsy, but Gino Garmon is investigating here on the island, supposedly working with the police."

"No shit?" Brie snorted. "Like he's ever investigated a *real* crime."

"Tristan said he'd been a cop."

I didn't know where Garmon had worked before he came to St. Claire. Maybe it was some small department in the middle of nowhere, or maybe he'd been fired because he was incompetent. Or he lied on his resume, or maybe . . .

"What are you writing? Weird." Brie frowned as she flipped through the pages.

I remembered the semicoded comment that might be about her father. Would Brie figure it out? Maybe.

I finally grabbed the book from her and held it in my lap. "Not me," I said. "I think—" I hesitated just a second. Should I clue her in? Brie was a kid—okay, she was starting college, but she *was* a teenager. Still, she had been here at the same time as Diana, and she'd already proven herself to be observant. She might be able to fill in some of the blanks.

She looked at me with suspicion, so I just blurted it out. "I think the book belonged to Diana Harden. The missing woman."

"The dead woman," Brie corrected me bluntly.

"Yes."

Brie nodded. "I saw her with a book. I thought she was writing in it—you're saying she wrote in *that* book." She reached for it again, but I held it away from her. She pouted. "Geez."

"Let me explain first." I wanted someone to confide in, but how did I explain my theory? "Diana was writing about people here at St. Claire. Staff and guests."

Her eyes widened. "*Really?* Now you *have* to show me."

"She wrote in sort of a code, and I don't think it's appropriate."

Brie stared at me in disbelief. "I'm eighteen," she said flatly.

I opened it to the middle and read one of the comments.

"'A trophy wife and juggling a bimbo. Viagra much?' Then she has a year, 2012, and drew what looks like a row of houses." As I said *year*, I wondered if I was wrong about that. Maybe the number meant something else.

Brie snorted. "Maybe the guy has a couple wives in different parts of the country."

"Or multiple mistresses," I said. I turned a couple pages and then read, "'How much will he pay to keep his secret?'" I looked at Brie and said, "That comment doesn't have a drawing, but it has a number, 522. I thought maybe a room number, so I tried one of the numbers, and it's not a room."

"Good guess," Brie said. "We're in a cabin. We don't have a number. It's called the Jasmine Suite."

"It's like she's writing whatever comes to mind when she sees someone. There are several notations that appear to be tracking individuals' net worth. They're vague, but I'm a financial planner. I recognize some of the shorthand."

"No names?"

"No, just these numbers and a few doodles." I turned to the front of the book and read the comment that I had been mulling over all night. "She circled a passage about the book's heroine, then wrote, 'Sounds just my type. I hope she's not *too* mad at me . . .'"

"Holy shit," Brie muttered. "That sounds personal."

"There's a heart next to it, so I'm thinking it's about a girl-friend, or maybe she just likes redheads? The heroine is a redhead." I bit my lip. I had been thinking of a possibility all night, and now it seemed so obvious that I wondered if I was embellishing the thought in my head.

"What?" Brie asked. "You thought of something."

"Amber is a redhead. And later in the book, Diana wrote that her #1 was going to be late, again with that little heart next to the comment."

"OMG, you think that Diana and Amber were an item?" Brie said excitedly.

"Jason mentioned that Diana was angry because her girl-friend was late to their vacation. But maybe I'm reading too much into this." I giggled at my unintentional pun.

"Don't you follow news?" Brie said. "Amber Jones has been seen with the hottest guys *and* the hottest girls."

I wasn't up-to-date on popular culture, unless it was about popular books and authors. Plus, I wouldn't call entertainment gossip *news*. "I didn't know she was that big an actress."

Brie laughed. "She's an extra. A couple of one-liners in mov-ies, but mostly she plays the victim on crime shows where she just has to lie on a slab and look like a corpse."

I pictured Diana's body and involuntarily shivered. "Well." I didn't know what to say. "I suppose we could find their social media accounts and see if Amber and Diana have been together." I considered Amber's argument with Parker. "Do you know any-thing about a thirtysomething guy who looks like a trust fund baby? Slim, sandy blond hair, has a dickhead vibe. First name Parker. He and Amber were arguing yesterday. Then I heard him talking to his father on the phone."

"Parker Briggs. *Total* dick."

"I overheard him telling his father that he and Amber were trying to fix their relationship."

"Really? Maybe." She wrinkled her nose. "I don't know."

"Have they been here before?"

Brie shrugged. "I've never seen them. But we come the same two weeks every year, right after school gets out. When Dad played ball, we came in December—really nice then. I mean, it's nice now, but June is also the beginning of hurricane season."

I must have looked panicked, because Brie laughed and said, "They don't have any major storms on the radar for the week."

That relieved me. I'd seen too many pictures of the aftermath of hurricanes. I didn't want to be in one.

I flipped pages on my notebook and started writing names and days. "Diana went missing on Sunday. Amber came over on the ferry with me on Tuesday, but Parker was already here. Do you know when he got here?"

"Monday," Brie said. "Word is that he made a last-minute reservation and was told there was nothing available. He made a stink, and Tristan freed up a room—they always have one or two for people like Briggs. St. Claire thrives on those elitist assholes, the ones who throw money around and have the clout to break a place."

"I know the type. But not everyone here is like that."

She shrugged. "Half and half."

"I chatted with Nelson and Anja Stockton. They seem very nice."

"Wannabe elitist assholes."

"And David and Doug came over with me on the ferry. They were friendly."

She shrugged. "Sure, I met them a couple years ago. Nice, but Doug has a stick up his ass. Makes sure that *everyone* knows that his husband saved my dad's career. He drops the name of every baseball player David performed Tommy John surgery on. And talks about their house and their vacations, and I want to ask, what are you compensating for, Doug?"

For a teenager, Brie was not only observant but insightful.

I made a note about Briggs. "So Parker arrived Monday. When did you get here?"

"Friday."

"And Diana got here Friday, too, right?"

"Yes. We were on the same ferry."

She looked over to what I was writing. "What are you doing?"

What should I say?

"Come on, tell me," she pushed. "It looks like a timeline."

"Diana was here for two days before she disappeared. If she really was blackmailing people, who? And—"

Brie leaned forward. "And you think someone here, on the island, killed her?"

I wanted to temper her enthusiasm—though I was just as excited.

"Maybe," I said cautiously. "But it could have been an accident."

"You believe that?"

I shook my head.

"Neither do I."

"What did Diana do on Friday and Saturday? I mean, on Sunday morning she went to St. John. That was, according to the newspaper, confirmed by the St. John police. You said she went to the spa on Friday, right?"

Brie nodded. "And she spent a lot of time lounging on the beach. That's where I saw her the most. Reading that book." She paused, clearly thinking about something specific.

"What do you remember?" I asked.

"Nothing," she said quickly.

It wasn't nothing. "Brie, don't hold back. I told you my theory."

"What if I saw Gino Garmon in a heated conversation with Diana on Saturday night?"

"The night before she disappeared?"

"Yep."

"Did you hear what they were arguing about?"

"No. It was late, and I was hanging out at the dock. It's peaceful there, no one's around, but it's off-limits to guests after dark. I was sitting on the back of the ferry looking at the stars, and they were on the beach next to the dock. I heard a shout, thought I was busted, but when I looked over, it was Gino and Diana. He was angry. She was laughing. Then she got mad and pushed him. He walked away first. But I couldn't hear what they were talking about."

And now Gino was investigating Diana's death. That seemed like a huge conflict.

"What do you know about CeeCee and Trevor?" I asked.

She shrugged. "I don't think either of them have been here before. They came in late Friday night."

"Can you find out if Trevor's married?"

Brie grinned. "Easy-peasy." She pulled out her phone, then groaned.

"What's wrong?"

"Sherry. Shit." Brie rolled her eyes. "My dad thinks we need to spend girl time together. He just texted me, reminded me I'm supposed to be back in fifteen minutes so we can 'do some-thing.' Like what? *Talk?* I can't stand her."

I thought back to my brief encounter earlier today. "She's kind of possessive about your dad."

"Right?" Brie said. "You saw it too. I mean, she's had two husbands, you know. I don't trust her."

I had an idea. "I'm going hiking with CeeCee this afternoon. We're meeting at the bar. I don't know why I agreed, except I felt kind of bad for her because she's so friendly and her boyfriend is working all day. Why don't you and Sherry join us."

"You wouldn't mind?"

"You'd be doing me a favor."

Brie grinned. "She'll hate it! Perfect." She typed rapidly on her phone with her thumbs. I was fast, but Brie beat me. "Now she can't get out of it, because she won't say no to my dad." She turned her phone so I could read the messages.

DAD: Remember, you and Sherry have a girls afternoon.
　😎 Don't be late. 🕐
BRIE: 🙁

DAD: Give Sherry a chance. It's important to me. 🙏
BRIE: I know
BRIE: hey there's this hike I really want to do totally easy
   trail so tell her to wear good shoes k?
DAD: Great idea! I'll tell her. 😄 I'm meeting up with Da-
   vid and Doug, I'll see you both when you get back. 👋

I laughed and handed her back her phone. "Your dad likes emojis."

Brie sighed dramatically. "I regret showing him how to use them. I've told him less is more, but whatev. He's like at that awkward age between Gen X and Millennial."

"We need to do some research," I said. "If we learn more about the people on the island, maybe we can figure out what Diana's shorthand means."

"Like?"

"Trevor's background, and maybe Gino Garmon. Where was he a cop? And if Amber and Diana were together."

"Anyone else she wrote about?" Brie glanced at the book.

"Maybe, but I'm still putting it together." *If* Diana had been writing about Andrew and Sherry, I didn't want Brie reading about it without me knowing exactly what she meant.

"I'm not your Girl Friday," Brie said. "Think of me as Dr. Watson. If I'm going to help you—and I can run circles around you on the internet—then I want to know what you know."

She turned her phone around again, and there was an Instagram post of Amber Jones and Diana Harden, arm in arm, at some charity event.

My mouth fell open, and I grabbed her phone. "How'd you find this so fast?"

"What can I say? Cyber-sleuthing is in my blood."

The picture had been taken at a children's charity event in New Orleans six months ago. It was posted on the charity page, and only Amber was identified.

Brie took her phone back. "I'll see what I can find on Parker Briggs too."

"Be careful with him," I said, suddenly wondering if we should even be doing this. I was dragging an eighteen-year-old into something that could turn dangerous.

Because *someone* had killed Diana Harden.

"Of course," she said.

"I'm serious. If I'm right and Diana was blackmailing someone here, on St. Claire, then they're still here. Because everyone who was on the island Sunday is still a registered guest."

My words sank in.

"Okay, I get it," Brie said, and got up. "I'll be in full stealth mode." She was halfway across the patio when she looked over her shoulder with a smile. "One thing about teenagers? No one here pays us any attention."

CHAPTER
TWELVE

"Women can be just as dangerous as men."
—Holly Jackson, *A Good Girl's Guide to Murder*

I ARRIVED AT THE Blue Dahlia a little early, hoping Jason would be at the bar. Instead, the same girl from this morning was working. I tried not to show my disappointment.

"What would you like, Ms. Crawford?"

It still unnerved me that every staff member knew my name even if I hadn't met them.

"I'm about to go on a hike. I'm not that hungry, but feel like I should get something."

"I know just the thing—no alcohol. I call it Callie's Energy Blast. Delicious, and also good for hangovers."

"I don't have a hangover, but I'll take one."

Trying not to seem like I was super interested in the answer, I asked, "When does Jason come on?"

"He was supposed to relieve me at one but needed to talk to security, so he said he'd be late." She glanced at me, lowered her voice. "We're not supposed to talk about what happened last night."

"I was there," I said.

Callie nodded. "I heard. It's *awful.*" She glanced around, leaned over, and said quietly, "I overheard the police talking at the dock early this morning. They said she was strangled."

I pictured the scarf around her neck. "So it wasn't an accident."

"She could have fallen off a boat somehow, got tangled in something."

"But wouldn't the captain or another passenger have alerted the authorities?"

"The police are questioning all of the boat owners on St. John. That's where she was when she disappeared."

Did everyone believe that except me? While I might not be a nautical expert, I just couldn't see a body floating from St. John to here—from one small island to a smaller island twenty miles away, separated by a vast body of water?

"Could she have rented a boat?" I asked Callie. "Because I don't think her body could have floated all the way here."

Callie's eyes widened, and I thought about how my comment must have sounded. Before I could backtrack, she said, "Oh, I hadn't thought of that. Yeah, she could have, but God, I hope not, because then how did she die? You know? If she was strangled *here*?" She shivered. "I'm sure the police will figure it out."

"Yeah, me, too," I said, though I didn't believe it. Because it wasn't the police investigating here, on St. Claire. It was Gino Garman, security chief, who was seen arguing with the victim the night before she disappeared. If Diana *had* rented a boat on Sunday, why hadn't the police learned of it in the two days she'd been missing?

Still, this *was* the Caribbean. Everyone acted more relaxed and casual than any place I'd visited. Even my Grams, who turned having fun into an art, would have found this island too relaxed. She'd have been the daredevil to take Jason up on hang gliding lessons just to get her adrenaline pumping.

Callie handed me her to-go "energy blast" smoothie just as CeeCee walked into the Blue Dahlia, dressed in khaki walking shorts and a tight tank top under an unbuttoned lightweight shirt. She wore cute ankle boots, a big hat, giant sunglasses, and a designer backpack over her shoulders.

I felt out of place in my T-shirt, shorts, and well-worn sneakers.

"Hi, Mia!" she said enthusiastically. "Are you ready? I'm *so* excited."

"I'm ready, but is it okay if Brie and Sherry join us? They were also planning to hike."

I saw Sherry trudging toward the bar, not looking happy at all. Brie was a couple feet in front of her, grinning slyly.

"Of course!" CeeCee said. "The more the merrier!"

Every sentence was an exclamation. It was exhausting just listening to CeeCee.

Brie came up and quickly started talking. "Are you going up to the peak too? Great." She winked at me "Sherry, Mia and CeeCee are joining us. This'll be fun."

Sherry looked from me to CeeCee and then to Brie. Did she suspect that we'd set her up?

"Yes," she said after a moment. "Sure."

CeeCee clapped her hands. "This way, girls!" She led us through the lodge and out the back to the base of the mountain trail. "It's no fun hiking alone, and now it's a party!"

"Trevor doesn't like to hike?" I asked.

"Sure he does, but he's always *so* busy with work. He doesn't have much free time."

I wished I'd had time to dig a little into Trevor. I didn't even know his last name. CeeCee didn't seem to fit with him, so I was guessing either he was divorced and playing the field with a younger woman, or he was married and a cheater.

She had to know if he was married, didn't she? He hadn't been wearing a ring, but would a woman travel this far with a man if she didn't know his marital status? Maybe. Not every woman lacked the spontaneity gene like me. Or binge-watched true crime documentaries and pictured how an affair could go horribly wrong. Sometimes, I thought *Fatal Attraction* should be mandatory viewing for everyone over eighteen.

I glanced back to where Brie and Sherry were only a couple steps behind us. They weren't talking. I caught Brie's eye—she knew what the goal was, to find out as much about Trevor as possible to figure out if Diana had been blackmailing him. She nodded, caught up to us. "CeeCee, I *love* your boots. Where did you get them?"

She looked down, laughed. "I've had them forever! Aren't they cute? I got them in this little boutique in Charleston when I was there on business."

"What kind of business?" I asked.

She hesitated as if she wasn't expecting the question. "Then? Um, I worked for a decorator."

Brie started chatting with CeeCee, so I held back with Sherry. "It's so pretty here," I said, motioning to the flowering trees that lined the trail.

"Yes," Sherry concurred.

"This is my first vacation in years," I said.

Sherry shot me a side glance. "And you came here alone."

"My boyfriend and I broke up a few months ago."

"St. Claire is not a place for singles," she said. "I don't think you'll find a new boyfriend here."

The comment was snide and rude, and I really didn't know how to respond.

"I'm not looking for a relationship," I said, sounding more defensive than I wanted to. I forced joy into my voice. "I just came to relax."

She harrumphed and stopped to take a picture. I kept walking, not caring if I left her behind. Sherry called out, "Brie, look at these flowers! Let's take a picture for your dad."

Brie waved at her. "Maybe later!" Then she continued her conversation with CeeCee. I was right behind them when Brie asked, "How did you and Trevor meet? He's so serious, and you're so much fun."

CeeCee grinned. "Trevor isn't serious *all* the time. He's just in the middle of a big land deal and has to be in all these *meetings*. He never should have switched to cash basis accounting. He has to jump through all these hoops to prove his net worth to his bank."

Her comment surprised me. CeeCee didn't seem like someone who understood the pros and cons of accrual basis versus cash basis accounting, but she was right that determining net worth was much harder under cash basis. Maybe something she picked up working for the decorator.

"Is that where you met?" Brie asked. "Through work?"

"I guess, sort of! I work for a caterer, and we served one of his corporate meetings." She put her hands over her heart. "It was love at first sight!"

Decorator to caterer?

Brie and CeeCee were chatting about the island, and Sherry remained ten feet behind me, so I just tried to enjoy the hike. I thought about what CeeCee said and wondered what she meant by it. She might understand a lot more than she let on. She might not be as . . . okay, *dumb* is a mean word. But why would someone who's smart want to act like they weren't?

Maybe I was reading too much into the conversation.

I heard CeeCee talking about the sunset cruise tomorrow and how she hoped Trevor would finish his work so they could go. "I don't want to go alone," she said. "It's supposed to be *so* romantic. If he finishes this big deal, he'll be happy, and then we'll have fun!"

I had read about the sunset cruise, and like CeeCee thought it sounded too romantic to go on by myself.

Sherry said, "Too bad it's couples only, Mia. The cruise is a highlight of St. Claire."

I hadn't realized she'd caught up with me. She made a point of looking down at her left hand and tilting her bare fingers in an odd, flashy manner. Suddenly, I realized she expected Andrew to propose to her. Was that why he'd brought her to the island? I glanced at Brie. Did she suspect?

Neither Brie nor I liked Sherry, but I tried to be objective. Sherry Morrison was very pretty, with flawless, creamy skin, large, dark eyes, perfect bone structure. Taller than me and always impeccably dressed, even when casual. Clothes, jewelry, makeup—always appropriate for the occasion, never too much or too little.

We came off the trail at the top of the northernmost peak, a flat area roughly the size of a football field.

We could see *everything*.

To the south was the bulk of the island—lush and green with flashes of color where a flowering tree had exploded in growth. Below was the resort, laid out like a child's toy, the main lodge overseeing the myriad of cabins and cabanas, the blue of the pool sparkling in the sun.

To the east was the ocean, calm and vibrant—so light and clear in some spots I could almost see the sand beneath—edging the shoreline for at least a quarter mile. Then the sharp contrast of darker blue water as the shore fell away to the deep.

The ocean wrapped around the northern edge of the island like a glove, water on three sides, making me feel isolated. A flash of me standing here, on this island, in the middle of the ocean gave me a sense of vertigo and smallness—a speck of dust on the vast earth.

The wind whipped around us, but there was a picnic area with heavy wooden tables. Signs warned us away from the north side of the clearing, proclaiming steep drops and rocks below. I had no intention of getting that close to *any* edge of the clearing.

I realized that this was the cliff that Jason had hang glided from. I could make out the dock to the south, where I'd arrived yesterday.

"I brought snacks," CeeCee said, and opened her large backpack. "They made them for me in the restaurant. Isn't that nice?" She pulled out containers with fruit, sandwiches, and pasta salad and laid them out on one of the three tables. "And champagne! There's plenty for all of us."

She popped the cork and giggled when bubbles overflowed. "Sorry."

CeeCee seemed harmless, except for that out-of-character comment and her strangely deep understanding of finance.

"This was thoughtful," I said. The hike had made me hungry, the crepes now a distant memory.

"I knew I'd be *starving*," CeeCee said as she opened up the containers. "Help yourself."

Brie went over to the edge of the cliff and made me nervous. She had her phone out and was taking pictures. Sherry went over to Brie, and as CeeCee chatted, I watched as Sherry drew out her phone and took a selfie of her and Brie. Sherry laughed, looking like she was having a great time, but as soon as the phone camera went off, her dour expression returned. She said something to Brie. Brie shrugged and turned away.

Sherry sat on the bench across from CeeCee and me.

I took one of the plates and put two of the small sandwich triangles on it, some fruit, and a large heaping of the delicious-looking pasta salad.

CeeCee said, "Sherry, we should all get together before we leave. Trevor is *such* a baseball fan."

"Sure," Sherry said, and smiled at CeeCee. "That would be fun."

She was a lot nicer to CeeCee than to me. Because I was single and unattached? Did she consider me a rival?

I looked around and thought it might be fun to come up here with Jason. He didn't work mornings, so maybe for an early lunch. I didn't really know him, and even though we'd almost kissed, I felt like I should learn more about him before throwing caution to the wind and sleeping with him.

My face heated at the thought.

CeeCee said suddenly, "Mia! You didn't tell me that you're the one who found the body last night." It was so out of the blue it took me a second to process what she'd said.

"Me? No. I mean, I was there, but I didn't find her."

"I heard it was Diana Harden," she said. "The guest who went missing. I *told* Trevor that something must have happened to her."

"I'm sure it was an accident," Sherry said.

"Did either of you meet her?" I asked.

CeeCee nodded, eyes wide, as she bit into a mango. "We

arrived on Friday, but later than everyone else. Trevor had a meeting, so the resort was kind enough to send a helicopter for us Friday night. There's a helipad on the top of the mountain."

I looked around and didn't see it.

"There." CeeCee pointed south. I still couldn't see anything through the trees. "It's used mostly by Ethan Valentine, we were told, but he sometimes lets VIPs use it. I was scared. I don't like flying, and a helicopter is *a gazillion* times more dangerous than a plane. But ten minutes later, we were here!"

"Was she on the helicopter, too?" I asked, then remembered that Brie said Diana was on the ferry with her.

"No. Only Trev and me. But it was *really* late, and I was hungry, so we went to the restaurant, and Diana was there by herself. Reading, but also . . . well, she wasn't very nice."

"How so?" I asked, curious.

"We had just ordered and were having wine, a really, really yummy prosecco, and she comes over and talks to Trevor. Completely ignores me, except, well, she gave me a mean look. I know, I know, that sounds *totally* childish, but it was mean, and I almost cried." She blinked, looked from me to Sherry.

"Trevor and Diana knew each other?" I asked.

"Yyyessss." She drew out the word as if hesitant about saying anything.

I pushed. "How?"

CeeCee bit her lip. "Well, Trevor said they had met once through mutual friends, but he didn't really know her. Claimed she had wanted to do a business deal with him, but it was too small for his company. They only handle big projects. I don't remember the details. He didn't tell me much, but when he turned her down, she was really angry." She frowned. "I don't know why people are so mean all the time. My mama always said if you can't say something nice, keep your mouth shut."

I tried not to sound too curious but couldn't help myself. "What did Diana say?"

I willed her to tell me, but didn't push, not wanting to come off as nosier than I'd already been.

"Well, she didn't actually *say* anything. It was like, she just completely cut me out of the conversation. She turned her *back* to me."

"Rude," Sherry said.

You're one to talk, I thought.

"It was like I was nobody," CeeCee said, "and I know I shouldn't be upset about it, but I was tired, and she was mean, and I said something to Trevor. He promised she wouldn't bother us again."

Promised? I wondered what he said—or did—to keep Diana away from CeeCee.

"And," she continued, "she didn't." She nodded forcefully and drained her champagne.

The takeaway was that Diana had known Trevor before they saw each other on the island. She knew something about him . . . and his business. Had she been blackmailing him? I wanted to review her notes again. Maybe there was some clue I missed. If she wrote about him and I had a detail, I might be able to break her code.

Sherry got up and walked toward Brie, then Brie immediately came over to us, plopped down next to me. "Look," she said, and showed me the photos she'd taken on her phone.

"Nice," I said. "I like how you framed the resort here. Your camera is better than mine."

"Maybe I'm just a better photographer," she said with a laugh.

"You are," I concurred. "I point and shoot and sometimes get lucky."

Brie showed me an app she had on her phone and explained how she used it to edit her photos. CeeCee asked Brie to show her how to take better selfies, and Brie was happy to demonstrate. She tilted her head toward me, held the phone high, and said, "Smile!" *Click click.*

"The trick is coming from above, not below, but hold your arm like this—" she demonstrated "—so you don't get a weird angle and the camera doesn't go out of focus."

CeeCee practiced making duck lips and acting sexy and coy. "Trevor will love these!"

Brie said, "No duck lips. It's so 2010."

"What?" CeeCee's lips quivered.

"Smile wide, like this." Brie demonstrated.

"Really?" CeeCee copied her, looked at the picture. "You're right! So much better!" She leaned over and hugged Brie. "Thank you!"

"Sometimes, it's a plus being the youngest in the room."

CHAPTER
THIRTEEN

"A good detective never overlooks the small details."
—Robert Crais, *The Last Detective*

THE HIKE BACK DOWN the mountain went much faster, and the four of us parted by the waterfall in the lodge. Brie said, "See you later at the beach party, Mia?"

"I'll be there," I said. I didn't really have a choice since all the restaurants were closed for the weekly Caribbean luau. It was late afternoon, and the resort was surprisingly quiet. Staff was setting up for the party on the beach side of the pool deck, a couple of people I didn't recognize sat in the Blue Dahlia (Jason still wasn't behind the bar), and two families with kids ate together in the restaurant.

I wanted to find out what Trina, the woman who ran the gift shop, knew about the origin of my book. How had it ended up on the free beach reads table? Did housekeeping find it in her room? Was it left on the beach or in one of the bars? I would imagine if the killer knew it existed, he would have destroyed it as possible evidence.

Someone tore a page from the book. That person could have killed Diana and then taken the evidence.

I walked into the gift shop and froze. Amber Jones was talking to Trina in a raised voice.

"What do you mean, you don't know?"

I bristled at the tone. The four years I was in college, I'd worked at a local bookstore and detested entitled, bitchy customers who talked down to me or anyone else on staff. When had general politeness disappeared from our culture?

"Housekeeping said they bring books left behind to *you*." She waved her finger in Trina's face to punctuate *you*.

Trina cleared her throat. "Ms. Jones, yes, books that have been left by guests are put on that table." She gestured toward the *Beach Reads!* sign. "But we don't inventory them, and I don't know where—"

"That's unacceptable. I spoke to the head of housekeeping and they don't keep records either! This resort is a complete *mess*."

"I can contact Mr. Dubois. I'm sure he can help—"

"*No one* has been able to help."

Amber turned around and almost walked right into me as she left. No apology. She looked at me as if it was my fault she wasn't looking where she was going.

Trina smiled at me, but her eyes were teary. "May I help you, Ms. Crawford?"

"Are you okay?" I asked.

She nodded but didn't say anything.

I glanced at where Amber had gone. She strode down the wide tiled corridor heading south, toward the road that led to the dock. Then she stopped and pulled out her phone and appeared to be texting someone.

I rethought my plan. Was Amber looking for Diana's book? Did she know that Diana had been writing in it? If Amber knew about the book and understood its value, then she must have known about Diana's blackmail schemes.

Why hadn't I thought of that connection this morning? If Diana Harden was blackmailing people on the island, and Amber was her girlfriend as Brie surmised, it made sense that Amber would know what Diana was up to.

Did that make Amber an accomplice? Was she, too, in danger? And where did Parker Briggs fit into their scheme?

"Do you need something?" Trina said.

"Yes, sorry, I just came back from a hike. I'm a bit ditzy." I smiled, hoping it looked natural as I began to piece together small details. "I wanted to buy presents for my assistant and my grandmother, but I might not have room in my luggage. Do you ship?"

"Yes, we package up anything you want here, and it goes out the next day. Are you still looking, or do you know what you'd like?"

"Looking," I said. I wanted to buy gifts, but it wasn't the primary thing on my mind right now. I was keeping one eye on Amber and trying to figure out how to get information out of Trina.

Be bold, I told myself. *Channel Elle Woods.*

"Have you heard anything about what happened to Diana Harden?" I asked as I casually flipped through a colorful book about the history of St. Claire. At the surprised look on her face, I quickly said, "I know she was killed, and, well, I guess I'm a little scared." I put a hint of worry in my voice, hoping that disguised my excitement. "I saw her on the beach. I talked to Tristan and he was very nice, but didn't have anything new to share. Trust me, my imagination is probably far wilder than what really happened."

Trina glanced behind me, then to the side, then leaned forward until her face was only inches from mine. "She was strangled," she whispered. "And she was wearing the same dress she left the island in. So they think she was killed on St. John."

"And floated here? That seems like a long way." I didn't buy it. Common sense said she was killed on the island or near the shore.

"My roommate who is in housekeeping? Well, she heard from the ferry captain that Ms. Harden told him not to come get her, that she'd take a water taxi back because she didn't know how long she'd be. The police talked to the water taxi drivers. No one brought her back, but there are private boats, too. So we think that Ms. Harden hired someone and got herself killed."

"But why would someone kill a guest if they were complete strangers?" I thought of several reasons. A serial killer. A rapist. An accident that was covered up.

Trina whispered, "I know she's dead, and I feel bad about that, but she was rude. Extremely demanding and treated staff like we were servants. I mean," she added quickly, "we are happy to serve all the guests here, whatever you need."

"I know what you mean. I used to work retail."

She bit her lip and looked worried. "I shouldn't have said anything."

I gave her a reassuring smile. Out of the corner of my eye, I spied Amber stuff her phone into her pocket and practically storm out of the lodge and down the gravel path that bordered the road. "It's okay, I won't say anything. Everyone here has been more than hospitable. I should shower and dress before dinner. I'll be back to buy presents later."

I followed the path Amber had taken, vaguely hearing Trina call after me that my room was in the other direction. I waved to acknowledge that I heard her, but continued following Amber, her bright blue sundress and white hat easy to spot. With her red hair, she looked like a walking American flag.

Suddenly, Gino Garmon stepped in her path. I froze, then quickly hid behind a large plant, hoping I was too far away for either of them to see me, but wishing I was closer to hear what they said.

I peered through the large banana leaves. They appeared to be in a heated conversation. Gino wore sunglasses, his mouth in a firm line, and Amber stood with her hands on her hips, as if lecturing him. Then he stepped forward and said something. She didn't step back. She didn't look intimidated, and poked his chest while speaking emphatically, then brushed past him and continued down the path toward the docks.

He watched her go, then punched a golf cart with his fist, leaving a clear indention. He shook out his hand, wincing in pain.

What was *that* about?

I wanted to follow Amber, but Gino would see me. By the time Gino went back into the security office, Amber was gone, and I didn't see which path she took.

My cell phone rang as I was walking back to my cottage. I answered the unfamiliar number.

"Hello?"

"Ms. Crawford?" a female voice asked.

"Yes?"

"This is Anita from the spa. You had a 4:00 p.m. massage with Ginger. Will you still be making the appointment?"

I'd completely forgotten that I'd made the appointment last night before going to the lagoon. It was five after four, but I said, "Yes! I'm sorry, I was on a hike." I immediately turned down the path toward the spa.

"No trouble at all. I'll tell Ginger to expect you shortly."

After hearing staff talk about how Diana had made Ginger cry, I had made the appointment in the hopes that I could get her to talk about Diana.

I stepped into the waiting room with its relaxing color palette in subdued greens and grays. Floor-to-ceiling windows looked out at a well-tended flower garden. A gentle stream of water cascaded down one wall, and faint nature music played from hidden speakers. I spotted a discreet camera mounted behind a hanging fern.

A moment after I stepped in, a door opened, and a petite Asian woman said, "I'm Anita. Please follow me."

We walked down a wide hall with sliding bamboo doors. Faintly scented oils and lotions tickled my nose. Anita opened one of the only doors that had an actual knob. We stepped into a room with comfortable chairs, a drink center with iced water and a chilling bottle of champagne in an ice bucket, and another waterfall flush against the wall. "Through that door—" she motioned to the left "—is the changing area. Leave your clothes in one of the lockers and use one of the robes hanging on the wall. Through that door—" she motioned straight ahead

"—is a restroom and private shower stalls. Feel free to refresh yourself. When you're ready, Ginger's parlor is right across the hall in room 4. She'll be waiting for you."

"Thank you," I said.

I poured a glass of lemon water and drank heavily, then stepped into the bathroom. It was a full bath, with two rainfall showers separated by a clouded glass block wall for privacy. Plants grew everywhere, and the skylight provided enough natural light that I didn't need to flip on the light switch.

I took a quick shower because I felt sticky, then used one of the huge bath sheets to dry off. I stepped into the changing area and almost screamed.

Sherry Morrison was there dressing.

"I'm sorry. I didn't know anyone was in here."

She gave me a half smile that felt fake.

"I just had a massage," she said.

"How was it?" I asked conversationally. I was trying to be polite, though I couldn't help but think about Diana's negative comments that I suspected were about Sherry.

"Amazing. I was here my first day, and it was to die for, and I'm coming back on Friday for a full makeover." She looked me up and down, head to toe. I felt super awkward wrapped in a towel.

"It was fun hiking with you and Brie," I said.

"Let's cut to the chase," Sherry said, pinning me down with a cold stare. "I know *exactly* what you're up to."

"I—what?" I was at a complete loss.

"This little innocent girl next door persona does not work on me. You befriended Brie thinking that would give you a leg up with Andrew. He's *mine*, and you need to back off."

I was speechless. Where had she got the idea that I was interested in Andrew Locke? Because we had a conversation? Or because Brie and I were friendly?

I hadn't been expecting this confrontation, and I didn't know how to respond. I thought back to the hike. Brie did kind of give Sherry the cold shoulder, but did Sherry think *I* had something to do with that?

"I know women like you, *Mia*," she snapped. "Single, coming to St. Claire, clearly looking for a sugar daddy. Not going to happen with *my* boyfriend."

"I don't want your boyfriend."

"I need to bond with Brie, and you're getting in the way."

"That's not my intention," I said trying not to let my voice quiver. "Brie and I are closer in age, and—"

"Oh, *please*. You're not *that* young. Stay away from Brie, and stay away from Andrew. *I mean it.*"

The cold anger on her face threw me. Before I could respond, she walked out.

I had been afraid my perception of Sherry Morrison was tainted by Brie's feelings toward her dad's girlfriend, but clearly Brie had reason to dislike her other than the mere fact she was dating her dad. I put Sherry high on my list of people to google when I got back to my cottage.

Anyone who felt so threatened by a virtual stranger might have enough anger to kill.

IT TOOK ME a minute to calm down after the confrontation with Sherry before walking across the hall to Ginger's suite. "I'm sorry I'm late," I said to the petite brunette with pale eyes. "I took a shower because I felt icky after my hike."

"Do not worry," she said in a soft, soothing voice, and motioned for me to disrobe and lie on the table. "When you reserved the massage, you indicated no allergies to any scents?"

"Correct."

"Do you have a preference? Or would you like unscented oils?"

I hadn't thought about scents. I didn't know what to say. Was I supposed to look at a display, like nail polish when I got a pedicure and picked a color? I rarely even wore perfume.

"Do you have plans this evening?" Ginger asked, recognizing my indecision.

"The luau . . . then I'm meeting someone on the beach." I wondered what Jason would like?

"A romantic interlude?" she asked.

"I hope," I said before I could stop myself. "I mean, I don't know, just, um, maybe something light and fresh?"

"I have just the oil," she said. "It's my special blend. I call it sea jasmine. Not too strong, but wonderfully calming when I add a hint of lavender. It's fresh and romantic."

"I trust you," I said, and hoped my trust wasn't misplaced.

"If you'd be more comfortable in a towel," Ginger said, and motioned to a fluffy stack of white towels on a shelf.

I realized she was waiting for me to lie down. I hadn't had a massage in years, but was glad I had a female masseuse. I took a deep breath, smiled. "I'm fine." I shrugged off the robe and lay face down on the table, which provided an open space for my face so my spine remained straight.

As soon as Ginger's small, strong hands started rubbing my muscles, I moaned.

"You are tense," Ginger said. "Relax, clear your mind. Think of the ocean, the gentle push and pull of the waves." As she spoke, she moved her hands slowly and firmly over my upper body muscles. She was amazing. And the oil was perfect, floral and salty, not too strong, and oh so relaxing. I almost forgot why I'd made this appointment in the first place.

Fifteen minutes into the process, when Ginger told me I was still tense, I found the opening I needed to ask her about Diana.

"I guess I'm tense because of last night."

"Oh?"

"I was on the beach. When the Kents found Diana Harden's body."

Her hands paused. Then she cleared her throat and said, "That must have been awful."

"And I'm trying to forget, but I can't."

"I can imagine," Ginger said and moved from my shoulders to my right arm. "Relax, Ms. Crawford."

"She came here before she disappeared," I said.

"Mmm-hmm," Ginger said vaguely.

"Did you help her?"

"Uh-huh," Ginger answered in the affirmative. "If you want to relax, you need to empty your mind."

She turned up the nature sounds, and it was impossible to ask questions without practically shouting. By the end of the hour, she hadn't shared anything I didn't know. I had no idea what Diana had said or done that had made this sweet woman cry.

I did finally relax, as if I was melting on the table. When Ginger was done, I was half-asleep. She said in a soft, soothing tone, "Stay here for a few minutes. I'll be back with a refreshing smoothie."

"Mmm-hmm," I said because I couldn't speak.

I thought about what the honeymooners had said about a couples massage, and then I pictured Jason on the table next to me, a grin on his lips, his eyes half-closed, his body naked. Instead of being nervous and unsure, I smiled as I remembered how he almost kissed me last night, the way he made me feel comfortable and desired. Maybe it was the island, maybe it was the freedom that I could do something spontaneous and not think about every way it could go wrong. I wasn't even all that upset that I hadn't been able to get Ginger to gossip about Diana.

My mind drifted to Amber and her conversation with Trina, demanding information about a book. I distinctly remembered at the Sky Bar that the three staff members talked about packing up Diana's room after she disappeared. If the book had been left in her room, they would have packed it up with the rest of her belongings.

Which suggested that the book had been found elsewhere. Maybe on the beach. That made sense with the damaged pages and sand. Yet why did Amber think it should be in the gift shop?

As security chief, Gino would have access to Diana's belongings. Maybe that's why Amber had talked to him. Had he allowed her to go through Diana's personal items? When she hadn't found the book, maybe she went to housekeeping then to the gift shop then back to Gino to complain it was still missing.

But *I* had Diana's book.

I needed to be more careful with it.

I RETURNED TO my room to get ready for the Caribbean luau. I really didn't know much about what Diana was doing, other than likely blackmailing people on the island. Now she was dead. Was it all that big a leap to assume that she was killed because she'd blackmailed the wrong person? I didn't think so. But because I didn't understand most of Diana's shorthand, I didn't know exactly *who* she had blackmailed—or attempted to blackmail. Just because she was tracking the net worth of her fellow guests didn't mean that she had confronted them with a deep, dark secret they would kill to keep buried.

Why write in a stupid code anyway? I thought as I applied a bit of makeup to my tan face—I'd definitely gotten some sun today, and it looked good. Mid-swipe with my bronzer, I remembered the missing page—the *stolen* page. I had an idea.

I quickly dressed, then retrieved the book and my notebook from the safe. After leaving them out when housekeeping was here, I'd decided to be more discreet.

I turned to chapter twenty-eight. I didn't know who had torn the page out, or why, but surmised it was because Diana had written something about them—and it was only on this page. How they knew, I could only guess. But there was a reason they took it, and I wanted to know what it was.

And I knew how to make the words magically appear.

I took the book to the desk and dug a pencil out of the bottom of my laptop case, then turned on the lamp. Every crime show I watched used this trick.

I tilted the page under the light to see if I could detect an impression on the paper. There was something here, but I couldn't read it. Carefully, I rubbed the pencil over the paper, then turned it again under the light, straining to read what Diana had written.

There were two distinct impressions. One in the margins on the front side of the page that had been torn out. I could barely make out the letters. There were too many missing letters, which I replaced with *x*'s hoping something would jump out at me. But the *x* could also mean a space.

I wrote them down, but they made no sense.

77 xxx emxxz $50 xxx xx 522 xxx carxx

The numbers were better defined than the letters, maybe because she was writing in script. I put it aside to look at later.

At the bottom of the back side of the page—at what would have been the end of the chapter—Diana had written a list of numbers.

11
19
157
52
210

I had no idea what they meant. A combination to a safe? My room safe required a six-digit code.

Maybe there was a hotel safe with a traditional combination? I still didn't think the numbers went into the hundreds. Lottery numbers didn't go that high, either.

She could have mixed up numbers to hide their meaning, but there were too many digits for a Social Security number or a telephone number. Unless there was an international code, which was usually two or three digits. So twelve digits would fit for some countries.

Possible, but why write it out in five lines? The number 11 could be Canada or the United States, but then there would be an extra number.

The last impression was a happy face. Two lines for eyes, a curve for the mouth, and a circle surrounding them. It was the deepest impression on the page, next to the numbers.

The numbers also didn't match with any of the other written numbers in the book, such as the 77 or 522.

I put my notebook aside. Whatever the numbers meant, they were the last thing Diana Harden had written in this book.

The party was starting, but I didn't want to be the first one to arrive, so I took a glass of water to my patio along with my laptop. After the late night and then hiking this afternoon, I was drained. I could fall asleep out here listening to the ocean. Maybe I wouldn't go to the luau at all.

I opened my laptop, and my finger itched to log in to the office just to make sure that everything was running smoothly. I was responsible for other people's money, and while I trusted Braden and I had left clear instructions for managing each client, I had this nagging feeling that I needed to double-check every account.

Or, rather, triple-check, because I'd double-checked the day before I left, when I was supposed to be packing.

"Stop," I told myself. Instead of hitting my employer website, I opened the search engine and typed Sherry Morrison.

Bad idea. There were a lot of Sherry Morrisons out there.

I typed: Sherry Morrison Andrew Locke

Bam. First link was a sports gossip magazine that had a photo of Sherry and Andrew at a football game last November.

The caption read: Former pitcher for the Dodgers and Braves, Andrew Locke, rooting for the Colts where his best friend and former college roommate Richie Dunn is the interim offensive line coach. Locke seen here with his girlfriend, Sherilyn Morrison, an interior decorator.

Within ten minutes, I'd compiled a long list of articles that Sherry was featured in—or, rather, her *boyfriend* of any given moment was featured in, where she was also mentioned. She had been attached to *nine* different professional sports players over the last ten years. Four, including Andrew, were retired.

I dug around a little more, curious as to why none of these relationships had lasted. That's when I found *three* separate engagement announcements. The first resulted in her first marriage at twenty-one, which had ended in divorce three years later. Her second engagement had been called off quite publicly when her fiancé—a professional football player—cheated on her. Her third engagement ended in her second marriage . . . and his death. They'd been married two years and two days when he'd died after a heart attack while they were on a romantic couples cruise for their anniversary.

Sherry had fought his adult children and ex-wife during probate, but his will was airtight, and she received only a small portion of his estate—the house and a million dollars. Not that a million was anything to sniff at, but considering the man had been a retired football player and was worth over one hundred million, her portion was a tiny fraction of his total estate.

One gossip rag had the dead husband's daughter ranting about Sherry being responsible for her dad's death.

"It wasn't an accident. It was murder."

But there had been no formal investigation. One article indicated cause of death was sudden cardiac arrest. The autopsy found signs of heart disease.

Every article mentioned that Sherry was an interior decorator, and she had an LLC under Prestige Design Group, but her webpage was bare-bones and hadn't been updated in years.

One divorce and one dead husband in ten years. The first marriage lasted three years, the second two years. Was Andrew Locke to be the third?

I didn't want to tell Brie about this, but at the same time, wouldn't Andrew already know that his girlfriend was divorced *and* widowed? It seemed like a topic that would come up in conversation, since it was all public. I wouldn't necessarily want to know about my boyfriend's ex-girlfriends, but I definitely would want to know if he'd been married before. That seemed important.

Maybe Brie knew. Maybe it didn't bother her dad. It just bugged me that Diana had written about Sherry in the book, and not in a flattering way. She wrote as if she knew specific dirt on Sherry.

Money or love? Money, of course—he's worth a small fortune. Does he know all the dirt on his new girlfriend?

No guarantee she'd written about Sherry, but who else here lived in Arizona and had brought their girlfriend to the island?

I might have to dig a little deeper on Ms. Sherilyn Morrison, interior designer.

My phone beeped with an incoming message, making me jump as I was so engrossed in online gossip. It was Brie. I felt surprisingly guilty—and protective—about what I'd learned about Sherry.

Where you at? I have some tea.

I let out a deep breath, my bangs fluttering up. Guess I was going to the luau after all. I responded:

Getting dressed. Be there in a few.

CHAPTER
FOURTEEN

"He made her more confident, more daring. He made her more . . . herself. Or at least the herself she wished she could be."

—Julia Quinn, *Romancing Mister Bridgerton*

THE WEEKLY ST. CLAIRE Caribbean luau was spectacular and, according to the brochure in my room, one of the highlights that guests most often mention.

I could see why.

Staff had transformed the wide patio that separated the pool from the sand with gazillions of tiny lights woven through the trees and lanais; candles floated in the pool, which was underlit with turquoise. Tiki torches framed the paths from the main lodge to the party. The sun hung low over the mountain but had not yet set, casting the most beautiful splash of pinks, oranges, purples, and indigo across the sky.

I pictured having my wedding reception right here, on the beach, by the light of a hundred torches, the amazing scents of steaming fish and barbecued steak making my mouth water.

Of course, I needed a husband to have a wedding reception. I didn't even have a boyfriend.

The party prompted the early closure of all resort restaurants and bars. Six temporary bars were set up, plus the main pool bar was open. It was a meet and greet, a celebration of the island. Endless food, drink, and a live band brought over from St. John.

I stood at the edge, feeling a bit out of sorts. The party was in full swing by the time I arrived. Apparently every guest was here. Dozens of people I didn't know mingled, groups of four and six chatting and drinking champagne or fruity beverages. More people joined the groups as I watched. I didn't recognize anyone.

Everyone was dressed in "island chic"—white shirts on the men, cute wraparound dresses on the women. Some flowered, some solid colors, all highlighting sun-soaked skin. Jewelry sparkled in the flickering light, again making me wonder what was real and what was fake.

I scanned for Jason and saw him at a temp bar across the way mixing what looked like a martini. His warm, sexy smile; his confident movements as he shook, poured, placed the drinks on napkins; his easygoing vibe even as he quickly served the older couple. My stomach fluttered—now I knew what the books meant by "butterflies." He turned his head, as if knowing someone was watching him. I attributed my heating blood to the warmth of the tiki lamp next to me. He caught my eye, and his smile widened. Was he thinking about our almost kiss? Was he thinking about what might happen tonight? I unconsciously licked my lips; when I realized what I'd done, I prayed he hadn't noticed. After all, he was at least twenty yards from me.

Then he winked, and I knew that he'd seen, that he knew exactly what I was thinking, and it pleased him. He motioned for me to come over; I walked forward as if he'd tugged on an invisible string.

I was almost there when a couple cut me off, and then I heard my name.

"Mia! There you are. *Finally.*"

Brie grabbed my arm and pulled me away—away from Jason, away from a much-needed drink after a very busy afternoon.

I didn't have an opportunity to protest, but I grabbed a glass of champagne from a roving waiter as Brie navigated through people until she found a vacant, partly enclosed lounge seat. I tripped and sat heavily on the pillow-strewn oversized chair, barely saving my drink from spilling.

"What?" I finally said.

"I've been *dying* to tell you what I found, but my dad insisted we have family time after the hike. Which was fine, because Sherry was getting a massage—" eye roll "—so it was just dad and me. But this is big!"

I wanted to tell her what Sherry said to me at the spa but decided to keep it to myself for now. If my idea about Sherry was off-base, I didn't want to cause problems in their family. Instead, I asked, "What did you learn?"

She glanced around to make sure no one was within earshot.

"First," she said, her voice low but excited, "Trevor Lance *is* married. *Second* marriage. He dumped his first wife—the one he met in college and had two kids with—seven years ago for Krystal Kline, a bikini and lingerie model. She turns thirty next month. He's fifty-one."

"I thought he was married, but—"

"*And,*" Brie interrupted, "Krystal is in Europe this week for a bachelorette party for her best friend. So he brings his mistress here?" She looked at me meaningfully. "Anyway, I don't think CeeCee knows, do you?"

It took me a second to catch up with her line of thought. I was trying to picture Trevor with a bikini model. He was nice-looking for an old guy, but I never understood why smart, beautiful women married guys old enough to be their fathers. Except for the obvious financial motivation.

"I don't know," I said. "Maybe. She's smarter than she sometimes acts. Would it matter if she knew he was married?"

"Well, *yeah*, if Trevor killed Diana."

"That's a big leap, and a weak motive," I said.

"Adultery is a great motive," Brie countered.

"Even if she does know, I suppose he wouldn't want his wife to find out," I guessed. "Did you learn anything else about him?"

She shrugged. "He lives part-time in Hilton Head, South Carolina, and Dallas, Texas. He's some big land developer, Lance

& Wong Development. Travels a lot—there were a lot of business articles about him doing this and that. I didn't read them in detail."

That was something I could do. If Diana *was* blackmailing Trevor, it might not be about his extramarital affair. Based on what CeeCee overheard, I wondered if Diana had known more about his business than Trevor wanted her to know. Diana had drawn little houses next to one of her comments about someone having an affair. If that comment *was* about Trevor and CeeCee, it would give me one more clue in deciphering her code.

"I'll look into his business," I said, but Brie wasn't listening.

"Gino Garmon," Brie said. "He's the one. *He* killed Diana."

I almost choked on my champagne. I looked around the edge of the canopy to make sure no one heard Brie; the closest people were fifteen feet away. I couldn't hear them, so I hoped they couldn't hear us.

"Shh," I admonished. "Why would you say that?"

"You're right. Gino was a cop. Eight years in Miami. There was an investigation into him skimming money from busts. He resigned, but I think he was *forced* to resign. Maybe they couldn't prove it, or they didn't want a big trial, or whatever. But the crime blog I read was pretty convincing that he was stealing."

"And they couldn't prove it?"

"Maybe he used it to buy drugs. Maybe he was keeping a woman in a fancy apartment, bought a Tesla, I don't know. But if he was stealing, maybe Diana knew about it."

That seemed far-fetched. "That information would have come to light before he was hired as head of security," I said.

"Maybe." She shrugged. "It's still suspicious."

I didn't see how something that was already known would make Garmon subject to blackmail.

"Do you know when he started working here?"

Brie thought on that. "He introduced himself to my dad when we were checking in four years ago."

"Anything else?"

"Isn't that enough?"

"The information is public, and he probably explained it away or passed the background check because there was no evidence, or maybe his boss gave him a good recommendation. That's not enough to blackmail him. Wait—" An idea formed.

"What?" Brie leaned forward.

"If the police in Miami didn't have evidence that he skimmed the money, but he resigned anyway, there may have been *another* reason. Did he come straight here from Miami?"

"No—there's a two-year gap."

"What did he do those two years?"

"Oooh, good question. I'll ask—"

"No. Don't ask anyone. He's investigating Diana's death."

"Which makes him doubly suspicious."

Brie's confidence that Gino Garmon was a killer started to rub off on me. Maybe because he was a jerk and I got a bad vibe from him. But we needed more than he *might* have been a dirty cop.

"You find out everything you can about him on social media," I told her, "but don't ask questions. If he *is* guilty, it could put you in danger." I drained my champagne and asked, "Did you learn anything about Parker Briggs?"

"Not much. I didn't really have the time. His family has a foundation, and Briggs is into all kinds of projects, like he funds ideas or whatever."

"A venture capitalist?" I suggested.

"Yeah, maybe?"

"Finance is my world. I'll dig around." It wouldn't be difficult. I'd love to do it myself, but since I was on vacation and didn't have access to all my resources, I'd ask Braden. He wouldn't mind a side project.

"So, what did you learn?" Brie asked.

I decided to share my confrontation with Sherry in the spa, but downplay it.

"I ran into Sherry after her massage," I said.

Brie rolled her eyes.

"She thinks I'm trying to come between you and her because I have the hots for your dad."

As I said it, I realized how silly it sounded and started laughing.

"Do you?" Brie asked seriously.

"No!" I glanced over at Jason. Brie smiled and playfully hit my arm.

"Teasing," she said. "Sherry is all oh, we should go shopping and get mani-pedis and all that. Do I look like a mani-pedi girl? And *hello*, I shop online. She only does it for my dad's benefit. She can't wait until I leave for college."

"I also witnessed a confrontation between Amber and Gino. I don't know what they were talking about, but Amber was looking for a book—I think *the* book."

"See? Gino again. He *has* to be involved." She frowned. "Amber knows about the book?"

"Diana must have told her, but she doesn't know *what* book—she saw me with it on the beach, didn't bat an eye."

"You need to keep it under lock and key."

"I have it in the safe."

"Gino is in security, and if he knows about the book, that's the first place he'd go. Hide it where no one would think to look."

"There's not a lot of places."

We both thought.

"I know," Brie said. "Tape it behind the dresser. People look *in* drawers, maybe even *under* drawers, but I don't think anyone would think to look *behind* a dresser."

I grinned. I couldn't help it. "You must watch a lot of crime shows."

She shrugged. "Just common sense."

It was a good idea. If someone was determined, they might find it, but short of carrying it with me wherever I went, it was the next best thing.

I glanced over to where Jason was working. He had a small crowd around him and seemed to enjoy his job.

I asked Brie, "Do you know anything about Luis?"

"Yeah, he's great."

"Does he live on the island full-time? He seems too old to have a job."

"He's ancient. He doesn't work here, though sometimes he helps out. He has full run of the place because he's Ethan Valentine's great-uncle. At least, that's the rumor—Luis has never said anything, and if you ask him about Ethan, he just smiles and nods and ignores you."

That surprised me.

"Luis lives in Ethan's house," Brie continued. "The big house on the cliffs to the south. I've never been there—it's off-limits. I heard a couple hiked over there once, and when they came back, they were told they were no longer welcome on the island. Given a full refund and shipped off the same day."

"That seems a bit excessive."

"Ethan Valentine is a total recluse. Like, a nerdy hermit. Honestly? I don't think he's there most of the time, just comes and goes without anyone knowing when. He has a yacht and a helicopter, and Kalise said he's a pilot, so he flies himself. Luis lives there full-time, has a golf cart he drives to get back and forth. At least, that's what I've figured out over the last couple of years since Ethan bought the island."

"And Ethan never comes here, even though it's his resort?"

"Nope," Brie said. "He's at his house, or off the island. He runs a mega-company. Maybe not Elon Musk, Jeff Bezos super mega, but big."

I hadn't really thought about Ethan Valentine and how he owned the island. It didn't seem important, but it was odd.

"Rumor is that when he bought the island, he wanted to shut down the resort," Brie said. "Kalise and Tristan, who've both been here forever, put together a proposal to revitalize the place and presented it to his team, and Valentine watched the video and said do it. So Kalise and Tristan run the place. Kalise says it's the best of all worlds—she feels like it's her resort because Valentine doesn't get involved in day-to-day management. When she wants something, she puts together a proposal, sends it to him, and he gives a thumbs-up or thumbs-down. She's never even met him."

"I wonder if they told Valentine about the murder," I mused.

Brie shrugged, then said, "What do you keep looking at?" She craned her neck.

"I'm not," I said and almost blushed. Yes, I had been checking out Jason across the way. I couldn't hear him, and I couldn't always see him through the crowd, but every once in a while, the crowd parted and I could watch him work.

He was a lot of fun to watch.

"Oh. My. God. You're hot for Jason."

"No!" Now I did blush.

"Yes you are. You can't stop staring at him." Brie nodded. "He's cute. Go for it."

"Stop."

She laughed. "You're what, thirty? And a prude?"

"No, and no."

She raised an eyebrow.

"I'll be thirty tomorrow, and I'm not a prude. Just selective."

"You selected well. I approve."

"I don't need your approval."

I didn't want to talk about my sex life with a teenager.

"What's our next step?" Brie asked.

"Hello, ladies!"

I yelped as Jason emerged from around the side of the canopy. Had he heard what Brie and I were talking about? He couldn't have—two minutes ago he was across the beach at the bar.

Brie laughed and said, "Are those for us?"

Jason held two glasses of champagne in one hand and a plate of hors d'oeuvres in the other. He placed them on the small table. Shrimp, stuffed mushrooms, steak bites, cheese, and crackers.

"Thank you," I said.

Brie took the glass of champagne as she got up. "I'm going to catch up with my dad. Later." She wiggled her fingers at us and left me alone with Jason.

Where I wanted to be. But not when all these people might see. *What do you plan to do? Jump him on the lounge?*

Maybe.

"Aren't you working?"

He sat down where Brie had been, then moved closer to me. Our knees touched.

"I'm entitled to a ten-minute break now and again."

"Oh. Thanks." I sipped, then picked up a cheese slice on a delicate cracker. "I went hiking up to the cliffs that you jumped off of yesterday."

"I didn't jump. I flew. Or, technically, glided."

I involuntarily shivered, remembering how terrified I'd been, even though I hadn't known who he was at the time. "Did you talk to the police about the body?" I asked, not meaning to be so bold.

"Gino Garmon is handling the investigation here. But I'm certain something happened on St. John. No one brought her back to the island."

"Don't you think that it's strange for St. Claire security to handle a murder investigation?"

He looked surprised. "Murder? They don't know what happened to Diana. Why do you think she was murdered?"

I forgot that I had made that leap, but Trina *had* overheard that Diana was strangled. Maybe Gino hadn't shared that information with the rest of the staff.

"Well, um, she's young. She's healthy, I presume. She left and disappeared and was found dead. And—I overheard someone say the police believe she was strangled." There. I could get it out there without ratting out Trina.

"I heard the rumor," he said, "but the police haven't confirmed it. It could have been an accident. St. John has some crime problems, though the police do a good job of keeping violence out of the tourist areas. You're not worried that something might happen here, are you?"

He took my hand and seemed genuinely concerned.

"No, just curious. I really want to know what happened to her." I looked at our joined hands and wished he didn't have to go back to work.

"If I promise to find out for you tomorrow, will you at least try to enjoy the luau tonight?" He squeezed my hand. "Please?"

"I'm having fun." I smiled to show him *yeah, having a great time.* I don't know if he bought it. "I like watching people," I admitted. "I'm not really into crowds, but I promise, I'm enjoying myself and looking forward to the lagoon tonight."

He smiled, leaned forward until his lips were almost on mine. If I edged forward an inch, they would touch. I held my breath.

Jason whispered, "I might be a little late because of the luau, but no later than midnight. I promise."

"Should I bring anything?"

Stupid question.

"Bathing suit optional."

Then he kissed me. His lips were warm, salty from the ocean breeze, a hint of coconut, and perfect.

Oh, God, *so perfect.*

I might have moaned out loud. I touched his shoulder, maybe to make sure I wasn't hallucinating. Maybe so I wouldn't fall over. He was warm and muscular, and if there weren't a hundred people on the other side of the canopy I don't know what I might have done.

Then he stood up. "I wish I had more time, but I have to get back to work." He sounded sincere. "I'll see you tonight."

He winked and walked away. I didn't say a word. I couldn't. He took my breath away.

Damn. I liked the daredevil bartender. A lot.

I watched Jason as he made his way back to the bar and relieved Callie. He turned and looked at me, gave me his award-winning half smile, and I waved back. Then he was busy with serving others.

Reluctantly, I averted my attention to the crowd.

Jane and Amanda would tell me to get out on the dance

floor, talk, be social. Instead, I sat here sipping champagne and people-watching. I wasn't sad and I didn't feel left out. I hadn't lied when I told Jason I didn't like crowds. I *did* like observing.

Quickly, I realized not everyone was happy *or* social.

Anja and Nelson stood off to the side, aloof, her with wine, him with beer, not talking to anyone *or* to each other. That seemed odd, considering they had been joined at the hip (though not as close as the honeymooners) since we arrived. I recalled the comment about Anja's mistake, and in light of reading Diana's comments, I wondered whether she could have been blackmailing them even though she'd disappeared before they arrived. Someone like Nelson Stockton might make the gossip rags. Maybe Diana knew they were planning the trip.

David and Doug were sitting together at the edge of the luau with a large group of people, all drinking and laughing.

CeeCee and Trevor were sitting with the honeymooners, which I thought was an odd foursome. For the first time, the Kents didn't have their hands all over each other.

I couldn't see any security personnel, including Gino Garmon. Kalise moved fluidly from group to group, the perfect activities director, making sure everyone was enjoying themselves. Tristan assisted staff at the crowded pool bar. Servers moved with grace through the throngs of people who seemed to pay them no attention, grabbing flutes of champagne or food from their trays.

I didn't see Amber or Parker. I hadn't seen Amber since this afternoon when she walked off after her confrontation with Gino, and I hadn't seen Parker since yesterday afternoon, before I went to the Sky Bar. But everyone else I'd met—and the many I hadn't—were here.

I walked over to the buffet and helped myself to a little bite of everything, then headed in the direction of David and Doug. They were comfortable, and I wouldn't have to talk—I could simply listen to the large group. Instead of cutting through the crowded dance floor, I walked around the perimeter of the party. I heard a familiar voice.

Sherry.

"I couldn't get away today," she was saying. I didn't see her or who she was talking to. She paused for a few seconds, then said, "I hired you. You'll do what I say." She was on the phone with someone. I still couldn't see her; she stood behind a vine-covered trellis. "Noon, tomorrow, same place."

I kept walking before she saw me, and I missed the end of the conversation.

Her tone had been . . . well, cold. Cold and all business. I worried about Brie and her dad, because Sherry was up to something.

Or maybe the call was innocuous, like a vendor in her interior design business. Clearly, my imagination was in overdrive. There *was* a killer on the island, so I saw—and heard—malevolence in every conversation.

Didn't mean Sherry was up to something.

Didn't mean she wasn't.

CHAPTER

FIFTEEN

"I do know that the slickest way to lie is
to tell the right amount of truth—then
shut up."

—Robert A. Heinlein, *Stranger in a Strange Land*

BEFORE I LEFT FOR the lagoon, I added Brie's notes to my own,
then emailed my assistant Braden and asked him to look at the
companies and public financial statements for Trevor Lance and
Parker Briggs. I did a quick search on both, but there was too
much information to go through tonight. I bookmarked some
of the articles to read later, including one about Trevor Lance's
divorce and remarriage. His ex-wife was older, attractive, classy.
His new wife was beyond gorgeous and had a lucrative career
as the face of a major cosmetic line. And yet he was here with
another woman.

I did not understand men. Sometimes, I didn't want to.

I was about to close down my laptop when I saw a message
from my boss, so clicked on it. Reading the message wasn't actually *working*, I told myself. It was probably a *have fun* note or a
group message about a new law that would impact our industry.

Hello Mia,

I just received the mock-up of our new masthead. Ron
and I also decided we needed to update our logo, and

what better time than when we bring on a new partner?
What do you think? We won't approve it without your
okay, of course.

I hope you're having a lovely time at St. Claire. Gayle
and I went two years ago for our thirtieth anniversary
and it was perfect.

Stuart

Attached was a JPEG. It took a couple seconds to load, but
then I saw the new branding for McMann & Cohn.

It was more contemporary than their previous logo, but still
retained the stately *we'll take care of your money* appearance. The
classy serif font had been replaced by an equally classy but less
rigid serif font.

McMann Cohn
Crawford

A thin line separated the original partners above my name,
but my name was spread out so that there was balance on both
sides of the line.

A second image was for the landing page on our website,
which incorporated the new masthead, but included our areas of
expertise: Financial Advising, Estate Planning, Tax Preparation

The color scheme was the same banker's green and black,
but they'd added a gold accent that popped in a professional way.

My mouth dropped open. This was happening. Could I
even say no *now*?

I was in shock, seeing my future laid out so clearly. I closed
the message without responding.

My vibrating cell phone jolted me back to the present.
Amanda's home number lit the screen.

"Amanda?" I answered, confused and surprised.

"Braden," my assistant said. "Why are you surprised? You just sent me an email."

"It's after eleven. I didn't expect you to get it until tomorrow."

"It's ten here in humid and rainy New York City."

I hadn't accounted for the time difference.

"Why are you emailing about work on your vacation?" he asked.

In the background, Amanda called out, "Why are you working, Mia?"

"I'm not," I said before Braden could repeat Amanda's question.

When I hired Braden three years ago, I knew he was not only perfect as my assistant, but perfect for my best friend. We had developed a symbiotic relationship because we had the same fiscally conservative investment backbone, and I trusted him implicitly. And if I was made a partner, Braden would be given a promotion and raise, which would benefit both him and Amanda as they wanted to start a family.

I had another person's fate and livelihood to consider as well as my own. I had to take the promotion.

"Mr. Cohn said no work while you're at St. Claire," Braden said.

"I'm not working."

"Then what's this about Trevor Lance and his company, Lance & Wong? And Parker Briggs—I think I've heard that name."

"It's not work," I insisted. "I can't explain in detail. This is sort of a pet project?" I said it as a question because I didn't know *what* to say. I had planned to send the email, have Braden do the research, and email me back data. I didn't want to explain myself.

Would Braden help me if I said, *I think a woman was killed because she was blackmailing someone, and Lance and Briggs are two of my suspects?*

"You don't want to tell me?"

He sounded almost hurt.

"I'm helping a friend. Please?"

"Of course," he said. "I'll get you the information by noon tomorrow. My time."

"While I have you on the phone, can I pick your brain about something else?"

"What do you need?"

"Hypothetically," I said, "if a cop was skimming money from drug busts, but it was never found and he doesn't have a drug problem, how could he hide it? I came up with a few scenarios—keeping the cash in a safe deposit box in the name of a friend or family member, investing through a shell corporation, keeping a mistress that no one knows about—"

"Is this about a book you're reading?"

I hesitated. "Um, yeah," I lied.

I don't lie well. I don't know if Braden picked up on my tone, but I was glad he couldn't see my face.

"All those are possible," he said. "But I guess if a cop is stealing from bad guys, he has a vice. If it's not drugs—are you sure?"

"Pretty sure."

"Then he needs the money for something else that isn't easily traceable."

"Something illegal," I said.

"That would be my guess. He's already committed a crime, right? So what's another crime?"

"Like prostitutes," I thought, and didn't realize I'd said it out loud.

"Why are you reading anything?" Amanda said in the background, closer this time. "Do I need to get Jane on the phone?"

"No," I said, realizing that Braden had put me on speaker.

"I'm serious, Mia. I told you, no books. You're supposed to have fun. Meet people. What happened to that Mayan god hunk you were talking about?"

"I don't want to hear this," Braden said.

"Are you having fun, or are you hiding in your room, reading?" Amanda demanded.

"I'm having fun," I said. "I went to a beach party tonight and talked to a lot of people."

"And the demigod?" she asked.

"You know I'll tell you everything when I get back," I said. "In fact, I'm heading to a late-night swim date in a few minutes."

"Ohmigod!" she squealed. "I have to call Jane."

We said our goodbyes, and I sighed. My friends could be exhausting. I hoped I had something to tell them about Jason when I got home.

Hey, girls! I had sex with a gorgeous bartender and solved a murder!

I thought about all the illegal ways that Gino Garmon could have spent the money he'd stolen.

Allegedly stolen.

I wish I knew how much money we were talking about, but Brie said there were no dollar amounts in the news articles. If you took the money before it was put into evidence, it would only be a guess. *My* guess was that he would pocket whatever was easy. A few hundred dollars at every scene . . . maybe a few thousand.

Drugs, prostitution, gambling . . .

Gambling.

I grabbed Diana's book and skimmed the opening chapters until I found what I remembered reading yesterday.

Totally broke, he'll help.

The number 77 was underlined. What did that mean? Maybe a dollar amount?

Was Diana referring to Gino Garmon? If he really took the money from the drug busts, why was he broke? What had he spent it on? Could he have lost it all gambling? That made a lot more sense than spending it on prostitutes and drugs.

Was he helping Diana? Was he part of her blackmail scheme?

Maybe . . . maybe they were blackmailing someone together and he didn't want to share the money. Had one of the people Diana was tracking paid her and—maybe—Gino killed her for the money?

Except, who would have a hundred thousand in cash lying around on an island? It would likely be an electronic transfer or something of value. Like jewelry.

77 . . . was that Diana's shorthand for Gino?

I was on the verge of something. Maybe the numbers did refer to people. If I knew one—if I assumed 77 was Gino—maybe I could figure out the others.

I skimmed through my notes. There were nine different numbers that didn't have a dollar sign attached. Had Diana blackmailed—or planned to blackmail—*nine* people?

I listed them on a separate sheet of paper. Then my phone vibrated.

Quarter to midnight. Time to meet Jason.

I hid the book, put my notepad in my laptop case, and left.

CHAPTER
SIXTEEN

"There will be a few times in your life when all your instincts will tell you to do something, something that defies logic, upsets your plans, and may seem crazy to others. When that happens, you do it. Listen to your instincts and ignore everything else. Ignore logic, ignore the odds, ignore the complications, and just go for it."

—Judith McNaught, *Remember When*

I DON'T KNOW WHY I was so nervous.

I was an (almost) thirty-year-old professional woman who is smart, pretty, and a good conversationalist. I was mature enough to make my own decisions, flirt with handsome men, and even have a one-night-stand.

I had never had a one-night stand in my life.

But my gut told me to let go with Jason, because he was exactly what I needed. This was my first and last fling before being chained to a desk for the rest of my life.

Then I reminded myself that I hadn't actually accepted the promotion. I didn't *have* to accept it. I could continue doing what I was doing for the company, handling my current accounts, not taking on bigger accounts or more responsibility.

Who was I fooling, though? I'd seen the masthead. Of *course* I would accept it. I'd earned the promotion. It would be not only out of character to turn it down, but short-sighted. When would I get another opportunity like this? Never. I would be a full partner with all the prestige and recognition and stature that went with my name not only on the door, but on the masthead. At the age of *thirty*.

I had *earned* it, I reminded myself again. I'd worked my ass off for five years not just because I liked my job—which I did—but because I wanted to work myself up into *this exact position*. Cohn and McMann were in their fifties. They would retire in the next ten years, and I would be running the entire company, bringing in junior partners the way Stuart Cohn had brought me in five years ago.

Would I be married? Would I have a baby? Would I be forced to live vicariously through Amanda and Jane because I had no time to date, fall in love, and have a life outside work?

All these thoughts ran through my head once more as I sat on the edge of the lagoon, letting the water roll up and tickle my feet. I considered that I might be melancholy because in thirteen minutes, I would be thirty.

I didn't feel thirty. Sometimes I felt like I was twenty-one and trying to figure out what I wanted to do with my life, and sometimes I felt forty, set in my ways and wanting to tell everyone to get off my lawn.

I had a dream, but I rarely thought about it and never discussed it with anyone. It was a foolish idea, completely irresponsible, impracticable, impossible. Not a dream for a fiscally frugal financial planner whom wealthy people trusted with their money.

The moon slowly came into view through the opening above the lagoon. The gentle waves glittered. For a split second, I felt wholly at peace. Very odd, since I was in the middle of a major life decision and had found a dead body last night.

This place was more magical than any place I'd ever been. The open cavern, soothing water, and especially the breathtaking beauty of the lagoon under moonlight.

This was exactly where I was supposed to be at this moment.

Here, I felt like I could actually acknowledge my dream—a dream that could never become reality. I almost wanted to toss a quarter in the water and make a wish. But I didn't know what my wish would be.

Instead, I picked up a shell—an unusually beautiful pink shell, about three inches long, wide and open on one end, spiraling to a point on the other. It was unique and imperfect. Staring at the shell, I pictured what I wanted—my wild dream that I would never, could never, pursue. Reluctantly, I tossed the shell, and the dream, into the water.

I let them go. I knew who I was and what I should do with my life.

"Penny for your thoughts."

I screamed and jumped up, tripped, then fell on my ass.

Jason looked sheepish, but he fought a smile. "I'm sorry. I thought you heard me walk up."

My adrenaline hit the roof. "Damn you!" I said, barely getting the words out because I hadn't quite caught my breath.

Now he laughed, reached down, and pulled me up.

He didn't let go of my hands. "I *am* sorry," he said softly. "You looked so beautiful sitting here under the moonlight, it took my breath away."

"Apology accepted," I said, my heart still racing, though no longer from being startled.

He reached into the picnic basket at his feet and brought out a cupcake. "Happy birthday."

I stared at it, blinking back tears. The last thing I expected was a birthday celebration. He pulled a small candle from his pocket, pushed it into the cupcake, then lit it.

"It's five after midnight. Make a wish," he said.

I didn't know what to wish for. I had just let my dream go in the ocean, but maybe . . . I could wish to forget about the outside world for the rest of the week. Maybe I could forget about Diana Harden and the people who might have killed her, forget about the drama with Sherry Morrison, forget about what was going on with all these people I would never see again. I wanted to just let myself go and have fun until I landed back in reality next Tuesday.

I blew out the candle.

He kissed me.

A light, promising kiss. And then another. I smiled when he stepped back, and I wasn't blushing. I knew what I wanted.

Jason spread a blanket on the sand, then unpacked the basket. He patted a spot for me to sit.

"Eat," he said, and motioned to my cupcake. He brought out a second cupcake and took a big bite.

You'd think after all the food I'd consumed at the luau that I wouldn't have room for a cupcake, but I did. It was a rich chocolate with a hint of rum and cherry.

"This is amazing," I said with my mouth full.

"I bribed the baker."

Somehow, that made me happy. That Jason, the bartender, would bribe a coworker to bake me a birthday cupcake.

"There's ten more in my apartment," he said. "They're yours for the taking."

My stomach danced with butterflies. I knew exactly what he meant. At least, I *hoped* I knew what he meant.

He poured two glasses of champagne and then clinked his glass to mine. "Happy birthday, Mia Crawford."

I sipped, warm and giddy and excited.

"So, what were you thinking about under the moonlight with such a wistful expression on your face?"

"It's not important."

"You looked sad. No one should be sad on St. Claire."

"I was offered a partnership. I'm a financial planner, you know, and it's a great opportunity."

"And that makes you sad? Because your company recognized your talent and wants to reward you?"

"No. Of course not. It's what I've wanted since I started. I like the partners, the other people who work there. It's a great business. I'm good at it. Really good."

"But?" he prompted.

I stared out at the water and thought of the shell I'd tossed back, a farewell to my dreams.

"Have you ever wanted something so much, but knew it was impractical and irresponsible to even try because it would never work?"

"You're confusing me, so you must be confused yourself."

"I can't explain it. You probably wouldn't think twice—just like you jumped off the cliff."

"Glided off," he corrected me. "Jumping would be dangerous. There are rocks below."

He was trying to lighten my mood, but I didn't smile.

"Get it off your chest," he said. "Maybe that will help you make peace with whatever is bothering you."

"Being here has helped," I said. I didn't want to tell Jason or anyone. Except . . . Jason was the safest person *to* tell. After this week, I would never see him again. "This is a magical place."

"Abracadabra." He touched my lips with two fingers. "Tell me your dream. It'll be our secret."

I didn't plan to say a word, but then lots of words came out, surprising me.

"I want to own a bookstore." Now that the words were free, I couldn't take them back. "I've loved books my entire life. My earliest memory is of my dad reading to me. I spent hours in the library, and I spent all my birthday money on books, at this little bookstore in Connecticut where I grew up. I love talking about books, sharing my favorite stories with anyone who will listen. I belong to two book clubs and record video book reviews, and when I'm not working, I'm reading.

"But small businesses fail at a very high rate," I continued. "Bookstores are more difficult than most. Rent alone is prohibitive because the profit margin is low—or nonexistent. Most new businesses fail in three years. I would lose my savings, have debt, and everything would be gone. I'd never recover." I shrugged. "So it's just a dream."

"Nothing is *just* a dream," Jason said. "Tell me what your store would look like. Where is it?"

"New York is too expensive, but that's the ideal place," I said. I hadn't meant to elaborate, but Jason seemed so interested in what I was saying that I couldn't help myself. "I'd want to own the building, maybe live upstairs. I want the feeling of Tribeca or Greenwich Village, the quaint buildings and store-fronts, the neighborhood feel. But not such an expensive neigh-borhood. When you first walk in, you'd see books people want to read—nothing stuffy, no political books, no air of superior-ity. I want fun books, mysteries and romances and feel-good biographies. I want cookbooks and adventures and uplifting self-help books. And a huge children's section with bean bag chairs for the kids, where parents would feel comfortable leaving their little ones so they can browse. A story hour once a week, maybe with a children's author coming in to read her favorite book. A café where friends can chat over coffee, a private room that looks and feels like an in-home library where book clubs can meet, or a writers' group. I want . . ." I stopped suddenly, just then realizing how long I'd been talking.

"Go on," Jason urged.

I shook my head. "It can't happen."

"Why?"

"Because I'd have to get a loan and deplete my savings, and the business would go under in three years. Then who would take care of my grandmother? I'd have to start at the bottom, rebuild, and never come close to where I am now. I have a great offer that ensures financial stability for the rest of my life. It would be irresponsible and foolish to turn that down on a whim that is destined to fail."

"Is it?"

Maybe not in Jason's world of hang gliding and island liv-ing, but in the real world? "Of course," I said.

"What if it's a success?"

"It's far more likely to fail than succeed. You don't under-stand."

He didn't say anything at first, and I worried I'd hurt his feelings.

"I'm sorry," I said, and meant it. "We're people who see the world differently. You're bold and brave and jump—*glide*—off mountains for the fun of it. You don't have anyone you're responsible for except you. I'm not brave. I'm—well, cautious. And that's okay. If I did something rash, I would be constantly worried, probably get an ulcer and start biting my nails." I tried to smile, but it felt lopsided.

Jason refilled our champagne flutes, then said, "I love that you're responsible and you think about others, like your grandma. I love that you take care of her and make sure she's happy in her golden years. Family . . . well, it's important, whether it's just one person or a huge extended family. But Mia, life is meant to be lived. There's no one right way to do it. The world needs people like you to keep the ship steered straight. And the world needs people like me to show people like you the possibilities."

He took my hand, kissed it. "What if you're more like me than you realize, and that's why your dream is so vivid? Maybe you have two angels on your shoulders. We won't call them an angel and a devil, because they're both good. One is telling you to stick with what you know, the tried and true, the security blanket. That you are damn good being the captain of your ship and keeping the boat on course, moving ahead, vigilantly navigating any obstacles in order to dock at the end and be satisfied with a life well lived. And the other is telling you to jump ship, take a sailboat through uncharted waters, the wind whipping you this way and that, because maybe it's the journey itself that makes life worth living."

He leaned over, hesitated, as his lips were only an inch from mine. I held my breath, mesmerized by his speech, the way he looked at me, his dark eyes on mine . . . then he kissed me, tasting faintly of chocolate and champagne. His lips warm and confident and oh so yummy.

"Maybe," he whispered into my lips, "your path doesn't allow you to take a risk with someone like me." He kissed me again.

"Or maybe," I said, my voice hoarse, my body leaning toward him, "you're the risk I need."

I put my glass down in the sand; it fell over, but I didn't care. He put his down too. Slowly, he pushed me onto the blanket, his lips on mine, his hands skimming down the side of my sundress. He moved his hands lower, over my ass, making me moan in anticipation of what I knew would be the best sex I had ever had in my life.

"You're not wearing anything under your dress," he said, sounding mildly surprised.

"You told me to be bold," I whispered, reaching for his face, his cheeks rough with a day's growth of beard.

This time when we kissed, something shifted inside, as if I had made a decision I didn't know I was making. Every muscle relaxed as I wrapped my arms around his neck, and his body molded across mine as if he had been created to fit right there with me. The sensation was heady, intoxicating, both familiar and completely foreign.

Unrushed, Jason unbuttoned my dress, his hand cupping my breast, making me gasp, then sigh. He kissed my neck, down my throat, until his mouth reached the other breast. The warmth of his breath, the moisture of his tongue, the sound of my own pulse beating in my ears, had me whispering his name, surprising me. At my urging, Jason continued to pay homage to my breasts, gently pulling down the straps of my dress until I was free. If I stood, my dress would fall, and I would be completely naked.

But he didn't rush. His body was built with coiled, lean muscles, tense and hard, and as he explored, I explored. His skin, his hair, his shoulders. He ran his tongue up my chest, to the sensitive skin under my neck, to behind my ear. He lightly bit my lobe, and heat rushed to every limb in my body.

"Oh, God," I gasped.

"We're just getting started," he said, a smile in his voice. He looked down at me, kissed me, watched me. "You're beautiful and you're smart. My favorite combination."

I blushed. Or maybe flushed, because if he had suggested we make love on the beach right then and there, I would have happily accommodated him.

"You're blushing," he said in awe. "You're perfect."

"Perfect?" I swallowed. "That sounds like a line."

"No line." He kissed my neck again. "Beauty is in the eye of the beholder, and I behold you to be perfect." He put his lips on mine, slipped his tongue inside just enough to tease. While his mouth occupied mine in a playful war, his hands ran down my back to my ass and pushed me against his clothed body.

Now he moaned, and I smiled. I wasn't the only one here who was ready for more than a make-out session.

He pulled his mouth from mine, but I urged him back, not ready to part.

"Mia," he said, my name sounding like a melody.

I looked up. The moon was directly overhead, washing over our bodies as if it were daylight. I had never been an exhibitionist, but at this moment, I didn't want to leave. I definitely didn't want to move away from Jason.

"I want you to know I don't do this," he said.

"Hmm?"

"I don't get involved with guests."

"Shh," I said, suddenly dreading that he was going to retreat.

"But I want you."

My heart skipped a beat.

"I just wanted you to know this is new to me."

"You're not a virgin, are you?"

He laughed, a deep, contagious laugh, and collapsed on top of me. "No, no, I'm not." Then he rolled me on top of him and pulled my mouth down to his.

I sat up and straddled him. The moonlight and sweat made Jason's skin glow and look ten times sexier than when I'd first laid eyes on him. My dress was bunched around my waist, and he still had on his shorts, but I hoped they wouldn't be on for long. His hands went to my breasts, and I leaned back to enjoy this moment in time.

I deserved to let go. To be free and not think about tomorrow or my job or decisions I needed to make. To enjoy being loved and pampered and . . .

And his fingers went under my dress and touched me between the legs, so intimate and daring.

"Oh. My. God."

I didn't remember ever feeling such overwhelming waves of lust. Every touch created a new sensation, and I wanted more.

"Can I—" Jason began.

"Yes. Anything. Now."

Did I speak? I wasn't sure. I hoped he could read my mind.

Jason rolled me back, his weight on top of me, his lips, his fingers making magic inside me to the point that I thought I'd completely lose it before he had a chance to unsnap his shorts.

Then his fingers stopped.

"Don't. Stop."

I moved to regain the connection. Then his fingers were gone, and he put his mouth to my ear. "Someone is here."

I froze.

Slowly, Jason pulled my skirt down and my dress up, secured my straps over my shoulders. He kissed me. "It's okay," he said. "I'm not done with you, but we don't need an audience." He buttoned my dress, and I shivered. I didn't know if it was from residual lust, the promise of more, or the fear of getting caught.

Then I heard the voices, and recognized the man.

Nelson Stockton.

Jason pulled me to sitting as Nelson and his wife Anja walked from the trail into the clearing.

"We're sorry," Nelson said in a subdued voice that echoed lightly off the rocks. "We couldn't sleep."

"It's fine." Jason's tone was rough around the edges.

I blushed. Yes, I was now dressed thanks to Jason, but it was clear what we had been doing and what we had been about to do. How long had they been there?

"We'll head back," Nelson said.

Anja smiled at me. "We are very sorry to disturb you."

"We're just talking," I said lamely. Jason put his arm around my waist, making it clear we weren't *just* talking. I'm sure my hair was a mess. My dress felt funny as if the buttons were askew.

"Continue your conversation," Anja said with humor. "Come, Nelson." She took his hand, and they went back the way they'd come.

As soon as they were out of sight, Jason laughed and buried his face in my neck. "That was a close call."

"What if we go back to my cottage?" I said, not laughing.

He stared at me. "Are you sure?"

"Stop asking me that. I'm sure. At least nobody will walk in on us there."

He jumped up, pulled me to my feet, and quickly cleaned up the picnic, not caring if sand was loaded into his basket along with the remnants of champagne and cupcake crumbs. With the basket in one hand, and my hand in his other, we hurried down the path. Then he made a detour. "Faster this way," he told me.

I didn't object.

In minutes, we were at my cottage from the beachside.

"You don't get lost, do you?" I said.

"Never," he said. "I've tried, but my sense of direction never lets me."

He sounded sad about that, as if he sometimes wanted to disappear.

"It's fun," he said.

"What is?" I asked as I reached into my beach bag to retrieve my key.

"Trying to get lost."

"Are you serious?"

"I'll drive someplace I've never been before, and just see things. No destination, no map. Take winding roads. I've gotten stuck a couple times, but never lost."

"But you could always pull out your phone and know where you are."

"It takes discipline to resist. It's part of the journey."

I pushed open my door.

"I'll admit," Jason said, "I don't have the discipline to resist you right now." He kissed me as I shut the door.

"I'm glad," I said, and led him from the sitting area into the main room.

I stifled a scream.

My room was a mess. The bed stripped, drawers opened, couch cushions askew. The glass slider was partly open. The mirror above the dresser was shattered.

I ran to the dresser and looked behind it.

The book was gone.

CHAPTER
SEVENTEEN

"All the secrets of the world are contained
in books. Read at your own risk."

—Lemony Snicket

JASON SAT WITH ME on the patio while Gino and his security team
took pictures and collected evidence. They found some fingerprints that they would send to St. John. The fingerprints were
likely mine. If I were going to toss a room, I would wear gloves.

Jason was a rock. After my initial shock that the book was
missing, I'd cried until I realized nothing of mine had been
damaged. Then I became confused. How did anyone know I
had that book—or why it was important? By the time Gino
and his team arrived, I was frustrated and angry at the viola-
tion of my space.

I'd told them that nothing was missing except a used paperback book I'd picked up for free in the gift shop. I didn't tell
them I had hidden the book behind the dresser. I didn't mention that the book had belonged to Diana Harden or that she
had written suspicious notes in the margins and I thought that
she had been blackmailing people on the island. I didn't trust
Gino. He had secrets, and one of those secrets could be murder.

Besides, he didn't believe me. He questioned why someone
would take a cheap paperback and not my laptop. So I kept my
mouth shut about my theory—someone had seen me with the
book, knew it contained blackmail information, and stole it.

Tristan arrived shortly after Gino. The manager looked distraught and wore pajama bottoms along with a misbuttoned shirt that he'd rushed to put on.

"I do not know *what* to say," Tristan began as he stepped out to the patio where Jason and I were sitting. "*Nothing* like this has ever happened on St. Claire."

Murder was worse than a B & E, but I didn't say it since the narrative coming from everyone who worked on St. Claire was *Diana Harden disappeared on St. John.*

Tristan continued. "I have my *best* housekeeping team coming tonight to make this right." He looked over his shoulder at the broken mirror and frowned.

Jason said, "Tristan, isn't there another room you can put Ms. Crawford in?"

"Of course, if you would be more comfortable in the main building, I can get a room ready—"

"I'll stay here," I said. "Thank you."

"Are you sure?" Tristan looked concerned. Was he worried that someone with ill intent would return or that I would leave a bad review on Trip Advisor?

"Yes," I said. "I appreciate you bringing in people to help me clean up."

"You will not do anything," he said and put a hand on my arm. "I feel awful, just . . . I don't know how or who or . . ."

"Tristan," I said, "it's okay." He seemed genuinely upset, and I wanted to reassure him. "I don't blame you or anyone other than the person who came in here."

"You are far too understanding," he said. "Give me one hour. You will never know anyone was here. Kalise is right now creating a new key card for you, so you can feel safe. Jason, can you stay with Ms. Crawford until we're done?"

"Of course," Jason said, his hand on my elbow.

When Tristan went back inside to talk to Gino, Jason said, "Why don't you come to my place? I'll sleep on the couch if you'd be more comfortable."

The offer endeared him to me, but I declined. "I'm okay.

Just really mad." Really, really, *really* mad. And a teeny-tiny bit worried. Who knew the importance of the book?

"I can stay here," he suggested.

"Under any other circumstances, I'd love that, but I wouldn't be good company right now." I took his hands. Damn, I had been *so close* to having what I knew—based on the way he kissed, the way he used his hands—would have been the best sex of my life. And now the moment was gone. Maybe we could re-create the magic of the lagoon before I left, but right now I was fuming. The idea that someone had been in my space, going through my things. Maybe it should have scared me, but instead of fear, all I felt was anger.

"Are you sure nothing else was taken? Why would someone take a book and not your jewelry or computer?"

Because the book had information, information that might point to Diana's killer. But I didn't say that.

"I don't know," I muttered, feeling a tiny bit guilty I didn't tell Jason the truth.

We sat on the patio and watched Tristan instructing a housecleaning crew. The security team left with Tristan, but Gino stood in the middle of the room, observing. I watched him. He gave no hint that he'd been here earlier, but I didn't trust him.

I shivered, and Jason wrapped his arm around me, taking it as a sign of me being cold and not creeped out by Gino.

"I'm really sorry this happened," he said.

In that moment, I saw a flash of anger in Jason's expression. Not once had he shown anything except calm and concern, until now. I touched his shoulder. His muscles were tense. The anger wasn't gone, just buried. This was a side of Jason I hadn't expected. There was fun Jason, romantic Jason, passionate Jason, concerned Jason. Now angry Jason.

There was far more to Jason Mallory than sexy, daredevil, fun-loving bartender.

I almost blurted out everything about Diana's book, including my theory that blackmail was always a great motive for murder. Yet . . . I pulled back. Because I didn't actually have proof of anything, even that Diana had written in the book.

But I wanted to tell him something, so after working through ideas in my head, I finally said, "I picked up the book at the gift shop, and someone had written in the margins. Maybe the notes were important to whoever wrote them."

His brows furrowed. "What kind of notes?"

I shrugged, feeling bad about lying to him. "They seemed like a personal shorthand. Some numbers and letters and doodles that really didn't make sense."

"And you bought it here, at our gift shop?"

"It was on the free table. I left the book I read on the plane and picked that one up."

At least I gave him *some* truthful information.

"Why wouldn't the person just ask you for the book back?" Jason wondered.

Because she's dead. But I just shrugged.

"You should tell Gino," Jason continued. "It might help find out who did this."

"He doesn't believe me."

"He does. He's an ex-cop and suspicious of everyone." Jason took my hand, kissed it. Leaned over, kissed me. "Are you *really* okay?" he whispered.

"Yeah." I would be, when everyone got out of my room. "It's still my birthday, so I was thinking about going on the sunset cruise tonight, if you're working it."

"I am." He smiled. He still looked worried, but a touch of his humor was back. "I'll be done thirty minutes after we dock. I have an idea of what we can do after the cruise."

"So do I," I said.

He grinned. "That, too, but something else. You'll love it. I promise." He kissed me again. And again. My tension drained away.

"I'll hold you to that," I said.

When the housekeepers were done, I thanked the women, and they left, followed by Jason and Gino. I double-checked the door and slid the security bolt. Then I made sure the glass doors were locked, closed the blinds, and fell face-first onto the bed.

I was exhausted.

I grabbed my cell phone on the nightstand to text Brie.

Then I stopped.

Brie knew I planned to hide the book behind the dresser—she had suggested it. Maybe she broke in and took it, but staged the mess to make it look like someone else had searched, so I wouldn't suspect her.

I didn't want to believe it. I hadn't let her see the book because I didn't want her to read the information that might have been about her dad and Sherry, so she had motive. But would she have broken the mirror? I didn't see her acting so *violent*. The beach thief who tore out the page didn't have motive—he'd already gotten what he wanted. Unless he thought there was more in the book about whatever Diana had written about him?

Yet anyone Diana wrote about could have seen me reading the book on the beach and come here to look for it. Maybe Amber figured out I had it.

I put my phone back down. The jury was out about Brie. I'd rather talk to her face-to-face than over text.

I stripped and took a shower. I didn't feel unsafe. The thief had taken what he—or she—wanted. I still had my notes, but I hadn't written everything down.

I bundled up in a robe, leaned into the mound of pillows on my bed, and looked through my notebook. The first couple pages were lists of books we were considering for book club and notes about books I'd read for when I recorded my video reviews. It wasn't until halfway through the notebook that I'd copied what Diana had written with my questions and impressions.

Brie knew where I'd hidden the book, but she also knew about my notebook. Amber knew about Diana's book, but she didn't know I had it unless someone told her I picked it up at the gift shop . . . or she saw me with it. Maybe Amber had enlisted Gino's help, and that's what their conversation had been about earlier. Maybe he recognized the book. The person who tore out the page on the beach might have decided they wanted the whole book.

Or someone else who had more to lose. Someone who had seen me with the book and knew its value.

Finally, I turned off the lights and tried to sleep. I wished I had taken Jason up on his offer to stay. I closed my eyes and tried to remember the lagoon, the blanket on the sand, kissing under the moonlight, how Jason had touched me, making me feel as if I were the only person in the world . . .

Someone had stolen my book.

Dammit. I couldn't even properly set up my subconscious for a satisfying dream.

I got up, turned on the lights, checked all the doors (again), and went back to bed with my notebook.

I looked at the numbers from the page the beach thief had stolen. I still had no idea what they meant, but if the thief had the page he wanted, why come back and take the whole book?

Diana Harden was blackmailing not one person, but several. And the book was the key as to *who* she was targeting. And I'd lost it.

She had gone to St. John for a reason. I needed to know why. Had she gone to meet someone on St. John? If so, who? Someone must have seen her, talked to her, known what she was doing on the larger island.

I pulled out my laptop and checked the ferry schedule. The ferry left St. Claire every three hours starting at 7:00 a.m. I definitely wouldn't be on that ferry, considering it was after three in the morning. I signed up for the next.

I didn't know if I would learn anything on St. John, but it stood to reason that Diana's Sunday adventure had something to do with her disappearance and subsequent murder.

I flipped to the last page I'd written on, and I'd circled the number 77 and written: *Is 77 Diana's shorthand for Gino Garmon?*

Why did that feel right? Because of the comments . . . or . . .

I flipped the page of my notebook and wrote out the alphabet, then wrote numbers next to the corresponding letters, one through twenty-six.

G = 7.
Gino Garmon = 77.

Did that work for all the numbers?

I took the two most commonly written numbers, 112 and 2012. 112 could be KB or AL. AL . . . Andrew Locke. That number was also on the page with Diana's notes about a house in Arizona and his girlfriend's dirty secrets.

2012 would then be TL. Trevor Lance . . . which would fit with what she wrote about a future deal, if she had in fact been in business with him or wanted to be, based on what CeeCee had said.

Another number . . . 522. If I'd broken the code, that would be Ethan Valentine?

My heart thudded. I had deciphered Diana's code. I still had a lot of analysis to do, and without the book to reference, it would be difficult with only my notes and memory.

I went back to the list of five numbers that had flummoxed me. Maybe they referred to people as well.

11 = AA
19 = AI
157 = OG
52 = EB
210 = BJ

I couldn't think of anyone I'd met or heard about on the island with those initials, but it was a place to start. Maybe I could find a way to access the registered guest list, or a list of personnel.

My cell phone rang, and I stifled a yelp.

I grabbed it, didn't recognize the number. Spam on an island. I almost didn't answer, but spam usually didn't come in the middle of the night.

"Hello?"

"How are you doing?"

It was Jason. I smiled in the semi-dark.

"Sleeping with the lights on. Or, rather, not sleeping."

"I can be there in ten minutes."

My heart skipped a beat, and I almost said yes. But I was tired, and I had plans tomorrow to figure out who these people were and if any of them had a motive to kill Diana.

"I'll be okay," I said. "Thank you, though."

"I talked to Tristan. He thinks someone wanted to intimidate you, maybe a mean prank."

"I think—" I hesitated, wishing again that I'd told him more about the book "—maybe whoever left the book in your gift shop just wanted it back." That sounded lame.

"I told him about the book. Tristan will follow up with Trina in the morning."

I almost wished he hadn't, but maybe then I'd find out if Trina mentioned the book to anyone.

"I had fun tonight," I said. "I'm really looking forward to tomorrow."

"You mean tonight?" he said with a light laugh. "The sunset cruise is a favorite of mine. You'll remember it forever, I hope."

"Maybe if it was just you and me," I said.

"Maybe before you leave, I can make that happen."

My heart did a little flip. "Good night, Jason."

"Good night, Mia."

CHAPTER
EIGHTEEN

"Everyone who keeps a secret, itches to tell it."

—Gillian Flynn, *Dark Places*

I WAS AWAKE FAR too early for the amount of sleep I'd had, but took the time to have a solid breakfast and drink multiple cups of deliciously rich coffee.

I had a plan: find out what the police knew about Diana's trip to St. John. I didn't trust Gino, and the St. John police might have valuable information. That, plus the information I had from her book, and I was confident that I'd figure out what happened to her.

My cell phone rang as I was walking to the ferry. Caller ID read *Grams*.

I still had plenty of time, so I sat down on a bench facing the ocean and answered.

"Hello, Grams," I said.

"Mia, is that you?"

"Yes. Is something wrong?"

"Wrong? Of course not! Happy birthday, sweetheart!"

I smiled. She had never forgotten a birthday or any other special occasion. "Thank you."

"What are you doing? You're not sitting in your hotel room reading, are you?"

"No, Grams. And it's not a hotel room. It's a charming

cottage right on the beach with a huge bed and my own patio and hot tub."

"When I lived in New Zealand, oh, gosh darn, when your dad was four, I think, we had a place right on the beach. A tiny room, barely fit a bed and table, but the view was amazing. I'd love to go back, but it's probably not there anymore." Then she said, "What are you doing right now?"

"I'm waiting for the ferry to St. John. It's a larger island about twenty minutes away by boat." The morning ferry had just arrived. Several people got off, mostly staff, and then I saw Anja Stockton. She must have gone over first thing in the morning.

"With someone?"

"Alone. Sightseeing and shopping."

"Alone?" Grams said. "Honey, aren't you having fun?"

"Yes, I am. I promise."

"Mia, what did I tell you—"

"Grams, you don't have to worry about me." I definitely wouldn't tell her about the break-in or the strangled woman who'd washed up on the beach, but I knew she wouldn't give up until I shared something. "Tonight I'm going on a sunset dinner cruise."

"Ohhh! That sounds like a wonderful way to spend your birthday. You promised me that you would put yourself out there."

I remembered how Jason kissed. Yes, I definitely had put myself out there, but if I told Grams about Jason, I'd never get her off the phone.

"I am," I told her.

"You are? You're not lying?"

"I wouldn't lie to you."

"But you're not posting anything to Instagram. I saw that reel where you talked about a book, and that's the only thing you've posted. How do I know you're having fun if you don't share anything? I've gone on that Instagram five times a day and nothing!"

Brie had found Diana's social media. Had she posted anything from the island that might help me make sense of her cryptic notes?

"Okay, I'll post something."

"Every day. I want to see the island."

"I'll post my view now. Check in five minutes."

"Thank you, dear."

Anja Stockton was walking along the water alone about thirty feet from me. She looked upset, as if she'd been crying. I hoped nothing bad had happened, and I considered reasons she might have gone to St. John so early. Was Nelson ill? Had something happened to someone in her family?

"You okay?" I asked Grams. "You need anything?"

"I'm good. The Paris theater is having a Cary Grant weekend, and on Friday they're playing *To Catch a Thief* in the afternoon, which is my favorite, and then *Charade* after dinner, which is Martha's favorite, so Martha and her sister and I are going to make a day of it."

"That sounds like fun," I said, and meant it. I loved classic movies. My cats were named Nick and Nora, after all. "Find out when they're having a *Thin Man* marathon. I'll go with you."

"You bet. Now, you go have fun, understand me? I love you, pumpkin."

"Love you too, Grams."

I ended the call and took a picture of the ocean, then another of the pool area. I posted both and wrote a sentence about the most beautiful place on earth. Grams would definitely like the pictures.

I started for the ferry again, but noticed that Anja was now sitting on a bench only a few feet from me, on the beach side of the road. My watch told me I still had time, so I went over to her and said, "Hi, Anja, are you okay?"

She looked at me, and I couldn't see her eyes behind large dark glasses, but her face was splotchy and damp. She wore a wide-brimmed hat and zebra-print wrap that hugged her elegant curves. Her huge diamond engagement and wedding rings sparkled when the sun hit her hand.

"Oh, Mia. I'm a mess."

I sat down even though she didn't invite me.

"I'm a good listener," I said. Maybe it was rude of me to in-trude, but Anja was clearly sad. I hoped it wasn't her husband; I know, I know, married people had problems. But I loved happy endings, and they had seemed so happy together.

She smiled thinly, took off her glasses, and ran her fingers under her red, swollen eyes, then put her sunglasses back on and sighed deeply. A full minute later, when I was thinking I shouldn't have bothered her, she said quietly, "It's been a rough couple weeks."

"I'm sorry, I didn't mean to pry, but I don't like seeing peo-ple so sad, especially in a place like St. Claire."

"You're not prying. You're kind, and I'm really tired of keeping secrets." She paused. "I don't fit in here. Nelson doesn't, either, but he doesn't care. It's one of the reasons I love him so much. I, unfortunately, care more what people think. I'm trying not to."

"Did someone say something to you? Was someone mean?"

"Here? No, St. Claire is lovely, even if I don't quite feel like I belong."

She reached into her oversized bag and pulled out a pop-ular entertainment magazine folded open to an article in the middle. A photo of Anja dominated one of the pages, clearly a professional shot. A box in the corner showed a much younger Anja, with big hair and too much makeup, grinning ear to ear, wearing a long blue dress next to a very tall, very wide young man in a white tuxedo that was too tight on him. The back-drop screamed *prom*.

She pushed the magazine into my hands. "If Nelson knew the only reason I went to St. John this morning was to buy that rag, he would be furious."

The headline blared:

ANJA BENOIT STOCKTON'S SECRET LOVE CHILD
WITH NFL LINEBACKER JAMAL WALLACE

"I don't need to read this. I don't follow celebrity gossip."

But my eyes flitted over the key words and phrases and put together part of the story. Anja and Jamal had been high school sweethearts when Anja got pregnant and gave the baby up for adoption.

"Nelson and I knew the story was hitting. He did everything in his power to stop it, but when he couldn't, he brought me here to St. Claire, to shield me from the gossip and reporters."

"I don't know why people feel the need to dig around in someone's past."

"It's my fault."

"It takes two to make a baby," I said.

"Not about that." But she smiled. "Jamal was a sweet kid. We grew up with next to nothing, but I had my looks and Jamal had football. He wanted to marry me and take care of us, but I knew our lives would be stuck forever in Zachary, Louisiana. It wasn't a bad place to grow up, but we had dreams, and a baby wouldn't fit into those dreams. So I told him I had a miscarriage, then went to live with my cousin in Atlanta, had the baby, and gave her up for adoption. I finished school there, ignored Jamal—kids today would say I ghosted him. I felt like a ghost for those two years."

She stared out at the ocean. I should say something, but I didn't know what to say. Having a child out of wedlock wasn't a scandal anymore, and it wasn't really a scandal twenty-five years ago, either. Yet she'd been so young.

"You know," I said, "it's really nobody's business."

She laughed, her response surprising to me. "Everything is everyone's business."

I looked back at the article, which had a definite slant against Anja. The gist was that a twenty-five-year-old girl named Rosemary Jackson was searching for her birth parents and found her father, Jamal Wallace, through an ancestry database. They met with the blessing of her adoptive parents, and Jamal was heartbroken because he'd been told by the birth mom that she'd had a miscarriage. An investigation uncovered that the birth mom was Anja Benoit, now Stockton, a successful model.

"Jamal is right to be upset," she said.

"I don't think so," I said. I could sympathize with both of them. I could feel empathy for the man who had been lied to while also understanding the reasons Anja had lied.

"I made decisions *for* him without discussing any of it *with* him. He's a good man. He wanted to do the right thing, and I lied to him. It has weighed on my conscience for years. It wasn't until Nelson that I learned to forgive myself."

"I, um, overheard you and Nelson talking the other day. He was upset."

"Yes. Like I said, he did everything to suppress the story, threatened to sue, offered to pay. He thought it would hurt me if this came out. There was even a woman who said she could bury the story—for a price. Nelson was going to pay her, but I put my foot down. It hurts, but not for the reason he thinks. I had been thinking for years about reaching out to the adoption agency to let them know if my daughter wanted to meet me, I would be willing. But I didn't. I don't regret my decision to give her up. I couldn't have given her the life she deserved when I was seventeen. Her parents are good people. But I regret lying to Jamal. Fear—it is a powerful emotion. So I dragged my feet for years and then *this*."

She took the magazine from me, stared at the photo of her and Jamal.

"Have you considered reaching out to her now?"

Anja didn't say anything, and I thought maybe my question was too forward.

After a moment, Anja said quietly, "What if she hates me for what I did?"

"What if she doesn't?" I said.

Anja leaned back and closed her eyes.

I thought back to Diana's book and the large dollar amount with the numbers 1419 underlined. Nelson Stockton. Was Diana the woman who claimed to be able to suppress the story for a fee? This story had been in the works for at least a few weeks, Nelson and Anja weren't on the island when Diana disappeared, and there would be no reason she'd get away with blackmailing him over Anja's situation when multiple people knew the story. But what if she had some pull with the publisher? Or if she gave information to the press when he didn't pay? Maybe Diana Harden and blackmail were old friends, long before she was murdered on St. Claire.

"Thanks for listening to me," Anja said.

"Of course," I said. "This was an awful way for the news to come out, but at least it's out. Now you can weigh your options and make a decision on your next step. For what it's worth, Nelson loves and supports you."

She smiled. "He's a good man. He knows Jamal, who was a rookie when Nelson was in his last year of playing. He said he would arrange a meeting between us. But Nelson hurts because I'm upset."

"How'd you know that Nelson was the one?" I asked quickly, before I could change my mind.

"There were a lot of little things," she said. "He'd been married for fifteen years and has twin sons, grown now. We met at a charity function many years after he lost his wife in an accident. I was speaking, to raise money for inner-city youth sports. He was also seated at the head table and convinced the organizer to change seats with him so he could be next to me. When he looked at me, I felt a little tingle." She laughed lightly. "At that point, I'd been a successful model and spokeswoman for years. I had always planned to marry and have kids, but felt it wasn't happening because of what I'd done to Jamal. Nelson's wife had been gone for a decade at that point, and he told me she'd spoken to him that night. He'd planned to just send a check and stay home. Then he heard her telling him to go because he would meet someone who would change his life." She smiled, and I couldn't help but smile, too. "I love him. It's as simple as that. He's not fancy, he has his flaws for sure, and he cares a bit too much about sports, but when he looks at me, I know he loves me. I feel at peace when I'm with him."

"He's perfect for you." I thought about how I tried to explain to my Grams and friends about what I wanted in a man. Not perfect, just perfect for me.

"He is," she concurred. "Speaking of perfect, I am truly sorry that we interrupted your romantic moment with Jason last night."

I barely stifled a groan.

She laughed, took my hand. "Darling, you are so cute. And he hasn't been able to take his eyes off you."

That surprised me. "What?"

"Every time you walk into his line of sight, his eyes follow you. He's smitten."

I had nothing to say to that.

"I think it's lust," I said, then backtracked. "I mean, we enjoy each other's company, but he lives here, and I have a career in New York, and we're just having fun."

"Honey, have all the fun you want. Career is important, but we can't forget that we're also women who crave love."

Love? *Love?* I wasn't thinking love. I was thinking one-night stand and getting this lust for Jason out of my system, then going back to New York and accepting my promotion and getting on with my life.

"I scared you," Anja said, squeezing my hand as she smiled warmly. "You never know when Cupid hits a bull's-eye."

CHAPTER
NINETEEN

"The problem with putting two and two
together is that sometimes you get four,
and sometimes you get twenty-two."

—Dashiell Hammett, *The Thin Man*

I WASN'T THE ONLY person on the ferry.

Sherry Morrison was drinking a mimosa in the cabin. She
stared out the opposite porthole, preoccupied. Our conversation—
or, rather *her* conversation—yesterday at the spa disturbed me. As I
was carefully walking around the deck to avoid Sherry seeing me,
CeeCee ran up the dock, her oversized bag bouncing against her
hip. "Wait for me!" She was breathless and collapsed on a deck chair.

I quickly slipped to the front of the boat and hoped neither
of them saw me. The last thing I wanted was to get trapped into
a social group. Fortunately, there was another couple on board,
and CeeCee talked to them.

The ride to St. John was less than thirty minutes over the
open sea, and when we docked, I let everyone else depart before
I took the short, steep hill to the main police station.

First things first. Find out what the St. John police knew
about Diana's death.

I quickly learned that crime fiction wasn't always accurate.

How many books had I read where the heroine goes into
a police station and sweet-talks her way into information? Or

waits until the desk sergeant steps away and quickly scans the computer for all the answers.

I was polite. Friendly. I *flirted*.

I got nothing. Nada. *Zilch*.

The police chief, who was in charge of the investigation, wasn't in the office. The cop sitting behind the desk—who looked younger than Brie—wouldn't even admit that Diana *had* been murdered.

"If you need information, talk to the security chief on St. Claire, Mr. Garmon. Would you like contact information?" he said in broken English.

No, I would not *like his contact information.* But I didn't say that. I smiled, thanked him for his time, and left.

The St. John police angle was a bust.

But I wasn't deterred. What did Diana do on St. John? She must have had a purpose here. Who did she talk to? Someone had to have seen her.

I went back to the dock and showed Diana's photo around to people who worked at the stands. Everyone was friendly— well, everyone wanted to sell me something. I politely declined, asked again. When no one admitted to having seen Diana in any of the shops or restaurants, I asked about private water tax-ies. Had the police already done this on Monday and Tuesday, after she first disappeared? Were they suspicious that someone like me was asking questions?

I'd been certain I'd find answers here on St. John, but after two hours of talking to damn near everyone in the commercial district, I had nothing. I was exhausted. The hills were killing my calves, and all I wanted was sit in my hot tub with a large bottle of wine.

I was alone on my birthday focused on the last day in the life of a dead woman. What happened to my resolve last night to put everything aside for the week except my own pleasure and happiness?

Someone broke into your room and stole your book, I reminded myself.

I walked down the narrow street feeling sorry for myself at the same time I was wondering what my next step should be. *Someone* had to have seen Diana on this island. She was a pretty blonde American. She would stand out.

I paused at the corner and caught sight of a restaurant on the hill with an amazing view of the bay. I was famished. I started up the hill but hesitated when I saw a familiar woman sitting on the deck of the restaurant.

CeeCee. Though I only saw her in profile, there was no mistaking her lush, thick bleached blond hair—pulled back into a high, bouncing ponytail—and large boobs framed by the tight sundress. She and an older woman were eating lunch under a wide umbrella. This restaurant was quite a distance from the dock and outside the main tourist area.

Maybe she had a friend who lived here? Or spontaneously invited a stranger to lunch. That seemed on point. Yet . . . CeeCee's demeanor seemed different. She wasn't using her hands in the flamboyant way she usually communicated. As I watched, she leaned back with a glass of wine and a relaxed smile. The other woman was in her fifties with a short gray-blond bob and a long, narrow face, dressed in a chic sundress. She looked like money.

I took out my phone and snapped a picture because I thought she looked familiar, but I didn't recall seeing her on St. Claire.

CeeCee turned toward the street as if she sensed someone watching her. I immediately ducked into a small, crowded shop to avoid being seen.

"Most private water taxis don't work out of the dock area," said a deep, feminine voice in heavily accented English.

I jumped, not expecting to see the large woman sitting on a bench on the balcony of the souvenir shop. She was in her sixties with wrinkled, tan skin.

"I'm sorry?"

"Bertha from down the street said you're looking for a private taxi. She saw you headed my way. She understands English, doesn't speak much. So, I figure you come to me to ask."

I showed her Diana's photo on my phone. "Did you see this woman on Sunday?"

She didn't answer my question. Instead she said, "Kids who want to make a quick buck off tourists aren't going to work the docks. They'd be run off by the cops and charter companies."

"Where are they? Another dock?"

The woman laughed. "They have don't have a license. They move around."

"I need to find who took this woman to St. Claire on Sunday."

The stranger stared at me long enough to make me squeamish. Was she lying to me? Trying to con me? Get me to pay for the information? Hell, at this point I'd give her near anything.

"You see anything you like?" she asked, her hand spread to encompass her small, enclosed shop.

Yep, money.

I walked through the crowded shop. Mostly junk—odds and ends, no organization, prices triple what they should have been. I truly panicked when I overpaid for anything.

But money talks.

I saw a bright turquoise shirt with a mermaid lounging on a rock, wearing sunglasses. *I swam with the mermaids, St. John, US Virgin Islands.*

My Grams would love it and wear it. It wasn't really wasting money on the tacky shirt if Grams got use out of it, right?

The woman smiled and pulled out a handheld card reader. I handed her my credit card. She rang up the purchase, put the shirt in a bag, and handed it back to me.

"Crusty over at Fish Bay sets up special trips," she said.

"Where is Fish Bay?"

"Down the hill, turn left at the yield, walk a mile, then up the hill, it curves around, then—"

"Do you have Uber on the island?"

"Better."

She whistled so loud my ears rang, then raised her arm straight in the air. She was leaning so far on the edge of the balcony, I thought she'd fall over the railing.

A tall, skinny kid on a bike with a rickety-looking seat attached rode up to the door. The seat didn't have a seat belt. I pictured my body flying off a cliff because he'd lost control.

"My grandson, Jorge. Twenty dollars."

I handed her back my card. She rang it up. I'd thought it would be safer not having cash on me; now I wasn't so sure.

Certain I was going to plummet to my death on a narrow, winding road, I reluctantly climbed into the seat and held on tight as Jorge headed down the hill toward the main commercial area. I slumped down to avoid being seen by CeeCee, but when I looked back at the restaurant deck and the bright umbrella she'd been sitting under, she and her guest were gone.

I sat up and glanced around. "You know we're going to Fish Bay, right?" I said, because this wasn't the direction his grandmother had pointed out to me.

"Yes," he said. "This is faster."

Fast was relative. We got stuck behind cars as they navigated through pedestrian, bike, and vehicle traffic in the main part of town. I'd made a huge circle, I realized, as the police station was to my left, and the dock where the ferry dropped me off was to my right. I pulled a visor out of my bag as the sun beat down on me; the only thing keeping me from heat stroke was the cool ocean breeze.

Jorge made a few quick turns that had my life flashing before my eyes, but then we were on a road with trees and bushes growing on both sides, interspersed with small houses, restaurants, and clearings where I could see the water.

It was pretty and more authentic than the ritzy St. Claire, but rougher around the edges.

We slowed down again as pedestrians crossed in front of us heading to the beach. The sun sparkled on the still bay, sailboats heading out or returning.

Sherry walked right in front of Jorge's bike, and I immediately dropped down into the seat. Sherry looked angry, and I didn't want her to see me. She might think I was following her, and after her over-the-top behavior at the spa yesterday, I didn't want a confrontation here.

"Watch where you're going, jerk!" she shouted at Jorge.

"So sorry, so sorry," he said.

"It wasn't your fault," I said automatically, though I don't know if he heard me.

I peered over the seat and watched as Sherry climbed into the back of a taxi. They turned at the next corner.

"Miz?" Jorge said. "Miz, you okay?"

"Can you follow that taxi?"

Had I said that out loud? I almost laughed.

"*Sí*, that one?"

He gestured to where Sherry's taxi had turned up the road.

"Yes. Please. I'll pay you." There had to be an ATM on the island.

He obliged.

Then I thought, *How am I going to get back before the ferry leaves?*

I should have thought this through. The farther we were from the tourist areas, the more I questioned my judgment. Why had I wanted to follow Sherry?

Because she's been acting suspicious. And that phone call last night.

I looked at my watch. It was 12:30. Her meeting was over. Except she looked angry, and the taxi wasn't going back to the dock.

It was probably nothing.

It might be something.

What was I doing? I wasn't a cop. I wasn't a private investigator. I wasn't even Miss Marple, who probably had the sense not to go riding on a bike to the other side of a foreign island with a stranger, following taxis to the isolated areas where she had no business being.

I was a financial planner who read too many mysteries. I was reading way too much into Diana's disappearance. It could have been an accident.

Sure, she was "accidentally" strangled with her own scarf.

Maybe her notes had nothing to do with blackmail.

But someone stole the book.

It was too late to back down now. I wanted to know what Sherry was doing.

And, to be honest, I was having fun.

The nice thing about St. John—at least from my perspective on the back of a foot-powered bike following a gas-powered vehicle—was that the roads were narrow and crowded, and no one drove fast because of the sharp turns. Jorge lost sight of the taxi a few times, but he wasn't deterred from our pursuit, and always caught up with it—usually because the taxi was stuck in traffic.

Then we were in the open near the top of one of the hills, where three roads came together. All around were lush green trees and bushes, and I couldn't see the ocean.

The taxi had parked near a food truck, but Sherry wasn't inside. Dammit! What could she be doing here? There weren't any businesses in walking distance except for the food truck.

"I'm sorry," I said to Jorge. "I shouldn't have had you come all the way here."

"It's fine," he said, though he sounded tired.

"It's probably too far to go to Fish Bay now," I said.

"No, that road—" he pointed "—all downhill to Fish Bay. You ready?"

"Yeah—oh, wait!"

Sherry walked out from behind the food truck. With her was a wiry-looking man with dark hair, sunglasses, and a moustache. He looked rough and edgy, or was that my imagination filling in blanks?

Sherry held out an envelope, which he took and immediately pocketed. No, not suspicious at all, handing an envelope to a strange man in the middle of St. John. She yelled at him, her face firm, angry, determined. He stood there and took it, his expression unchanged. He nodded as she went on a rant, then he said something to her. I couldn't read lips. That would have been a very useful skill.

Sherry strode back to the taxi, and the driver left.

"We done?" Jorge said.

"Yeah," I said. As discreetly as possible, I took a photo of the strange man. He retrieved the envelope from his pocket and pulled out a thick wad of cash. He counted it, nodded to himself, and pocketed the money. He tossed the envelope in the trash can outside the food truck, then went inside the truck, closed down the sides, and a minute later drove off.

"Do you know him?" I asked Jorge as he started pedaling in the opposite direction.

He shrugged. "No, miz. The truck? *Sí*. It's a, um, business with many food trucks."

I leaned back and wondered what Sherry Morrison was up to . . . and if it was going to hurt Brie.

FIFTEEN MINUTES LATER, Jorge emerged from a winding but downhill road to a flat area with a view of a small, narrow bay. Jorge pulled over under a large tree in front of a business that looked like a house with a sign that read "Fish Bay Fish Tacos."

"Crusty's here," he said. "Best food, cheap."

"Um, can you wait for me? I can pay you when I get back to your grandmother."

"ATM," he said, and pointed to a sign in the window that blinked *ATM* in red.

"Okay, I'll get cash. Can you wait?"

He smiled, put his feet up on his handlebars, and leaned back on his seat.

I entered the restaurant. No AC. A long counter separated the kitchen from the dining area, which was dotted with small, mismatched tables. Several people were eating, and no one looked like a tourist.

"What'dya haven?" The young girl spoke quickly, stringing her words together and pronouncing *having* as *haven*.

I looked at the handwritten menu on a chalkboard. Two items had already been erased for the day.

"Four special tacos? And um, two water bottles?"

I didn't know what was in the tacos, but the place, though too hot, smelled delicious.

The girl called out the order and rang me up, placed two small water bottles on the counter. The water cost more than the tacos.

"I need to talk to Crusty."

I was really hoping that Crusty wasn't the scary-looking man behind the counter who was currently making my tacos.

"Yep."

That was all she said.

"And is he here?"

"Nope."

"Where can I find him? Jorge's grandma—" I said when I realized I hadn't gotten her name "—told me I could find him here."

"Yep." She handed me back my credit card.

"When?" I asked, getting exasperated.

She shrugged. "He's on de boat now, twenty minutes? You want me call 'em?"

"That would be great," I said.

The cook hit a bell, and the girl reached back for my basket of tacos without looking. I took them to the ATM and withdrew two hundred dollars—Crusty might want money for information. Then I went outside, which was decidedly cooler than indoors. I climbed onto the seat of the bike cart and handed Jorge one of the water bottles, two of the tacos, and two twenty-dollar bills. He'd earned every dime.

"Gracias," he said.

I ate my tacos. They were fresh and delicious.

We were parked on the uneven base under a huge mampoo tree, its trunk thick and roots breaking through the ground in multiple places between us and the inlet. It was quite nice, I thought as I watched the boats. Jorge drained his water and leaned back, closed his eyes, his hat partially covering his face.

I didn't know what to do other than wait and reflect on

what I'd learned—which was not much, to be honest. I'd come here to retrace Diana Harden's steps . . . and only learned that CeeCee was having lunch with a girlfriend, and Sherry Morrison had given a shady-looking man cash. I still didn't know why Diana had come to St. John or what she did while she was here. I hoped I could get back to St. Claire with enough time to shower and change for the sunset cruise. Put all this unproductive sleuthing on the back burner and enjoy the evening with Jason. A thrill went down my spine remembering how he made me feel . . . I deserved him, didn't I? I deserved a night to let go and not overthink everything.

"There," Jorge said, interrupting my daydream. He motioned toward the inlet. A kid was scrambling up the rocks from the shore below. A fishing rod protruded out of his backpack, and he struggled to carry a large ice chest.

"That Crusty," Jorge said.

Crusty went into the restaurant. A minute later, the kid came out without the ice chest and climbed next to me on the cart, getting into my personal space. He couldn't have been more than twelve.

"I'm Crusty," he said. "You?"

"Mia," I said automatically.

"You need a ride?"

I pulled out my phone and showed him the photo I had of Diana Harden. "Do you know if someone took her to St. Claire on Sunday?"

He looked at the picture, and I couldn't read his expression. Then he said, "Fifty."

"Fifty what?"

"Fifty bucks."

"For?"

"I'll tell you who took her back."

He could be scamming me, and it would be my fault if I lost my money, but I had a feeling . . .

I only had twenties. I handed him two and said, "Forty. No bullshitting, okay?"

He pocketed the bills and said, "I took her."

I narrowed my eyes. "Are you lying to me?"

"Nope. She paid me two hundred to take her, and fifty to not tell anyone. I kept my mouth shut. But I heard she got dead."

"You should have told the police."

He shrugged. "I didn't kill her."

"And you took her to St. Claire."

"Yep."

"What time?"

He shrugged again. "Don't know. Sunset? My ma was pissed 'cause I got in after dark. I ain't supposed to be on the water at night. But two hundred fifty bucks? Sheee-it. It was worth the whoppin' I got."

"And you took her to the dock?"

He hesitated.

"Crusty, this is important. Did you take her to the main dock, or did you leave her somewhere else? Maybe meet up with another boat?"

He was looking at my small purse slung crossways over my body.

"No more money," I snapped. "Do you want me to tell the police about a kid named Crusty who scams tourists?"

He frowned, but Jorge laughed. "She's cool, Crusty."

"Please tell me," I said firmly.

Crusty sighed. "She wanted to go to Ethan Valentine's private dock on the south side of the island."

I wasn't expecting that answer. "Seriously?"

"Yep, not lying to ya. I left her right there on his dock. Swear to God, it's the truth." He made the sign of the cross.

I believed him. He had no reason to lie.

CHAPTER
TWENTY

"Was it a threat, or a well-meant warning?"
—Carolyn Keene, *The Secret of Shadow Ranch*

CEECEE WASN'T ON THE ferry returning to St. Claire, but Sherry Morrison was. She must not have seen me this morning, because she appeared surprised when I walked on board right before the boat left.

"What are you doing here?" she asked, accusation in her voice.

I smiled and held up the bag with Grams's new shirt. "Shopping. I wanted to get away for a while, see the sights. You?" I tried to keep my voice light and only marginally interested. I didn't think she'd seen me following her up the mountain, but I wasn't positive.

"Same," she said with cold eyes.

I didn't see any bags in the cabin, but didn't comment.

The captain came down from the helm and said, "You two are the only guests returning?" He glanced at the dock as if expecting someone else.

"Do we have to wait for the others?" Sherry snapped. "I need to get ready for the cruise tonight."

"Of course not," he said evenly. "There's another ferry run in two hours."

"We can wait," I said, mostly to irritate Sherry. "I mean, after what happened to Diana Harden, maybe we should."

The captain smiled, shook his head. "No, that's not necessary. I return in two hours. We'll be off in just a few minutes, and Gregory will be down with refreshments."

He went back to the helm, and Sherry stared at me. "You didn't have to offer to wait. Dammit, I have plans tonight."

"You're not concerned that a woman was murdered?"

"Hardly. She probably pissed off the wrong person."

I really didn't like this woman, but I bit my tongue. I might not like her, but I was also suspicious about her actions. I wondered if Diana had attempted to blackmail Sherry. Maybe that was what the money was for—murder for hire.

A chill went down my spine at the thought.

The engines started up, and a moment later, we were pulling away from the dock. Gregory, the server, came down with flutes of champagne and a tray of hors d'oeuvres. They served champagne like water.

I excused myself, went out to the deck, and watched St. John shrink as we left the bay and picked up speed. I hadn't brought a book with me. I *never* left home without a book, and yet I hadn't even thought about it today. Diana's disappearance and murder had consumed me, and whoever stole the book drew me deeper into the mystery. But tonight—tonight was Jason and me. I was excited . . . and a little scared. There was chemistry between us—we both felt it. I smiled, leaned against the railing, closed my eyes as the wind whipped my hair around. Wishing Jason was here, just the two of us.

I heard something—metal on metal, maybe—opened my eyes, and turned around.

I screamed, dropped my glass. It shattered on the wood deck. Sherry was standing right behind me, so close that she could have pushed me overboard.

"Didn't mean to scare you," she said in a tone that said anything but.

Gregory came from the cabin, saw the broken glass, and said, "Ms. Crawford, Ms. Morrison, be careful. I'll get the broom." He hurried away.

Sherry stared at me. "Stay out of my business. Stay away from my family." Her voice was low and menacing.

"Family?" I repeated, though I thought *business*. She had seen me following her. A lump formed in my throat. Where was Gregory with the broom?

She smiled. It was twisted and cruel. "Future family."

Then she went back into the cabin, leaving me perplexed and a lot worried.

ANDREW MET THE ferry when we docked. I watched from the deck as Sherry ran to him and kissed him with the passion of the honeymooning Kents. He responded in kind, put his arm around her waist, and they walked down the beach toward the resort.

I had a lot to think about.

I took the shuttle, and when it dropped me off in the roundabout, I headed straight to my cottage, avoiding three conversations.

Doug was his usual chatty self, but I bowed out of drinks by the pool because of a "headache." Brie tried to flag me down, but I waved her off, not wanting to engage in that conversation yet—though I knew I'd eventually have to ask her if she took the book.

And Mrs. Kent, the female half of the horny honeymooners, who was, surprisingly, not with her husband. In three days, I had never seen them separated.

"Have you heard anything about what happened to that poor woman?" she asked me as I passed her exiting the yoga studio, her skin glistening from exercise.

Okay, so I avoided two and a half conversations.

"No," I said, still walking.

She turned and walked beside me. "I talked to one of the maids, and *she* said that the woman was murdered." She whispered *murdered* like some people whisper *cancer*.

"That's the rumor," I said, trying to give off the aura that I was busy without being rude.

"I heard she had stayed in your room," Mrs. Kent said.

That stopped me, literally, and I faced her. "Really?"

"Don't you think that's creepy?" she asked.

If she had learned that Diana had been in my suite, maybe it was common knowledge. It *would* be common knowledge among the staff.

Maybe Brie hadn't been the one to take the book. Maybe it *was* Sherry, who could have easily known which cottage Diana was in. Or someone who knew what Diana was writing in the book and had been looking for it *in her room.*

But why her room and not the luggage in storage? I remembered the staff that first night I was here at the Sky Bar commented that housekeeping had packed up her room because she hadn't checked out. I'd thought maybe Amber asked Gino to look through the suitcase—or that he allowed her to do so. If she didn't find the book, the next logical step would be to search the room.

A lot of theories, but little evidence to back them up.

"Creepy," I agreed. "You okay after the other night?"

Mrs. Kent sighed. "Yes, thank you. I freaked."

"Justified," I said as I glanced down the path to my door. "I need to go, but maybe I'll see you on the cruise tonight?"

"We'll be there," she said and waved as I walked to my door.

I sat down at the desk and booted up my laptop. I'd been planning to research Ethan Valentine and dig deeper into Sherry Morrison, but I hesitated as I thought about the implications of Diana Harden having my suite before me.

Anyone *could* have seen me reading Diana's book on the beach—like Sherry Morrison—but that didn't mean everyone had seen me reading it, or knew what it was if they had. If the culprit knew Diana had written in the book and couldn't find the book in her belongings, they might have thought it was here. Which would clear Brie.

I had thought she might have taken it simply because she'd told me where to hide it. I didn't have to secure it to the back of the dresser, but it was a good idea in light of my suspicions about Gino. Was I giving her the benefit of the doubt because I liked her?

I couldn't help but think of all the mysteries I've read where the sidekick betrayed the hero. Brie had already called herself Dr. Watson. I haven't read every single Sir Arthur Conan Doyle story, but I don't think that Watson ever betrayed Sherlock Holmes.

I was no Sherlock, but I still had a hard time believing that Brie would have made such a mess of my room and broken the mirror. It was mean and borderline threatening.

The thief, when he or she couldn't find the book in Diana's luggage, could have thought *Diana* had hidden it. That put Gino and Amber at the top of my list.

I was about to text Brie and ask if she could meet before the sunset cruise, when I saw that she had texted me twenty minutes ago.

u mad? we need to talk.

I texted Brie and said one hour, Blue Dahlia. That would give me enough time to get ready for the cruise. She responded with a thumbs-up emoji.

Brie *could* have taken the book, but it now seemed unlikely. She'd come through with information about Gino Garmon, Diana and Amber's relationship, and Trevor Lance's marital situation. She would have just asked me to see the book.

After my experience with the police on St. John, I considered reaching out to Ethan Valentine directly. Except, what if *he* was involved? Crusty said he'd taken Diana to Valentine's private dock the night she disappeared. Maybe I should talk to Tristan. He would know if Valentine had been on the island Sunday. If he wasn't, then he had nothing to do with her murder. Or Luis, Valentine's uncle, would know. I doubted the octogenarian had strangled anyone.

I turned to my computer and searched for Ethan Valentine.

The first link that came up was his bio on the Valentine Enterprises website. It was surprisingly brief for a multibillion-dollar company. He founded the company to support video game creators by offering a full array of services from debugging a program to marketing and distribution. He purchased projects in the independent marketplace and repackaged them for mass distribution. There was nothing about him taking a sabbatical for three years on an island, and trade magazines referred to him as reclusive but engaged with his business.

I clicked images, and there were pictures of three different men named Ethan Valentine, none of whom could be the dot-com genius. The MIT student paper wrote a short article about Ethan Valentine:

> Computer science and engineering major Ethan Valentine sold a data compression program he developed in high school to Roland Briggs, the head of the Briggs fortune and a fellow MIT alum. While the details of the sale are not yet known, rumors indicate that Briggs paid low eight figures for the program. Valentine couldn't be reached for comment, but his roommate John Douglas said he wasn't planning to return to MIT in the fall. "Ethan has more ideas than anyone, and he plans on using this sale as seed money for his own company."

Briggs. That couldn't be a coincidence, right?

I did a quick search on Roland Briggs, and yes, he *was* the father of Parker Briggs, the man I'd spoken to, the man who had been arguing with his ex-girlfriend and Diana Harden's current girlfriend, Amber Jones.

That was a connection I couldn't ignore.

I didn't have time to dig into the finance articles, so I saved them to my desktop to peruse later.

I had just changed into a new dress when Braden called.

"You answered your phone too fast," he said.

"I'm getting ready for a sunset dinner cruise," I informed him.

"Then I won't keep you long. I looked into the two companies you asked about. Ninety percent of Lance & Wong Development, LLC, is their commercial real estate company, AV Properties and Trust, which has just under $16 billion in assets and a market value of $17.5 billion, according to Forbes. They have several major projects in the works, but the largest two are a $100 million project in Dallas and a $120 million project in Nashville."

A market value of $17.5 billion would make Lance's business probably one of the top twenty in the country. I asked Braden, "Anything sketchy about their business model?"

"They've been sued a half-dozen times but only lost once, a wrongful termination and breach of contract case against a small concrete company out of Houston. They have a mixed reputation in the real estate world."

"What about the other ten percent of their business?"

"I didn't really look at that. I can."

"No, that's okay," I said, though I wasn't certain if the information would be important or not. "What about Briggs?"

"Parker Briggs is the black sheep of the family," Braden said. "He's never held down a real job as far as I can tell. Ostensibly he works for his father, Roland Briggs, but there are more articles about him at parties and getting in trouble than there are about his business. Typical trust fund brat," Braden said derisively. "You know the type."

I did. Several of our clients had offspring like Parker Briggs.

"And Roland runs the family business?"

"Yes, with his daughter Abigail Briggs Horowitz and her husband, who is the company attorney."

"He's also a philanthropist, right?"

"Right. The Briggs Family Trust had a big write-up just last week on renovating the children's hospital in New Orleans."

Diana Harden was from New Orleans. No book detective believed in coincidences. "Oh?" I said.

"It's where they live. At least, the dad and the Horowitzes live there. I don't know about Parker. He gets around, and is seen often in New York, Miami, and Los Angeles—that's where he seems to have gotten into the most trouble."

"Would you say the Briggs family business is healthy?"

"They have A ratings across the board, and Roland Briggs and his daughter are well respected."

"Thanks." I hesitated, then just let it out. "Do you know much about Ethan Valentine? He got his start when Briggs bought his data compression software."

"Valentine Enterprises? Not much. Valentine keeps a low profile, but . . ." She heard him type on his laptop. "Business is very healthy. A few disgruntled board members because he's so reclusive, but they created and now manufacture one of the top video games in the world. Sort of like *Where in the World Is Carmen Sandiego* meets *Choose Your Own Adventure*, but with guns and bombs. They're coming out with a new edition at the end of the year. Preorders have already exceeded the last edition."

In the background I heard Amanda say, "Tell her to stop working and have fun!"

"I'm not working," I said.

"Neither of us believe that," Braden said.

"I'm *not*," I repeated. "In fact, I need to hang up right now and finish getting ready." I was going to be late meeting Brie.

I heard rustling on the other end. Then Amanda came on the line. "I want pictures," she demanded.

"To prove I'm having fun?"

"Yes."

I laughed. "I'll see what I can do. Goodbye." I ended the call and shut down my laptop.

I didn't know what, if anything, Ethan Valentine had to do with Diana Harden or Parker Briggs, but there was *some* connection to both, and now I was curious.

I felt surprisingly nervous as I applied makeup and fussed with my hair. This was it, I thought. I would put Diana Harden's murder aside, not worry about potential suspects, and think only of Jason.

I don't know why I was so nervous.

TWENTY-ONE

"If there's a justification for my actions right now, it's this: I have gone completely mad."

—Veronica Mars

BRIE WAS SITTING ON a recliner on the edge of the patio, drinking something pink. I sat on the chair next to her. "I'm sorry. I was talking to my office, and time got away from me." I looked at my watch. "Okay, I have twenty minutes before the shuttle leaves for the ferry."

"You're going on the cruise?"

"Yeah. Jason's working, and it's my birthday so . . ."

"Oh, happy birthday."

"Thanks. Thirty. I don't feel different." I think I'd felt—and acted—thirty from the minute I took my position at McMann & Cohn five years ago. I'd skipped over my fun twenties. The thought depressed me.

Brie stared at the water and drank her daiquiri.

"What's wrong?" I asked.

"I think my dad is going to propose to Sherry tonight. I'm just—well, it's fucked. Fuckity fuck fuck."

"Do you know much about her? Her background?" My mind raced. Sherry wasn't who she seemed. Her attitude with me, her sneaking around the island, paying a creepy guy cash for who knew what.

Brie shrugged. "Enough to know that she's awful. I don't want my dad to marry her. I *know* she's after his money. Okay, I don't *know*, but I *think* she is, and her last husband is dead, and I don't want my dad to . . . to . . ."

Her voice caught, and I said, "Have you told him how you feel?"

"Yes! No. Sort of. I mean, Sherry is the first woman he's ever brought *here*. I just think she's two-faced. She's fun and nice and all casual when she's with my dad, but when he's not around? She's conniving. Snotty. She criticized the housekeeping staff for being mediocre, that we didn't pay a thousand dollars a day to live in filth. *My dad* pays a thousand dollars a day. Not her. I don't think she has any money other than what she got from her husbands."

"Two-faced," I mumbled.

"What?"

"Diana wrote in the book that she was meeting 'two-face' at eight on Sunday. Maybe you're not the only person who thinks that Sherry is two-faced."

"You could be right. But we can't prove it." Brie was right, but I didn't discount the idea. She said, "You know, it's just been dad and me for years, and I don't want him to be alone."

"Give him more credit," I said. I hesitated, then told her what Sherry said to me in the spa. "She thought I was flirting with your dad, and that I had befriended you in order to get close to him."

"What?"

"Then I saw her today in St. John, and she was acting . . . well, suspicious." I didn't tell her what Sherry said on the ferry, or how she intentionally scared me. I still wasn't certain I hadn't turned a light warning into a serious threat. "I followed her."

"You followed her where?"

"I saw her in a taxi. She met up with a suspicious guy in the middle of nowhere and gave him an envelope of cash."

"I knew she was up to something! And?"

"I don't know. I wish I did."

"Mia," Brie said, and bit her lip. "Please don't be mad at me."

"You took Diana's book from my room." Instantly I was relieved. That meant it wasn't gone.

Brie frowned. "No! Why would I? Is it missing?"

"Someone broke into my room. They made a mess and took the book, which I'd taped behind the dresser, just as *you* suggested. Just tell me the truth. Do you have it?"

"No," she said. Then she glanced away. "Well, shit."

My heart fell. "I really hoped it was you. I would have been mad, but also happy that it wasn't gone."

"I *didn't* take it," she insisted. "But—I did go into your room last night. The patio door was unlocked. I shouldn't have, I know! But I wanted to see what you didn't want me to see."

I was confused. "What are you talking about?"

"Yesterday, you totally didn't want me to go through the book, and I thought there might have been something written in there about my dad that you didn't want me to know. The door was *unlocked*. And I didn't touch anything else. I looked behind the dresser. It was there. I read it, put it back exactly where I found it."

That had a ring of truth.

"How long were you there?"

"Ten minutes, twelve tops. I watched you leave, waited a couple minutes, then went in, figuring you'd be gone at least an hour."

I didn't like that Brie had violated my space or my trust, but I believed her.

"Okay," I said.

"I'm sorry," she said sincerely. "Did somebody really take it?"

"Yes." That put me back to thinking Amber, Sherry, or Gino. Gino had seen me with the book on the beach. Maybe because Amber had been asking about it, Gino had taken it upon himself to look for it.

My headache grew, and I rubbed my temples. It could be someone I hadn't thought of yet, someone else she had been blackmailing.

"Maybe you won't be as mad at me when you find out we didn't lose everything." She pulled out her phone. She scrolled through her images, then handed me the phone. "I took pictures of all the pages Diana wrote on."

My heart swelled, and I couldn't help but smile. "All is forgiven if you send those to me."

She immediately did, then pulled up one of the pages. "This is about my dad," she said, pointing to one of the first notes in the book listing values of property and net worth.

"I think so," I said. "The number 112? I figured out her code—at least some of it. 112—Andrew Locke. 2012—Trevor Lance. 77—Gino Garmon. 1419—Nelson Stockton. There's more. Some I can't figure out without a list of guests and staff."

"You think she was blackmailing all these people?" Brie asked.

I nodded. "Or planned to."

"And she's dead." Brie leaned back, finished her daiquiri. "I read what she wrote about my dad and Sherry. Diana thought Sherry's involved with my dad for his money. I have *always* thought she was a gold digger. Maybe she's running out of money. Maybe she's about to lose her house. That won't matter if she marries dad and gets half of everything that's his. She'll use him. My dad—he's an absolute great guy, totally generous and the best person I know. But he's way too trusting. He's like head over heels for her. He's going to propose. And I don't know what to do about it. I would die if anything happened to him."

Brie was on the verge of tears. My heart went out to her, and I understood why she went into my room to look at the book. If my dad were still alive, I would want to make sure anyone in his life loved him for him.

"We'll think on it," I said.

"You'd help me? Even after I betrayed your trust?"

I didn't like Sherry, and I really liked Brie. "Of course I'll help." I looked at my watch. "The shuttle leaves in two minutes. Can you walk with me? I want to show you something."

We walked toward the roundabout outside the lobby. I showed her the photo I took of CeeCee and the woman at lunch. "I think I know this woman. I've seen her, but I don't know who she is."

I handed Brie my phone.

"Oh. Yeah. I think . . . yep. That's Trevor Lance's first wife. Remember? I showed you that article about his new wife, the model who's in Europe right now, and it had a picture of his first wife, but she was much younger then."

I remembered now. I squinted at the picture. "You think?"

"Ninety-nine percent positive." She handed me back my phone.

I think she was right. I'd also glimpsed a photo of the ex in one of the articles about Trevor I'd read the night before.

"Why would his mistress meet with his ex-wife?" I wondered out loud.

"I don't get any of them. They're all dickheads."

I couldn't disagree with her.

The last person was getting on the shuttle. Henry waved at me, and I put up my finger to hold him.

"Tomorrow morning, let's go through these pages and my notes. Maybe between the two of us, we'll figure out exactly who else Diana blackmailed *and* what she had on Sherry, okay?"

"If you push her overboard, I wouldn't be upset."

I laughed, though I shouldn't have.

"Hey, look," Brie said, and pointed to the base of a trail marked *St. Claire Peak.*

Amber Jones—in chinos, a T-shirt, and sneakers—stood tapping her foot, her mouth in a thin line. I couldn't see her eyes shaded behind dark glasses, but she was clearly waiting for someone. As we watched, Parker Briggs strode up to her. He took her arm, and she hit his hand. He, too, was dressed in walking shoes and casual clothes. They didn't look like they were going on a romantic excursion.

"Didn't you say earlier that you thought Amber was looking for Diana's book?" Brie said. "Maybe she took it."

As we watched, Amber rummaged through her bag, and they walked up the pathway. They were too far away for me to see what she pulled out, but it looked like a book. The size of a trade paperback like the one that had been stolen from me.

"They're up to something," I said. "I think that's my book."

Henry honked, made a motion toward his watch. Doug waved at me from the shuttle to hurry.

"I gotta go," I said, torn about what to do. Jason was on that cruise. I really wanted to spend some time with him. And I'd told him I'd be there. "Keep an eye out for when they return, okay?"

"I'll follow them."

"No. That's too dangerous. We don't know what they're doing." But clearly, Amber wanted the book for a reason. What was in it that was so valuable? And why would they be going up the mountain at the end of the day? What was up there?

"Come with me," Brie said.

Henry honked again and called out, "Ten seconds, Ms. Crawford!"

"I thought you wanted me to push Sherry overboard?"

"I don't want you to get kicked off the island."

I bit my lip. Okay, Jason was working the cruise. He probably wouldn't have much time to spend with me anyway. And everyone else was couples. I'd be sitting at the bar watching him, out of place and stuck with nowhere to go and nothing to read.

"Okay," I said. I must have been completely mad to give up time with Jason to hike up a mountain following two possible thieves. "Let's do it."

I called out to Henry. "I'm sorry, I can't go. Something came up."

He looked put out, and I tried to apologize again, but Brie grabbed my arm. Amber and Parker were already out of sight.

As the shuttle drove off without me, I sent Jason a message.

Something came up. I'm really sorry. I'll call you later.

I didn't wait for a response and pocketed my phone. For some twisted reason, following Amber and Parker didn't seem scary or intimidating. I hadn't been lying to Grams or Amanda—I *was* having fun. I hated to admit it because it was probably the riskiest thing I'd ever done, but unraveling this mystery was the most fun I'd had in years—more so now that I had a partner.

We headed toward the trail.

CHAPTER
TWENTY-TWO

"Sometimes we need to take big risks if
we want to find out who we are."
—Meg Cabot, *Queen of Babble*

THICK TREES WITH HEAVY, wide leaves shadowed the St. Claire Peak trail. The dank dirt made me sneeze, and I quickly put a hand to my mouth, hoping Amber and Parker hadn't heard me.

"Don't worry," Brie whispered. "They're too far ahead of us to hear anything."

She couldn't know that, I thought.

Brie gestured to the packed dirt trail. Because it was damp, we could easily follow their tracks.

The trail wound up the mountain in a steady incline. I felt it in my calves, still sore from our hike yesterday and traipsing around St. John this morning.

Halfway up the mountain, there was a fork. Neither was marked. "Which one?" Brie asked.

It had only taken us fifteen minutes to get to this point, so it was still light enough to see. We could continue south or turn right. The right path was steeper, the southern path narrower. Both looked partly overgrown.

"To the right," Brie said, answering her own question. "See? Their tracks."

Their footprints were clear in the damp soil. Parker had been wearing Top-Siders. I could see part of the Sperry logo clearly in several spots. Amber was wearing Chacos. I recognized the sandal pattern because I had a pair myself.

I was impressed. "Good eyes, Brie."

"When my dad played ball, he sent me to camp for summer. I learned some cool stuff."

Though sunset was still two hours away, the farther we went, the darker the trail became. In a few spots, a railing marked a particularly precarious edge. Other sections we navigated through dense bushes. The trail lights weren't on yet, and we had to pay careful attention so we didn't venture down an unmarked path. The resort's outdoor lighting turned on one hour before sunset, and I hoped these did as well. If they didn't, we'd have to use our cell phone flashlights to find our way back.

"Where does this trail go?" I asked Brie, my voice low partly because of the environment, and partly because I didn't know how far Amber and Parker were ahead of us.

"There's a vista point about three quarters of the way up. Then there are three trails. One is usually closed. It goes to the helipad and then Ethan Valentine's house beyond that. One goes over the mountain, past the lake, and then down to the West Beach—I've been there many times, but we usually take a boat back. The path is fine to go down, but it's really tough coming back up."

"The third trail?"

"To the Sky Bar."

I frowned. "This isn't the way we went up the other night."

"This is the longer scenic route."

"The dark and scary route," I muttered.

"It's pretty in the morning," Brie said.

Voices ahead had us stopping. Brie clutched my arm.

At first, we couldn't make out exactly what they were saying. I motioned for Brie to stay, and I slowly crept down the path, careful where I stepped, hoping to hear. Instead of staying, Brie followed me.

"You're just making this up as you go along, aren't you, Amber?" Parker said.

"I'm not making anything up," Amber snapped. "She wrote in code. It's an educated guess. Do you have a better idea?"

"Fine, but I swear, Amber, if we don't find those documents soon, you're going to pay."

"Oh, shut up," she said, her voice fading as they walked away.

I wanted to follow, but the trail both straightened and widened. We might be seen.

"What do you think?" I asked Brie.

"They're looking for the documents you overheard them talking about earlier."

"Right, but why would Diana hide documents outdoors? Wouldn't they get damaged?"

Brie shrugged.

Though I didn't know what they were looking for, they *had* stolen my book, and I wanted to see what they were doing. We continued up the trail until there was a fork.

"Where's the path that goes to the West Beach?" I asked.

She pointed. "It's off-limits at night. Too dangerous."

"So, which way did they go? They must be going to the Sky Bar, right?" I said. "If they're looking for papers, they'd be protected from the elements there." But they must be well hidden if no one on staff found them.

"Hold on," Brie said, and disappeared down the path leading to the beach.

She returned a full minute later.

"Don't do that again," I said.

"They went down there. We need to follow."

I bit my lip and looked around, trying to come up with an excuse to head back.

"Come on," Brie urged. "We have more than an hour before sunset, and nearly two before it's totally dark."

"Fine," I said reluctantly. "But we head back *before* official sunset. I don't want to get lost up here or fall off a cliff." And maybe I could salvage my evening with Jason.

Brie saluted and led the way.

"What's so important," I wondered out loud, "that Parker would come all the way to St. Claire to get it?"

Brie shrugged. "Money? Financial documents? Diana likes to blackmail people. Maybe she took something to blackmail him with."

Parker and Amber weren't here when Diana disappeared, so they weren't killers, but *would* they kill for these papers?

My head was spinning with the possibilities.

Fifteen minutes later, we hadn't caught up with them, couldn't hear them, and warning signs started to pop up along the path.

ST. CLAIRE TRAIL CLOSED AT SUNSET.

DANGER! STEEP DROPS AHEAD.

DANGER! NO SECURITY RAIL.

LAKE ACCESS WITH ST. CLAIRE PERSONNEL ONLY

"We need to go back," I said.

"Not yet," Brie said.

Did Brie have a death wish? I didn't. It's why I didn't hang glide, I obeyed all the rules of the road, and I paid attention to danger signs telling me that, well, something was dangerous.

Brie stopped abruptly, and I almost ran into her.

"Wh—" Then I almost stopped breathing.

Below us was the mountain lake we'd been warned to avoid. It was the most beautiful site on an island of beautiful sites.

The volcano was inactive and had been for thousands— maybe hundreds of thousands of years (I'd taken one geology class in college and hadn't paid much attention). Like Crater Lake in Oregon, but much, much smaller. To the east was a steep, smooth rock face that ended in the highest point on the island. To the west was a waterfall, the running water I'd been hearing for some time. The lush shorelines of the lake had trees and bushes of all sizes, untouched. It was like stepping back in time.

But what made this scene particularly gorgeous was the setting sun—it lit the cliffs in spectacular color, so bright and sparkly I was nearly blinded, considering the dark path from which we'd emerged.

"There's only one way to get out of the lake," Brie said reverently, as enamored as I was by the sight before us. She pointed toward the far southern shore, where there was an alcove. "I've been swimming over there—there's a cool lagoon. You can't quite see it from here. But most of the lake is off-limits because the waterfall is dangerous, especially after a storm. It goes straight down to the ocean."

I stared and saw a wire crossing the lake. I blinked; that couldn't be a zip line?

I followed the thick wire up until I saw a clearing only fifty feet away from us, with a metal and wood contraption where the wire was attached in multiple places, until it wound into one thicker wire.

"Hell no," I said.

Brie followed my gaze, then grinned. "Zip-lining! I was terrified my first time, too, but it's a lot of fun. You just have to remember to disengage the harness and let go between twenty and fifty feet from shore. Otherwise you hit land and could break something. But it is *so* thrilling."

"Never," I said. I estimated the distance from one side to the other to be at least three hundred yards—maybe more.

"The view is to die for," Brie said. "You have to try it. You land in that lagoon. From there, it's just a short hike to the West Beach, and a boat takes you back to the resort."

"Over my dead body," I muttered, then squinted and shielded my eyes from the sun. "Wait—are there people over there?"

Brie held her hand above her eyes, narrowed them. "They walked all the way around. Idiots! They're never going to get back up in the dark, not without risking their necks. They'll have to go the long way."

A flash of memory hit me. I pulled out my phone, but the

images Brie sent me hadn't all downloaded. "Brie—let me see your phone. The book."

She gave me an odd look, then took out her phone, brought up an album, and handed it to me, squeezing in to watch as I scrolled through the pages. There were fifty-seven photos, meaning Diana had written on fifty-seven pages—fifty-eight if I counted the page that was torn out. I stopped when I came to a page that had a word underlined. *Moon*. I remember when I saw this and thought it was strange to underline just a word. I flipped further and stopped. "There!"

Lagoon had also been underlined.

"I don't get it," Brie said.

"Diana underlined or circled random words in the book. What if they weren't random? We know her numbers stood for people on the island. What if the words she circled also mean something?" I gestured to the lake and noticed that the sun was rapidly falling, casting odd shadows around us. "There's another lagoon on the island. I've been there. It's closer to the resort." Unless Amber and Parker checked it out earlier, or lagoon was just one part of the code.

"There's at least a dozen words underlined," Brie said. "How do we know what they mean?"

"We should head back," I said. "Write them all out, and maybe the answer will be obvious."

"They already did that," Brie said, gesturing across the lake to the lagoon, where we could no longer see them. "They know what they're looking for."

"Diana was here for two days. Would she have come all the way up here to hide papers? She would have to retrieve them at some point, right?"

"Maybe, but Amber thinks they're up here."

"Or maybe she's trying to convince Parker of that. We're not going to get over there and back before dark. I certainly don't want to fall into the lake."

"You have a point," Brie conceded.

"The most logical place for any documents would be in her belongings that housekeeping packed up. That would be the first place to look. Amber didn't find the papers *or* the book, so she broke into the cottage where Diana had been—my room— thinking Diana hid something there."

"I'm with you. And?"

"Wouldn't you keep something important or valuable close to you? Maybe she was killed for the documents, and the killer has them."

"And Amber and Parker are on a wild goose chase?"

"It's possible." Which meant *we* were also on a wild goose chase.

"Or she *did* hide them and told Amber she hid them, which is why Amber's going through all these lengths to find them," Brie said.

"That's possible too," I agreed. "Logically, it would be a place someone wouldn't accidentally discover, yet easy for a guest to access."

I craned my neck, but Amber and Parker were no longer in sight. "Do you think they're okay?"

"Sure," Brie said. "There's another way up to the Sky Bar from the West Beach, but it's going to be a bitch of a hike, especially at night."

I didn't like those people, but I didn't want anything bad to happen to them. "If they're not back by the time we are, we should tell Tristan or Kalise where we saw them."

"They can sleep on the beach," Brie said. "Serves them right for being so sneaky."

"Let's not tempt fate," I said, pointing to all the danger signs. "We should go."

"Let's use the Sky Bar trail," Brie said. "The bar is closed tonight because of the cruise, but the road is easier to walk down and better lit."

"I'm all in," I said.

We backtracked until we hit the three-way fork, then headed north to the Sky Bar.

The path was mostly straight and flat. The ground lighting came on as we walked, and I noticed signs of construction—a clearing to the left, a large toolbox with a lock on it, and some orange netting to block off part of the area. A huge pile of branches and leaves was pushed to one side, weighed down by tarps.

"What are they doing up here?" I asked.

Brie shrugged. "My dad said something about building a cell tower. There's a couple other private islands in the area, and I guess they don't have good internet. St. Claire is in the middle and has the highest peak, so a cell tower would make sense. And give St. Claire better reception."

"I haven't had a problem with reception at the resort." But I remembered I'd had none when I shot my video review at the Sky Bar the other night.

"It's glitchy," Brie said, "but usually the rooms are fine. Anywhere else and it's hit or miss. Wow, look at the sunset."

Because of the clearing, we could see the ocean from the path. "It's sad that they're going to put a tower here," Brie said. "It'll totally ruin the view."

We watched as the sun brightened the western sky.

"Hey, want to take a selfie?" Brie said. She pulled out her phone and motioned for me to turn around.

I wasn't great at taking selfies, but Brie knew what she was doing, so we had fun with it. She took several photos and grinned. "See, you *can* lighten up."

"Can you take one of me so I can send it to my friends? And my Grams. She called me today and wants me to post more on social media."

Brie laughed. "My grandma doesn't even know how to use her smartphone."

"I taught Grams, and sometimes I think she knows how to use hers better than I do."

Brie took a few pictures. Then she said, "Okay, loosen up, relax. This isn't your senior portrait."

I rolled my eyes, and Brie laughed. "Oh, oh! Make a circle

with your arms. The sun is at the perfect angle! Okay—okay—take a step back. One more—got it! You're slaying it. Now squat and put your hand up like you're blowing a kiss, but face south. Yeah—lower your hand just a bit—great!"

"Are you studying photography in college?" I asked.

"Naw. Pre-med. Photography is a hobby."

"Pre-med?" I said. I don't know why that surprised me.

"Yeah. I want to cure cancer."

"That's really awesome."

Brie shrugged. "Somebody has to do it. Why not me?"

I stood, but my foot slipped. Then the rest of my body followed my foot, and I screamed.

CHAPTER
TWENTY-THREE

"We all do things we regret. It's part of growing up."

—Sue Grafton, *F Is for Fugitive*

I LANDED WITH A thud on a bed of damp leaves, which thankfully cushioned my fall but covered me in mud.

I looked up and at first couldn't see anything. Then the sky came into focus, a darkening blue as the sun was quickly disappearing.

The wind had been knocked out of me. I tried to call up to Brie, but no sound came out, just a strangled gasp. My ears rang as I took stock of potential injuries. My arms moved without pain. Good. Legs? Check. Neck? I moved it slowly back and forth. A little twinge, but nothing serious. I stretched, feeling my ribs, but there was no major pain indicating a cracked or broken rib.

"Mia? Mia!"

"I'm okay," I said, the words a whisper. I coughed, cleared my throat, and shouted up, "Brie? I'm okay!"

I stood, my feet sinking into the mud, my limbs heavy with it. Ugh.

"Can you climb out?" Brie asked.

"Maybe," I said. The hole was about twelve feet deep, but it was too wide for me to shimmy up. Even if Brie reached down,

I wouldn't be able to reach her hand, and the chances were high that I would pull her down with me.

I took out my phone and turned on the light, though it took me a couple of tries because my fingers were wet and slippery. I looked for a ladder, footholds, anything to hoist myself up and out.

Nothing.

I was stuck.

I did *not* want to be stuck. There had to be a way.

"Can you see a ladder up there? Remember the tools we saw? Go look there."

"I'll be right back."

Brie walked away. I stood in the muck feeling absolutely, totally, *completely* foolish.

"Mia?" Brie called a few minutes later.

"Don't come too close," I said. "I don't want you to fall, too."

"There's no ladder, no rope. Maybe if I lie down, I can pull you out?"

"No," I said. "It's too deep."

The hole was for the foundation of the cell tower. There had been orange warning mesh around the tools, but the mesh that was supposed to block off this hole? It was down here, at the bottom, where it did no good to warn anyone.

"You need to get help," I said. "Don't tell anyone we were following Amber."

"Of course not. I'll be as discreet as possible. We were on a hike, and it was getting late, so we cut through here. Total accident. Are you sure you're okay?"

"Nothing's damaged except my pride."

"It won't take too long," Brie said. "I'll try to get a cell signal at the Sky Bar. You have your phone? Light?"

"Yeah. It's at fifty percent. Go." The faster she got help, the faster I'd get out of here.

"Okay," Brie said, and then I heard nothing as her footfalls disappeared.

I wanted to cry. It was my thirtieth birthday, and I was stuck in a muddy hole at the top of a mountain when I *should* have been on a cruise with the sexiest man on the island.

I stared up at the sky that was now dark. Stars twinkled brilliantly, and if I hadn't been stuck in the bottom of a twelve-foot hole, I would have enjoyed them.

How foolish was I? I'd followed Amber and Parker deep into the island, two people who didn't like each other and had broken into my room and stolen my book. I went to St. John to talk to the police as if I, myself, were an investigator. I went on a bike with a kid I didn't know, following Sherry around the island. He could have left me in the middle of nowhere—or worse. I'd dragged an eighteen-year-old college girl into the middle of this mystery and put her in danger as well. I literally saw a dead body and thought I could solve the crime? Why was I more invested in finding out what happened to Diana—and what she had been doing on the island—than I was in exploring my feelings for Jason Mallory?

My imagination had not only gotten away from me, it had landed on Mars then taken a side trip to Jupiter. Gino Garmon wasn't a killer. He was the head of security. He'd been a Miami cop and was more than capable of working a murder investigation. And just because Diana Harden had paid a kid to take her to Ethan Valentine's dock didn't mean that he'd killed her. He probably wasn't even on the island. And all those people Diana might have been blackmailing? What if I was wrong? What if her shorthand had nothing to do with blackmail and was just nasty gossip?

CeeCee was a typical trophy girlfriend of an asshole fifty-year-old walking midlife crisis. I'd read far more into her offhand accounting comment than I should have. Who cared if she met with his ex-wife? Maybe the ex was just warning her away. Yet I was having my assistant in New York research Trevor Lance and Parker Briggs! I was wasting his time—and mine.

Who did I think I was? Miss Marple? Veronica Mars? I was more like the fumbling Clouseau, tripping my way into a pit.

But unlike the endearingly clumsy French detective, I was ill-equipped to solve the crime.

I was a grown woman with a grown-up job. I didn't have time for mai tais and sexy bartenders and solving crimes. This wasn't me.

I was Mia Crawford, CPA, Financial Planner: intelligent, responsible, diligent.

My name was going to be on the fucking *door*.

Tears burned, and I felt totally, one hundred percent sorry for myself.

I didn't want to be on the door. I would have no life. But if I didn't take the promotion, who was I?

Not knowing the future was far scarier than staying on the path I'd forged. It was safer to do what I'd always planned.

It felt like an hour since I'd fallen down here, literally hitting rock bottom, but when I looked at my phone, only fifteen minutes had passed since Brie left to get help. It was a good twenty-minute walk down the mountain, longer in the dark. So I shined the light around the hole and tried not to be squeamish. I pushed a bunch of fallen leaves into the corner and sat on them. The leaves and I slowly sank into the mud.

When I got out of here, I would tell security about Diana's book, that Amber stole it from my room, and what I thought Diana Harden had been doing. I'd show them the pages Brie photographed and tell them about the kid who brought Diana back to the island. Then I was done with playing Nancy Drew.

I had five more days on this island. Tomorrow morning I was going to forget all about Diana Harden and blackmail and Amber and cheating Trevor Lance. I was going to swim, drink, eat, and have sex with Jason Mallory. Maybe a five-night fling. I wanted to have sex on the beach, in the ocean, and in my hot tub. I wanted to get drunk and have fun and not think about Diana Harden.

Then I would return to the real world, accept my promotion, and forget all about St. Claire.

"MIA! MIA!"

It had taken Brie forty-two minutes to get down to the resort and return with help.

"Still here," I called from the pit.

The ground lighting on the trail above me cast odd shadows all around. Then the lights grew brighter, and someone shined a spotlight down into the hole. I shielded my eyes.

I heard Brie talking, but not what she said. Then several people came to the edge. "Hold tight, Ms. Crawford."

I couldn't see the face, but it sounded like Henry, the jack-of-all-trades from shuttle driver to bellhop to tour guide.

"Not much else I can do," I mumbled, then said clearly, "Thank you."

"We're going to lower a ladder down. Are you injured? Do you need help climbing up?"

"I'm okay. Just dirty." And cold and hungry, but I didn't say that.

A minute later, two men lowered a ladder and held it against the side of the hole. "Okay," Henry called. "I can come down and help."

"I'm fine," I said, and started up the ladder. Sore and bruised, but nothing was broken.

When I reached the top, two men I didn't recognize held out their hands and helped me climb out.

Tristan rushed over and said, "There was security netting blocking off this entire area! What happened?"

"It wasn't here," I said. I glanced at Brie. What exactly had she told them? "The netting ended over there." I gestured. "I'm sorry, I didn't see the hole. We were taking pictures, and—"

Why was I apologizing? It wasn't my fault. Sure, I was clumsy and didn't look where I stepped, but the netting ended twenty feet away.

"I am *so* glad you were not more seriously hurt."

Brie said, "We were on a hike, and it was getting dark, and I've been on this trail a hundred times, so I said let's cut through here and go back by way of the Sky Bar road."

"The resort is putting in a cell tower. It was supposed to be done before now, but we've had a few . . . well, you don't care about that. On behalf of St. Claire, I am *so* sorry."

That's when I saw Gino Garmon.

"Why were you up here in the first place?" Gino asked. "You were scheduled to be on the sunset cruise."

I was taken aback by his gruff tone.

"Um, I changed my mind," I said lamely.

He narrowed his eyes.

"Gino," Tristan said, "let's dial back the tone, okay? Ms. Crawford just went through a traumatic experience. This wasn't her fault."

Brie said, "Besides, it was all couples on the cruise. Mia and I thought it would be more fun to hang here."

"Of course, we completely understand. There is no reason to apologize, and we're blocking off this trail tonight. I'm so glad you weren't hurt."

I thought that the reason he might be upset had more to do with liability than my predicament. He'd given me three days free for finding a dead body; what would he give me for falling down an unmarked hole?

I walked stiffly toward the three golf carts that were at the head of the trail. We were much closer to the Sky Bar than I'd realized.

Henry said, "Mr. Dubois, Tim and I will close the trail and put up the netting tonight."

"Thank you," Tristan said. "Talk to me before you clock out, please."

Gino took my arm. "Let me help you, Ms. Crawford," he said with what I could only describe as a growl.

"I'm fine," I said, but he didn't let go as he ushered me quickly to one of the carts.

"Tristan, I'll take Ms. Crawford to the nurse to get checked out," Gino said.

"Thank you, Gino," Tristan said. "Ms. Crawford, please let me know if you need anything at all."

"I don't need a nurse," I said as Gino not-too-gently escorted me into the cart. He climbed into the driver's side, and I looked back at Brie. Her eyes widened, not quite sure what was going on. I willed her to hurry, but Gino drove off before she could catch up to us.

"Tell me what you were really doing up here," Gino said.

"I told you."

He was driving too fast down the mountain. Sure, the road was built for a wider shuttle, but the golf cart was small, no seat belts, and I could just picture us going off the edge. I didn't think we'd die . . . but it was definitely steeper than a twelve-foot drop into a muddy pit.

"Today I received a call from my good friend Juan Diego, the St. John police chief. I was shocked to learn that one of the guests from St. Claire had come in asking about Diana Harden's death. They didn't take your name—they have more important things to do than appeasing nosy Americans. But every man there noticed the pretty woman with honey-blond hair and big brown eyes. And you were one of only five guests who went to St. John today."

My stomach twisted like taffy as my life flashed in front of my eyes for the third time in one day. My dad, my Grams, and Jason, who I was supposed to have an island affair with before going back to my normal life. Was I going to die before I had sex with him?

"Stay out of my investigation," Gino snarled, interrupting my fear-induced fantasy. "This does not concern you, and if I find out that you lied to me about anything, there is nothing—nothing—I won't do to find out what you're really up to."

He pulled up at the resort and stopped the cart.

I didn't like being scared, but I also didn't like men who went out of their way to intimidate women. It took all my strength to look him in the eye when I said, "I don't know what you're talking about, Mr. Garmon. I'll walk to my cottage *alone*."

I got out, surprised my knees didn't completely buckle, and headed straight to my room.

I felt Gino's eyes on my back for a long, long time.

CHAPTER
TWENTY-FOUR

"One day you will kiss a man you can't breathe without, and find that breath is of little consequence."

—Karen Marie Moning, *Bloodfever*

WHEN I PUT MY nearly dead phone on the charger, I noticed four texts from Brie, each sentence a separate message.

> omg are you ok?
> seriously what a dick
> i can't come by my dad is NOT happy
> ttyl

The first two were sent thirty minutes ago when Gino pulled me away from the others. The last two were sent only a couple of minutes ago.

I felt bad putting Brie in this situation in the first place, but I was too overwhelmed by the events of the evening—of the last two days—to think about anything but a hot shower. I *really* needed to decompress.

The bathroom mirror was not my friend. Caked mud everywhere I could see, leaves in my hair, my dress—the first time I'd worn it—a lost cause, stained and torn. Why hadn't I changed when Brie and I decided to follow Amber and Parker? I loved this dress.

I turned on the glorious rain shower, stripped off my clothes and, near tears, threw everything in the trash. I stepped under the hot spray and winced when the water hit dozens of small cuts, but I didn't move until the water ran clear. Slowly washed my body and hair, thinking about what Gino had said and how his subtle threat both scared and angered me.

When I was stuck at the bottom of that damn hole, I'd been ready to turn over everything I had to Gino and Tristan and be done with it. But how could I turn over what I knew of Diana's book if Gino was the one who killed her? I didn't *know* he'd killed her. Maybe he was just a jerk. Yet he was pushing so hard on the theory that she'd been killed on St. John, maybe to divert attention away from him? And if I told him about the young teen who had brought Diana back to the island, would he be convinced that Diana had died on St. Claire—or would I put the kid in danger?

He had motive and opportunity, and his behavior was more than a little suspicious. He had purposefully intimidated me, and I couldn't discount his heated conversation with Amber *and* the argument Brie had witnessed between him and Diana. Plus the threat. *Especially* the threat. That he would do anything to find out "what I was up to" could just be macho crap, but it was the way he said it. He *wanted* to scare me.

And clearly, I couldn't trust his good friend Juan Diego, the St. John police chief.

Would Tristan listen to me? He had shown nothing but concern for my well-being and that of his staff and guests. My initial fear that he might be inclined to cover up a murder because it would be bad publicity seemed weak. It was more logical that he'd want a quick, quiet resolution to head off bad publicity. I needed to think how to approach him with what I knew.

Then there was Sherry. Where did her bizarre behavior fit in? I understood the insecurity and overprotectiveness toward her boyfriend. Some people are just wired to be possessive. But she'd really overstepped at the spa, then intimidating me on the ferry. She was up to something, but was it dangerous? Had

Diana blackmailed her so she hired that creepy guy on St. John to kill her?

While I was stuck about what I *should* do, I knew what I *shouldn't* do, so that was a plus, right?

Food. Sleep. Then maybe a solution would present itself in the morning.

I regretted picking up the damn book in the first place. If I'd never seen Diana's musings, never suspected blackmail, never followed Amber and Parker up the mountain, I would be naked with Jason Mallory right now.

When I stepped out of the shower, I felt more human. I dried off, lathered my body with lavender-shea body lotion, then brushed out my hair, leaving it wet down my back while I wrapped myself in one of the plush bathrobes.

A brisk knock on my door made me jump.

I held my robe tight against me and looked through the peephole.

Andrew Locke?

I opened the door. "Can I help you?"

"We need to talk about my daughter," he said. He made a move to come inside, then hesitated and asked, "May I?"

I nodded. He stepped inside and stood in the small sitting area, clearly uncomfortable. I offered an olive branch. "Brie is terrific," I said. "I like her a lot. We kind of bonded, I guess because we were both raised by our dads."

I was nervous, so I rambled. I could see why he might be upset that his daughter was hanging out with someone who got her in trouble with resort security.

"I don't want to make a big deal about this, but I'm very concerned about what happened tonight. My daughter says you were hiking, but she didn't tell me she was leaving the resort, and I didn't know where she was. She could have been hurt—you both could have been hurt. I talked to Tristan about the situation. He blames himself and staff for not clearly marking the pit. I don't blame you. It was an accident, and Brie wasn't injured. Still, I think you should minimize your time together."

I blinked, not knowing how to respond. He was chastising me in the nicest way possible, so there really was nothing to say. If he was over-the-top angry, I could easily point out that Brie was an adult and could make her own decisions about who she socialized with. But he was being a dad, and I thought about my own dad and how concerned he had been for my well-being. He would have done the exact same thing as Andrew.

So I nodded in agreement.

"Thank you, Mia."

I opened the door to let him leave, then said, "I really do enjoy spending time with Brie. This vacation is unusual for me, and I'm here alone. She's one of the few people who has made an effort to include me. I didn't mean to overstep."

"I appreciate that," he said, then smiled. "Brie is a great kid, isn't she? I know she's eighteen and going off to college, but she's still my little girl. She wasn't happy that I brought Sherry with us, but I'm hoping that now that we're getting married, she'll accept her. Sherry can't replace her mother, I know that—Brie knows that. It's a new beginning for both of us."

Brie's fears were right—Andrew had proposed to Sherry.

"Congratulations," I said automatically. "I didn't know you were engaged."

"Tonight. It was a bit spontaneous, but I've had the ring for a few weeks, and it seemed like the right time. I hope Brie can forge a relationship with Sherry like she did with you." He held out his hand, and I shook it. "I'm glad you're okay, Mia."

He left, and I closed and locked the door. Okay, that was a lot to unpack from a short conversation. *Steer clear of my daughter, she's a great kid, by the way I'm getting married.*

A little weird, but he was so nice about it. Did he think I was a bad influence? A small giggle escaped me. *Me*, Mia Crawford, doing anything that wasn't proper, legal, and right. I couldn't even have a successful one-night stand.

No, he was just worried about Brie and all the bad things that could have happened to her on an island that had already coughed up one dead body.

My head hurt. Tomorrow was soon enough to make decisions.

I had five minutes to order room service before they closed the kitchen. I should have been starving, but my stomach was still twisted in knots between Gino intentionally intimidating me and Andrew Locke playing protective dad and me being trapped in a muddy hole for what seemed like hours but was only forty-two minutes. I ordered a shrimp salad and bottle of pinot grigio because there was no way I wanted to go to either of the restaurants or the bar and eat alone. Or, worse, have people ask about what had happened.

I had a voicemail on my cell phone. Tears welled as I listened to Amanda, Braden, Jane, and her fiancé singing happy birthday. They laughed at the end, and I smiled through my tears.

"Thank God you didn't answer, or we would be on the next plane down to St. Claire!" Jane said.

"Love you, Mia!" Amanda trilled. "Take pictures! We need *all* the deets."

"Bye!" the four said in unison, and then there was silence.

A rush of complex and unexpected emotions ran through me as I stared at my phone.

I came to this island for a week of sun, sea, and sex. Everyone told me how easy it would be to find an unattached guy. Then there was Jason, who said he had plans for us tonight, who kissed like a dream, and instead of meeting him on a romantic cruise, I pursued two people because I thought they'd broken into my room and stolen my book.

Was I so insecure and unsure about my decision to let myself go wild that I intentionally sabotaged the one opportunity I had to enjoy the moment and not think about the future?

Except . . . I really detested people like Diana Harden who used people's faults against them. When I first read her notes, I'd admired her boldness and observations. Now I realized she was trouble. Not that most of the people she was blackmailing were any better than she was.

Then I thought of Anja Stockton, who had made a difficult

decision but ultimately what she felt was the best decision for her and her baby. She didn't deserve to be humiliated or blackmailed or threatened. What of the other people Diana was blackmailing? Maybe they made a mistake. Maybe there was more to their stories just like there was more to Anja's.

Then I thought of Sherry and whether the dirt Diana had on her had driven Sherry to murder.

Did Diana deserve to die for it? Why did I even care?

I stood in the threshold of the open sliding glass doors and listened to the waves. I heard music far away at the Blue Dahlia. Distant laughter. I realized in that moment that I *did* care. I didn't like what I knew about Diana Harden, but she didn't deserve to be strangled. I remembered the personal notes she'd written, about being lied to and betrayed. While that might not justify her actions, it made sense that she would want to expose liars and cheats.

What secret was so dark, so dangerous, that murder was the only answer to keep it hidden?

A knock on my door made me yelp. I chastised myself. It had to be the room service I ordered. Thinking about murder had me jumpy. I closed and locked the glass doors, then went to the peephole and did a double take.

Jason.

I opened the door. "I—Jason. Hi."

Smooth, Mia. Very smooth.

"Are you okay? I heard what happened tonight."

He tilted my chin up and looked at me closely. The intimacy of the gesture surprised and warmed me. "You're hurt." He touched one of the cuts on my cheek. "Did you see the nurse? I can send her over."

"I'm fine." My voice squeaked as his touch was more intimate and sweet than I expected. "I'm sorry I canceled on you tonight. I'm glad you're here."

"I can't stay," he said. "I wish I could." He seemed so concerned, like he really did care about me and what had happened.

"You have to work?"

"Tristan called a full staff meeting tonight. He wants to find out exactly how the hole was exposed and set up better safety protocols. It could have been so much worse. You're sure you don't need the nurse?"

"Nothing's broken. I just feel stupid and klutzy."

"It wasn't your fault."

He hadn't been there. He didn't know that Brie and I had been following two thieves.

"I certainly regret not going on the cruise."

"I missed you," he said with a small smile. His fingers were at the back of my neck, playing with my hair, then skimmed my jawline. I almost didn't breathe. I certainly didn't want him to stop. "I was walking through the kitchen and saw that you ordered room service, so I told the staff I'd bring it to you." He motioned to a cart next to him that I hadn't noticed. Because what red-blooded woman would notice *anything* when Jason Mallory touched her? "May I?"

I nodded, surprised and endeared and feeling romanced.

Jason wheeled in the cart and positioned it by the glass doors. "You can leave it outside when you're done. Staff does a round-up between midnight and one, and again in the morning."

"Thank you," I said.

"I'm glad you're okay," he said. "Happy birthday."

He looked at me as if he saw the whole me, inside and out. My stomach flipped, my lips parted, and I couldn't stop staring.

"I really want to stay," he whispered, his fingers caressing my cheek.

"I wish you could stay, too," I said with quiet confidence. Something about Jason . . . he brought out feelings in me I didn't know I had. A deep longing for something . . . *more*. For something different than I'd settled for in the past.

Someone who was perfect for me.

The thought crashed into me and I pushed it aside, because this was a vacation fling, not a permanent relationship. It couldn't be.

His slightly lopsided smile made those stomach flips jump higher into my throat.

Then he kissed me.

A self-satisfied sigh escaped my lungs as my eyes closed, and in that moment, it was just Jason and me. His hand on my face, his lips on my mouth, my head empty of every single thought I'd ever had. All I did was feel . . . then he adjusted the kiss, took it deeper, warmer, *hotter.* My hands went to his shoulders, then his neck, the ends of his hair, soft curls that wrapped around my fingers. He smelled so good, like coconut and bay rum and the sea.

"Mia," he whispered into my lips, then stepped back. His eyes were glassy, his breath had a hitch to it, and I knew then it wasn't just me. He felt it too, the attraction, an itch that I desperately wanted to scratch. "I don't want to go."

"I don't want you to go."

"I have to. Dammit."

"Duty calls."

Then he pulled me against him, and this wasn't *just* a kiss. This was . . . *more.* More passion, more need, more intimacy. He pressed his body against mine, and I felt every muscle, every rock-solid piece of him, and he moaned.

"Damn," he whispered. "Tomorrow." Another kiss. "I promise."

"I'll hold you to it," I whispered, and let my hands fall to my side.

He looked at his watch, swore again, kissed me again. "If I don't leave now, I'll have hell to pay."

"Go." *Stay.*

"Sweet dreams, Mia." And he left.

I loosened my robe because I was overheated. Damn was right. I hadn't been kissed like that in a long, long time. Ever. I had never been kissed with such intensity that I believed every second the man truly, fully wanted to be with me.

It was terrifying and one hundred percent thrilling.

I poured the wine, took a long swallow. Forced my heart

rate to slow. It took a minute. Okay. Tomorrow. Anticipation was supposed to be good, right?

Damn Tristan Dubois calling a nighttime staff meeting. Otherwise Jason and I would have been making love right now.

I sat down and poured more wine, then took the domes off the plates. The shrimp salad made my stomach growl. I was hungrier than I thought. The second plate was bread and butter. And the third was a small fruit tart with a card addressed to me.

I opened the envelope.

Dear Mia,

I have tomorrow night off. Meet me at the dock at 6 pm for your belated—and private—sunset cruise. You won't regret it.

Love, Jason

I don't know why I kept staring at the *Love, Jason.*

We had nothing in common. He was a bartender who took risks, had no future plans. No plan for disasters.

I didn't take risks. I had my future planned from now until I died. I had plans for every imaginable disaster.

He lived in paradise. I lived in New Jersey and commuted to New York because it was cheaper than a New York apartment.

Love, Jason was just a signature, like I might write on a note to a friend. Casual. It meant nothing.

But that kiss, that perfect, delicious kiss, meant something. That kiss was . . . damn. It was everything I have ever wanted in a kiss. It was the kiss to end all kisses. The kiss I had been waiting for my entire life.

No man has ever kissed me like Jason Mallory.

And when I left St. Claire, I knew I'd never find a man who could.

CHAPTER
TWENTY-FIVE

"Life is infinitely stranger than anything
which the mind of man could invent."
—Sir Arthur Conan Doyle, *A Case of Identity*

AN ANNOYING, STEADY NOISE broke into my subconscious, pulling me out of a deep sleep. I groaned, managed to open my eyes a slit and look at the digital clock. 8:03.

I put a pillow back over my head, but a knocking noise cut through the layers of feathers and cotton.

I sat up, dropped the pillow, and heard my name outside the glass doors. I'd lowered the blinds, hoping to sleep. My entire body ached as I pushed the button to open the blinds.

Brie stood there and motioned for me to open the door.

My knees creaked as I hobbled the ten feet over to the door and opened it. I turned and shuffled back to the bed and collapsed, face-first.

"I'll make coffee." Brie walked over to the kitchenette.

"You shouldn't be here." My voice was scratchy.

"I'm *so* mad at my dad," Brie said. "I didn't know he was going to talk to you until Sherry told me. I would have come last night, but we got into it and—well—they're getting married."

She blinked back tears.

"He told me," I said.

"I told him it wasn't okay to act like a Neanderthal and embarrass you, embarrass *me*, like he did."

"He was nice and apologetic, but worried. He's right—if you'd fallen and were hurt—"

"I didn't, and I wasn't, and you weren't, and I swear Gino made a much bigger deal about it than it was."

"Why did Gino talk to your dad anyway?"

"Because he's a jerk."

I told her what Gino had said to me driving back to the resort yesterday and the veiled threat.

"That's so totally messed up," Brie said.

"Your dad's right. You can't be in the middle of this, and he doesn't even know what we're doing. Unless you told him?" I was relieved when Brie shook her head, though in some ways I wanted a neutral third party to assess what we knew.

"Nope. My dad is a great guy, but he's very much law and order. Let the authorities handle it, he'd say, and then totally side with Gino because he's in charge."

"What do you think of Tristan?" I asked.

Brie shrugged. "He's fine. I don't really *know* him. You'd think he was fake, always asking is everything good, are you happy, please come back, can we get you anything else to make your visit perfect. Total kiss-ass. But he's also nice when he doesn't have to be. Like last night, he drove me back, and he seemed genuinely interested in me, not in a creepy way." She paused. "After Ethan Valentine bought the island and renovated everything, and it was our first time back, Kalise told my dad that she and Tristan had a lot of autonomy to make the resort work, but if it failed, there would be no second chance. I think you falling in the hole really shook him up."

I understood Valentine's thoughts on the matter. He was an entrepreneur and would expect success; he wasn't in hospitality, so he would keep on or hire the best people to run the business. If it failed, you cut your losses. You don't pour good money after bad. You don't factor in sunk costs when making a business decision. It was a rule of thumb I followed when I gave advice to my clients.

"It's a lot of pressure, but this year Kalise seems more at ease, so I think things are going well. And the resort is sold out for the next year."

"How do you know?"

Brie grinned. "People say a lot of shit around me when they don't know I'm listening."

"Was the resort thriving before Valentine bought it?"

She shrugged. "It was old. A bunch of rooms couldn't be rented because of plumbing issues, and the cottages were crappy. But the beach is gorgeous, and the pool has always been nice, and it's private. We came because Dad and I have a lot of memories here. Now, in addition to the resort getting a total facelift, they also have more stuff to do—the Sky Bar is new, they put in more trails, completely redid the cottages, have the sunset cruises, the luau, fishing trips, better food, expanded the spa. Tomorrow we're going to an uninhabited island and snorkeling. I did it last year, and it was awesome. You should come."

I hesitated, thinking about how her father might not approve.

Brie seemed to know what I was thinking and said, "My dad and Sherry are coming. And—" She bit her lip and looked at her mug.

"And?" I prompted when she didn't finish her sentence.

"I need to find out what Sherry is up to. Like, Tristan acts fake but he isn't? She acts authentic, but it's a lie. She doesn't love my dad, but he doesn't see it. He's lonely because I'm leaving, and that's why he proposed. She says what he wants to hear."

"She seduced him."

"Yes! He's not that old—only forty-two. I'm not opposed to him remarrying, just not *her*."

I wondered if I believed that. Brie might not think any woman was good enough for her dad. It had just been the two of them since she was five. Still, Sherry's background and behavior *were* suspicious.

"Maybe you should talk to your dad about how you feel," I said.

Brie snorted. "Yeah, nope. Awkward."

"It doesn't have to be. Maybe something along the lines of, 'Dad, I want you to be happy, but I don't think Sherry's the woman who can do that for you.'"

She blanched. "Oh, God, no." She shivered as if imagining the conversation. "Anyway, maybe you can help."

"Me? How?"

"Break them up."

I laughed. I couldn't help it. "That's not me."

"I don't mean throw yourself at him," Brie said with an eye roll, "but find something on her."

"We already did."

"But he *knows* all that. I mean, she made it sound totally normal that she's divorced from one rich guy and that her second rich husband is dead from 'natural causes,'" she said with air quotes. "But it's *so* not normal. I think she blew through all her money, so she's hunting the Next Rich Guy to support her. I can't let that be my dad."

"You think Diana knew something about Sherry that she didn't want your dad to know?" I asked.

Brie nodded and pulled out her phone. She read, "'Money or love? Money, of course—he's worth a small fortune. Does he know all the dirt on his new girlfriend?'"

It was one of the first comments Diana had written, followed by financial details.

"This is my dad," Brie continued. "She's talking about my dad and Sherry. Using your code, Sherry would be number 1913—she wrote that number twice. Did you notice this?" Brie turned her phone to face me.

Diana had written: Small fortune from 1913 with patience.

"What if," Brie said, "Diana approached Sherry and blackmailed her? Remember when I told you that Sherry and I went to the spa Saturday and saw Diana there?"

"Yeah," I said, vaguely remembering the conversation.

"Well, Sherry was tense and told Diana they'd catch up later."

"And you asked if she knew her." The conversation was coming back to me. "She said a business thing years ago and changed the subject."

"Exactly. But what kind of business? Sherry has an interior decorating company in Arizona and does next to nothing with it, and Diana sold antiques in New Orleans or something. But they're the same age. Look at this."

Brie flipped through her screenshots and found one she had highlighted, turned her phone so I could read.

There was a symbol that looked vaguely familiar, like Greek letters, and then Diana had written: Wedding bells in the near future. For old times' sake I'll wait to get paid. Can't wait to tell my #1.

"I think #1 is Amber," Brie said.

"I think you're right," I said. "She mentioned her #1 being late."

"These are Greek symbols. Delta Gamma. A sorority. So I did a little research."

"They went to the same college."

"No, but they are both thirty-two *and* members of the same sorority, though different colleges. They could have met, or known of each other, right? And Diana must have known something serious about Sherry." Brie paused, then added, "Do you think Sherry killed her?"

I had been suspicious of Sherry because of her actions. But now that Brie said it out loud . . . maybe.

"I don't know," I finally said. "If the secret was bad enough?" I rubbed my eyes and poured more coffee. "I followed her yesterday on St. John."

"Yeah, you told me. She gave some sketchy guy cash."

"That, and on the ferry coming back, it was just her and me, and she told me to leave her family alone."

"That woman!" Brie exclaimed. "I'm not her family. I can't let her marry my dad. I need to tell him about the creep."

"We don't have proof. We barely have circumstantial evidence. Maybe if we can find evidence that she knew Diana and didn't say anything? Yet, that seems weak."

"Going to St. John yesterday? Totally *not planned*. And she didn't come back with anything—no shopping spree. She told my dad she went sightseeing, but she was paying off some guy? For what?"

"I don't know." I sounded like a broken record. "Don't say anything, because we don't have enough information. I can possibly look at her finances, but I have to think about how to do it."

"I can get you anything you want."

"I can't legally access her accounts without her permission, and I'm not going to lose my license. There are some things that are public record. I just don't know if I'll be able to find something to help make your case."

"I don't want her to kill my dad," Brie said. "And I really think she might if she doesn't get everything she wants."

Her fear sounded real.

"Let me see what I can learn," I said. "We have time before the wedding, right?"

"They're talking about August, right before I go to college. *Six weeks* from now."

"That's fast."

"Way fast. That's why I need you to break them up."

"Brie—"

"Not seduce my dad or anything."

"Oh, darn," I said sarcastically and rolled my eyes.

"But she really doesn't like you. Maybe we can find a way to make her explode so my dad sees her for who she is. I'll think on it."

I changed the subject and asked, "How do we find out if Ethan Valentine is on the island? Maybe his uncle Luis?"

Brie shrugged. "Luis is great, but he's kind of . . . I don't know, an odd old guy. He talks in riddles half the time. Kalise thinks he's going senile. She worries about him."

"I didn't see signs of senility," I said. I knew enough of my Grams's friends and neighbors in her senior housing to know the ones who were just forgetful and those who showed early signs of Alzheimer's. "Would Tristan have his schedule?"

"Oh, I'm sure."

"Maybe we can access it."

"Why?"

"If Ethan Valentine was here Sunday, Diana might have spoken to him. He may be the last person to see her alive."

"You think he killed her?" Brie exclaimed.

"No. I don't know. I don't know *him*. But she went to his private dock and then was never seen again. Maybe he was home and told her to get lost or get off the island because she violated his privacy. Or maybe he wasn't home." I thought a moment. "What do you know about how the resort office runs?"

"They don't have a big staff. It's Tristan, Kalise, and two others, I think, full-time in the office. Then security. There are three security officers on duty at a time, but they're stationed in a different building."

"We need information."

"You want to break in."

"Maybe." I couldn't believe I was suggesting something so . . . sneaky.

"Great idea. I'm in."

"We could get in trouble."

"Only if we get caught." Brie jumped up. "Let me find out who's in the office and when they leave, and I'll text you."

"I just want to find out Ethan Valentine's schedule," I said. "If he was there, then I think we need to go to the authorities and tell them about the kid who brought Diana back to the island. And if he wasn't, I want his contact information. Maybe with all his resources, he can figure out why she went to his house."

AFTER BRIE LEFT, I dressed and headed to the Blue Dahlia. The crepes cart was gone, but I grabbed a muffin and coffee from the buffet, then sat down in the corner and reread my notes. I resolved to gather as much information as I could about Diana Harden and her book, then talk to Luis and Tristan and figure out if we should take the information to the reclusive resort owner.

On my phone, I scrolled through Diana Harden's Instagram page. Diana hadn't posted much from the island, only five pictures in the two days she was here. But they told a story. I just didn't know exactly what story.

A photo of her painted toes while she lay on a beach recliner, the brilliant ocean beyond.

One of the resort—a rather boring straight-on shot, the resort looking like a mansion surrounded by trees.

A white dahlia in a vase, clearly taken in the bar, with the focal point a wasp in the center. It was the most artistic shot.

A woman smoking alone behind the resort. I couldn't see her face, and the shadows hid details, but she was very skinny with short hair and looked like she was wearing a St. Claire uniform.

The last photo was taken at night, and it took me a minute to realize that it was taken from the end of the dock, facing the resort, trying to get in as much of the island as possible, but without focusing on any one detail.

The one oddity was that all the pictures had been posted the same day—Sunday. But that didn't mean she'd taken them on the day she disappeared.

None of the pictures were captioned, so no clues there. I guess it's supposed to be artistic to just post a picture without captions or hashtags, but it was annoying when I needed more clues as to who Diana was blackmailing—and where she'd hidden the documents that Amber and Parker were looking for.

I looked around the bar, and it took a minute, but I found the vase that was in Diana's photo. I inspected it. Maybe she left clues in these locations? I picked up the vase; it was heavier than it appeared. Nothing underneath—no writing, paper, message of any kind. I put it back down. Either I was way off track, or Amber had already found any message Diana had left.

"Lose something?"

I jumped, whirled around, and put my hand to my heart. "Luis! You startled me."

He grinned. "Sorry. Come have a drink with me?"

"It's ten in the morning."

"Island time," he said, and I followed him to the bar.

Callie came over and said, "What can I get you, Luis?"

"Coffee with a splash of Jack, por favor."

Callie put a mug on the bar, filled it with rich-smelling coffee, and poured Jack Daniel's into an oversized shot glass. She smiled at me. "Same?"

"Just the coffee, with sugar."

Callie placed a steaming mug in front of me, and I savored the smell before I sipped.

Luis's "splash" was the entire shot.

Maybe I wouldn't have to sneak around the office if I could get Luis to talk.

Keeping my voice low, I asked, "I have a couple questions?"

Why was I so nervous?

"I might have answers," he said with a smile.

"Well, I, um." I cleared my throat. "I was curious if you had a run-in with Diana Harden. The guest who ended up killed?"

That sounded *so* bad.

"A run-in? I don't know what you mean."

"Well—when I went to St. John yesterday, I uncovered some information that I don't think the police know."

"Oh?"

I couldn't tell if he was just being polite or was really interested.

"I found a boy who said he brought Diana to Ethan Valentine's dock on Sunday evening. Around sunset."

"Aww. I see."

But he didn't elaborate. So I continued. "Ethan Valentine is your great-nephew?"

"Yes, that he is."

"I was reading a book the other day, the book someone took from my room. Someone—I think Diana—had written in the margins, and there was a reference to you being nosy. She wrote it, not me!" I added quickly.

He laughed, and I was relieved I hadn't insulted him.

"Yes, I see why she might think so."

But again he didn't elaborate.

"And, well, because Diana went to Valentine's dock, I wondered if you had seen her. Or maybe Mr. Valentine is on the island."

"Mr. Valentine." Luis laughed, his eyes sparkling. "Oh, my dear boy Ethan."

Odd comment. "Was he at his house Sunday night? Maybe . . . well, I'm not insinuating anything, just that he might know something."

"He wasn't home," Luis said. "But I saw Ms. Diana."

"You did?" That shouldn't surprise me, since Brie said Luis lived in Ethan's house on the cliffs. But why didn't the police know?

"Yes. She walked up the stairs. I said hello. She wasn't very nice. She pounded on the door, and I said no one was home. She did not take the information well and left."

"But you were there," I said, partly confused.

"Yes, I was enjoying the sunset from the deck. Maybe you can join me one night before you go. There is no better view on the island, and this island has many beautiful views."

"That's very kind of you," I said. I bit my lip. "Did you tell anyone that you saw Diana that night?"

"Of course."

When he didn't say anything else, I prompted, "The police?"

"Police? No. No one asked. I didn't really think about it until after her body was found. Then I told Gino, of course."

Had Gino told St. John police? Why would he, if he was the one who killed her? Most of the evidence against Gino was barely circumstantial; this was damning.

Trevor Lance rushed into the bar. He looked exhausted, and also angry.

He immediately came over to me. "Mia, right?" he demanded.

"Yes," I said automatically.

"Where's CeeCee?"

He encroached so far into my space I saw the vein pulsing in his neck.

"I—I don't know?"

"Do you or don't you? You went to St. John with her yesterday, and she never came back. What happened?"

My mouth opened, but I had no words.

Callie came over. "Mr. Lance, can I get—"

He put his hand up to silence her. That rude gesture settled my nerves. "Trevor," I said, "I did not go to St. John *with* CeeCee. We were on the same ferry. That's it."

"She told me you two were going shopping and having lunch and would be back late. That was fine because I had work to do. But she never came back. The captain said she didn't return, and I swear, if you don't tell me where she is, I'll—"

Jason came up behind me and put his hand out, effectively forcing Trevor to take a step back. "Tristan told me that he's in contact with St. John police," Jason said. "Gino, our security chief, is retracing her steps. We'll find her."

"Like you found Diana Harden?" Trevor snapped.

He was more angry than worried, I realized.

"Did you and CeeCee have an argument?" I asked before I realized I'd opened my mouth to speak.

Both Jason and Trevor stared at me, surprised that I'd asked.

"We have not, though that's not your business."

"Then why are you so angry? Maybe you should go to St. John to look for her."

He reddened. "You have some explaining to do—"

"Ms. Crawford doesn't owe you anything, Mr. Lance," Jason said firmly. "You will back off, and if you have any questions, speak with Tristan."

Trevor looked like he wanted to hit Jason. Then he stormed off.

Jason said to Callie, "Call Tristan. Tell him what just happened."

She nodded and got on the phone.

He looked at me, his green eyes clouded with concern. "You okay? He didn't hurt you, did he?"

I shook my head. "What happened? Is she really missing?"

"I don't know the details. Tristan has been on the phone with everyone he can think of today. You were friendly with her?"

"We talked a couple times. She was outgoing and very nice." I bit my lip.

"What are you thinking? Did she say something? Did Lance hurt her?"

I shook my head. "I don't know. But—yesterday I was on a bike taxi getting a, um, tour around the island," I fibbed, "and I saw her having lunch with a woman who I think is Trevor's ex-wife."

Jason looked confused. Then his eyes narrowed. "How certain are you?"

"I saw an older photo. Brie and I were being nosy about Trevor and CeeCee and looked him up. I'm almost positive it was her."

"I'll tell Tristan. You don't have to be in the middle of this." He rubbed his hands up and down my arms. "You're shaking."

"That was just so unexpected. I'm better now."

"It was completely out of line. He won't be allowed back."

"Must be nice that Tristan trusts your opinion."

Jason smiled. "I'm a good judge of character. But management listens to employees. It's something I appreciate. Otherwise I might not have stayed here so long." He kissed me. "You sure you're okay?"

He kissed me in public. At the bar. Where everyone could see. He wasn't worried about getting in trouble with management? "Yeah," I said, not quite knowing what to make of this. "I'm looking forward to tonight."

"Me, too." He kissed me again. "I'm going to help Tristan and Gino find CeeCee, and let Tristan know who she had lunch with. I don't know if it matters, but we'll get to the bottom of it. Six tonight. Don't be late."

"I won't," I said, and smiled as he left.

I turned, expecting Luis to still be sitting on the stool, but he was gone.

I asked Callie, "Where did Luis go?"

She shrugged. "I didn't notice. Probably going down for his late morning nap." She smiled. "He really just comes and goes. Sometimes I don't see him for days. Other times he sits under a tree for hours at a time. He's odd, but I really love him. St. Claire wouldn't be the same without Luis."

CHAPTER
TWENTY-SIX

"A successful theft is an anonymous act.
The absence of a mark."
—V. E. Schwab, *The Invisible Life of Addie LaRue*

I CALLED THE SPA to see if I could get in before my date with Jason tonight. They were completely full, but the receptionist said if I wanted a mani-pedi, I could come in at five, when they usually closed. I thanked her but declined—I didn't want to be late meeting Jason. Instead, I signed up for a yoga class that started in an hour, then went to the gift shop and bought presents for my friends, Grams, and my cat-sitter. Trina promised to ship them the next morning.

I rounded the corner toward the yoga studio, figuring I'd go early to stretch and relax, and nearly ran into an upset Doug.

"Hey," I said. "Are you okay?"

He blinked and sighed. "It's been a long day."

It was not even eleven in the morning.

I didn't forget how kind Doug had been when I first arrived. I hated seeing anyone so sad, especially in such a beautiful place.

Putting aside my yoga plans, I linked my arm in Doug's and said, "Coffee?"

He glanced at me like a sad puppy. "Maybe a Bloody Mary?"

"Sure."

We walked to the poolside bar. This early it wasn't crowded, mostly young families with kids enjoying the pool. We walked across the bridge that led to the bar—at this bar you could sit out on a platform in the middle of the pool, or swim up and drink. We were the only ones at the bar.

The bartender—older, brown skin, close-cropped white hair and a neatly trimmed mustache—came over with a smile.

"Hi, Charlie," Doug said. "Two Bloody Marys, please?"

"Coming up, Mr. Butcher."

"Doug. I told you, *Doug*."

Doug smiled and turned to me as Charlie made the drinks. "I absolutely *do not* want to come back here."

"What happened?"

"What *hasn't* happened? Five years we've been coming here, and now David gets his nose out of joint because we're hanging around with our friends *too much*. *Literally* that's why we come, and he's never had a problem with it before."

"Have you talked to David about it? Does he have a specific reason it's bothering him this time?"

"No, because David doesn't like to discuss. He likes to direct. Inform. Explain. Assume."

"What exactly did he say, Doug?"

"Nothing!"

I waited until Charlie put the Bloody Marys in front of us. I wasn't a big tomato juice girl. I picked the celery out of the large plastic cup and bit it, sampling the mix. Okay, not bad. I took a small sip.

Doug drained a third of his before putting his cup down.

I said, "I'm not married, and I haven't been in a serious relationship in a while, but are you sure David didn't say something? Maybe he didn't explain in detail, but he must have said *something* for you to think he's not happy."

"Literally, he said, 'Why are we spending all our time with Jim and Josh?' And we're not."

"Name three things you've done with just David."

"I don't understand what you mean." He sounded snippy.

"Maybe he wants more alone time."

"We're social animals. We *like* people."

"Maybe you're more social than David?"

"It's why he loves me," Doug said defensively. "Because if it weren't for me, David would be all work, no play."

"Consider that maybe he's more introverted, and introverts need their downtime. I'm speaking from experience here," I added. "Being around too many people, always having to be *on*, is exhausting."

Doug frowned, bit into his thick bacon slice and chewed.

"You didn't answer my question. Are you saying you and David have done nothing alone?"

"Of course not." He pouted.

"Well?"

"We enjoyed our hot tub last night. Alone."

"That's one."

Doug wrinkled his nose. "We went on a hike Wednesday afternoon. It was lovely. Then—" He stopped.

"Then what?"

"Well, Jim and Josh were heading to the gym, and we joined them."

"Planned?"

"No, and I don't even *like* going to the gym. I suggested it because David complains if he doesn't work out every day."

"That's one and a half things," I said.

"Why doesn't he just talk to me?"

"You should talk to him," I said. I thought of all the misunderstandings between people I knew—misunderstandings that would be resolved if one person just stepped up and asked a question.

"I shouldn't have to," he muttered.

"No one said marriage is easy," I said. I thought of Anja and Nelson and how supportive they were of each other during a really difficult time. I thought of Henry and his wife creating a second life working here on the island after their kids grew up. And how Braden and Amanda completed each other.

But I wasn't married and had never been in that serious a relationship. Most of what I absorbed came through romance novels, and they were fiction, hardly manuals for a successful long-term relationship.

"Just saying," I continued, "you could be right, and David could be right, or you could both be half-right. But if you don't work it out when the problem arises, then your frustrations will fester. Basically—you shouldn't be here talking to me. You should talk to your husband."

I couldn't believe I was giving relationship advice. Me, Mia Crawford, whose last relationship lasted a year only because we saw each other twice a month, at most.

I gave good advice, though.

"You're right," Doug said.

"Go," I said.

He drained his Bloody Mary and gave me a hug. "You're good people, Mia."

"You too."

Alone, I sipped my drink and enjoyed the sights and sounds of the kids in the pool. I'd missed the yoga class because of my impromptu meet with Doug, but I enjoyed people-watching here at the pool bar since it wasn't crowded.

"Another?" Charlie asked, motioning to my empty Bloody Mary.

"I'm good for now," I said, and ate the last of my celery.

I thought about Adam. Why hadn't I cared when we split? Because I didn't care about *him*? I liked him . . . but I didn't feel deeply for him. I never really put my heart on the line because I didn't care what happened between us.

I cared what happened with Jason. Even knowing it was short-term, I felt something deep inside I couldn't explain.

I thanked Charlie and rose from my seat. Then I spotted Amber Jones walking briskly down the beach from the north shore, near where Diana's body had been found. She looked a mess, far from the classy actress I'd met on the ferry three days ago. In fact, she wore the same clothes she had on when Brie and I followed her last night. She would've had to circumnavigate most of the island to come back from the north. Had she been in the jungle all night? Where was Parker Briggs? I meant to tell someone that Brie and I had seen them on the opposite side of the lake. Then it completely slipped my mind after I fell into the pit.

I made a beeline toward Amber. She didn't see me at first, almost walked right into me, then stopped as if just realizing I was approaching her.

"Amber, what happened?" I asked.

She poked me in the chest. "You!"

"Me?"

"Don't think I don't know what you're doing, *Mia*." She said my name like it was a curse.

"What did I do?"

She narrowed her eyes. "Where is it?"

Was she talking about the book? I was certain she and Parker had taken Diana's book from my room. Was I wrong about that?

"Where's what?"

"You know what I'm talking about! Don't play stupid."

"I really don't." I felt hot and cold at the same time. If not them, then who took the book?

"You found the file, didn't you? I swear, if you don't give it back, I'll—"

"File? What file?" I said, more angry than intimidated. And wholly confused. I didn't even know what the documents Diana had hidden were. Why on earth would Amber think I had them?

She growled, fists clenched, and stomped her feet in the sand, then winced. I noted then that she wore no shoes, and her feet were cut up.

"Amber, I don't have what you think I have," I said.

"I don't believe you," she whispered.

"You stole my book," I said, deciding to lay it all out.

I paused a beat, waiting for her to deny it or explain; she did neither.

"We both know that Diana was blackmailing people on the island," I said. "But *I didn't find anything*. Whatever Diana was up to, she didn't leave very good clues. So go ahead, keep it, I don't care. But you might think about what was going on with her, because *someone* killed her. And if you didn't know already? Everyone who was on the island Sunday *is still a registered guest*."

Except CeeCee, I realized as if I'd been stung. CeeCee had disappeared yesterday. Just like Diana. Was she dead . . . or was she fleeing? Fleeing Trevor . . . or running from the law because she was a killer?

Amber stared at me with a flash of concern. Then she said, "Just stay out of it. This really doesn't concern you." She hesitated, then softened her voice. "And if you *do* find the file, I will make it worth your while to return it to me."

"What's so important about this file?"

"Let's just say Diana took something that neither of us quite understood the value of. And I need to get it back as soon as possible."

To give to Parker, I thought but didn't say. Diana took a file from Parker, and he needed it back before he met with his father on Monday, I deduced. Diana and Amber had been in on it from the beginning, but didn't realize the repercussions of their actions. Did they intend to blackmail Parker? My guess was yes. Or . . . maybe they intended to blackmail someone else with the contents of Parker's file. But with Diana dead and the file missing, Amber was on the hot seat.

"Like I said, I don't have any files. Good luck."

Amber stomped off.

"What was that all about?" Brie came up behind me, making me jump.

I told her what Amber said and what I thought it meant. "I think she was out all night."

"She looked it," Brie said. "Come on, we don't have much time."

"For?"

"You want to know how to find Ethan Valentine? We have to do it now. There's a staff meeting in five minutes. It's our best chance to get into Tristan's office and find Valentine's contact information."

I hesitated, realizing this whole thing was quickly getting out of hand.

"What?" Brie said. "I thought this was the plan."

"Yeah, but—"

"No buts. We're doing this." Then she turned and started walking as if she knew I would follow her.

Which I did.

CHAPTER
TWENTY-SEVEN

"Being dead means never having to do
anything sneaky."

—Lawrence Block, *Burglars Can't Be Choosers*

I WAS NERVOUS. I HAD never broken into someone's office before.

Brie led me through the main lodge. The administrative offices were in a one-story building south of the lodge, attached by a portico. Two golf carts were parked under the roof.

"Wouldn't a staff meeting be in the offices?"

"Too many staff. They're in the library on the second floor."

That stopped me. "There's a library? Like, shelves with books and comfy chairs and quiet music?"

"Yeeeaaah." Brie eyed me suspiciously. "It's open to guests, except when they have staff meetings."

"Wow."

"Not now. I'll show you later if you want."

"I wish I'd known."

"Focus, Mia."

I redirected my attention to the administrative building. It looked closed.

"How are we going to get in?" I looked around. The main door was visible to anyone who walked by, from both the roundabout and any of the south-facing windows. "Anyone could see us walk through the door."

"Stop being so obvious!" Brie snapped. "Just chill. There's

more than one entrance. We're going to walk by, then take the trail on the other side of the building to the back."

"The security office is on that side."

"They're in the staff meeting too, except for one guy. As long as we don't bring attention to ourselves, he won't even notice us."

"And if he does?"

"The path curves around the back of the resort. We're just going for a walk on this beautiful day."

Brie linked her arm in mine, and I groaned. "I hate this plan."

"Trust me."

I didn't really have a choice at this point.

"Where is everyone?" I asked as I realized I didn't hear voices or laughter or splashing in the pool.

"Staff meeting. Told you."

"No, like, everyone else."

"Oh. Well, there's a scuba lesson at the dock, and Kalise took a group hiking up to St. Claire Lake. But you're right, it's quiet."

"You seem to know everything that's going on."

Brie shrugged. "Like I said, we come here every year, and it's not a big island."

One person sat at a desk in the security office. He looked up when we walked past. I froze. Brie smiled and waved to him, and we kept walking.

He waved back, practically blushing. He was young, couldn't be more than twenty, I thought, and I noticed Brie had straightened her spine and tucked her long hair behind her ear as we walked by.

Brie had more natural flirtatious charm than I did.

"You going out with him?" I whispered.

"No," she said curtly, but glanced at him. So did I. He immediately looked down at his desk, pretending to be busy.

"He's cute."

She shrugged, then steered me to a patio attached to the administration building. Neatly trimmed flowering hedges grew under the windows and vines spiraled up lattices attached to the stucco.

Brie immediately grabbed the knob and opened the side door.
"They don't keep it locked?" I asked.

"Shh," she said, and we stepped inside. The door swung closed
behind us.

We stood in what appeared to be a staff break room with a
couple tables, couch, refrigerator, and counter. As my eyes adjusted from the sun to indoor lighting, I listened.

Except for the hum of appliances, there was silence.

Brie walked quickly through the break room and into the
hall. The administrative building was completely open with a
lot of space around each large desk, and a central conference table that would sit eight. One office had a door in the back, and
that's where Brie led me.

The door was open, but the light was off.

"You get the info. I'll watch for anyone coming back," Brie
said.

"What if there are cameras in here and we're already busted?"
I whispered.

"I checked. There aren't. I don't know how long we have,
so let's go."

She walked through the office and stood to the side of the
main door so no one would see her if they approached.

Now or never, I thought. There was enough ambient light
that I didn't flip the switch, which might draw attention.

Tristan's office was immaculate—a desk with neatly arranged
file folders, a computer, and a phone. A printer on top of a short,
locked filing cabinet. His chair was ergonomically designed. I
didn't sit. My heart pounded so loudly in my ears that if Brie
screamed, I didn't know if I would hear her.

The computer screen came on when I touched the mouse.
Thank God it wasn't password-protected, because I doubted
anyone under fifty had a Rolodex anymore.

I quickly opened the contacts tab and scrolled for Ethan Val-
entine. I took a picture of the screen—his name, an address in
Miami, the address here for St. Claire, a phone number with a
Miami area code, and an email. That was it.

I closed down that tab and opened Tristan's calendar, hoping to find information about Valentine's schedule. Nothing referencing Valentine. I felt like a voyeur and closed the calendar. A glance out the door showed Brie was still on sentry duty, looking nonchalant, like she might be waiting for Tristan to come back so she could talk to him.

How could I find out if Valentine was on the island short of hiking to his house? I clicked on the finder and skimmed for anything that might be his schedule. Nothing jumped out at me. So I clicked on Tristan's email and . . .

It was password-protected.

I was about to leave when I saw a file labeled *Employees*. I hesitated, then clicked it. Inside the file were files for each employee, last name, first name. I shouldn't do this . . . but I did. I found Garmon, Gino and clicked it open.

There were multiple documents including application, references, performance reviews. I opened his application and scanned it. He'd left Miami two years before he started here. He'd been a private investigator for those two years . . . was that a real job or a fake job? Because wouldn't it take time to get his license and build his clientele? Did he not like being a PI, or was it a temporary gig while he found something else? I took a picture of his references, closed the document, opened the most recent performance review.

"Mia Mia Mia." I heard Brie repeat my name in a low voice.

I looked up, and she was motioning for me to come.

I took a picture of just the first page that popped up, quit the program, and ran out of the office, panicked.

"This way," Brie whispered, and we turned into the break room just as two people walked through the main door, chatting.

Brie opened the back door, and we exited. Brie turned right, away from the buildings, down the path that circled the back of the resort.

"Shit," I muttered. "That wasn't much time."

"Short staff meeting, I guess," she said. "Did you get his schedule?"

"Couldn't find it, but I have Valentine's contact information. And was reading Gino Garmon's file when you alerted me."

"Anything?"

"He was a PI for two years before he got this job. I have his references. Maybe I'll call them, see if anyone knows about why he quit the force."

As soon as we were out of sight of the buildings, I breathed easier. "That was way too close," I said.

Brie giggled.

"And fun," she said.

"Maybe for you," I said, trying not to laugh. "My heart is still pounding."

"Mine too."

We cut through the back entrance of the resort, and I grabbed a premade wrapped sandwich from the buffet. There seemed to be food available 24/7.

"I worked up an appetite," I said, then laughed out loud.

"Ms. Crawford, Ms. Locke," Tristan said as he approached us. I froze.

He knew. He had cameras in the office. Someone saw us. *He* saw us. I was going to be kicked off the island before I solved this mystery *or* had sex with Jason. A double tragedy.

"Hiya, Tristan," Brie said with a casual smile. "What's happening?"

How could she be so calm?

"I was looking for Ms. Crawford," Tristan said.

"Me?"

"I wanted to first apologize that you were made uncomfortable by another guest this morning. I have spoken to Mr. Lance, and he is leaving the island tomorrow."

"You didn't have to send him away," I said. Thank God he didn't know that we'd broken into the office and accessed his computer. "He was just worried about CeeCee."

"Perhaps," Tristan said, "but either way, he's leaving of his own volition. And to put your mind at rest, Ms. Tremaine is safe and sound. She flew back to the States yesterday afternoon.

I haven't spoken to her personally, but I received confirmation from St. John that she took a ferry to St. Thomas and then boarded a nonstop flight to Miami."

"And she didn't tell her boyfriend?" Brie said. "Cold."

"I will be following up with her personally to ensure that she is truly all right, but I know you were concerned, and I hope your mind is at ease."

"Yes, thank you," I said, though I still thought it was strange for CeeCee to leave so abruptly. "It's been a bit disconcerting considering what happened to Diana."

He shook his head. "Absolutely awful."

"Are the police or your security any closer to finding out what happened to her?"

"They are still working on retracing her steps," he said. "I don't want to speak out of school here, because again I don't have confirmation from St. John, but she was spotted on the far side of St. John, in Coral Bay. Why, I won't speculate. The police will find the answers. They are diligent, if a bit slower than we would like."

He sounded more confident than I felt.

"I'll admit when I heard CeeCee went missing yesterday, I thought something might have happened to her."

He reached out and patted my arm. "I'm so sorry. I promise here, on St. Claire, you are perfectly safe. I truly hope the police find out exactly what happened so that our guests can rest easy."

Brie said, "Gotta go, Tristan. Thanks."

We walked to my cottage, and it wasn't until we stepped inside that I finally relaxed. "Wow, I thought for sure he'd caught us."

"I thought you were going to spill everything," Brie said. "You don't lie well, do you?"

I shook my head. "So CeeCee went home. Huh."

"You're thinking something."

"Her lunch with Trevor's ex-wife," I said. "And a couple small things she said that made me think she's not the airhead everyone thought she was."

"And?"

"I don't know. Something's off there." I shrugged, then said, "I thought for five seconds that maybe CeeCee killed Diana."

"Really? Why?"

"Blackmail. But it doesn't make sense because nothing I read implies that Diana had blackmailed CeeCee—it's Trevor who's cheating on his wife." CeeCee's code would be 320, and I didn't recall seeing it in the book.

I pushed CeeCee and Trevor to the back of my mind and looked at the contact information for Ethan Valentine.

"What do you think we should do?" I asked Brie.

"I guess the question is, what do you think Valentine can do?" Brie said. Smart question. I didn't know.

Because Valentine's schedule wasn't on Tristan's computer, we didn't know if he had been on the island Sunday, though Luis had said he hadn't been at the house Sunday when Diana showed up.

"I'll sleep on it tonight," I said.

Brie raised an eyebrow. "Is that what you're going to do? Sleep?"

I blushed fifty shades of red. "Eventually," I stammered.

Brie laughed. "Go get ready for your hot date. I'm going to see if I can convince my dad to have some one-on-one time with his favorite daughter. Maybe I can figure out a way to break them up. Don't forget snorkeling tomorrow. Ferry leaves at ten."

CHAPTER
TWENTY-EIGHT

"Curiouser and curiouser!"

—Lewis Carroll, *Alice's Adventures in Wonderland*

AFTER MY SHOWER, I WAS relaxing on the patio when Braden called.

"Is everything okay?" I immediately asked, almost jumping out of my recliner.

I could think of a hundred things that might have gone wrong at the office. I began to panic because I hadn't been watching the news, I hadn't read even one financial paper since I'd arrived on the island, and my neglect meant I'd let all my clients down.

"Fine," he said, sounding odd. "Are you okay?"

"You're calling me on a Friday afternoon. I thought the stock market crashed or something."

He laughed. "Mia, the world is running surprisingly smoothly right now. No major or minor upheavals in the market. I've reviewed all client accounts per your instructions, and there are no issues. I adjusted Mrs. Grossman's portfolio as you indicated and sent her a revised statement."

"Thanks," I said, and relaxed. "I know you're on top of everything. I just worry."

"You wouldn't be you if you didn't," he said. "I'm calling because you wanted information."

"Right." I'd forgotten. "Sherry Morrison."

"I emailed you a bunch of stuff, but the gist of it is that she's in financial hot water. She filed for Chapter 13 bankruptcy last year. I pulled the filing and sent it to you, but the basics are she's being forced to sell her house to pay for her debt. The problem is she doesn't have much equity—she took out a second mortgage with really bad terms shortly after her husband died. The only reason to accept those terms, in my opinion, was because her credit was shot and she had erratic income. I could run her credit—"

"No, I don't want to cross a line. I'm doing this for a friend, but I don't want you or me to get into trouble. You're sure it's *her* Chapter 13?"

"Yes. A lot of credit card debt, the two mortgages, and tax liens."

"Did you find out anything about her employment? She has a business."

"I don't think she does much business. She doesn't advertise. Her website was last updated three years ago. Did you know that she's been seen on the arm of a bunch of different professional sports players?"

"I know," I said.

"What's really going on?" Braden asked.

"I'll tell you everything when I get home."

"Are you sure you're okay? You sound preoccupied."

"I'm great. I'm relaxing on my own private beach. I have plans this evening I'm really looking forward to." I might or might not tell him about falling into the pit.

"Well, then, I'll see you next week."

I ended the call and realized my trip was half-over. Yet . . . the resort was giving me three free days for finding a dead body. Depending on how things went with Jason tonight, maybe I should ask to extend my vacation by three days. Considering I had rarely taken time off for the last five years, I knew Stuart wouldn't care. He'd probably be thrilled.

A flood of anxiety washed over me. I *needed* to be in the office next week. I trusted Braden, of course, but I had duties and responsibilities and clients who depended on me. If I told them

I would be back from my vacation on Wednesday, I needed to be back from my vacation on Wednesday.

The thought of going back to my office was borderline depressing.

I pushed all that aside and realized that I was hungry. I hadn't finished the sandwich because I'd been too nervous after Tristan flagged us down. I didn't know what Jason had planned, but I didn't want to be hangry when we met up. I headed to the Blue Dahlia for a snack and a second drink to settle my nerves. Not nerves—it was more the thrill of anticipation as I let my mind wander back to that kiss last night.

It was surprisingly quiet as I walked to the bar. No kids playing, only a few people lounging on the beach. The pool was unmoving. Two people sat at the pool bar, and four women in yoga clothes were the only guests at the Blue Dahlia, drinking and eating appetizers from the perpetual buffet.

I made myself a small plate of food and sat at the bar, where Callie was still working, and asked her for another of her delicious spritzers.

I went through the images of Diana's book on my phone, working through all the angles. There were a lot of reasons to blackmail someone—adultery, stealing from a business partner, some unknown crime, more. Or, as Anja was going through, exposing a long-held secret that would hurt people but wasn't a crime.

Secrets . . . Ultimately, blackmail came down to a secret that someone was willing to pay to keep buried. But how long would someone pay? At some point, the truth would get out . . . unless the blackmailer was confident that Diana was the only one who knew the secret.

I thought about Gino, and then remembered the pictures I took on Tristan's computer. They were difficult to read because I hadn't taken the time to zoom and focus, and at first I didn't see anything of interest. But the last line of the performance review was interesting.

Discussed repeated trips to St. Croix. Gino assured me he is no longer gambling.

Gambling would explain a lot. It might explain why he left the police force, if he was taking money from busts and spending it on cards or horses. It would also explain what Diana might have on him. The big question was, *how* would Diana know about Gino Garmon? Did someone tell her? Had she researched staff before she arrived? Most of the guests were wealthy, so she might have been in their same circles or read gossip rags or could call friends for dirt. But staff was distinctly different.

Out of the corner of my eye, I saw movement near the bar. A staff member came in with supplies. He was of slight build, an older teen. There was something familiar about him—it was the way he moved.

A flash of me treading water after jumping into the ocean that first day . . . and the person who was going through my things. I'd had a sense it was a *he*, someone not too big. Someone who moved like a teenager . . .

"Hey, you—" I glanced at his chest. He wore a thin jacket, and I couldn't see his name tag.

He looked at me, eyes wide, and I knew this was the kid who had torn the page from my book.

Then he turned and walked away as if I hadn't spoken to him.

I glanced around for Callie, but she was talking to the older women. I pursued the kid. He walked briskly through the center of the resort, not running, but with purpose—and the purpose was to avoid talking to me.

"Hey!" I called. No one was at the registration desk, and I didn't see any staff around to help. The kid entered the spa, and I followed.

He wasn't in the lobby. I opened the door to the treatment rooms, and he wasn't in the hall, but I remembered from my massage that there was another exit.

I left and ran around to the back just as he exited the building.

I grabbed his arm. "Stop," I said in my sternest voice. "Do I need to take you to security?"

Eyes wide, he shook his head rapidly back and forth. "What? I didn't do anything."

"You tore a page from my book. Why?"

"Me? No."

But he averted his eyes, clearly lying. I wasn't a good liar, but this kid was even worse.

"Yes, you. Someone else stole the book from my room. Or was that you, too? Did you steal the wrong page, so took the entire book?"

"I didn't! I swear. Please—I'll lose my job." His eyes darted left and right as if looking for an escape.

"I won't tell security if you tell me why you took that page."

His lip quivered. He genuinely looked terrified. "I can't. He'll—look, ma'am, I'm sorry. I don't have the page. I—I—I gave it to someone. And I—I didn't take the book. I swear, I didn't take the book, just the one page."

"Who did you give it to?"

"I can't." Then he kicked me in the shin and ran.

CHAPTER
TWENTY-NINE

"Life is an adventure to be lived, not a series of repetitive days to survive."

—Lucy Score, *Riley Thorn and*
the Dead Guy Next Door

I HAD A BRUISE on my shin from where the jerk kid kicked me.
It blossomed into a dark purple blotch pretty quick.

I didn't want to go to Gino, but someone needed to know
what happened. I considered telling Jason and asking him what
to do about the situation, but I didn't want to drag him into this.

I headed over to the administrative office and found Tristan
and Kalise both working. "Hi, do you have a minute?" I asked.

"Of course," Kalise said with a smile. "You look very nice
this evening."

"Thank you," I said. "I had an issue with one of your staff
members." I'd thought through how I wanted to address the
situation. If he was concerned about losing his job, maybe the
kid would tell his boss the truth.

Kalise and Tristan exchanged a glance. Then Tristan said,
"Please, come to my office. I'm so sorry for any trouble the staff
has caused you."

Tristan closed the door behind us and motioned for me to
sit in a wicker chair across from his desk. I squirmed a bit, remembering how I'd sneaked in earlier and invaded his privacy.

"I don't want to get anyone in trouble," I said, though I

didn't completely mean it—my shin still hurt. "But maybe if you talked to him, you could figure out why he was going through my things."

Tristan sat in his chair and looked concerned. "A staff member went through your personal items?"

"Yes," I said. "A young employee—twenty, maybe—with light brown skin and short, dark hair. My height. The first day I was here, I saw him going through my bag when I was in the water. When I got to shore, he was gone. The next day, I discovered a page had been torn from the book, and I remembered that a young man had been in my things. Today I saw him and asked him about it, and he ran from me."

"You think he took your book?"

The way he said it, I thought he was humoring me, and I realized how absolutely ridiculous I sounded. We were talking about a twelve-dollar paperback I'd gotten for free, and I was acting as if he were a jewel thief.

"No." I knew Amber had stolen my book, but maybe she'd hired him? The kid said *he*, so maybe Parker hired him to tear out the page . . . the more I thought about it, the more I wished I hadn't come here. "Maybe," I clarified. "But he ran from me, wouldn't tell me why he went through my bag on the beach." I stopped short of telling Tristan his employee had kicked my shin because I didn't want him to lose his job. I just wanted to know what was going on.

"Is anything else missing?" Tristan asked.

"No. And I don't want him in trouble, but I'd like to talk to him, get his side of the story."

"And you don't know who?"

"He worked this afternoon stocking the bar, and he might have been on the ferry when I first arrived." Certainly Tristan would be able to look at employee records and figure out who I had seen.

"Let me see what I can do," Tristan said. "I can't promise there will be no disciplinary action. St. Claire takes pride in our staff, our hospitality, and never should anyone feel unsafe."

A murdered guest made me feel a lot less safe than a book thief, I thought.

"I just want to talk to him," I said.

"No promises, but I'll see if I can identify him and possibly arrange a meeting."

"I appreciate it." I thanked him and left.

I really didn't know what to do. I looked at my watch and realized it was nearly six. I would have to run to the docks to meet Jason on time.

I started walking briskly when I heard my name.

"Ms. Crawford!"

I turned and saw Henry standing next to one of the shuttles. I approached, and he said with a knowing smile, "Your chariot awaits."

He knew. He knew about my date with Jason. I wasn't keeping it a secret—Brie knew—but I didn't exactly announce it. And Jason had kissed me at the bar, and any number of people could have seen. Was I blushing? Yep, I was. Maybe Henry would think I'd gotten too much sun today.

"Um, thank you," I said, and climbed in.

He chuckled, and we started down the narrow road to the dock. "Jason is a good man. You'll have fun tonight."

My blush deepened as I remembered exactly how good I'd felt when Jason kissed me last night, with all the unspoken promises behind the kiss. I realized that spending the day looking for clues to Diana's murder was partly to distract me from my nerves about tonight. A thrill ran up my spine, and I willed my stomach to settle.

"I missed the cruise last night, and he said he'd take me out." That sounded stupid. I might as well have worn a neon sign announcing that I was going to have sex with Jason Mallory tonight.

"Awful what happened on the mountain. It's all blocked off now. No one else will get hurt. Mr. Tristan spoke with the contractors—they return next week after equipment is delivered. They'll investigate what happened, but they think that the orange fencing wasn't installed properly—the men they hired draped it between the trees and didn't stake it down. There was rain Monday morning, the day before you arrived, and some heavy winds." He shook his head. "I'm glad you weren't seriously hurt."

I hadn't thought that it had been intentionally removed because there was no way that anyone would have known Brie and I would be walking along that path at the top of the mountain. But I was still relieved that they'd figured out it was shoddy work.

"I think Jason feels sorry for me that I spent my birthday in a muddy pit," I said, trying to make light of the situation.

"Oh, no," Henry said as if I had been serious. "I've never seen Jason excited like this. He's giddy. And if I'm honest, I know a bit about what he has planned."

My heart raced. "What?"

"It's a surprise," he said with a grin.

"I don't like surprises."

"You will like this one."

Did everyone on the island know I was going out with Jason tonight?

"Don't look so nervous," he said with a chuckle. "You'll have fun, I promise. I can't remember the last time Jason had a date on or off island, and he's pulling out all the stops."

I had nothing to say to that—I didn't know what I *could* say. This whole week had taken on a surreal feeling. It was like watching myself eat, drink, and be merry without really being a part of the island life.

Henry stopped at the dock.

"There's no boat," I said.

"The ferry left ten minutes ago with our day workers returning to St. John."

"But then why did Jason ask me to meet him here?"

"There's more than one boat on the island," he said.

I heard a motor before I saw it. But it wasn't a boat that pulled up onto the shore; it was a Jet Ski.

"No." I didn't realize I had spoken out loud until I heard my voice.

Henry laughed and waved at Jason, then headed back to the resort, leaving me there. With Jason and a Jet Ski.

Jason jogged up the beach and took my hand. "Ready?"

"No. Not at all." I needed an excuse. I looked down at my clothes. "I'm wearing a dress."

"You have a bikini underneath, right?"

I nodded.

"I listen, Mia. You don't like helicopters, small planes, hot air balloons, or hang gliding. Got it. The Jet Ski stays firmly on top of the water. It's gassed up. You will love it, I promise."

It terrified me. Jason's ear-to-ear grin was contagious, though. He was excited, and that made me a little (very tiny bit) excited too.

I slowly said, "Oh-kay."

He opened a metal box on the edge of the deck and handed me a life vest. I held it awkwardly.

"You've never put one on?"

"Never had the need to."

He laughed, took it from me. "Take off your dress."

I blinked and pictured us lying naked in the sand.

"What?" My voice sounded like a croak.

"I have a dry box. It'll be safe and sound in there."

Skeptical, I took off my bag, then my dress. I was wearing a neon-pink bikini and suddenly felt self-conscious. But Jason put my dress over his shoulder and then put the life vest on me like a dinner jacket. He expertly buckled me up in the front, testing each strap. He was standing very close, and when I looked at him, he kissed me. "Smile, Mia."

I did. A small one. Then he tickled me, and I burst out laughing. "Stop!"

He gave me one last poke, then kissed me quick. He grabbed my bag with his left hand, and my hand with his right. We walked down the beach to the Jet Ski.

"Aren't we having dinner?" I hadn't finished my snack plate. I'd be hungry before dark.

"We are."

I looked around. Henry was already gone, and I didn't hear or see anyone else.

He glanced at me. "You don't like giving up control, do you?"

"No," I admitted. "I like having a plan."

"Which is a great character trait for a financial planner. But tonight, trust me, okay?"

"I do." It was true. While it scared me to leave the evening completely in Jason's hands, it was also exciting.

Jason opened the seat and put in my dress and bag, then closed and secured it. He climbed onto the front of the Jet Ski, motioned for me to sit on the back. "Hold on," he said as he started the motor.

I let my hands rest lightly on his hips.

"Tighter," he said. Then we were moving *fast*. "I won't let you fall, but you need to hold on."

I clung to him to avoid being thrown off the back.

"Jason!" I screamed.

I couldn't hear him, but we were so close, my body vibrated with his laughter. He drove fast out of the small bay and headed out to sea.

I closed my eyes and clutched Jason, scared to death that I would be thrown off and drown. I could swim and I had a life vest, but when you were moving at a hundred miles an hour (okay, probably closer to twenty, but it felt like a hundred), your life flashed in front of your eyes.

All I saw was my neat and tidy desk at work, with my perfectly arranged files and color-coded notes. My two cats, Nick and Nora, meowing at the door of my apartment when they heard my key in the lock. Then I saw Grams over my coffin, shaking her head, Jane and Amanda on each side of her, all of them looking sad. Not because I was dead (though I'm sure they would all be sad at my demise), but, Grams said as she pet my cats, "Poor Mia, she never lived."

Yes I did! I wanted to scream, but Nightmare Grams was right. I was scared of living.

Suddenly, the Jet Ski stopped.

"What's wrong?" I asked. "Are we sinking? Did it break? Do you have a radio? How far are we from shore? Can we swim back?"

"Open your eyes," Jason said.

"No."

"Mia," he said softly. "Open."

Slowly, reluctantly, I opened my eyes.

We were a good distance out to sea. I could see the entire island before me. The resort looked like a tiny dollhouse. The sun was barely behind the island, glorious colors framing the mountain peaks like a halo.

It was gorgeous and romantic, and I had no words.

Jason put his hands on mine, which were still tightly wrapped around his waist.

"Sometimes," he said almost too quiet for me to hear, "I come out here and sit until it's almost dark. It makes me feel small, but in a good way. My problems are smaller, my worries disappear . . . it's freeing. When I get back on the island, solutions to my problems magically appear." He chuckled. "Because I took the time to clear my mind and not overthink everything."

I realized then that I didn't really know Jason. Not who he was inside and what he might worry about. He was friendly and intelligent and had opinions about things like extreme sports and taking risks and even my own dream of owning a bookstore. A dream I had never told anyone until Jason. Maybe because he was a stranger . . . maybe because I would never see him after this week.

But I didn't know Jason's dreams, or his fears, or how he grew up or even where he grew up. I didn't know if he had brothers and sisters, what he did before he started working on St. Claire, and if he had plans for his future.

"I can see why you love this island," I said. "Why you work here."

"It won't last forever," he said.

"Why? Henry seems very happy. He talked about how much he and his wife love working at the resort and how good management is to them. Housing, a month paid vacation."

I felt Jason laugh more than heard it. "Henry and Millie are empty nesters. Did you know Henry used to teach high school biology in the States? And Millie owned her own business, alterations and dry cleaning. One of her kids took over, Henry retired early from teaching because he didn't enjoy it anymore, and they started working here. He once said he'll never retire from the resort because he doesn't feel like he's really working."

I didn't realize Henry had not only completely changed careers, but chose to do something simpler for probably less money. Though with the kids out of the house and free housing on the island, maybe they didn't need as much to be comfortable. I'd always thought of my career trajectory as having to keep moving up the ladder, making more money, putting more into my retirement so that I *could* retire and support myself. I had never before considered maybe doing something different, something I loved, after my career was done.

Like opening a bookstore in thirty years.

"I could stay here for hours," he said, "but I'm hungry, and you're probably hungry, too. The sun is disappearing, and being on a Jet Ski at night is dangerous."

"Even for you, Mr. Risk Taker?"

"I take risks, but not stupid risks."

"Too bad we can't eat out here," I said jokingly.

"We're going to jet around the island. I have a picnic set up for us on the other side. Ready?"

I squeezed him and he drove south, parallel with the island. This time, I didn't close my eyes. The front shield helped keep most of the water spray off my face, and I saw the island in all its glory. The pristine beaches, neatly docked boats, inlets, and green mountains with occasional bursts of color where flowers had taken over an area.

The southern tip of the island was a paradise within paradise.

A beach spread out from the base of a cliff that had to tower ten stories up. There was a dock here, too—as big as the one that serviced the resort—with a boat house. Stairs had been built into the cliff. I would be terrified to walk up them—how were they even secured?

At the top of the stairs was a deck with a one-hundred-eighty-degree view. It had to be spectacular. The house was wood and glass, no lights on except white string lights wrapped around the deck and trees. Behind the house, the mountain gently sloped up to the peak, but based on maps of the island I'd seen, there was a narrow road that went from the house to the resort.

Ethan Valentine's house.

I wanted to ask Jason about him, but talking was impossible over the noise of the Jet Ski. Jason navigated around protruding rocks, then around to the west side of the island and up to a man-made break.

The southern half of the island was narrower than the northern half. Jason slowed, then stopped as we approached a boat anchored a couple hundred yards from the beach. The boat was lit up, visible even though the sun had just started to dip into the ocean, making me think there was a party going on.

"Someone else is here?" I asked when he stopped. I tried not to show my disappointment that we wouldn't be eating alone.

"I brought the boat earlier, then went back to the resort to pick you up."

"Why?"

"I needed to get the food over here. Plus, remember? No Jet Skis at night."

"And how are we going to get back?"

He laughed. "The boat. Anytime we want. We're on no schedule. No one is expecting me or you." He ran his hand up and down my leg. My heart skipped a beat, thinking about the lagoon the other night and how close we'd been to having sex before we were interrupted. "Can you wait a few minutes to eat?" His voice was low, sexy, teasing.

"Sure," I said, sounding far more confident than I felt. I pictured having sex on the Jet Ski, and I didn't quite know how it would work. I supposed I could sit in the front, face him, pray we didn't topple over . . .

"I want to show you something, and we don't have a lot of time before the sun goes down."

Jason turned the Jet Ski toward the inlet and stopped on narrow beach. He helped me off the Jet Ski, and I wobbled as if just getting off a horse. Before I fell on my ass in the sand, he caught me and kissed me.

"One sec."

He pulled the Jet Ski a few feet up the beach, took my sandals from the dry compartment, and slipped them on my feet.

"I feel like Cinderella," I said.

"I am honored to be your Prince Charming." He bowed deeply, then took my hand and led me toward the cliff.

It looked like there was nowhere to go, then Jason led us around a huge boulder, revealing the opening to a cave.

I froze. It was dark and scary and not like a place I wanted to explore.

Jason faced me, took both my hands.

"Trust me," he said.

"Where does it go?"

He didn't answer me, simply stared at me with an expression that said *this is your choice.*

His expression also said that my decision now was about more than whether to go into the cave. It was about trusting him—and trusting myself. About whether I was going to always play it safe, or take a risk . . . even if it was a small risk.

Jason was with me. The risk didn't seem so great with him by my side.

I leaned up and kissed him. He looked surprised, and that's when I realized he'd been the one who had initiated each of our make-out sessions. I was a very willing participant, but I hadn't spontaneously kissed him until now.

I was glad I did. Something shifted between us. I felt closer to him, as if we shared something unspoken.

Holding hands, we entered the cave.

The sand was rockier, large shells littering the mouth of the cave. A stream of water flowed into the ocean behind us. The cavern was completely dark for a minute, but I swallowed the fear, my hand tightening in Jason's.

Then suddenly, we stood in the open.

It wasn't a nearly enclosed cavern like in the lagoon on the north side of the island; instead, it was a park, open to the sky, a thin waterfall streaming down the rock face. Bushes grew out of the cliffs, and trees towered all around us. In the middle where the water fell was what looked like a small lake. I watched as it streamed out the way we'd come in. The setting sun reflected off the cliffs, casting a surreal glow and multitude of gold-tinged colors all around.

"It's—" I had no words. For a bookworm like me, how could I not think of a word other than *beautiful*? We stood in a snow globe without snow. Or the Garden of Eden.

"I know," he whispered.

I leaned against Jason, my back to his chest, his arms wrapped around me, his chin resting on the top of my head. We stood together in the middle of this amazing spot, watching as the light changed with the falling sun. Just when I thought it couldn't get more beautiful, another ridge or tree was highlighted as the angle of the sun changed. The chirping birds faded as they nested for the night.

I didn't want to leave. There was something spiritual here, as if this spot made me part of the island itself.

Jason slowly turned me to face him and kissed me. It was a light kiss, a long kiss. A kiss that had no urgency, but was full of desire. My lips parted. His hands went to my back and pulled me tighter against him, but still his lips were light, teasing and loving at the same time.

"We need to go," he said, sounding sad.

"Mmm-hmm."

"I have a whole evening planned for us."

"Mmm." I held him tight, put my hand on his chest. "If we must." Then I thought about the cave. "Do we have to worry about the tide?" I said, suddenly thinking we were going to be trapped in here with rising water.

"It comes in, but it doesn't flood the cave unless there's a storm. We're safe."

With a final look at the beauty of the area, we turned and walked back through the cave, emerging on the beach as the sun finished its descent. We took a minute to watch it melt out into the sea. The sky exploded with color. I've watched many beautiful sunsets, but this I would never forget.

Jason pulled the Jet Ski back into the water and climbed on. I heard a motorboat but didn't see anyone.

"What the hell?" Jason said as a small boat sped away from his larger one. It had been behind the yacht.

"Who is that?" I asked. A figure was behind the wheel, but he or she was in all black and wore a helmet.

"I don't know, but I don't like this," he said. He turned the ignition. The Jet Ski sputtered, stalled. He tried again, then frowned, breathed deeply. "Do you smell gasoline?"

"Yes," I said.

We got off and Jason checked the tank. "Dammit, someone drained the tank. It's empty."

"Why would anyone do that?" I asked. Silly question. He didn't know any more than I did.

"We can't stay here," he said. "The tide comes in all the way to the edge of the cliff." He looked at the cave. "I would say we could go back into the cave, but we would be trapped in there at high tide. Can you swim to the boat?"

"Yes," I said. "It's not too far."

He looked miserable, as if all his plans had been destroyed. I was more angry—and a little scared—wondering why someone would sabotage Jason's Jet Ski.

And who knew we were here.

Anyone could know. At least, anyone who'd helped Jason put this all together.

"I need to pull the jet up behind the rocks, to the mouth of the cave," he said. "It should be safe there overnight. Wait here."

When he returned, he said, "I am *so* sorry."

"It's not you. It's whoever sabotaged us."

"When we get to the boat, I'll radio security about what happened. I don't want this to ruin our night."

I wondered if whoever had messed with the Jet Ski knew I'd been asking questions about Diana Harden. I hadn't exactly been subtle. But why? I didn't *know* who'd killed her. I only suspected. Gino Garmon was at the top of my list, but Sherry Morrison had been acting just as strange, and she definitely had secrets, even if I hadn't figured them all out yet.

And then I thought about Amber and Parker. They knew I'd once had the book. They could think I was looking for the documents Diana hid somewhere on the island, and sabotaged us to prevent me from finding them—not realizing that wasn't my plan tonight.

I wanted to tell Jason everything I knew about Diana Harden's life . . . and death. About her book, why I thought Amber and Parker had stolen it, about her blackmailing people—one of whom had most likely killed her.

Jason said, "We need to swim over before there's no more light. Ready?"

"Let's go."

The water was cool when we walked in. Jason said, "It drops off quickly here, unlike the other side of the island. So be careful."

He started swimming, and I followed. He continually looked back to make sure I was behind him.

The current pushed against me, so by the time I reached the boat, I was drained. Jason was already there, holding on to a ladder. When I reached him, he pulled me up. I was out of breath and shivering.

"I have towels and robes in here," he said as he led me into the cabin.

A table, complete with flowers and unlit candles, stood in the middle, and a bottle of champagne chilled in a bucket secured to the corner. He opened a cabinet and retrieved two fluffy towels. We dried off, and then he handed me a robe. "You can take off your bathing suit if you want—you might be more comfortable."

Even though the situation was less than ideal, I felt a jolt of anticipation as I thought about being naked under the robe.

"I'll radio in, explain what happened. Then—if you're still up for it—I did plan dinner." He smiled. "I promised to feed you."

"I'll hold you to it," I said. "After that swim, I'm starving."

TEN MINUTES LATER, I came out of the stateroom wearing the robe with nothing underneath. There was a bedroom and bath, and I tried not to think about what we might do later in that bed. I'd found a comb in the bathroom and made myself partly presentable, brushing the worst of the tangles out of my hair.

Jason wasn't there. For a split second, I panicked that whoever had disabled the Jet Ski had returned and done something to him.

I heard footsteps on the deck above, so climbed the stairs and called out. "Jason?"

He turned to me. "Radio is busted. Literally, someone ripped all the wires out, destroying them. I tried to put it back together, but then realized the cables were also cut. I inspected the boat—we're not taking on water, the anchor is secure, and we have a generator for the lights—but the gas tank is empty, too. I'm so sorry."

"Don't apologize," I snapped. "This isn't your fault. I was thinking—could someone be trying to sabotage the resort?"

He looked surprised. "Why?"

"I don't know, but first one of the guests is killed. Then I fell into the hole because the security netting was gone. And now your Jet Ski and boat are disabled. Have there been other accidents over the last few weeks?"

He shook his head. "Nothing that comes to mind."

"Are we safe here?"

"Yes. I promise. I checked the weather before I planned this excursion, and there are no storms expected in the next twenty-four hours."

"Do you have a cell phone?"

"Even if I did, it won't reach anyone on the other side of the island. It's one of the reasons the resort is putting in a cell tower next to the Sky Bar, so the west and east coasts can more easily communicate."

"If we can't reach anyone, how are we going to get back?"

"Henry knows where I planned to go tonight, and Kalise—I had to ask permission to take the boat. If we don't show up by morning, they'll come look for us."

"Okay," I said, getting comfortable with the idea of spending the night on the boat. If I was going to be stranded anywhere, I was glad it was with Jason. "Let's eat."

"You're not freaked out?"

"No." I paused, considered, realized that I was telling the truth. "I'm okay. Really. I'm definitely hungry, and I have some things to tell you."

"About?"

"I might know part of what's going on. I didn't tell Gino Garmon everything I knew about Diana Harden when he asked."

Jason stared at me to the point that I felt distinctly uncomfortable. "Did you know her?"

I shook my head. "I never met her alive, but I feel like I know her." Now or never, I thought.

"Diana Harden was blackmailing people on the island. I found her notes. They were written in the book that was stolen from my room Wednesday night."

CHAPTER
THIRTY

"Then I realize what it is. It's him. Something about him makes me feel like I am
about to fall. Or turn to liquid. Or burst
into flame."

—Veronica Roth, *Divergent*

JASON HAD THOUGHT OF EVERYTHING.

The evening was a little chilly, though the sea was calm.
He set up the meal in the main cabin, a table for two, champagne, and steak salad with fresh rolls. It was perfect—hearty
and healthy and very delicious.

I told him everything I knew over the meal. About how I'd
found the book, what I'd read in the pages, why I believed that
it belonged to Diana Harden and that she had been blackmailing
at least one person. I would have shown him the pictures except
that my phone was in the seat of the Jet Ski. I explained how
one of his staff members had torn out a page my first day here,
and why I thought Amber and Parker had stolen the book—or
hired the kid to do it. They were looking for documents that
Diana had hidden somewhere on the island, and thought clues
were in the book—which was why Brie and I had followed
them yesterday, and that's how I ended up falling in the hole.

I told him I didn't trust Gino. I didn't tell him Brie and I had
broken into Tristan's office for Ethan Valentine's information—
that was really crossing a line I still wasn't comfortable with.

I told him about why Sherry Morrison was giving me weird vibes, about her money problems, but also admitted that she was possessive of Andrew and thus might just not like me on general principle. I'd already told him about CeeCee's lunch with her boyfriend's ex, and what Tristan told me of her departure.

"When she disappeared on St. John, I thought she might have been a victim, like Diana," I said. "I'm glad she's okay, but I still think she had a secret."

"Like?"

"Like she's not exactly who she appears to be."

He listened to everything I said, asked a few questions, didn't call me foolish or make fun of my amateur sleuthing.

"And because of all these things, you think someone might be sabotaging the resort."

"I don't know—I only had that idea because of what happened to your Jet Ski and boat. I still think that Diana was killed because she had blackmailed someone. She had information about a lot of people. I figured out who most of them were because her number coding system is pretty simple, but there are a few I couldn't find—I mean, the initials don't match to anyone I've met here. She tracked guests' net worth, property values, and made comments about bad behavior."

"You've been working this vacation, haven't you?" He smiled, and I didn't feel awkward anymore.

"Brie helped me. But I don't want to get her in trouble," I added quickly. "Her dad was angry about what happened yesterday."

"I won't say anything." He crossed his heart.

"CeeCee wasn't who she pretended to be, and it's really bugging me. Trevor's a wealthy man, involved in commercial real estate among other things. The commercial real estate market is depressed right now, and it's not a good investment, but his company is working some other ventures."

"This is your world."

"Financial planning, maybe. I know good long-term investments. Maybe CeeCee is in league with someone to steal from him, like a honeytrap."

"A honeytrap?"

"You know, where a woman seduces a man—"

"I know what a honeytrap is," he said with a chuckle.

"Anyway," I continued, "maybe that was why she left." I thought about her meeting with his ex-wife. "She met with his ex-wife and disappeared."

"You said honeytrap . . . what if that's exactly what it was? Maybe she was hired by his ex-wife to take something from him? Money or information."

"Yeah," I said thoughtfully. "Maybe that is what she was doing."

"I bet you could figure it out pretty quick."

"How?"

"Like you said, you know good long-term investments. You could probably look at his portfolio and projects and see what might be valuable to someone else."

"I could," I agreed.

"But tonight, let your brilliant mind rest. Forget all this, okay?"

I nodded.

"What were you doing on St. John?" Jason asked as he poured us both more champagne.

"Promise you won't think I'm ridiculous?"

"I don't think you're ridiculous in the least." He took my hand, kissed it.

"I thought I could get information about Diana's murder investigation from the police because I think Diana was black-mailing Gino. And if she was, he shouldn't be investigating her murder," I said.

"You think Gino killed her?" He sounded surprised, but not like I was completely crazy.

"I think," I said slowly, carefully, "that he has done a lot of things to make me believe he's guilty. Some of her notes referenced him—he's 77 for Gino Garmon. The first day I arrived, he asked about the article I was reading describing her disappearance. Told me not to worry about it, but it was the way he said it that made me suspicious. He's in charge of the investigation, and then he threatened me when he brought me back to the resort last night."

Jason's spine straightened. "He threatened you?" His voice was low, and for the first time, I saw something more in Jason than his carefree manner. I saw a backbone that I didn't quite expect.

"He knew I'd gone to St. John and talked to the police, made a point to tell me that it would benefit me to stay out of the investigation. It was the way he said it."

"We need to tell Tristan about this," Jason said. "He's the manager. He's in charge of staff, including security."

"I have no proof of anything."

"Doesn't matter," Jason said. "He shouldn't have intimidated you like that."

Jason was right, but what if I was wrong? "I don't want to ruin his career because I let my imagination get away from me."

Jason laughed. "Mia, you're the most down-to-earth, logical person I've met in a long, long time."

I don't know why, but that made me happy. Maybe because he said it as if my personality delighted him. Maybe because he believed me about Diana and didn't dismiss my many theories.

"I try," I said lightly.

"I like that you're straightforward and honest. It's refreshing."

I was practically beaming. I cleared my throat and said, "Dinner was delicious. Did you make it yourself?"

"Not really."

"What does that mean?"

"I had the kitchen prepare everything. I just put the salads together."

"You put the salad together *very* well." I smiled.

He took my hands and said, "Are you sure you're okay being stranded out here tonight? I promise, someone will come for us in the morning."

"I'm fine," I said. "I'm not alone, am I?"

I was nervous. Flirting didn't come easy to me. And while we had kissed—dear Lord, had we kissed—I was still uneasy about my ultimate goal: casual sex with one of the hottest men I'd ever met.

Then he brought my hand to his lips and kissed my palm, and my nerves disappeared. I gasped from the sensation of his tongue as he licked my fingers.

"I want to show you something," Jason said, and I nearly stopped breathing.

He got up, quickly put the plates on a tray, and led me up to the deck. We went all the way to the top of the cabin, where there was a wide platform. He pressed a button, and all the boat lights turned off.

"Look," he said, and pointed to the sky.

It was so dark, I couldn't see the island at all, except for a very faint row of lights at the very top, blinking red likely to warn low-flying planes that there was a mountain.

The sky was awash with light, millions of stars, more than I had ever seen in one place. I was in the middle of the ocean and felt as if Jason and I were completely alone in the world.

"Oh. My. God." I didn't know if I'd spoken until Jason kissed my ear.

"It makes you think, doesn't it?" he whispered.

"I can barely form a thought, and I didn't even drink that much."

"Nothing we do changes the stars. I look up and think of all the people who never see outside themselves, never stop moving long enough to take in this ancient sight. The stars we're seeing are already gone, burned up, burned out, but their light remains. It's why I think everyone should live their dream, because if you find joy in what you do, when you're gone, you'll leave a light in your place that everyone who comes after you will see. Just like the stars."

I turned around so I could face him. The moon had not yet risen, but the stars gave enough light that I could see his eyes as he stared at me. I kissed him.

Jason wrapped his arms around my waist and pulled me close, deepening our kiss, champagne mingling with salty air. I couldn't get enough, didn't want to get enough. The gentle waves of the ocean undulated beneath us. The boat moved up and down, slowly rocking, seducing both of us.

"Here?" he whispered at the same time he untied the sash on my robe, revealing my naked body.

"Yes." Because I didn't want to wait to go downstairs. I wanted to make love now, here, under the stars, in the middle of the ocean without thought of murder, blackmail, or tomorrow.

I especially didn't want to think about tomorrow.

His hands were on my hips, then on my ass, then up and down my back as if he wanted to touch me everywhere all at once. He wore a T-shirt that hugged his lean muscles; I pulled it up, touched his warm skin, breathed in his scent.

All doubts disappeared when his hands cupped my breasts and we both moaned. We wanted each other, we craved each other, and that made all the difference in the world.

"Off," I said of his shirt, and he pulled it off. I unsnapped his shorts, and they fell to the ground. He stood there completely naked in the starlight, and if I could hardly breathe before, I was breathless now.

Jason was perfect.

Tight, lean muscles. Tan, from both heritage and time in the sun. His hair had dried curlier than usual after our swim. His expression was part desire, part whimsy, part earnestness. He wanted to make me happy. It was etched across his face. He seemed both confident and cautious at the same time—or I was seeing a reflection of my own wants and fears.

Jason was perfect in his imperfection. He had a two-inch scar on his abdomen where his appendix must have been removed. His face wasn't perfectly symmetrical—his right eye closed a little more than his left. His nose had been broken at least once, the bridge slightly bigger than it should be. But all those minor imperfections gave him character and made him more gorgeous.

I might have stared too long, because he put his hands on my face and said, "You okay?"

"Perfect," I said breathlessly.

He smiled slightly, a crooked, perfect smile, and kissed me.

We fell to our knees, and he pushed the robe off my shoulders. The cool ocean breeze made me shiver, so he pulled me to him. "If you're too cold—" he began, then put his mouth on my breast and his hand between my legs, and I would have fallen over if he wasn't supporting me.

The boat rocked beneath us, and soon we were adding to the movement as Jason murmured, "You first."

"No," I said, my voice raspy as his fingers worked magic. "Together." I gasped as one finger slowly penetrated me.

"You first, then together."

Two orgasms? I had never had two orgasms in one night. None of my boyfriends seemed to care after they had one, and I figured I was lucky to get one in the first place. I must have tensed, or he might have read my mind.

He dropped his hand, and I groaned. He turned me to face him and said, "Want to go for three?"

"I don't—I don't think I can."

"Four."

I laughed. It was a strange sound, not really a laugh, sort of a yelping giggle as I moved closer to him.

"Are you daring me?" he asked with a wicked grin.

"Of course not."

"You are," he said. "I don't know if I told you, but I'm very competitive." He kissed me as we knelt against each other. Then he put his hand back between my legs and slowly inserted one finger. Then two. His thumb touched my sweet spot, and I gasped and tried to pull away, the sensation of his fingers almost too much. But he held me close, his mouth on mine, warm, as urgent as his fingers, the boat moving, rocking gently beneath us, and I arched my back as I exploded.

He held me tight as the wave of heat rushed through me and turned me to mush. I looked up at the stars, my vision blurred. He was kissing my neck, soft kisses. Then he licked the tender spot behind my ear, and I shuddered.

"Oh, my. Oh, Jason. I. Wasn't. Expecting. That."

Before I could catch my breath, he had me on my back, tucking my robe under my head. I stared at him, the stars all around his silhouette, and knew he wasn't joking about a second orgasm. I wanted him fully, and I would do anything he asked at that moment. My mouth parted, and he leaned over me. "You're beautiful, Mia."

It might have been a line, but I'd already had one orgasm, and he could feed me any line he wanted if he could coax out another one.

"You're uncomfortable," he said.

"Huh?"

I couldn't feel much of anything but Jason's body on mine.

The roof of the cabin was about the size of a double bed. He kissed me, then rolled over, taking me with him, so I was on top.

"Better," he said.

Having all this access to him and his body was rather intoxicating. I didn't know what to touch first, so I touched everywhere, moving my hands slowly down his chest to his thighs, brushing them against his warm, hard penis. His hand started moving frantically around the deck.

"What? Did I hurt you?"

"Condom. Pocket. Now."

I found his shorts and the condom. Ripped it open. He tried to take it from me, but I held it away. "Allow me," I said.

"Oh God, Mia," he said, his muscles bunching in his neck as I took charge.

I had never been this bold, this brave, in my life.

I had never felt this sexy before, or this desirable.

And then, I slid down onto him, my breath hitching in my chest with each inch. Jason's hands held my hips firmly.

"Don't move," he said. "Give me one sec."

He moved inside me, and I involuntarily clenched. He moaned, took in a deep breath, slowly let it out. His hands, still on my hips, pushed me up, then back down.

I didn't need to be told twice.

I moved to find better leverage, put my knees on either side of him, then found the railing above his head. I held it tight as we moved together, first slowly, then faster, our rhythm in sync. No awkward fumbles. Had our bodies known each other in a previous life? I felt like I was with a stranger . . . and with someone I had known forever.

And I was on the verge of another orgasm. I wanted to let go. I wanted to scream with the overwhelming lust that unexpectedly flowed through me.

"Jason," I gasped.

"Now," he said.

I sank down on him, one final plunge, and I screamed into the night. His body convulsed beneath mine as I collapsed on top of him.

We lay like that for five, ten, fifteen minutes? I didn't know. Time stopped. Then a breeze rolled over me, and I shivered, remembered that I was naked and sweaty. We shifted, Jason adjusted himself, and we leaned against the railing, my head on his chest.

"Wow," I said, my mouth dry.

"Definitely," he said.

The ocean seemed lighter around us, and I bolted up. "Is someone coming?"

"No," he said, and pulled me back down to him. "Look."

He gestured toward the island. It appeared to be glowing. As we watched, the moon rose. It was two days shy of a full moon and cast a blue-gray tinge on the world around us.

"You're cold," he said.

"I don't want to move."

"I promised you another orgasm," he said. "Let's try the bed."

"You actually promised me two more," I teased, and kissed him. "I won't hold you to it."

"Is that a dare?"

"Maybe."

"I accept the challenge, Mia Crawford."

He helped me up, and we went down to the stateroom.

Jason finished the challenge to my complete and total satisfaction.

THIRTY-ONE

"For there to be betrayal, there would have
to have been trust first."

—Suzanne Collins, *The Hunger Games*

JASON WAS RIGHT: A BOAT came for us just after dawn the next morning while we were eating the dessert we hadn't gotten to the night before. Dessert for breakfast was the perfect end to the best night I had ever had in my life.

The ferry captain, Eli, was piloting a speedboat. We came out onto the deck and waved at him. Eli wasn't alone. Tristan and Kalise were both with him.

I wore my bikini under a St. Claire polo shirt Jason had found for me, and I—straitlaced, good-girl Mia Crawford—wasn't even embarrassed. I didn't regret one minute of last night, and judging by the very energetic way Jason had woken me up this morning, neither did he.

"What happened?" Tristan asked as he and Kalise boarded the boat. They both looked concerned, as if Jason was their son who had been out all night without calling.

"Someone sabotaged the Jet Ski and the boat, dumped the fuel, and then disabled the radio."

"What?" Kalise said at the same time Tristan said, "Who would do that?"

"Someone in a black scuba suit with a mask was on a small boat when we came out of the cavern. It looked like one of the boats we have for guests. I couldn't even say if it was a man or a woman. We were too far away."

"No one checked out a boat yesterday afternoon," Kalise said. "But they often forget to tell us."

Tristan turned to me. "Ms. Crawford, I can assure you that life on St. Claire is hardly as precarious as you have experienced."

"I'm fine," I said. *More than fine*, I thought. I was floating.

Multiple orgasms. I thought they only happened in fiction. I was blissfully wrong.

"This is just unacceptable," Tristan said. "We'll find who did this. They will be fired if staff, banned from the resort if a guest. Maybe prosecuted! This could have ended so much worse."

Jason said, "It's okay, Tristan. Really. No one was hurt, though I'd like to know who sabotaged my equipment." Jason called out to Eli, the boat captain who pulled up beside them. "Do you have extra gasoline?"

"Yes, enough to get you back to dock," Eli shouted.

"Great. Can you get me fueled up and then take Ms. Crawford back to the resort?"

"Absolutely," Eli said.

"I can stay," I said. I didn't want to leave, and that made me feel all lovestruck and needy. But I didn't care.

Four orgasms. And one more this morning for good measure.

"Give us a sec," Jason said to Tristan, then took my hand. We walked to the opposite end of the boat while Eli fueled.

"You okay?" he asked.

"Yes, of course I'm okay. More than okay."

I wanted to kiss him . . . but suddenly felt a bit self-conscious since we now had an audience.

He put his hand on my chin, made me look at him. "Mia, I had an amazing time last night, even with all the disasters. You're incredible in every way."

I searched his eyes and saw truth. He rubbed his thumb over my lips; I kissed it. "It really was a fantastic night." I sighed. "But you're right, I should go back with Eli."

"I won't be long, but I have to figure out what happened here and retrieve the Jet Ski."

"I'd like to know, too." Emboldened by the way he looked at me, and the way I felt inside, I said, "Tristan offered me three free days after finding Diana's body."

Jason smiled. "Really? I'll take a couple days off, and we can go island hopping."

My heart twisted. "Well, I have to get back to work. I have responsibilities, and I could probably work remotely, but the internet here is spotty, and I need a secure connection because of the financial end of my business. But I'll plan another vacation soon. Like a long weekend. And . . . maybe you can visit sometime. If you're ever in New York."

A frown touched his lips, and I think he was really disappointed that I was leaving. "It wouldn't be a problem to get you into Ethan Valentine's house, if you want to stay and need to work. He has state-of-the-art everything, and, well, I know he wouldn't mind. I'll, um, talk to Luis, ask him."

"That's really nice of you. I'd heard rumors that he wasn't friendly—that two people were kicked off the island because they hiked to his house."

"I don't remember that," he said. "But seriously. I don't want you to leave Tuesday."

My heart did a flip. "Maybe."

"I hope you stay." He ran his fingers between my breasts. "I enjoyed everything about last night. Talking to you. Making love." He kissed me.

"You're a distraction," I said with a smile.

"A *good* distraction?" he asked whimsically.

"Very good." I took his hand from my breast because all this touching was making me horny, and I wasn't generally the type of girl who got hot and bothered with fun petting. Clearly, Jason changed everything I had thought about sex and foreplay, and for the better. *That* was an understatement.

"I meant to tell you last night when we talked about Diana's book and then . . . well, we were *distracted*." He grinned and kissed my neck; I continued. "When I went to St. John, I learned that one of the water taxis—not a registered service, one piloted by a kid not even old enough to drive—brought Diana back to the island on Sunday night. He left her at Ethan Valentine's dock."

Jason froze, took a small step back. "*What?*"

"Yeah, it sounds bizarre, but I believe him. He knew details, like the time he left and what she said, and that she paid him extra to keep quiet. I don't think that Mr. Valentine was on the island last weekend—not positive, but Luis said *he* was there when she arrived, and he told her no one was home. But there must have been a reason she went there. Maybe she planned to blackmail him."

Jason looked preoccupied.

"You okay?" I asked.

"Yeah. Sure. Just thinking."

"Even though someone took the book from my room, I have pictures of the pages she wrote on. She wrote about Valentine—he's number 522—but her note was cryptic."

Jason was looking over my shoulder, an odd expression on his face. I said, "I'm sorry. Are you friends with him? Would he be upset?"

"Not exactly friends," Jason said. "I need to talk to Tristan about Gino and everything you told me. Don't worry, you're not getting anyone in trouble. But we need to figure out what's going on with him, because he has been acting odd, and not just with you."

"Whatever you think is best," I said, relieved that I had shared this burden with someone I trusted. "But be careful, okay? Someone here killed Diana. I don't want you or anyone else to get hurt."

"I'll find you later," he said. Then he kissed me, but it was a quick, friendly kiss, not a romantic kiss. "You be careful too, until we know what's going on, okay? What are your plans? Just so I know how to reach you."

"I promised Brie I'd go on the snorkeling trip."

"Good. You'll have fun. I'll see you when you get back."

"Okay."

I must have sounded concerned, because now he leaned into me and gave me a hug, then kissed me. "*If* you want to see me," he added with a sly grin.

"I don't know," I teased. "Last night is going to be hard to top."

"I love a challenge."

"Jason? Ms. Crawford?"

Tristan walked around the deck and saw us in an embrace, averted his eyes. I stepped back; Jason took my hand and pulled me to his side.

"A problem?" Jason asked.

"I don't know yet. I was just on the radio with Gino. He's identified a person of interest in the murder of Diana Harden."

"Who?" Jason and I said simultaneously.

"A staff member. He's new this season, and I was looking to speak to him about the break-in in your room, Ms. Crawford."

The skinny teenager I confronted yesterday.

"But—" I began, and Tristan cut me off.

"I don't know if I believe it, but I couldn't find him yesterday after I spoke to you, and when I went to his apartment, he wasn't there. Eli said he'd gone to St. John on the evening ferry, so I asked Gino to look for him, just to talk to him. When Gino searched his room, he found Ms. Harden's cell phone."

"What would be his motive?" Jason asked.

"I don't know," Tristan said, his face pinched with worry. "She was a disagreeable guest. Maybe he thought she'd have him fired. She complained about several staff members during her short time on the island, though I didn't field a complaint about him specifically."

"Who?" Jason said again.

Tristan didn't look like he wanted to say, but cleared his throat, put his head up, and said, "Georgie Arendt."

"Georgie?" Jason shook his head. "He's a good kid. He wouldn't hurt a fly."

"I'm only telling you what we know right now. Maybe he has a good explanation. Maybe he was scared after his confrontation with Ms. Crawford."

Jason looked at me as if I'd kicked a puppy.

"It wasn't really a confrontation," I said. "The first day I arrived, I saw a young man going through my bag on the beach. Later, I realized that a page was torn out of my book, and when I saw Georgie, I recognized him. I tried to ask him about it, but he ran. I think he was scared of someone. He didn't act like he'd killed anyone."

I agreed with Jason; Georgie didn't look like someone who could kill, though not all killers looked capable of murder.

He *had* run. Maybe he knew the killer, and that's why he was scared. Maybe he knew that *Gino* was the killer, so when Gino started looking for him, he ran for his life.

I glanced at Jason and suspected he was thinking the same thing.

Eli called out from the other boat, "You're all good, Jason! Ms. Crawford, care for a ride back?"

Jason said, "Go, we'll talk later. I'll have your things brought to your room." He squeezed my hand, but his mind was clearly a million miles away.

BACK AT MY COTTAGE, I showered, dressed, then headed to the restaurant because I was starving. While the tiramisu we had for breakfast was terrific, I needed real food and filled my tray at the buffet. I sat in a corner and watched the birds fly from tree to tree, chirping happily. A lot like I felt. If I could sing, I might have joined their melody.

"Ms. Crawford."

I looked up to see Trevor Lance standing across from me.

"Can I help you?" I asked formally. He didn't look as intimidating as yesterday; in fact, he looked as if he hadn't slept all night.

"You indicated yesterday that you had seen CeeCee on St. John. Can you please elaborate?"

His voice was calm, but forced, as if he was trying to be super polite when he really wanted to hit something.

"I saw her having lunch with a woman."

"Did you know the woman?"

I bit my lip.

"Please, this is important," he said.

"It was your ex-wife."

He didn't look surprised; in fact, he looked almost relieved. "Thank you," he said quietly.

"Is something wrong?"

He put his hand on the chair across from me as if he were going to sit down, but he merely leaned on it, looking defeated. "I've been had, Ms. Crawford." I couldn't tell if his eyes were red from tears or rage. "It serves me right."

"Did CeeCee steal from you?"

He laughed humorlessly. "Technically, yes, but it wasn't her idea. I should have seen it coming."

"Your ex-wife." I didn't realize I'd spoken out loud until Trevor nodded.

"Funny thing is," he said wistfully, "I still love her."

"Your ex."

He looked a million miles away, but he nodded and turned to leave. I asked abruptly, "Did Diana Harden blackmail you?"

He harrumphed. "She tried, saying she would call Krystal—my wife—and tell her about CeeCee. I said go ahead, I wasn't the only one on vacation with another woman."

Then he left.

Brie found me as I was thinking about the exchange with Trevor Lance.

"Tell me *everything*," she demanded, grabbing a grape off my plate.

"What?" I asked, confused.

"Come on! Everyone heard you were stranded on the other side of the island last night with Jason. What happened? I want details."

"Nope."

"Nothing happened? Don't believe it."

"I'm not giving you details."

"One thing. Just give me one juicy tidbit so I can live vicariously through you."

I said, "Jason is a romantic."

"Duh. That's not a detail."

"He kisses better than anyone I've ever kissed," I said honestly.

"Kisses," Brie said bluntly. "Just kisses?"

I made a motion of zipping my lips and throwing away the key. Brie laughed. "Okay, fine, don't share. You have ten minutes to finish up." She ate a strawberry.

"Ten minutes for what?"

"Snorkeling. You promised to help me with Sherry."

I groaned.

"You *promised*," Brie whined. "Just a little flirting. I'm not asking you to sleep with him."

"Brie!"

She laughed. "I know you can do it. You flirted with Jason."

I did a lot more than flirt, I thought, and bit my lip. "That's different. I'm going to see Jason again. I don't want him to think I'm flirting with other men."

"You *really* like him."

A lot. More than I wanted to, if I was going to be honest with myself. Not that I would say that to Brie.

"But you are coming with us snorkeling, right?" Brie pushed.

"I said I would."

"You don't want to."

"I don't know what we can do that's going to show your dad Sherry's true colors." I told her what Braden said yesterday about Sherry's finances. "I have no legal way to go deeper into her finances, but she's in bankruptcy and has to sell her house."

"It's something."

"She could have a sob story or a legitimate reason like her mother had expensive cancer treatments or even that she was conned. She already hates me, so I can't befriend her. She thinks I'm trying to steal your dad from her."

"What if . . . oh, light bulb!"

I didn't like Brie's tone. "What?"

"You don't have to do anything. But we can make Sherry *think* you're flirting with my dad . . . and that he's receptive."

That seemed far-fetched. "How?"

"Leave it to me."

"Brie—"

She put her hand up. "I know what I'm doing. You just need to be yourself. Change nothing."

"All right," I reluctantly agreed. "But if this works, I have something for you to do. I have an idea how we can find the documents that Amber and Parker are looking for."

"Whether it works or not, I'm all yours. Now eat fast. We have to be at the dock in five minutes."

CHAPTER
THIRTY-TWO

"Everyone has a plan until they get punched in the mouth."

—Lee Child, *The Affair*

I DIDN'T THINK THAT Brie's plan was going to work, but I didn't say anything because she was ultra-confident.

Instead, I did exactly what she told me to do, starting with sticking by her side and laughing at her jokes, both the good and bad.

There were two distinct groups on the snorkeling trip. Two families with a gaggle of kids between the ages of eight and twelve who all stuck together and outnumbered the adults, then the rest of us. Sherry, Andrew, and Brie; Doug and David; and the horny honeymooners, who seemed to have tamed their PDA. They still couldn't keep their hands off each other, but they didn't have their lips locked half the time.

It was a beautiful day, and while I *was* tired, I was glad I'd come. The island was a thirty-minute ferry ride. Though uninhabited, there was a permanent cabana, a dock and boathouse, and a row of portable toilets. The island was a government-owned nature preserve; St. Claire maintained the facilities and paid a fee for use.

The reefs were along the eastern side of the island, so we walked fifteen minutes with our gear. Kalise provided a safety lesson, then a bit of history about the reef and the island itself.

Doug had brought an underwater camera and seemed especially excited about the trip. When I caught his eye, he pointed to David, who was listening intently, then gave me two thumbs-up. I supposed that meant he and David had worked things out. I was glad.

St. Claire had amazingly clear water. But this place, which Kalise called Pedro Point, had water so clear we could see details on the sandy bottom far from shore.

Kalise brought the kids and parents to one area, and the rest of us went with staff farther along where it was less noisy, but no less beautiful. Brie and I hung back with the others, and we watched Sherry cling to Andrew, walking a dozen feet ahead. He didn't seem to mind, and I—not for the first time—thought Brie might be too close to the situation. She loved her dad and didn't want anyone to take her place. It was normal, and she'd outgrow it.

Except . . . I didn't like Sherry, either, and I didn't trust her. She was mean. And her attitude on the ferry back from St. John was definitely suspicious.

Brie started laughing and playfully hit me. "Are you serious?" she said.

It took me a second, but I caught up. "Totally," I said with a snicker.

"And?"

"And?" What was I supposed to say? She wanted to make Sherry angry or jealous so she'd do something to irritate Andrew, and I didn't actually have a story I was telling.

"What'd you say to her?" Brie made a purposeful glance toward Sherry, so I followed her gaze and realized that Sherry was looking back at us.

"Oh, I said . . ." Then I whispered nonsense into Brie's ear.

This whole farce seemed childish, as if we were gossiping behind Sherry's back, and no way would she fall for it . . . except that her face reddened, and she clutched Andrew tighter.

Okay, maybe Brie did have a good idea.

"See?" Brie said.

"Yes."

Suddenly Brie started laughing again, and this time Andrew turned around, a broad smile on his face. He stopped walking and waited for us to catch up. "Having fun?" he asked.

"Absolutely," Brie said, moving into the narrow space between Andrew and Sherry. "You know, Dad, I'd love to go to that great fish restaurant on St. John before we leave. Where we went to celebrate my sixteenth birthday?"

"Sure, we still have a few days."

"Mia, you have to join us," Brie said. "That's okay, Dad, right? Mia's leaving on Tuesday."

He hesitated a moment, and I wondered if he regretted asking me to steer clear of Brie. "Sure," he said.

"Maybe it should just be *family*," Sherry said.

Brie shot her a look that Andrew couldn't see, then said to her dad, "That's a great idea, Sherry. Thanks for suggesting it. Just me and you, Dad. We have a lot to talk about before I go to college."

"That's not—" Sherry said, then cut herself off when she realized what Brie had done.

"I don't want to think about you leaving just yet," Andrew said, and kissed the top of Brie's head. "It's been you and me for a long time, kiddo."

Brie discreetly winked at me.

Brie, Andrew, and Sherry went to a different section of the reef, and I stood with David because Doug was off in his own world with his camera. I couldn't see the Kents anywhere. We chatted for a bit. David gave me some pointers, then he joined Doug, leaving me alone. I didn't mind as I happily floated atop the reefs, looking at the colorful fish and interesting plants. The water was so amazingly clear and refreshing I could have stayed here all day, especially once I got the hang of breathing through the tube. I daydreamed about Jason, wondering if maybe we could come here alone before I left. I didn't know the rules, but Jason liked to break rules, and this was one I would happily break—alone on an uninhabited island with the guy I lov— liked. Liked a whole lot.

I wasn't so naive to think that there was a bright future for us, but I wanted to see him away from St. Claire, to find out if I still felt this tug in my heart. I didn't really *know* him, though I knew quite a bit. The way he viewed life, both as something to fully live and recognizing that he was a small part of a bigger whole. He'd romanced me with both his words and his body.

I wanted to do it all over again.

Suddenly, I couldn't get any air.

My tube was clogged or something, but I didn't panic because I was literally swimming just below the surface. Yet when I tried to emerge from the water, something pushed me down. Now water flooded my snorkeling tube. I kicked away, jammed my toe against the reef. I finally surfaced, coughing and sputtering.

Sherry stood in the water, glaring at me.

"What the hell?" I said.

"I don't know what you mean," she said.

"You pushed me down!"

"You're mistaken." She made a point to look around. No one was nearby. No one had seen.

In a low voice, Sherry said, "Stay out of my way. I know exactly what you and that little brat are up to. It won't work."

"You really *are* insecure."

"You have me all wrong. I have more confidence in my little finger than you could ever have. Andrew is *mine*. We're getting married. You and Brie will not stop it. He's already irritated that Brie hasn't welcomed me with open arms, and he thinks she's being selfish. He has needs that only I can satisfy."

"Two husbands, one dead," I said, sounding a lot braver than I felt. But there was space between us now, and I could scream before she could do anything to me. "What did Diana have on you? I mean, you were in the same sorority, after all."

Her face darkened. "Stand down. This doesn't concern *you*."

Suddenly, her face changed, all sunlight and joy. "Andrew, over here!" She waved at someone behind me.

I turned and saw Andrew and Brie swimming toward us.

"They want us to head back early," Andrew said. "There's a storm coming in—nothing big, they said, just overnight rain—but the ocean is getting choppy."

As if on cue, wind came in off the ocean and chilled me, and I spotted distant clouds to the east.

Andrew and Sherry went ahead; I hung back with Brie.

"What happened?" she said.

"I really don't like Sherry. She called you a brat."

"Really?" Brie laughed, but I didn't think the situation was funny.

"Diana had something on her. I think she's dangerous."

"Like, killed Diana dangerous?"

I didn't respond because that was exactly what I'd been thinking. Tristan said they had a suspect, but I didn't see that young man Georgie killing anyone. I'd really thought it was Gino . . . but now?

"I don't know. But she's definitely up to something."

"I'm going to tell my dad."

"We have no proof. We need to find something first, something tangible."

"How?"

"By figuring out every line Diana wrote in her book to see if it points to specifics."

"I'm in," Brie said. "But aren't you going to see Jason again tonight?"

"I plan to," I said, finally smiling again. We emerged from the ocean and headed up the beach toward the dock. "But we have time this afternoon. Can you come by?"

"I'll be there as soon as I take a shower."

THE WAVES WERE choppy as we headed back to St. Claire, the dark clouds coming toward us faster than we were moving, but the captain assured us that we'd all be back at the resort before the first raindrop hit the island.

Everyone was inside the cabin except Brie and me. I'd had it with Sherry. She deliberately cut off my air supply when we were snorkeling, but I couldn't prove it. I was more concerned about Brie and what she would face when they returned to Arizona.

"I have to convince my dad that she's bad news," Brie said.

"Tomorrow there's a big dinner and dance up at the Sky Bar," I said. "If we spend this afternoon and all day tomorrow trying to find what Diana knew about her, maybe we can expose her."

"What if we ask Amber?" Brie said.

"Are you serious?"

"We know they were involved. Amber knows about the book and probably also the blackmail, and she only seems to care about finding the documents. What if we figure out where the documents are, and trade that information for dirt on Sherry?"

I liked that option. "We have to find the documents first."

Lightning flashed in the distance. "Wow," Brie said. She craned to see St. Claire. It was at least ten minutes away.

Several people from inside the cabin came to the deck to watch the lightning show. It was pretty spectacular, though a little creepy. I was glad we'd be back at the resort soon. Brie went to her dad, and Sherry immediately followed, kissed Andrew, then leaned against the railing.

Brie said something, but I couldn't hear it. Sherry looked angry and Andrew confused.

The ferry slowed a bit as we neared the island. Then a wave had the boat moving up and down to the point my stomach was a little queasy. I took a couple deep breaths, getting my bearings. Then I heard a scream and a splash.

"Sherry!" Andrew shouted. "Woman overboard!"

A bell rang, the ferry's engine cut off, and David grabbed a life preserver and rushed over to Andrew. He tossed the ring out to where Sherry was flopping in the water. She struggled to swim toward it, and I noticed there was blood on her head.

Andrew kicked off his shoes and jumped into the water. He swam over to Sherry, bringing the ring to her. She grabbed it with one hand, then clung to Andrew with the other. She was sobbing and gulping for air as the waves became more violent from the incoming storm.

I went to Brie's side. "What happened?"

"I don't know. One minute she was standing there. The next, she fell through the gate."

I noticed then that one of the railing gates was unlatched. If someone had leaned against it, they easily could have fallen over the side.

"You didn't—" I said quietly.

"No!" Brie said when she saw what I pointed to. "*She* did it."

"Why?" I asked.

"For attention? Dammit, she set this up, I know it."

We watched as David and one of the crew helped Sherry back onto the boat, and then Andrew followed. Sherry wrapped her arms around him, sobbing.

"Let me check your head," David said. "You must have hit it falling over."

"It'll be okay," Andrew said to Sherry. "You're okay, thank God."

Sherry looked directly at Brie and me, smiled slyly, then buried her face in Andrew's shoulder.

WE DOCKED AT three that afternoon. The sky was no longer blue, and darker clouds looked ominous on the horizon with lightning flashing in the distance. I was exhausted and tired. A hot shower, then Brie and I would come up with a plan to beat Sherry.

Then I'd spend the night with Jason. That made me smile.

I was the last in line as we walked up the dock to the waiting shuttle. The kids had run ahead along the beach to the resort without their parents.

Andrew had his arm around Sherry and she now sported a

bandage on her head, which I thought was overkill. Brie stopped and walked over to the side of the dock to take a selfie with the storm clouds as a backdrop.

"Brie, hurry up, Sherry needs to get into some dry clothes and relax."

Brie looked at me and rolled her eyes.

"Ohmigod!" Doug shouted. "Is that a person?"

Everyone turned to the southernmost edge of the dock. Eli and two of the deck hands jumped off the ferry and joined the group. They all stopped at the edge of the rocks that led down to the beach.

Something was wrong. I hurried over to Brie's side as David and Eli climbed down the rocks. Brie took my hand and squeezed.

The fall wasn't steep, though it could be dangerous because of the rocks that had been built up to create a breakwater between the dock and employee housing.

There was a body on the rocks. A seagull stood on his head. David reached the body and shooed the bird away.

That's when I recognized Gino Garmon.

He was very, very dead.

CHAPTER
THIRTY-THREE

"Instinct is a marvelous thing. It can neither be explained nor ignored."
—Agatha Christie, *The Mysterious Affair at Styles*

THE RAIN STARTED BY the time I reached my cottage.

Gino was dead. My number one suspect in the murder of
Diana Harden was dead.

It could have been an accident—he fell and hit his head.
But the drop wasn't far, and he'd just accused a twenty-year-old
staff member of murder. If Gino was guilty, he'd successfully
pinned the murder on someone else and then accidentally fell
to his death? I didn't buy that. If he wasn't guilty . . . did that
mean the kid had killed him? Would everyone now be looking for Georgie because he was suspected of killing two people?

I shivered, thinking about how I'd confronted the skinny
young man. He hadn't seemed dangerous; he'd been terrified.

Maybe it was an accident. People do wild things when confronted with jail. He could have pushed Gino to get away. Gino
fell and hit his head. A short but deadly drop on the rocks.

None of this sat right with me, but I didn't have any
answers—and I didn't think that Diana's book had the answers,
either.

On the desk next to my closed laptop was my dress, neatly
folded, and my cell phone. A note was folded on top.

I opened it.

Mia~

> Your things, as promised.
> All staff is working to secure the resort before the storm.
> It won't be severe, a mild tropical storm that should pass by
> morning. I'll come by when I'm done.

Love, Jason

I smiled and set his card aside. My phone was nearly dead, so I plugged it into the charger. A text popped up from Brie.

I hate her! I'm coming over now.

Poor Brie. I hoped we could find something on Sherry serious enough that at least Andrew would postpone the wedding. She hadn't killed Gino, so she probably didn't kill Diana, either—though she was up to something.

I remembered the creepy guy she met with yesterday and the money she gave him. Maybe she *was* a killer . . . and hired a guy to do the dirty work.

More likely Gino was hired . . .

I straightened. Hired by Parker Briggs because Diana had stolen documents from him? That seemed plausible, I thought. And Parker was here now, looking for the documents. Maybe Gino was supposed to get them, and when he couldn't find them, Parker had to come to the island himself.

I wished I knew what she'd taken that might be worth killing for. I feared I'd never know, a story without an ending.

I showered, dressed, the pounding rain making me a bit nervous. Though it was only four in the afternoon, the day had darkened, and I watched sheets of rain fall straight down around my covered patio. I was hungry, but I didn't want to leave.

Someone pounded on my door. I found Brie there, drenched.

I pulled her inside.

She looked like a lost puppy and dripped on the floor. I grabbed a couple towels from the bathroom and tossed them at her.

"What happened?" I asked.

"Sherry happened," Brie said. "They're getting married."

"Right, but—"

"They're getting married *tomorrow*."

That seemed sudden. "Tomorrow?"

"Sherry went all emotional on my dad and manipulated him. I don't know why he agreed—I went to take a shower, came out ten minutes later, and he told me they were getting married at the Sky Bar tomorrow at sunset! That he wants me to be his best girl and stand up for him. It's happening too fast, and I can't stop it."

She started crying, and I hugged her.

"We'll think of something."

"No, we won't! She's going to win, and I can't do anything about it."

"Brie, don't give up. Tell him what you're feeling. That it's happening too fast."

"I did. Sort of. I mean—damn, it's all my fault! She deliberately fell overboard because I put her on the hot seat. I confronted her with the fact that she knew Diana Harden. Basically said why didn't you tell us that you and Diana were in the same sorority? And Dad was surprised. He started asking her about it because she specifically told him she'd never met Diana. And Sherry was trying to come up with a lie, and then wham, she falls through a gate that should have been secure. I *know* she did it on purpose. But Dad won't listen now, because he *loves* her and she almost *died*." Brie rolled her eyes, but her expression was heartbroken. "Right. Almost died only a couple hundred feet from shore? She hit her head on the boat, and according to *her*, she could have been knocked unconscious and *drowned*. I wish she had!"

"You don't mean that."

"I do," she insisted, wiping tears from her face. "I told him it was too fast, too much, and he needed to think about it. He said he didn't want to wait, that this week has taught him that life is too short. Then—then—"

"What did you say?" I pushed when she pursed her lips.

"He asked Sherry to leave for a minute, and he hugged me and said he loved me, that he had always listened to me and made changes in his life for me because we lost Mom. And now I'm an adult, and he wants to share his life with Sherry. And what could I say? What could I do except agree? I don't want him to hate me!" she sobbed.

"He never would," I told her.

"Whatever she said or did or does in bed, I don't know, but she has him wrapped around her little finger, and I don't know what to do."

She was about to sit on my bed, then realized she was still wet.

I retrieved sweats and a T-shirt for her, and she changed in the bathroom. Then we sat at the table in silence.

"We'll find something on her," I said quietly.

"I don't know if he'll even believe me." Brie frowned and stared out into the darkening day.

I opened my notebook and looked at everything I'd written about Diana's notes in the book. Then I pulled out my phone and scrolled through the pages Brie sent me, looking for anything related to Sherry Morrison—or her code, 1913—or the Delta Gamma letters. Diana knew that Sherry had a secret—a secret that she was willing to pay for? Or kill for?

Gino Garmon was dead. He could be the killer. He had motive, opportunity, and he was an angry guy. He could have used the poor kid Georgie to steal the page from my book. Was Gino's death an accident? Or did he have a partner? Could that scrawny, scared kid have killed Gino? Or someone else?

Sherry also had a motive, but she couldn't have killed Gino—she was on the snorkeling trip with us. My head was spinning.

Was Sherry's secret recent or old? Other than the initial comment about her gold-digging, and the note with the Delta Gamma letters that read, *Wedding bells in the near future. For old times' sake I'll wait to get paid,* there was nothing else that even marginally related to Sherry.

"I think you're right," I said to Brie.

"About?"

"We should talk to Amber Jones."

Brie sat up straight, didn't look as depressed. "Really? Now?"

"We'll go to the restaurant. She's staying in the lodge some-where. Maybe we can figure out what room."

"Leave that to me," Brie said. "Let's go."

It was still raining. We ran down the waterlogged path un-til we reached the main lodge.

The restaurant was packed with more people than I remem-bered seeing in one place at the resort, even at the Sky Bar the first night. The sky windows were closed, and all the external doors had been shut, but the lights were bright and music played. We passed the arcade where most of the kids were entertaining themselves. The buffet was elaborate and smelled amazing.

"They really know how to do a storm right," I said.

We helped ourselves to food and sat down at one of the few vacant tables. I looked for Amber or Parker. Amber wasn't there, but Parker was sitting at the bar, shoulders slumped, back to the room. Charlie, not Jason, was working the bar.

Brie was watching her dad and Sherry talking to Tristan. "Probably planning the wedding," she muttered.

"Amber's not here," I said.

Brie stuffed a shrimp in her mouth and said, "I'll find her." She got up before I could warn her to be careful.

Jason walked in through the lobby. He was wet and looked beat. I jumped up and went over to him. "Hey."

"Hi," he said. "It's miserable out there."

I looked him over. "I can see."

"But the resort is secure. Employees who were off-duty went back to their apartments, and those who are working will crash in the library upstairs because the lodge is booked. No one should be out on the beach tonight." He touched my damp hair. "You went out?"

"Only from my room to here."

"Still up for having me come by later?"

"I'm counting on it," I said.

"Good." He seemed preoccupied.

"What's wrong?"

He looked around, then took my arm and escorted me into the bar. He bumped fists with Charlie, then took me into the stock room and closed the door.

"Georgie didn't kill Diana," he said. "He reached out to me. He's terrified. He told me he stole a page from your book because Gino asked him to."

"Where is it?" I asked.

"He gave it to Gino. Gino burned it right in front of him."

"But Gino's dead."

"They're saying it's an accident," Jason said. "But they had to remove the body because of the storm, so if there was any evidence on the rocks, it's gone now."

"Do you believe that? That it was an accident?"

"I don't know. But if it's not, the police are going to look at Georgie, because Gino already called in an APB on him. He's twenty years old, Mia. His whole life is turned upside down. And I don't know how to prove he didn't do anything wrong."

"One of the nice things about the American legal system is that you're innocent until proven guilty, right? The police have to prove he killed Diana."

"Gino found her phone in his apartment, turned it over to Tristan."

"Gino *said* that's where he found it," I told him. "What if— what if Gino was framing him? And Gino's death really was an accident? If Georgie comes clean and explains everything, that might clear him."

"He's scared and hiding."

"He called you, right?"

"Yeah," Jason conceded. "But that doesn't mean he'll reach out again. I tried calling Georgie after I heard about Gino, and he didn't answer."

I reached out and touched him. "I'm sorry."

"I feel helpless." He started rubbing my arm, as if to both

seek and give comfort. It endeared him to me in a way I couldn't explain, even to myself. "He just started here this season, but he's a hard worker. Born in Miami and saving money to go to college."

"The worst thing he can do is hide from the police," I said. "That makes him look guilty."

"I'll try to find him. Maybe I can talk sense into him," Jason said. "Thanks for listening."

He leaned in and kissed me, caressing my face in a romantic gesture. Now I knew what swooning felt like in all those historical romance novels I'd devoured in college, because my knees wobbled, and I wanted to fall into his arms.

"Please be careful," he said. "I still don't know exactly what's going on here, and I'm not ready to sign off that Gino's death was an accident."

"You be careful too."

"I'll be by around ten, if that's not too late."

"Anytime," I said, and hoped I didn't sound desperate.

He kissed me again and said, "We should probably leave before I need to lock the door." I blushed, and Jason laughed softly. "I love how you're so shy about these things."

"What things?" I said, trying to force my body to behave.

He pushed me up against the door and pressed his body firmly against mine. I gasped, then said, "I wasn't shy last night."

"No, you weren't," he said, and kissed my neck. I closed my eyes and let all the feelings wash over me. Lust. Need. Excitement that we were making out in the storeroom.

What if someone needed another keg?

Jason laughed into my neck. "You just realized anyone could find us making out in here, didn't you?"

"Okay, I'm not as much into PDA as some."

"That's okay. I like it. I like you. Tonight."

"Tonight."

We left, and I realized I was in way over my head with Jason Mallory, but surprisingly I didn't panic.

I didn't know if that was good or bad.

BRIE WASN'T BACK when I returned to our table. I finished my champagne, still a little overheated from the make-out session in the storeroom. I thought about poor Georgie and wished I hadn't told Tristan about his confronting me. Tristan brought in Gino, and Gino then ended up dead.

I remembered the missing page. I couldn't read most of it even after I rubbed a pencil over the impressions, but there were a few letters that popped out.

I flipped through my notebook until I found what I'd written. A lot of blanks that I had marked with x's, but I now rewrote it without the missing letters.

77 emz $50 522 car

The 77 was definitely Gino Garmon. All the other coded numbers fit for Andrew, Sherry, Amber, Trevor, the others. The only coded numbers I didn't have names for were the list of five numbers that had also been on the missing page.

"Emz" was embezzlement, in shorthand. I couldn't see all the letters, but it worked in context. And I thought "car" with the missing letters was "cards"—he was stealing money, embezzling, because of a gambling addiction. Tristan knew he had a problem, which was why he asked about his trips to St. Croix on the employee evaluation.

It made a lot more sense that he lost his job as a Miami cop because of gambling. He had debt, he was stealing, and Diana knew all about it and was blackmailing him. 522—that was Ethan Valentine. She could have threatened to tell the resort owner about his gambling problem, which may have prompted a full audit of the resort.

Motive and opportunity, I thought, proud of myself.

How did Diana know about Gino's problems in the first place? Had she connected with him in the past? Or knew someone who was?

Where did Georgie Arendt come in? He'd admitted to

taking the page from my book, and he called Jason and told him he did it for Gino. Maybe Georgie wasn't the clean, honest kid Jason thought he was. Maybe he was in on something with Gino. Something that could have pushed him to kill his partner.

I wasn't going to figure this out just staring at my notes. Instead, I focused on something more fun and less dangerous: finding the documents Diana had hidden somewhere on the island.

I had been thinking about this ever since Brie and I had followed Parker and Amber to St. Claire Peak. They were using the book to find out where Diana had hidden the documents she'd stolen from Parker, but they didn't know how she'd coded the information. The list of numbers in the margin had been torn out with the evidence about Gino's gambling, but I had recreated them from the impression they left on the page beneath. And I wondered if they weren't names of guests and staff, but a different code—one that led to treasure—namely, the file Diana had stolen from Parker.

11
19
157
52
210

They weren't number codes for the people she was blackmailing, I realized as I stared.

They were page numbers.

I flipped through the images that Brie sent me, and on those pages, a single word had been circled. I wrote them down in order.

score
child
rice
king
jewel

I had no idea why she circled these words, but I was sure I was on the right track. I read the paragraphs around these words, and they told a story specifically about the heroine's search for the missing treasure. I wish I had the book so I knew where the treasure had actually been found in the story.

I hit myself and went to my e-reader app on my phone—something I rarely used—and bought a copy of the book. It took several minutes to download because the internet was slow, but when it finished, I immediately scrolled to the last two chapters and read as fast as I could.

The characters had found the treasure on a boat, locked in a box. The bad guys had killed Gabrielle's mentor who'd found the treasure, but they couldn't get it off the island, so hid it in a box on a public ferry.

There were several boxes on the St. Claire ferry, which would be safe, dry, and semiprivate to store documents that Diana planned to retrieve in a day or two. She easily could have hidden them the morning she left for St. John.

But it was night. It was raining. No way I could access the boxes now. It would have to wait until morning.

Brie waved at me, and I went to her. "I think I know where the documents are," I said.

"Good. I have Amber's room number."

"Don't tell her, because I want to find them first. I mean, if it's something illegal, we need to turn it over to the authorities. But we can use it as leverage for information she has about Sherry."

The lodge had four stories. We went up the stairs to the second floor. I glanced into the library and sighed.

"It's beautiful," I said.

Brie nodded. "It's nice. But staff is sleeping in there tonight. We'll check it out tomorrow."

Amber was at the far end of the wide hall. I knocked on the door. I heard a loud curse behind the thick door, and then it flew open.

"Yeah? Oh. You."

Amber didn't look like her beautiful, put-together self. Her hair was dull, her eyes shadowed, and her face sallow.

"Are you okay?" I asked.

"Great!" she exclaimed sarcastically, throwing her hands in the air. She grabbed a wineglass and drained it, then poured another glass, but the wine bottle was nearly empty. She drank it anyway, then slammed it down on the table.

Brie and I glanced at each other, then stepped inside and closed the door.

The lodge suites were oversized hotel rooms with a plush sitting area separating the sleeping area and a small alcove set up as a den. A balcony would have a view of the ocean, but the shutters were closed because of the storm.

"I'm really sorry about Diana," I said, wondering if she was grieving.

"Diana," Amber said. She was on her way to being drunk, but I don't think she was yet there. "Love her, hate her. I wish she were here so I could tell her what an idiot she is!"

"Tell us what happened," I said.

"You know!" Amber sat heavily on one of the love seats.

I sat across from her, and motioned for Brie to stay near the door. I didn't know if Amber was dangerous or volatile, but I didn't want Brie to get caught up in anything.

"She came here with documents she took from Parker," I said.

"Teach him a lesson, she said, for cheating on me."

I was confused. "I thought you and Diana were involved."

"We are. Were. *Everyone* betrayed me except Diana. She's *always* been on my side, and I loved her for it. And she got herself killed!"

Tears welled in Amber's eyes. She got up, walked to the mini-bar, and opened a fresh bottle of wine.

"So she stole something that Parker wants back, but hid it," I said.

"At first I was all in, but then . . . Parker found out. Sunday he came to my house and said he was going after Diana."

I must have gasped audibly, because Amber then said, "He didn't *kill* her. He couldn't even get here until Monday. He wouldn't dare hurt her until he got his files back. Then he might have pushed her off a cliff."

"What's in the files?" I asked.

"I don't know! Diana looked, of course. She called me and said we had everything to take Parker down. Parker would have his comeuppance, and we'd drink champagne and celebrate. We weren't even supposed to come to St. Claire. We had a trip planned to *Europe*, but she said someone *here* would be interested in the documents. I don't even know what that means! But when *Parker* found out that Diana had come *here*, he blew his top."

"So Parker knew who Diana wanted to give the files to," I said, trying to keep up with Amber, but she was very confusing. Maybe my assessment of her partial sobriety was off.

"Hell if I know! But yeah, sure. Probably. And give? No. Diana did nothing without getting something in return."

"Do you have any idea why they're important?"

"Something to do with Ethan Valentine, but I don't even think he exists. No one has seen him for *years*."

Valentine. Diana had gone to Ethan Valentine's house the night she disappeared. Luis said he wasn't home, but maybe she planned on selling the documents to him.

"*Apparently* . . ." Amber said, and drank half the wine, some sloshing over the sides without her noticing. "Ethan had a falling out with Parker's father a few years ago, which is why he bought the island, to lick his wounds. Diana knew all about it. She knows everything. It's because of her business."

"Antiques?"

Amber blinked at me, then burst out laughing. "What made you think that?"

"The article in the St. John paper?" I said, trying to remember exactly what it had said.

"That's her *family's* business. She sometimes works for them—she has a great eye—but Diana doesn't have to do anything. She's loaded. She goes to parties and charity balls all over the country and knows everybody."

"Which is why," I said, "she knew secrets about so many people here on St. Claire."

"Diana is—was—the smartest person I've ever known. I'm going to miss her so much." Amber collapsed on the couch, the tears rolling freely.

I didn't know how smart it was to blackmail people—clearly, it hadn't turned out well for Diana. I said, "Diana and Sherry Morrison belong to the same sorority."

"Delta Gamma. Me, too, though I dropped out of school when I got a recurring role on a crime show." She beamed. "It's how I met Diana."

"But Sherry and Diana didn't go to the same college."

"No, but we knew each other through the national office."

"You know Sherry?" Brie said, taking a step forward.

Amber rolled her eyes. "*Scary Sherry.* Keep your men far from that one."

"Why?" Brie demanded. I winced, but Amber didn't seem to sense the change of tone.

"Because Sherry is after one thing: marrying rich. She did it once, got a good settlement in the divorce, did it again and the guy croaked. Now she's getting married again! Poor guy. Idiot."

Brie opened her mouth, and I interrupted whatever she planned to say. "Sherry has convinced Andrew Locke to move up the wedding to tomorrow," I said. "We'd really like to stop that. Do you have anything you can share about her? I mean, I read the book. I know Diana was waiting for the marriage to get paid for something. What's that something she's keeping secret?"

Amber opened her mouth, closed it. Looked from me to Brie. "Why?"

"He's my dad," Brie snapped.

"Oh. Sorry."

"Tell me," Brie said. "You can't let her manipulate him like this!"

"He's a big boy. If he gets sucked into her games, that's on him."

"You know something! Please tell me."

"Why? You two haven't helped me with anything. I have no fucking idea where Diana hid the documents, and if I don't find them by tomorrow? Parker will ruin me."

These people all deserved each other, I thought. But if I walked away now, Brie would be hurt. And while Andrew might be naive, he didn't deserve to be manipulated by Sherry.

"I have an idea where the documents might be," I said.

Amber jumped up, then wobbled on her feet and grabbed the couch. "Tell me! Where?"

"We need to know what you have on Sherry."

"So you can take the information and then get the documents and screw me over? No thanks."

"You can come with us. Tomorrow morning. We can't go in the storm anyway."

"Are you bullshitting me?"

"No."

I hoped she believed me.

"I'll tell you this," Amber said a moment later. "I have a video of Sherry five years ago with a group of us on New Year's Eve in New York City. She'd divorced her first husband and had set her sights on number two. She was drunk and very chatty. All I'll say is, any man who watches it would never marry her."

"You *have* to send it to me," Brie pleaded.

"When I get the documents. Parker is flying home Sunday. If he doesn't have them, he'll destroy my career."

"Maybe you should find out what they are and destroy him," I surprised myself by saying.

"Mutually assured destruction? No thanks. I like my career. The only reason I wasn't here with Diana last weekend was that I had an audition."

"Tomorrow morning, 9:00 a.m.," I said. "Meet us downstairs in the restaurant."

"You'd better be there."

Brie was near tears, but I ushered her out.

"We could have waited until she passed out and gotten the video from her phone," Brie said.

"We're going to find the documents at dawn, well before we meet with her. I want to know what they are and why Parker Briggs wants them so badly before I turn them over."

"What about my dad?"

"Diana's phone was recovered in Georgie's apartment. The police couldn't get here because of the storm, so it has to be in the security office, don't you think?"

"We break in and get it!"

"No, I'm done breaking in—I'm still worried someone is going to find out we were in Tristan's office. But we might be able to access it, if we're smart. Let me think on it, okay?"

I looked at my watch. It was already after ten. "I have to go. Six thirty tomorrow morning, we'll get answers."

THE RAIN LULLED me to sleep, and it wasn't until my phone rang that I jumped up, remembering that Jason was coming by.

"Hello?" I answered groggily.

"It's me," Jason said. "I'm at your door. I woke you?"

"No. Yes. I mean . . . one sec."

I ended the call and went to the door. Jason stood there drenched. The rain was still falling, though not as heavily as before. "Come in."

"Sorry I'm late. We had one small disaster—a tree came down and blocked the road from the dock to the resort. We had to get it moved—in an emergency, we need to use that road. Everything else can wait until tomorrow to clean up."

"Do you want a hot shower?" I asked.

He smiled slyly. "Will you join me?" He stepped forward and kissed me. His lips were cool and wet. His hair dripped on mine. "Please?"

This guy made me feel so . . . desired. Special. It felt right, so right, and I had never quite felt like this before, as if we clicked together, two mismatched pieces that fit perfectly.

Jason gently nudged me toward the bathroom, all the while

kissing me, tugging at my robe until it fell to the floor, revealing the sexy sheer nightgown I'd bought just for this trip.

"Wow," he said as he looked at me from head to toe and back again. "You're beautiful, Mia."

I sucked in my breath, surprised that I didn't feel self-conscious or embarrassed.

"You're beautiful too," I said, then smiled and laughed. "You know what I mean."

Jason turned on the water, then stripped out of his wet clothes and draped them on a drying rack. He pulled my nightie over my head and placed it on the counter. "You won't need that tonight."

He backed me into the shower, under the jets, all the way to the wall, until our bodies were firmly pressed together as the warm water flowed over us.

Only once in my life had I had sex in the shower. It had been awkward and unsatisfying.

This was anything but awkward, and when Jason fell to his knees to focus on my pleasure first, it was not only satisfying, but unexpectedly wanton and hot.

I wanted him again.

Last night was romantic and sexy. Last night was about exploring and learning each other's bodies, a little awkward, but fun and special.

Tonight? It was as if we hadn't seen each other in weeks and had pent-up lust that only the other could satisfy. After Jason brought me to a sharp, unexpected orgasm, he fumbled for a condom he'd put on the counter. He made love to me up against the wall, holding one of my legs with his right hand, and holding on to the support bar with his left. I couldn't move, pinned between the cool, hard tile and Jason's hot, hard body. When I reached around to hold his ass so I didn't slip and break the connection, he groaned, released, and sighed into my neck.

"That was too fast," he said. "I couldn't help it. I've been thinking of you all day, thinking about this, about making love to you, and I came like a horny teenager."

"Are you saying you're done for the night?" I teased.

"Absolutely not," he said, and I felt him harden against my stomach. He looked down at me with the sexiest smile I'd ever seen, a sparkle in his eye. "Are you?"

I shook my head.

He turned off the water, picked me up, and carried me to bed, neither of us caring that we were wet.

We both acted like horny teenagers. I didn't realize how much fun sex could be.

CHAPTER
THIRTY-FOUR

"Friendship is a combination of art and craft. The craft part is in knowing how to give and how to take. The art part is in knowing when, and the whole process only works when no one is keeping track."

—E. L. Konigsburg, *The Mysterious Edge of the Heroic World*

MY ALARM WENT OFF at six. I groaned, then quickly shut it off for fear of waking Jason.

I rolled over, but my hand hit warm, damp sheets.

I turned on the light, and Jason wasn't there. Instead, there was a note on the nightstand.

Far from worrying it was a Dear Jane letter, I smiled. After last night, there was no doubt something special was brewing between us.

I opened the paper.

Darling Mia ~
There is nothing I want to do today except stay in bed with you. Or the shower. Or take a walk to our lagoon and make love to you under the moon tonight.
But duty calls, and it's all hands to clean up after the storm.
Please stay the extra three days. I'll move heaven and

earth to make sure you have a place to work if you need it, but I don't want to give you up at night. There's a lot I want to tell you, things I want to share with you that I've never wanted to share with anyone else. Stay.

Love, Jason

I ran my finger over *Love, Jason* and smiled. Was I falling in love? Or was this just residual joy from a night of wild sex? Isn't that what my goal was, to have mindless sex with a hot guy, then go back home, accept the promotion, and continue a normal, steady life?

Except . . . sex with Jason wasn't mindless. It was mind-blowing. I didn't have one-night stands. I always went into relationships with the idea that the guy was *the one*, that the good outweighed the bad. And always, I was disappointed—especially in bed.

I'd had more orgasms with Jason in two days than I'd had in the last two years. I didn't know if that was a testament to my own lack of sexual prowess or to the lack of skill of those I'd dated.

Maybe there was more to sex than inserting A into B. I was attracted to Jason, physically and intellectually. I don't know why that surprised me—just because he was a bartender didn't mean he couldn't be smart. Jason was not only intelligent, he was also thoughtful, contemplative, philosophical. I wanted to listen to him, talk to him, have meaningful conversations about life.

And yes, have sex with him as often as physically possible.

Maybe this was love, because I had never felt this strongly for any of the men I'd been involved with—after five days or five months.

I wandered into the bathroom, startled at what a mess I was. My hair, which I hadn't dried last night, was tangled and flat on one side. I had a faint red mark on my breast from when Jason had nipped me, and a bruise on my arm where I'd accidentally banged it on the nightstand when I reached for my phone to look up what a reverse cowgirl was—I'd read about it in several books and decided we should try it, but I wanted to do it right. I didn't realize there were a lot of right—and wrong—ways to do it. But I think we had our most powerful joint orgasm when we got it absolutely right.

After, we slept spooned together for an hour before I woke to Jason hard against me.

"I can't get enough of you," he had said, and kissed me. *"I have one condom left."*

He rolled on top of me, and we made love slowly, gently, because all our fun and games had left me sore. He knew how to be tender, and somehow, those touches, those kisses, light and urgent at the same time, told me everything I needed to know about Jason—and me—and what we might have together.

I took a quick shower mostly so I could do something with my hair. I didn't think I would be able to shower again in this room without thinking about Jason and me against the wall.

I was drying my hair in a blissfully hazy state when there was pounding on my door.

I opened it to Brie. "You said six thirty!" She walked in. One look at the bed and she said, "Ohmigod, he's not still here, is he?"

I blushed, then bit my lip to keep from laughing. "No. He had to work. I need five minutes."

Brie made coffee for us. I finished drying my hair, then put it up in a stubby ponytail and dressed in walking shorts and a tank top.

"How's the weather?" I asked with a glance outside my glass doors.

"A little cool, but clear. It's supposed to warm up later. It's kind of a mess, though—lots of branches and leaves everywhere. They have six people working on cleaning the pool right now, said it'd be open by eight. No serious damage."

I grabbed a lightweight sweatshirt and pulled it on. "Okay, first we check the lockboxes on the ferry."

I took the to-go coffee cup Brie handed me. We left via the beach to avoid people. The last thing I wanted was for Amber to see us walking down to the dock right now. Hopefully, she was so hungover that she was still sleeping.

The morning was beautiful, the air fresh and invigorating, much needed after limited sleep last night. Not that I was complaining about it, considering how I'd spent the hours.

An unusual amount of kelp had been washed up on the beach by the storm, and staff was cleaning it up.

"I didn't realize how many people worked here," I said.

Brie shrugged. "I heard Kalise say they called in everyone today, and right before I went to your room, I saw the ferry come in from St. John and dozens of people get off, all employees."

It took us fifteen minutes to reach the dock. Fortunately, it was empty—the ferry was docked, but no one was on board. Still, we quickly jumped on board and went inside the cabin.

"Where do we start?" Brie asked as we looked around.

"Anyplace that can hold a file, I guess. Boxes, drawers, the kitchen, under seats—places that wouldn't be regularly accessed. You take the cabin. I'll take the helm and kitchen."

"It's called a galley," Brie said.

"Galley," I repeated, and went up to the helm.

There were many cabinets, and some of them were locked. I didn't see how Diana would get into a locked cabinet, but when I couldn't find the documents, I thought maybe she'd somehow gotten hold of a key.

"Brie?" I called.

She walked to the stairs and looked up at the helm. "Nothing?" she said.

I shook my head. "Some of the cabinets are locked."

Brie smiled and pulled a set of keys out of her pocket.

"You took someone's keys?"

"Maybe. When Eli was having coffee in the restaurant, I distracted him, then took his keys. We'll return them to security on our way back, say that we found them on our walk or something."

"You're going to get us in trouble," I said, but took the offered keys.

We opened every locked cabinet. Tools, maps, equipment, and in the galley, food, champagne, glassware.

No documents.

"Plan B," Brie said.

"Which is?"

"We find Diana's phone, or steal Amber's."

It was almost nine. We didn't really have a choice.

This time, I had the plan. I had said no more breaking and entering . . . but plans change.

BRIE WENT INTO the security office. The young guy who had flirted with her the other day was there at the desk. As we suspected, everyone else was out working on cleanup.

As soon as Brie gave me the signal, I went into the security office through the back. The door was unlocked. Otherwise this would have been a very short excursion.

I snuck into the security building and went straight to Gino's office.

I closed the door but didn't turn on any lights. The morning daylight from the window—which faced a thick garden—was enough to see.

I was uncomfortable being in the dead guy's office, so I planned to be quick. The phone wasn't in any obvious place, but his bottom desk drawer was locked. The common metal desk was similar to my first desk when I interned at a CPA office. They were the easiest locks to crack. I lay down on the floor, shimmied under the desk, and used a letter opener to jimmy the lock mechanism under the drawer. It popped open.

Inside was exactly what I was looking for: a smartphone in a sealed plastic bag. Now I really was committing a crime—it was evidence in a homicide investigation.

Well . . . not technically. There was no label on the bag stating that it was evidence. I couldn't know for sure it was Diana's.

The phone was dead, and I didn't have the passcode, but I had a plan for that.

Get Amber to unlock it for me. But first, we needed to charge it.

I pocketed the phone and was about to leave when I heard voices.

Brie was talking loudly, though I couldn't hear exactly what she said.

Dammit, someone was coming.

I was about to get up, but the voices were right outside Gino's door. Brie and Tristan.

I crawled back under Gino's desk and made myself as small as possible. If he walked around the desk, he would see me.

Please don't come in. Please don't come in.

The door opened. Tristan said, "Yes, of course, Ms. Locke. Two minutes."

"Okay, I'll wait."

"Talk to Benji. I'll be right back."

He closed the door.

"Gino, you really screwed this up," Tristan muttered.

I closed my eyes, willing myself to just disappear. I almost laughed at the absurdity of it. What had I been thinking? Committing a crime, all to help Brie break up Sherry and her dad?

There was rummaging in the file cabinet. "Damn you, Gino . . . There it is."

The file drawer slid closed, and then a shredder engaged. One. Two. Three sheets. The door opened, closed.

I didn't breathe until I couldn't hear him anymore.

I waited until Brie sent me a thumbs-up emoji signaling the coast was clear, and then I left.

WE CHARGED DIANA'S phone to twenty percent in my room, then went to meet Amber. We were late, but Amber wasn't there. We headed up to her room and knocked. She was just getting dressed, and I said, "Ready?"

"God, I feel like shit."

I saw two empty wine bottles, and a third that was partly empty. I'd feel like shit too.

I glanced at Brie, and she nodded. I led Amber down the hall. Brie stayed at the door, her foot preventing it from closing, and as soon as Amber wasn't looking, she slipped inside.

I showed Amber the words I'd found, and how each paragraph was about the treasure hunt in the book, which ended with finding the treasure on a public ferry, so I suspected the documents were stashed on the St. Claire ferry.

She said, "That's it. Diana is always doing shit like this. I should have known. But—those numbers weren't in the book. Where did you find them?"

"A page I tore out," I fibbed.

"I knew there was something missing!"

Amber and I walked to the ferry, then repeated everything Brie and I had done—searching every box, every nook and cranny. The documents didn't magically appear.

"Someone got them first," Amber whined.

"Or maybe she retrieved them on Sunday when she went to St. John," I suggested. "She could have done anything with them." She was on St. John the entire day. Where else could she have hidden them, I wondered.

"I'm so screwed," Amber groaned.

Diana might have hidden the documents, or planned to hide them, but ultimately had them with her when she was killed, and they were now in the hands of her killer.

If Amber had been truthful, those documents could have gotten Diana killed. Not by Parker Briggs, but whoever she planned to sell them to.

"Amber," I said as we walked back to the resort, "I told you everything. We really need that video of Sherry."

"I don't have it. It's on Diana's phone, and I don't know where the hell that is."

"If I can get to her phone, can you retrieve it?"

"Sure, but it still doesn't help me."

"I'm not giving up, but we have to stop Sherry from marrying Andrew."

She eyed me suspiciously. "Do you have Diana's phone?"

"I know where it is."

"Give it to me."

"I want the video."

"Not until I get the files!"

We walked up the stairs to the second floor. Housekeeping was cleaning out the library after staff had stayed there overnight. I glanced through the double doors and saw floor-to-ceiling bookshelves and a huge nautical display for an ancient ship. Lots of comfy chairs and couches, and a computer station on the far wall. Windows opened to a balcony and the ocean.

And something clicked.

I thought of the circled words.

score
child
rice
king
jewel

She didn't hide them on the ferry; these weren't context clues to the story. She intentionally circled *these* words as the clue to where she hid the documents.

Lucy Score. Lee Child. Anne Rice. Stephen King. Lisa Jewell. All popular authors. Authors who would very likely be in this library.

Documents would be safe in a library. But where?

Amber was rambling, and I realized I'd fallen behind as I stopped to stare through the door. I ran to catch up with her. Brie was standing outside her door. She gave me a subtle thumbs-up.

It paid to have a smart, techie teen as a friend.

WE LEFT AMBER at her door, then grabbed food on our way back to my room. As soon as we were inside, Brie said, "You were right. She had the video on her computer. I sent it to myself."

"She's a liar," I said, "so anything she told us is suspect. But I figured she had to have it because Diana would have shared it with her. It wasn't passcoded?"

"It was, but it autofilled because the computer was just sleeping, not shut down."

"Did you delete the sent file?"

"Of course. She would have to be a computer genius to know I accessed it, and she's not, so we're fine. And even if she knows, what could she do?"

"You didn't look at it?"

Brie shook her head. "I started to, but I got cold feet. What if it's not as damning as Amber implied? What if it's worse?"

"Let's watch it together."

Brie brought it up on her phone. The video was a bit shaky, but mostly clear. A younger Sherry Morrison sat in a penthouse with the New York City skyline behind her. There were bottles of champagne and wine scattered all over. Four young women could be seen in the video, but more could be heard in the background. Sherry wore a Delta Gamma sweatshirt. She was very pretty—that wasn't in dispute—with perfect skin, big eyes, good bone structure, shiny light brown hair. The girl next door with brains was the vibe she had, and I saw it now as well.

"When was this taken?" I whispered, though I didn't know why I was whispering.

"December 31, five and a half years ago."

So Amber hadn't lied about that part.

Sherry was saying, "It was a good settlement, not great. Enough to tide me over until I reel Tom in."

"Tom?" a voice off camera said.

"Tom Jorgenson."

"The ex–football player?"

"He was interested when I was married to Bruce, but I had to play it cool. Flirt, but not enough to give Bruce the idea I was going to leave. Couldn't risk my prenup."

Giggling. The girl next to Sherry said, "I made sure my prenup had enough loopholes that I won't lose as much as you did."

A scowl crossed Sherry's expression. Then she smiled darkly and said, "You were always the smartest girl in the house, Liz."

Laughter from whoever was videotaping—likely Diana because I didn't see her on the recording, and she had sent the video to Amber.

"I'm actually having fun," Liz said. "I might stick around for a while, as long as he continues to satisfy me in bed and keeps an open bank account."

Raucous laughter.

Sherry said, "Not me. After Monroe broke off our engagement so he could marry that little whore who stole him, I realized that there is always something better out there."

"Why Tom?" a woman asked. "He's twice your age."

"Not quite," Sherry said with no self-awareness at all. "He wasn't my first choice. I tried for Andrew Locke a few weeks ago—had a mutual friend introduce us. But he has a kid, and the last thing I want is a teenager in the house, especially this one—he worships her, and no way am I playing second to a little brat. Tom has two kids. They're grown—no problem there. And when I'm done with Tom, Andrew's kid will be gone, and that'll be the perfect time for me to slip in."

"You have it all planned perfectly," the video maker said in what I thought was a snide voice, but Sherry just laughed.

"Yes, Diana, I do. And after Andrew, there will be plenty more to choose from. Men are *so* easy to manipulate. It's just a matter of finding out exactly what they want and giving it to them."

She was drunk, but this video was damning.

"Oh, Dad," Brie said, tears in her eyes. "I—how can I show him this? It'll break his heart."

"How can you not?"

Brie squeezed her eyes shut and nodded.

I hugged her, and a minute later, Brie jumped up. "Okay. I have to rip the Band-Aid off. But . . . alone. Because I don't want her in the room making excuses, I don't want to get in a fight with her. I just need to show Dad and let him see the truth for himself. Sherry has a spa treatment at one, but Dad went to St. John earlier to get something. I don't know when he's going to be back."

"Go to the dock and wait for him."

"What if she goes to meet him?"

"If you see her, call me. I'll think of something—maybe ask Kalise to grab her for a fitting or whatever. Or ask Jason to distract her."

"Okay, I'll let you know. What are you doing?"

"Going to the library. I have an idea about the documents, but I need to ponder it a bit more."

"You think they're in the library?" Brie asked.

"Yeah, I do. But I have no idea where."

I FIRST WALKED through the Blue Dahlia; Jason wasn't there. I asked Callie for one of her yummy spritzers and asked, "Is the Sky Bar party off because of the wedding?"

"Oh, no. Kalise refused to do that, because Mr. Locke and Ms. Morrison didn't plan for a wedding when they booked the trip. However, she's a romantic at heart, so she's setting up the Sky Bar to have the wedding an hour before the party officially starts. All guests are invited, and they'll have a special dance for them and everything."

"Oh. Good. I didn't want to miss tonight, I heard so much about it, and I'm leaving Tuesday." I didn't know if I was leaving Tuesday—I might end up staying for the extra three days. I was trying not to think about it. I had responsibilities . . . but I wanted to spend more time with Jason. Tomorrow morning would be soon enough to make the decision.

I told Callie, "Jason said he was working up there tonight. You too?"

"Naw, I rarely work nights. Charlie will take the extra

hours—his wife is pregnant with their first kid, so he needs the money."

She put the spritzer in a to-go cup. "How'd you know?" I asked.

"You didn't sit down."

I thanked her and walked through the lobby and up the stairs to the second floor.

The library was empty. Good.

I pulled out my phone and looked at Diana's writing, and the list of words that I thought for certain was a clue to the location of the files. Slowly, I roamed the shelves, flipping through all the books written by these authors, and no papers fluttered out to the floor.

But this *felt* right.

I looked again at Diana's social media pages, willing the photos to reveal something to me.

The five photos that had no caption. They had to represent a book, *the* book where she hid the file.

I closed my eyes and put myself in Diana's shoes. She liked puzzles and codes and secrets. What did the pictures tell me? Something was on the edge of my memory. Something familiar.

I looked at the pictures again.

A photo of her painted toes—she had a tattoo on her ankle. A rose with thorns.

The resort.

A white dahlia with a wasp as the focal point. A wasp . . . that was important.

A skinny woman smoking alone.

The last photo, dark, trying to take in the entire island. The dock looked like a bridge from this angle.

Oh. My. God.

I had read the book only once because it was dark and depressing, but it had been one of the most popular books of its time, and then a movie. It was the wasp that convinced me. Everyone remembered the dragon tattoo because of the title, but Lisbeth Salander—a rail-thin antihero who smoked—also had a wasp tattoo.

I hunted for the book.

CHAPTER
THIRTY-FIVE

"It often seems to me that's all detective work is, wiping out your false starts and beginning again."

"Yes, it is very true, that. And it is just what some people will not do. They conceive a certain theory, and everything has to fit into that theory. If one little fact will not fit it, they throw it aside. But it is always the facts that will not fit in that are significant."

—Agatha Christie, *Death on the Nile*

THE SKY BAR WAS lit up so brightly that I was pretty certain Jason and I would have been able to see it if the party had been two nights ago while we were on the boat.

I was on the first shuttle up to the Sky Bar with only a handful of people. I kept looking at my phone, but Brie hadn't texted me for help—I hoped she was okay.

When I stepped into the open-air bar, my mouth practically fell open. It was stunning.

Kalise had gone all out in one day to make Andrew and Sherry's wedding as beautiful and luxurious as possible. Balloons, elegant streamers, flowers, artfully arranged potted plants. The altar was raised a foot with a beautiful jasmine-covered arch for the bride and groom to stand under. Chairs were arranged to watch the couple, with the backdrop being the western view and the soon-to-be setting sun.

Unlike the other night, when the space had been arranged like a cocktail party with tall, round tables interspersed throughout the area, tonight five tables that each sat twelve people had been set up.

I walked around and looked for my name tag. I was at the table farthest from the dance floor and band—the dance floor that currently had a couple dozen chairs arranged to watch the nuptials, but would quickly be cleared for dancing. I didn't recognize most of the names. A small table for two was set near the bar, with a small wedding cake and his-and-hers champagne flutes.

Kalise really had thought of everything.

I found Parker's and Amber's names on two separate tables. Wouldn't it be fun to see their reaction when I revealed the files?

Parker Briggs was an asshole. I hope he lost everything.

I quickly moved their cards to my table, removing a couple I didn't know. I glanced around and hoped no one saw me.

Luis walked over and smiled at the flowers and altar. "I haven't seen you in a few days," I said.

"I've been around," he said cryptically. "A wedding tonight."

"So it seems," I said.

"I think I'll have a beer. Join me?"

I linked my arm in his, and we walked to the bar, where Jason was preparing the tools of his trade. Jason looked up, smiled at me. That smile . . . he brightened my world. Corny, yeah. Sure. But that didn't make it less true.

Jason turned to Luis. "Beer?"

Luis nodded once, and then frowned. "Jason, Jason, Jason," he said with a sigh, then picked up his beer and went down the trail that led to the bench I'd sat on my first night here.

Jason watched him leave with a blank expression.

"Did I miss something?" I asked.

"No. I didn't do something he wanted me to do, and, well, I'll make it up to him."

"I like him. And I'm sure he'll forgive you." I smiled and

said in a flirty tone, "Do you think you can mix me up your better-than-I've-ever-had sangria?"

He winked. "Anything for you."

This week had flown by, but at the same time, I felt like I'd been here for a month. I wanted to take Jason up on his offer to use Ethan Valentine's secure internet and work from here the rest of the week. I pictured myself with my laptop on Valentine's deck with that amazing view. Then I imagined myself in bed with Jason every night.

Jason poured me a frothy glass of sangria, his fingers brushing against mine, before he went back to others who were demanding his time. He was so confident, comfortable. He seemed to be a truly happy person. Because he took risks and had fun? Because he lived one day at a time? Because he didn't worry about his retirement thirty years from now?

Could I love a man who had no thought for the future?

I froze. Love? Where had that thought come from?

Where? Maybe in bed last night when I didn't want to let him go. Maybe this morning when I read his note that ended *Love, Jason.* Maybe the first night we almost kissed in the lagoon after he caught me skinny dipping.

Maybe all the romance novels were right and Jason was my destiny. The one perfect person for me.

Quickly, I slid off the stool, these emotions foreign and confusing. What if he didn't feel the same? What if, for him, it was just a fling? A fun, sexy fling, and I'd leave, and he wouldn't remember me in two weeks?

Stop, I told myself, but then I glanced over at him. He was looking at me with a serious expression. When he met my eyes, he blew me a kiss. My stomach fluttered. Unbidden, the song from Cinderella popped into my head.

So this is love . . .

I couldn't stop staring, certain he would think I was jumping ten steps into the future if I told him. I didn't take risks, and love was the ultimate risk.

Jason broke eye contact when Doug and David went up to

the bar. Relieved, I turned and saw Parker and Amber walk into the open room together. Both looked miserable.

I went over to them and smiled. "Hi, Amber. Glad you could make it to the party tonight. It should be fun."

Parker scowled at me and went to the bar. Charlie went over to serve him as Jason was busy at the other end.

Amber said, "I need a drink."

She, too, went to the bar.

I'd thought for ten seconds about giving Amber the documents I'd found folded in the pages of *The Girl with the Dragon Tattoo*, but considering what they said, I couldn't in good conscience keep the information to myself. I would be an accomplice to fraud, now that I knew the truth.

I sidled over to the appetizer table and made a plate, more from nerves than hunger. The truth—the *truths*—would come out tonight. But I began to worry about Brie. She hadn't called or texted me. I hoped her conversation with her dad went okay. I hoped she wasn't upset.

Kalise walked onto the small stage where the band had set up and took the microphone.

"For our early arrivals, in ten minutes, please have a seat for a brief but joyous wedding at our beautiful Sky Bar. Then we'll take a few moments to remove the chairs and set up the buffet for dinner."

Where was Brie? Where were Andrew and Sherry? Had they not told Kalise the wedding was off? Had Brie not convinced her dad to dump Sherry?

I approached Kalise. "I haven't seen the bride or groom."

"Ms. Morrison is in the tent." Kalise motioned to the opposite side of the space, in the direction of the hole I'd fallen in. "And Tristan is escorting Mr. Locke. Please, be seated."

"I'm waiting for Brie," I said.

I walked out of the main area to where the shuttle dropped people off. A minute later, I saw Tristan driving one of the shuttles with Andrew in the back. Brie wasn't with him.

I texted her.

Where are you? Your dad is here at the Sky Bar dressed
in a suit.

No response. My stomach fell, and Parker Briggs's crime
was no longer my first priority.

I walked over to Andrew as he got out of the shuttle.
"Where's Brie?" I asked.

He glared at me. "I should be asking you the same question."

"She was going to meet you at the dock this afternoon."

He looked both sad and angry. "She won't come. What did
you say to her?"

I was confused. "Nothing. I told her to meet you at the dock,
and . . ." My heart fell. "Andrew, something's wrong."

"I understand you and Brie are friendly, but this is my life,
and Brie is an adult, as she has told me time and time again this
week. She has chosen to boycott my wedding."

"Maybe you should postpone," I said. "She's your daughter.
She loves you—"

"I need you to back off, Ms. Crawford."

"Something's wrong," I said. "She would be here."

He pulled out his phone and read from it. "'Sorry, Dad, I
can't support you and Sherry. She'll never replace my mom.'"

"She didn't write that," I said automatically.

"She did, and I think you had something to do with it."

Brie was in trouble, I knew it, but I had no idea where to
start looking.

"Didn't she show you the video?"

"I don't know what you're talking about."

Tristan was watching us, a concerned look on his face. "Mr.
Locke? We're ready."

"Thank you, Tristan," he said. "David and Doug Butcher
agreed to be our official witnesses."

"Very well," Tristan said, and led Andrew to the altar.

I couldn't worry about the mistake that Andrew was making—
I needed to find Brie.

I ran to the tent where Sherry was getting ready, pushed

through the opening. "Where is Brie?" I demanded. "What did you do to her?"

Kalise and Mrs. Kent were helping Sherry with her dress and hair.

Sherry preened in the mirror. "I've been here all afternoon."

That look . . . that smug expression of victory. "You hired that thug on the island to do something to Brie. I swear, if you hurt her, I'll—"

Kalise stepped in front of Sherry as I was about to slap her. "Ms. Crawford, perhaps you should leave until the dinner begins."

I spun around and walked out, straight to the bar. "Jason," I said. "Brie's in trouble. I don't know where she is."

He said something to Charlie, then came out from behind the bar, and we ran over to the closest shuttle.

"What happened?" he asked as he jumped behind the wheel.

I told him everything about the video and Brie's plans to talk to her dad that afternoon. "But she never met him at the ferry, and she hasn't answered my calls or texts all afternoon. Sherry did something. She gave money to a man on the island. What if he hurt her? What if—oh God, she killed Diana and now she killed Brie, and—"

"Slow down," Jason said as he sped down the road. "You're jumping the gun here."

"The video. We have a video that Diana blackmailed Sherry with." I told him that Diana had planned to wait until after the wedding for her "payday," but Sherry was just biding her time. "Who else has motive?"

"Anyone else she apparently blackmailed," he said.

A golf cart was speeding up the hill toward us. A wild-eyed Brie was driving it.

"Stop!" I screamed, not knowing if I was yelling at Jason or Brie. I threw my arms up, expecting a collision.

There was no crash. Brie stopped the cart and ran over to us. She was soaking wet and had blood on her cheek and arm. "What happened?" Jason asked. "Who did this?"

"That . . . that . . . the guy. Sherry hired. I. I got away."

"You're wet," I said.

"She has my phone! The video! I lost it, and my dad—"

"I have Diana's phone," I said. "I'll make Amber give me the passcode."

Jason drove us back to the Sky Bar as fast as he dared, where Andrew and Sherry were already standing at the altar. I ran to Amber at the bar and opened my purse to show her I had the file. "Diana's passcode or I give these to Ethan Valentine."

"Dragon," she said automatically, holding out her hand.

I ignored her hand, typed in the code, and handed the phone to Brie. She'd be able to find the video faster.

"Dad, wait," Brie cried out, running down the short aisle.

Sherry's expression was a mix of shock and rage and calculation.

Andrew's eyes widened at his daughter's state. "Brie! My God, what happened? Are you okay?"

"I'll tell you everything, but please, watch this first."

"Andrew, she's clearly making a scene to delay the inevitable. I love you. Let's finish our vows, and then we'll have a family vacation, just the three of us."

Sherry smiled broadly, but her eyes were full of fear.

Brie ignored Sherry and held the phone out to her father. She turned the volume up to max, and Sherry's voice was picked up through the microphone.

"And when I'm done with Tom, Andrew's kid will be gone, and that'll be the perfect time for me to slip in . . . And after Andrew, there will be plenty more to choose from. Men are *so* easy to manipulate."

Complete silence. Everyone turned in unison and looked at Sherry.

"It's fake," Sherry said, her voice unsteady.

Andrew looked from Brie, to Sherry, back to Brie. "No," he said quietly, "it's not." He put his arm around his daughter and walked her back down the aisle, not giving Sherry another glance.

I loved happy endings.

Sherry stormed off the altar. "Andrew!"

Amber stuck out her foot, and Sherry tripped over it, taking the small wedding cake and champagne flutes down with her as she fell.

Kalise rushed to Sherry's side and helped her up, then hurried with her back to the tent.

Tristan motioned to the band, and music started. Then people began to chatter, staff came out to remove the altar and chairs, and within five minutes, there was no trace that a wedding had even been planned for the evening.

Something bugged me, though, and I couldn't figure out what. I mulled things over.

Sherry could have killed Diana to keep that video hidden, but she must have known it had been shared among other Delta Gamma sisters. And based on Diana's comments, she was willing to wait for her payday.

I don't know why, after days of thinking that Gino was the most likely suspect in Diana's death, I was suddenly concerned he wasn't guilty. If not Gino, that meant Georgie, a kid barely out of his teens, might have done it.

What had I missed?

The honeymooners came over and sat down across from me.

"You heard about Gino?" Mrs. Kent said.

"One of the other staff members killed him! Killed that woman too!" Mr. Kent exclaimed.

"We don't know that," I said.

"That's what everyone is saying," Mrs. Kent said.

I felt for Georgie. Everyone thought he was guilty.

Tristan sat down next to me. "Hello, hello, hello," he said to everyone at the table. Parker and Amber sat at the end. Amber was looking at me, imploring me to give her the papers. I shook my head. I knew what the papers meant, and I was pretty certain that when the truth came out about what Parker Briggs did to Ethan Valentine, he would have no clout to kill her career.

"How are you this evening, Ms. Crawford?" Tristan asked.

"Great," I said.

He nodded, steepled his fingers in front of him. "I'm glad to see you've bounced back from your ordeal the other night. And this little hiccup tonight, hopefully everyone will have a pleasant evening."

There had been a lot of "hiccups" recently.

"I heard the police have a suspect in Diana's murder," I said to Tristan. I made sure the rest of the table could hear me. I wanted to see their reactions. Mostly, I wanted to see Amber's reaction. She still hadn't told anyone that Diana was her girlfriend, and she didn't seem to be all that broken up about her death. She was more concerned about what Parker might do to her career—even though she was sitting with him at the table.

These people were *so* unlikeable.

"Yes," Tristan said, "I knew between Gino and the St. John police that they would resolve this situation. I'm still shocked that Gino is dead. He was more than a colleague. He was a friend."

Mrs. Kent said, "I heard it was a staff member who killed her."

"That is who the police suspect," Tristan said, his voice calm and clear. "He's not on the island. No one has anything to worry about. In fact, St. Claire is giving everyone a complimentary weekend to use anytime in the next two years. This week has been highly unusual, and on behalf of the staff, we want you to leave feeling refreshed and satisfied."

He smiled broadly, the consummate salesman.

Sherry burst out of the tent, Kalise at her heels. "You've all ruined my life!" she exclaimed. "But I'll come out on top. I always do."

"Shut up," Amber snapped at her.

"Oh, Amber Jones," Sherry mocked, "the actress, the model, the *whore*."

"Pot, meet kettle," Amber said.

"Get a lawyer," I told Sherry. "I have photos of you paying a man on St. John, and when Brie makes her statement and identifies him in a lineup, I'm pretty certain he'll squeal to avoid serious jail time."

Sherry stared at me with deep hatred. "*You.*" She rushed me, but Jason intervened and motioned for staff to remove Sherry from the Sky Bar.

Tristan jumped up and announced, "Dinner is served." He motioned to the servers to take care of our table first.

I had to hand it to him. Tristan did a good job of mediating what could have been an awful scene.

The food smelled amazing as the servers placed a perfect plate of steak and seared fish in front of me. I sampled a bite of each and almost moaned. Delicious.

But I couldn't stop thinking about what Parker Briggs had done to Ethan Valentine. I didn't know if he would go to jail for it, but he would definitely be censured by his board, and no one in the financial world would trust him.

Stealing intellectual property was a crime.

I couldn't give Amber or him the papers and let the truth remain buried. It would make me as awful as they were. So I said, loud enough for Parker to hear, "Tristan, do you know how to reach Ethan Valentine?"

"Of course, I can reach him at any time, but why would I need to?"

He sounded nervous. Maybe he hadn't told Valentine about Diana's murder or everything else happening on the island—including Gino's embezzlement of funds, if I had read Diana's notes correctly. But he would definitely want to tell Valentine about what I'd found.

I pulled the papers from my purse, held them up. "Mr. Valentine might be interested in these documents," I said loud and clear. I handed them to Tristan, confident that he would be the best person to get them to their rightful owner.

Tristan looked at them, confused.

I could feel Parker's and Amber's eyes on me, and it was clear Parker recognized what I had.

"Those are mine!" he screamed. "I will sue you, you little bitch!"

He jumped up, knocking several glasses over, scrambling to take the papers from Tristan, who dropped them as he put his hands up to defend himself. I quickly bent down and gathered up the pages, frustrated that Tristan didn't understand what they were.

Jason rushed to my side in a protective gesture. "Watch it," he said to Parker with a ferocity I didn't expect from him. "You're on thin ice, Briggs."

Parker did a double take as if he, too, couldn't believe the cold anger radiating from the bartender. He stared at Jason as if it was the first time he'd ever laid eyes on him. I really hoped Jason didn't get himself fired.

Parker made a move toward the papers, and I put them behind my back.

"She stole those papers from me!" Parker said.

"Diana stole them," I corrected him. "And now I know why."

"Diana stole them and blackmailed me," Parker said, the veins bulging in his neck. "When I wouldn't pay, she came here and hid them. They're still mine."

Tristan couldn't mask his interest. "What are they?" he asked.

I said, "Documents that prove Parker Briggs stole an idea from Ethan Valentine three years ago."

Tristan looked at me. Then his eyes flickered to Jason.

"Ms. Harden had them? That's why she was at his house?"

Everyone was arguing around the table, David and Doug in shocked surprise, Mr. and Mrs. Kent with loud chatter. Then Parker made another move to grab the papers from me, stumbled, and fell into the table, causing it to collapse, plates and food flying. Mr. Kent grabbed his wife and whirled her away in an impressively smooth move. Luis scooted his chair back but didn't get up. Amber started talking at the same time Parker wailed, and I couldn't understand what either of them were saying.

"Jason," I said over the commotion as something clicked in my mind. "Did you tell anyone that Diana went to Ethan's house on Sunday night?"

He shook his head. "No."

"You didn't tell Tristan when I left the boat?"

"I was worried that someone was trying to sabotage the resort. We talked about that—about the cell tower, the boat, and Georgie—" Jason narrowed his eyes at Tristan, as if he'd had the exact same thought I had.

I turned to Tristan. "How did you know Diana was at Ethan Valentine's the night she died?"

"I— That's not what I meant. Kalise! Leesa! Clean up!"

"Tristan?" Jason demanded. "What did you do?"

CHAPTER
THIRTY-SIX

"You don't have to justify yourself to me.
You did what you did."

—Sue Grafton, *A Is for Alibi*

TRISTAN KILLED DIANA HARDEN. I was sure of it.

And he killed Gino Garmon to cover it up. All the puzzle pieces fell into place, mostly. He was trying to protect the island's owner from blackmail, not realizing that the documents Diana had would help Valentine in the long run.

"Nothing!" Tristan exclaimed. "Everyone, sit down. Kalise! Bring a team over to clean this up, get new plates. Everything is fine!"

No one moved.

Tristan was sweating.

"Tristan," Jason said firmly, "what happened?"

"Nothing!" Tristan said, and plastered a smile on his face. "Nothing at all. This is a misunderstanding."

Said every guilty person ever, I thought.

Little facts began to fall together. "Amber used to date Parker, but he cheated on her."

"I did not!" Parker said.

"Did too, asshole," Amber said. "Me. You cheated on *me*." She ran her hands over her body as if to emphasize the absurdity of anyone cheating on her.

"And Amber and Diana have been friends and lovers for

years," I said. "They were in the same sorority. So I think Amber and Diana hatched a plan, and Diana seduced Parker."

He harrumphed, but then glared at Amber. "I knew you were behind this."

"Fuck you," she said.

"Diana stole the papers from Parker," I continued, "and Amber claims she had no idea what was in them, but I think she's lying."

"Am not," Amber said unconvincingly.

Everything was finally fitting into place, and it had to come out. "She and Diana thought Ethan Valentine would pay for the evidence that Parker stole his ideas and sabotaged his relationship with Roland Briggs, his father."

"My dad loved Ethan more than me," Parker wailed.

"Diana hid them," I continued, "maybe because she thought Ethan would have just taken them without paying if he knew she had them. Or, more likely, because Amber called her and told her Parker was on his way to St. Claire."

"Or because she just loved her stupid games," Amber said in a tone that was both admiring and sad. Maybe she really had loved Diana, in her own shallow way.

"You knew Diana was blackmailing people here on St. Claire. You argued with Gino Garmon because he was one of the people she had something on."

Jason looked at me. "What?"

"The page that Gino had Georgie steal from the book had notes related to Gino embezzling money—I think from the resort—and losing it in cards. It's in shorthand, and I'm missing some letters because I could barely see them, but that's the gist. I could prove it if I could look at the resort books. I am a CPA, after all."

Something else clicked. Georgie knew what was written on that page. Gino might have destroyed it, but Georgie was still a threat to him. Had Gino gone after the kid and Georgie killed him in self-defense? Or maybe Georgie understood the importance of Gino's embezzlement . . . and that someone was covering it up.

"Jason, do you know where Georgie is?"

"I'm trying to find him," he said.

"Because he might have figured it out, and that's why he's in hiding," I said.

"And that's why he killed Gino," Tristan said with an air of finality.

"No," I said. "Georgie had no reason to kill him."

"To protect himself!" Tristan said as if it was a foregone conclusion. "Because he killed Diana!"

"I thought Gino killed Diana," I said, "because of whatever she was blackmailing him with, but Amber also knows. And if Amber knows, Parker knows, and Gino didn't kill them."

"True," Amber said. "Diana called me Saturday and said Gino paid for her silence. She was so good at digging up dirt." She sighed again in admiration and wiped a tear I was half-sure was fake away from the corner of her eye.

"Which is why you had him go through Diana's belongings to look for her book. When he couldn't find it, you searched my room."

"I saw you with it. I knew Diana had left notes in the margins. I needed to find out what happened to the files she took. She always set up these little scavenger hunts. She loved the games."

"Why did you care?" Doug spoke up for the first time. "You wanted to screw your ex over. Why not just let him suffer?"

"Because—" she began.

"Shut up," Parker said. "Remember, your career!"

"Screw you," Amber said, but took a couple steps away from him. "If his father finds out, he'll cut him off. And Parker threatened my career if I didn't help him get the files back. He has nude pictures of me that I let him take because I was a fool. Said he would release them. Well, fuck it. I don't care anymore. I'm gorgeous. I'm talented. I'll always have another role, clothed or naked."

"On your back," Parker muttered.

She lunged for him, but Mr. Kent and David pulled her away.

"Diana must have reached out to Ethan to tell him what she had," I said. "And that would be through you." I turned to Tristan. "Everyone knows you're the only one who is in contact with Ethan on a regular basis."

"Did she?" Jason asked him. "Did Diana talk to you about those documents?"

"I—I—yes," he said haughtily. "She said she had a deal to make. I didn't think it was worth Mr. Valentine's valuable time, so I told her I wouldn't."

"What did she have on you?" I asked him.

"Nothing. That was it. I was shocked when she disappeared. Shocked!"

"She was murdered," Jason said bluntly.

"Georgie. Or—or maybe Gino did it and blamed the kid," Tristan said hurriedly. "Because of the gambling."

I shook my head. "No. Too many people knew about his gambling. You knew too. Because your finger is on every single aspect of St. Claire. You love this resort. Gino embezzled money from the resort. You must have figured that out."

"I will order a full independent audit of St. Claire immediately!" he exclaimed.

"And you knew that Diana went to Ethan's house on Sunday and couldn't find him there. The only way you could know that is if you saw her Sunday night. Yet you didn't tell the police that you saw her. You said she left on the ferry and didn't return." It was so clear now that I said it. "You lied to the police."

"No. You have it all wrong."

I glanced at Luis. "Luis, you told Gino about Diana, didn't you?"

"Yes, after her body was found," Luis said. "Poor girl."

"Gino really was investigating her murder," I said, somewhat surprised. Maybe his threat to me, though nasty, was intended to be a warning because he knew a killer was on the island. "Did Gino figure out you killed her, so you had to silence him, too?" I said to Tristan.

"Tristan," Jason said with an air of authority. "Why did you kill her?"

Tristan was backing up as if cornered. "I . . . I . . . I did it for you!" he shouted. "To protect you, Ethan!" He put his hand to his mouth, turned, and ran down the trail that led to the lake.

Jason ran after him. I was missing something, but with all the commotion, I didn't know what I thought I heard. Tristan killed Diana to protect Ethan? From what? Learning the truth about what Parker did to him?

I heard a scuffle and grunts down the path. "Someone, call security! The police! Jason needs help." I ran after them. I didn't know if anyone followed me, but I couldn't leave Jason to fend for himself. What if he was hurt? What if Tristan had a weapon? A gun?

My heart pounding in my chest, I ran as fast as I dared on the muddy trail, grateful that there were lights. The security netting was up around the hole along with a wooden barrier. Jason disappeared from view up ahead, where the trail forked. I heard him yell at Tristan to stop.

The tools were still next to the pit. I grabbed a hand spade, the only thing I could carry and might be able to use as a weapon because it had a pointed tip, and I followed the men.

"I did it for you!"

Is that what Tristan said?

I reached the trail that edged the cliffs above the lake and slid to a stop on the slick path. Up the trail that Brie said led to the helicopter pad, Jason and Tristan were in a wrestling match. Right on the edge of the zip line platform. Tristan was trying to push Jason over into the lake. The roar of the waterfall terrified me.

Tristan kicked Jason in the stomach, and he teetered on the edge. Then he fell.

"Jason!" I screamed.

Tristan grabbed one of the dangling zip lines and sped down the wire holding on to the harness, but not taking the time to buckle up. I ran to the platform, fearing Jason had fallen all the way to the lake. Could he survive that?

When I reached the platform, I saw Jason barely holding on to the edge of the wood. I lay down and put out my hand.

"You can't pull me up," he panted. "Pull down the trolley, please! The thing that looks like handlebars."

I saw it, did what he said. I pulled it down, but the weight of Tristan going across had the heavy line bouncing up and down.

"Now!" Jason cried out.

I pulled as hard as I could, getting the trolley within a foot of where Jason grasped the edge of the platform, and he reached up and grabbed the handle. Suddenly he was flying in the air down the zip line, completely out of control with no safety harness.

Paralyzed, not knowing whether I should run back for help, I watched as Jason sailed over the water. One hand slipped off, and I screamed as Jason wobbled precariously. Halfway across the lake, he lost his grip and fell. I watched him hit the water.

Without thinking, I grabbed the last trolley, held on tight, and followed him, praying he had the strength to swim to the shore and not be sucked down the waterfall. Had he made it far enough across? I didn't know. I didn't want to lose him now, not like this.

I screamed as the trolley rolled down the wire, gaining speed, clutching the handles because my life depended on it. I squeezed my eyes shut and prayed and screamed and begged as I flew through the air, going faster and faster and faster . . . how the hell would I stop when I reached the other side? Was I going to crash into a tree?

Open your eyes! I told myself.

I didn't want to, but I did, because I needed to see where I was going.

I was halfway across the lake. Suddenly, the weight of the line changed, and I bounced up so quickly that one of my hands slipped. I thought, *This is it. I'm going to fall and die, splat on the water.*

But I held on and was reaching the shore quickly. What had Brie told me when she explained zip-lining?

The line dipped down until I was almost touching the water. I could see the shore. It was only a hundred feet away and getting close fast.

"You just have to remember to disengage the harness and let go between twenty and fifty feet from shore."

I had no harness, so I just let go.

I splashed into the water and went down. The lake was deep, even here fifty feet from the beach, and I fought to come back to the surface. Breaking through, I gasped for air. I was alive.

Jason. He'd fallen farther back than I had.

I swam to the shore, my arms and hands aching from the zip line. But I made it and collapsed onto the shore.

I heard moaning behind me.

"Jason?" I called out.

I half crawled until I could push myself to standing. It wasn't Jason. It was Tristan. His leg was at an odd angle.

"My leg. It's broken," he said.

"Good," I said. "I swear, if you killed Jason, I will make sure you get the death penalty, you bastard!"

I turned and looked out at the lake, searching for signs of life. The setting sun reflected off the cliffs, but the lake looked dark. I didn't see him. I feared he really was dead.

Tristan was sobbing. "I did it for you, Ethan! She knew who you were. That's why she came to me. She knew you were Ethan Valentine, and she would have spread it far and wide. It would have hurt you, destroyed what we built here on St. Claire! I did it for you!"

I couldn't have heard that right.

Tristan was delirious.

Then I remembered his words before he ran. He had been looking at Jason when he said, *"I did it for you, Ethan."*

Finally, Jason emerged from the water, staggered up the shore, and collapsed.

I ran over to him. "Are you okay? Oh God, I thought you were dead."

He coughed, shook his head. "I made it. You did too." He pulled me close and hugged me tight as we sat in the sand. "Mia."

I hugged him back, my eyes burning with tears.

"Where is he?" Jason asked.

"His leg is broken," I said. I had all the pieces of the puzzle now, but was I putting them together wrong?

Tristan dragged himself over to us. "Ethan, I'm sorry. You have to understand."

"I don't," Jason—*Ethan*—said. "I don't understand how you could kill anyone and think you'd done it for me. Did you kill Gino?"

"He stole from us. He took fifty thousand dollars from our accounts!"

"You mean he stole from me," Ethan said, his voice low and angry.

"This is my resort, my resort!" Tristan cried. "I built it. Every room has my loving touch. Every meal I personally approve. This is my baby, and he stole from me! Then he said he knew I'd killed Diana and expected me to pay him!" Tristan was laughing and crying at the same time. "It'll be fine, I promise. Gino proved that Georgie killed Diana, and then Georgie killed Gino, and it's fine. It's what happened. Everybody knows that's what happened."

"No, Tristan, that isn't what happened," Ethan said. "You killed them both."

He pulled me close. I was . . . I don't know what I was.

"Mia, I'm sorry."

"No. No." I shook my head. I didn't want to cry. Not here, not in front of this man I didn't even know.

I pulled away, tried to get up, my legs rubbery.

"Mia, please listen," Ethan said.

I found my strength and started walking down the beach. There was a trail here. I'd seen it on the map. And I could go

the long way back to the Sky Bar. I didn't care how long it took.
I didn't want to be anywhere near Jason.

Ethan. Ethan Valentine.

Jason had lied to me.

Ethan had lied to me. I hit my head with my palm, trying to
bang sense into me that Jason didn't exist, that ultra-rich Ethan
Valentine had just . . . just what? Toyed with me? Laughed behind my back? Knowing who he was and what he did and what
he had, and I was . . . just me.

Even when he'd had the opportunity to tell me the truth,
that whole night on the boat when we were alone, or the next
night when we made love until we ran out of condoms, he'd
lied to me.

"Mia, please stop. Listen."

I stopped walking, turned around, and he almost ran into
me. "What, *Ethan*?"

"I'm sorry," he said simply. He didn't try to justify what
he'd done. He didn't try to explain . . . because there was no
explanation.

He was a fraud. Jason Mallory didn't exist.

I shook my head. "I can't. Not now. Not ever."

"I have no excuse. Other than my Uncle Luis, Tristan is the
only person who knows who I really am. I didn't want anyone
to know. I've been in limbo for the last three years."

I racked my brain for hints of the truth that I should have
caught. Some cryptic comments from Luis, maybe, but he was
an old man. How Tristan seemed to defer to Jason on the boat
when they came to rescue us, rather than the other way around.
Jason's assurance that I could use Ethan Valentine's secure internet if I wanted to stay for a few extra days.

I felt so foolish. I'd bought into a fantasy, hook, line, sinker.

I thought I had fallen in love. But you can't love a fictional
character; they couldn't keep you warm in the middle of the
night.

Maybe because I couldn't speak, Ethan kept talking.

"When Parker Briggs took my idea and all my documentation,

I said fuck it. That arena of cutthroat business is draining. I needed to get away. I bought the island and expected to tune out for a few months, figure out what to do. But then I found I could run Valentine Enterprises from here. I had good people to take over the day-to-day operations. I made decisions and reviewed projects and went to board meetings via Zoom, but I almost never had to show myself. When I had to, I made the connection poor and put on fake glasses just in case someone recognized me. I've changed—LASIK surgery. I started working out and built up muscle, grew out my hair, got tan."

"Everyone knows Clark Kent is Superman," I said. "Glasses are hardly a disguise."

"People see what they want to see," he said. "No one pays attention to bartenders, wait staff, housekeepers. So I asked Tristan to give me a job as Jason Mallory. I needed the time to just . . . I don't know, figure myself out. I got to help make St. Claire thrive, and people didn't know who I was. It was . . . heaven. For the first time in my life, I was truly free."

I'd only seen one old college picture of Ethan Valentine. I didn't see him in Jason. He had changed over a decade.

"Nothing's changed," I said. "Except a few dozen people now know who you are."

"I don't care about that. I don't care about them. I care about *you*. Don't walk away."

"What did you think would happen, *Ethan*." His real name still felt foreign on my tongue. "That I'd come visit every year, we'd have great sex, then I'd go away and you could continue this farce?"

"No. I was hoping you'd stay for a few extra days, work from my house, and then I'd tell you."

"Oh, now you're saying you always planned to tell me?" I shook my head. The tears were there, burning, but I didn't let them fall. "I don't believe you."

"It's the truth," he said quietly.

"You lied to me. We talked, we made love. I thought—no. The time to tell me was before I fell for you. I can't *trust* you."

"I don't have any more secrets. Ask me anything, anything at all—I'll tell you."

"How am I supposed to know if what you tell me is the truth when you're so good at lying?"

I ached. I was humiliated. Mostly? I was so damn sad.

I'd fallen for him, hard.

I'd fallen for a lie.

"Let me make it up to you," he whispered. "Please, Mia."

"You can't," I said. And walked away to find the beach, to find my way back. Somehow.

This time, he didn't follow.

CHAPTER
THIRTY-SEVEN

"And above all, watch with glittering eyes the whole world around you because the greatest secrets are always hidden in the most unlikely places. Those who don't believe in magic will never find it."

—Roald Dahl

I WAS PACKED HOURS before I was supposed to leave for St. John to catch my plane home. Henry had already picked up my luggage to take to the ferry.

I stood on my patio and stared at the ocean. This, I would miss. The sea. The colors. The smells.

But I wouldn't miss this feeling that I'd been had.

It had been a whirlwind after Tristan was arrested for murder. Talking to the police well into the wee hours of Sunday night. Talking to curious guests all day Monday. I tried to avoid them, but that didn't work. So many people came by my cottage to talk about what had happened at the Sky Bar that I finally went to the Blue Dahlia and drank heavily, answering any question people had. For hours.

"Did you know that the bartender was Ethan Valentine?" Doug had asked.

"No."

"When did you suspect the resort manager had killed Diana Harden?" the honeymooners asked.

"When he slipped up," I said. *"I heard what he said, that Diana had been at Ethan's house on Sunday night, and knew he'd done it."*

"How are you holding up?" Anja asked. *"If you'd like, you can come back to my suite, away from people."*

I looked at her and smiled, though I wanted to cry. "I'm okay."

I wouldn't be okay for a long, long time.

I was about to go back inside when Luis walked up from the beach.

I was mad at him, too.

"Hello, Mia," he said, and sat down on one of the chairs.

"I'm going home," I said, making no move to sit down.

"Please?" He motioned to the other chair.

"I don't want to talk to you. You lied to me as much as your nephew."

"Great-nephew," he corrected me. "Though you probably don't think he's all that great right now."

My lips twitched, but I refrained from smiling. Instead, I sat. "You almost told me at the bar the other day." I'd been replaying our conversation, and there were a few hints. But I hadn't caught on.

"Ethan made a mistake."

"A big mistake," I said.

"He cares for you."

My heart clenched. "I fell in love with Jason."

I said it out loud. Saying it hurt even more.

"They're one and the same."

"No, they're not. Jason is who Ethan wants to be. It's fake. He's pretending. I can't trust him because I'll never know who he really is."

The uncertainty would turn me inside out. I needed order in my life. Firm expectations. A reliable job that required discipline, following the rules, respect. A life with friends who counted on me, and who I could count on. Responsibility to others, like my Grams. Who needed me to be grounded, not foolish. Who needed to be able to trust me and my word. I did not need a billionaire fraudster who went to great lengths to deceive me and everyone around him.

"Don't we all spend our entire lives trying to figure out who we are?" he asked.

"I know who I am," I said with a lot more confidence than I felt.

"Is who you are who you want to be?" Luis asked, again with the riddles.

"I don't play what-if games," I said. "People don't change, and they shouldn't. People need to be dependable."

"You're right, people don't change," he said. "Not where it counts. Your values. Your loyalty. Your loves. But sometimes, we don't know who we really are, deep inside, until we face challenges and obstacles we've never faced before."

Luis stood, his knees cracking.

"Do you need help?" I asked, jumping up to offer him my arm.

He smiled, patted my shoulder. "I was right about you from the day I met you, Mia Crawford. Don't be a stranger."

Then he shuffled away.

I WALKED TO the ferry after saying goodbye to Callie, to Henry, to his wife Millie. Kalise gave me a hug. I was about to board the shuttle when Brie ran over and wrapped her arms around me.

"Hey," I said. "You okay?"

"Sherry left yesterday, thank God. And my dad is okay. We're okay."

"I'm so glad." And I meant it.

"He's a little sad. He feels like he's been had."

I felt the same way.

"He's pressing charges against the guy who grabbed me," Brie continued, "and maybe he'll flip on Sherry."

"You never told me what happened."

"You had a lot going on," she said. "I can't believe I missed it."

"I don't want to think about it. What happened that afternoon?"

"I was waiting for the ferry so I could show my dad the video when that creepy guy docked his boat. I told him the ferry would be back in a few minutes. He said he wouldn't be long. I kind of recognized him, but didn't realize it was from your photo until it was too late. He hit me and put me on the boat. Tied me up, but not very well. I pretended I was unconscious, then jumped overboard. It took me a while to swim to shore."

"That's dangerous."

"I wasn't really thinking. By the time I got back, I realized he had my phone, my dad had already returned on the ferry, and I thought they were already married. I was frantic. I'm just so glad I made it in time, and you were there to help me stop her."

"I'm really glad you're okay," I said, and meant it. For everything that had happened this week—the good and the bad—I'd made a great friend in Brie Locke.

"Sherry literally flew from St. John to Atlanta, where she was arm candy for a basketball player at a charity function last night," Brie said. "She had to have been working him like she was working my dad."

"He'll find someone who loves him for him."

"Yeah. I think so. I just want him to be happy. If it's not going to be with a woman, it'll be with baseball, his second love. He's taking a coaching job for U of A. I'll live on campus. He's going to get a house. I'll have my own space . . . but I can see him whenever I want."

"That's great," I said. "Maybe he'll find someone when he least expects it."

"I'm going to miss you, Mia. Do you think I can come visit sometime? I love New York."

"Anytime. I mean it, okay? You have all my social media profiles, email, phone number." I smiled. "I'm going to miss you too. You're the little sister I never knew I wanted."

She laughed, then glanced around and said quietly, "You're going to forgive him, right?"

"I don't know. I'm too raw right now."

"Stay."

"What?"

"He told me he asked you to stay for a few days."

"That was before I knew he was Ethan Valentine."

"If you stay, maybe you can figure it all out."

I shook my head. "I have work. Responsibilities. So does Ja—Ethan."

"Well, for what it's worth, he's really sad."

I wished I could just forget everything and forgive him. I wanted to. But there would always be that tingle in the back of my mind wondering who Ethan Valentine really was. Until he knew who he was, I couldn't know him.

"When Ethan figures himself out, then, maybe, we can talk," I said. "I fell in love with Jason Mallory. I don't even know who Ethan Valentine is."

Brie said, "Did you hear what happened to Parker Briggs?"

"Just that he and Amber left early yesterday."

She pulled out her phone, brought up an article from a gossip rag. "This literally came out first thing this morning."

PARKER BRIGGS OUSTED FROM FAMILY COMPANY AFTER ACCUSATIONS HE STOLE INTELLECTUAL PROPERTY AND PASSED IT OFF AS HIS OWN.

"Good," I said. "He's an ass."

"Definitely."

I hugged Brie again and climbed into the shuttle. Henry chatted about a variety of things but thankfully didn't bring up Ethan.

I thanked Henry and headed to the dock. Anja and Nelson were there as the ferry pulled into port.

"Are you leaving, Ms. Crawford?" Nelson asked in his deep, commanding voice.

"Yes. My vacation is over."

Anja hugged me tightly. She was shaking. "Are you okay?" I asked.

"No. Yes. I don't know." She glanced at the boat. "My daughter—she's agreed to meet me. And—my ex-boyfriend. He, they, um." Tears welled in her eyes.

"They're on the ferry," Nelson said. "We thought having a couple of days to get to know each other here, without fear of paparazzi and rumors, would help everyone."

"I'm so happy for you," I said to Anja.

"I want her to like me. But I need her to forgive me."

"Today, or tomorrow, or next year, she'll understand why you did what you did. It's hard to walk in other people's shoes."

I thought of Ethan. Should I give him a chance? Maybe . . . no. Yes. Damn. I didn't know. I had too many things going on in my own life. I couldn't help him navigate his personal crisis.

I watched a pretty young woman exit the ferry, followed by a man larger than Nelson. I walked away and let the family work things out together.

The captain came up to me. "Ten minutes, Ms. Crawford?"

"Thank you."

I walked along the beach next to the dock. Breathed in the last of the scents of St. Claire. This was it. I was going home. To my job, my Grams, my friends, my cats.

My name was going to be on the door. I would get a raise and more responsibility. And that was going to have to be enough.

I was walking up the beach toward the dock when a shiny seashell caught my eye. I squatted and picked it up. It was a pink conch shell that looked exactly like the one I had tossed into the lagoon my first night here. It couldn't be the same. That was silly. I stared at it and remembered why I'd thrown it in.

I'd tossed it in because I knew my dream was just a fantasy.

And yet, here it was.

I put the shell in my pocket. I'd keep it as a memory of what might have been.

I heard Anja laugh, and when I turned, I realized that it was her daughter laughing at something as they climbed into the shuttle. I was happy for them.

I boarded the ferry. I was the only one going home today. I stood at the bow of the ship and didn't look back. I didn't want to. Leaving had suddenly become bittersweet.

Then I saw him, Jason—*Ethan!*—sitting on a Jet Ski in the middle of the ocean. I stared as we passed. The ferry wasn't going fast, but Ethan rocked in the wake.

He blew me a kiss.

I hesitated, then "caught" his kiss in my hand. I held it, but I didn't know what to do with it.

I watched until I could see him no more. Then I faced forward again and headed home.

CHAPTER
THIRTY-EIGHT

Six Months Later

"Sometimes the dreams that come true are
the dreams you never even knew you had."
—Alice Sebold, *The Lovely Bones*

I STRAIGHTENED THE STACKS on the table of "Staff Favorites," my hand running over the embossed cover of *Deadly Treasure*, thinking about all the trouble this book had caused.

The book *didn't cause any trouble*, I thought. It was the book's owner.

None of my customers knew what had transpired on St. Claire last summer. I'd told Jane and Amanda most of it. Everything, in fact, except about my broken heart. Because even though Ethan Valentine's lie had hurt, I knew he didn't lie to hurt *me*. He lied because he didn't like who he had become and wanted to be someone else.

That I understood.

I'd fallen in love with a fictional person.

But I *had* fallen in love, and I think Jason Mallory fell for me. Too bad he wasn't any more real than the heroes in the books I surrounded myself with.

Beach Reads and Mysteries had opened for business the first weekend in November. Now, the weekend after Thanksgiving, we were getting more traffic with holiday shoppers and people from the neighborhood enticed by either our creative window display—thanks to Grams—or the scent of spiced cider that filled the large space.

It was everything I had ever dreamed of owning.

Nooks to read or chat; a small café with local-made pastries, salads, sandwiches, and of course a coffee bar. There were books everywhere, but also gifts for your favorite book lover. Shirts, book bags, handmade bookmarks, fabric book covers. The children's section was perfect for little people to explore, and tables were strategically placed with hidden power strips so older kids could study.

And an idea I stole from St. Claire: thousands of tiny white lights winding through the shop. Around the pillars of the open ceiling, draping down the bookshelves, decorating the plants, and framing the windows. They made me happy, and several times a day, I heard customers exclaim when they noticed the small details that made my store unique and inviting.

I might have fallen in love with a fictional person, but he gave me the world by opening my mind, and my heart, to my dreams.

Jason had told me—no, *Ethan* had told me—that my dream store should be a destination. It should fill readers with the desire to browse and buy, to provide peace like their favorite comfort read, or open whole new worlds with books that entertained, that made them laugh, cry, feel.

It did just that.

I hoped it did. I'd put all my money into this place and taken out a loan for the building.

I wasn't a *complete* idiot. I didn't open in Manhattan—that would have cost five times more. I didn't even open in New Jersey or back where I grew up in Connecticut.

Instead, I'd found a corner building four blocks from the beach in Miami, Florida.

Downstairs was my bookstore; upstairs I leased to an accounting firm because having another source of income never hurt. It wouldn't cover the mortgage on the building, but it was enough so I didn't panic every time I got the bill.

And, I bought a house. A tiny two-bedroom house near the beach where Grams and I lived and shared a single bathroom. It had a porch and a small yard, and I built a catio for Nick and Nora. They seemed to like it.

I knew that opening a small business was one of the riskiest gambles anyone could take. I knew most closed within three years. Many owners were left with nothing to show for it. I had invested everything I had into this business—not just money, but my time, my dreams, my tears, my fears, and my whole heart. For the first time in my life, I was taking not only a risk—but a risk that could wipe me out. A risk that, if I failed, would hurl me to ground zero. Worse. It was a risk that I wouldn't be able to bounce back from if I didn't succeed.

But every time I walked into my bookstore, I smiled. I might fail, but if I didn't even try, I didn't deserve my name on the door.

And it was.

BEACH READS AND MYSTERIES
MIA CRAWFORD, OWNER & MANAGER

My heart was full.

Well, almost full.

Grams worked part-time for me, and between living together and working together, sometimes we butted heads—but I felt closer to her than I ever had before. Jane and Amanda were mad at me for moving to Florida, but they had already visited twice, and Jane decided to move her destination wedding to Miami. Mr. Cohn and his wife came to visit when they were on vacation. He had been so disappointed that I'd quit, but told all his clients and my former clients about my new endeavor. Word of mouth—whether to sell a book, or sell a bookstore to readers—worked. My mail-order business to New York was extensive. Best of all, he'd taken my recommendation to promote Braden, who was thriving in my former position.

"Mia!" Grams waved at me as I was writing up our weekly

newsletter that highlighted new releases, upcoming events, and recommended reads.

I looked up, and she was talking to one of our regulars. I was giddy we *had regulars*. We'd been open for a month, and Mrs. Jansen came in almost every day for coffee. I'd already ordered six books for her.

I approached with a smile. "Do you have a question?"

"My granddaughter is thirteen. She says she's too old for YA, but her mom doesn't want her reading books that are too old for her, if you understand what I mean." She mouthed S-E-X.

"What does she normally like to read?"

"She likes drama, but she also likes mysteries. She read *Nancy Drew* when she was little."

"I have just the author for her. Young adult, but for older teens. Light on the romantic entanglements, but a lot of drama and mystery."

I told Grams to find her Holly Jackson in our YA section, and the two women went off, chatting about Nadine's "adorable" granddaughter. That would be me.

I almost laughed. I didn't consider myself *adorable*, but I was definitely happier these days, even with the stress of running my own business.

Because no one could be sad when surrounded by books.

And I was even trying my hand at writing one. I didn't know if it would go anywhere, but I found spending a couple hours a week in a fictional world I created was even more freeing than reading about worlds other authors created.

"Excuse me, but I'm looking for a book on ways to show I love you."

That voice.

I turned slowly as the world seemed to stand still. As the voices in the store fell away and my vision blurred.

Ethan.

I opened my mouth to say something, but I didn't know *what* to say, and I'd never expected to see this man again.

The sexiest man I knew. The man who knew how to kiss

me senseless and exactly where to touch me. The man who had freed me from the shackles of my self-made prison and opened my mind to possibilities.

The man who had lied to me.

Ethan Valentine wore a suit. It was a very nice, lightweight tailored suit with a pale pink shirt that looked impeccable on his well-toned body. But his tie? Pink flamingos wearing Santa hats. Something Jason Mallory would wear, if he wore a tie.

He put his fingers to my lips. "I love that you opened this store. I love that you told me the truth about me. I love your big whiskey-colored eyes and your warm laugh and the way your nose wrinkles up when you think someone is being rude. I love your bravery and your caution. I love your ability to see people for who they are. I love the way you make me feel."

I couldn't speak even if I'd wanted to.

"I love you, Mia, and I want to spend every day showing you that I love you."

"I don't have a book on that," I whispered, my voice catching.

Ethan smiled. "Maybe I should write it."

"Maybe you should," I said.

"I've been dreaming about kissing you, but I was afraid you might slap me."

"I won't slap you."

He leaned forward and kissed me. It was as good as I remembered.

Better.

I love you.

I loved this man, but was I certain I loved Ethan Valentine and not Jason Mallory? Was I positive this was it? How could I know? How could I know what *he* really felt? Were they just words, or did he mean them?

I looked in his deep green eyes, searching for something . . . and I saw it. I saw love.

Wasn't life about risks and rewards? Hadn't I proven that by giving up a stable career for my dream? Ethan said he loved me, and his eyes told me he wasn't lying.

I pulled Ethan to me and kissed him back. His mouth opened, and we were liplocked in a kiss that rivaled all of our other kisses. I wasn't dreaming anymore; Ethan was here, with me, and he loved me.

He touched my cheek, kissed my neck, my ear, then wrapped me tight into a hug and whispered, "I will make it up to you, Mia."

"Okay," I said, because my heart was still pounding in my chest. I had changed so much over the last six months, but it had all started with this man pretending to be someone he wasn't, showing me that I was pretending to love my carefully planned life.

"Are you allowed to take a break?"

"It's my store. Didn't you see my name on the door?"

He smiled, his eyes sparkling, and looked around appreciatively. "It is definitely you. You have help?"

"My Grams. And, um . . ." The names of my full-time employees completely slipped my mind. I didn't even remember who was working today.

"What's upstairs?"

"Accountancy group."

"And where do you live?"

"Two blocks away. I don't own a car."

"Want to give me a tour of your daily walk?" His fingers entwined in mine, and he pulled me to him again.

"You love me," I said, a statement.

"I do."

"How did you find me?"

He tilted his head. "I *am* Ethan Valentine."

I grinned.

"What?" he said. "Tell me what you want. It's yours."

"You."

"Me?"

"Yeah. I think I love you too."

"Think?"

I *knew* I loved him. I'd fallen in love and walked away because I didn't know who I really was that last day on St. Claire.

Now I knew who I was. And judging by Ethan's attire and self-confidence, he knew exactly who he was.

"I hope you know for sure, because I just opened an office here in Miami."

"You did?" That surprised me. "What about St. Claire?"

"I still own St. Claire. Kalise is running the resort solo and promoted two staff members as her assistants. My Uncle Luis is also keeping an eye on things. He told me to tell you that he wants you to visit soon." He paused, asked, "Do you miss it?"

"Sometimes," I said honestly. "St. Claire is special."

"We can go back whenever you want. That is, if you *know* you love me."

I tried to maintain a stern face, but I couldn't, and my grin widened. "I know I love you."

He smiled. "Good. Because we hired another sexy bartender to replace Jason, and I don't want to have to compete for your affection."

I laughed, wrapped my arms around his neck, and said, "Let's start the tour in the bedroom."

ACKNOWLEDGMENTS

When I took on the task of writing *Beach Reads and Deadly Deeds*, I knew it would be a slight deviation from what I normally write, so I devoured dozens of books—romances, mysteries, romantic mysteries, romantic comedies, and even a few YAs—recommended to me by my darling daughter Mary and her best friend Mia Phillips. I will forever be grateful that they helped expand my reading palate by introducing me to their favorite books. And a special thanks to Mary, who listened to me rattle off dozens of title ideas I didn't love, then said, "What about *Beach Reads and Deadly Deeds*?"

Friends are worth their weight in gold, and writer friends are doubly valuable. I have been blessed to count Toni Causey as my go-to gal when I get stuck. She read a very early first couple chapters and gave me valuable input. More important, she gave me the confidence I needed to dispel my doubt demons and tackle this super-fun project.

As always, I'm grateful to Crime Scene Writers, a group of selfless experts in all things crime and punishment who answer the most arcane and bizarre questions from writers. A big thank you to real estate broker Christina Kremidas, who taught me so much about how commercial real estate works in New York City that I decided to change a plot point to avoid leasing a building there.

Thanks to the energetic and creative team at Assemble Media who trusted me when this story went in a slightly different direction than they expected, and provided excellent notes early on that helped me write Mia into one of my favorite creations I hope you love as much as I do.

I think my editor was surprised when I came to her with the idea to write a romantic mystery, but April Osborn, Dina Davis, and the team at MIRA were super supportive from beginning to end. I've said time and time again, that a good editor is a godsend for an author, and April's notes were exactly what I needed. This book is so much stronger because of her editorial guidance. I also want to give a shout-out to the art department, who has done an amazing job on my covers and never seem to complain (at least to me!) when we come back with, "What if we tweaked this . . ."

As I was reflecting on my partnership with my agent Dan Conaway and Writers House, I realized we've been together for fifteen years this summer. Fifteen years and more than thirty books. Dan, thank you for keeping me grounded and being my advocate. I wouldn't be here without you and the WH team. Also, thanks to Dan's assistant Sydnee Harlan for her diligence, and for reading the first draft and giving me some on-point notes, especially about the ending!

As always, my family is my foundation. Without them, I would be lost. I love you—my husband Dan; my kids Katie, Kelly, Luke, Mary, and Mark; my grandson Colton; and my mom, Claudia. You all bring me joy.